Pra[illegible]

"One of the m[illegible]
can do is to e[illegible]
exploration of thought-provoking issues
and science fiction is the perfect genre to do
so. A good example of this is Keith Brooke's
latest novel, The Accord."
– **SF Signal** on *The Accord*

"First and foremost a superbly written
novel, featuring beautiful prose that instantly
hooked me from the powerful opening page
and kept the pages turning...
Highly, highly recommended."
– **Fantasy Book Critic** on *The Accord*

"The premise is good, the setting
impressively realized and immersive,
and the story reads like nothing else
on the shelves right now."
– **SF Reviews** on *Genetopia*

"If this sounds like something you've read
before, it isn't. The strangeness of this
disturbing future world is clear from the
book's opening scene... Keith Brooke is
remarkably adept at envisioning an almost
unrecognizable far future."
– **Fantastic Reviews** on *Genetopia*

Also by Keith Brooke

The Unlikely World of Faraway Frankie
The Accord
Genetopia
Lord of Stone
Expatria Incorporated
Expatria
Keepers of the Peace

Collections

Liberty Spin: Tales of scientifiction
*Faking It: Accounts of
the General Genetics Corporation*
Memesis: Modification and other strange changes
Segue: Into the strange
Embrace: Tales from the dark side
Head Shots
Parallax View (with Eric Brown)

As Editor

*The Sub-genres of Science Fiction:
Strange divisions and alien territories*
Infinity Plus (with Nick Gevers)
Infinity Plus Two (with Nick Gevers)
Infinity Plus One (with Nick Gevers)

As Nick Gifford

Erased
Incubus
Flesh and Blood
Piggies

Harmony

Keith Brooke

SOLARIS

For Debbie, always

First published 2012 by Solaris
an imprint of Rebellion Publishing Ltd,
Riverside House, Osney Mead,
Oxford, OX2 0ES, UK

www.solarisbooks.com

ISBN: 978 1 78108 001 6

Copyright © Keith Brooke 2012

The right of the author to be identified as the author of this
work has been asserted in accordance with the Copyright,
Designs and Patents Act 1988.

All rights reserved. No part of this publication may be
reproduced, stored in a retrieval system, or transmitted, in any
form or by any means, electronic, mechanical, photocopying,
recording or otherwise, without the prior permission of the
copyright owners.

10 9 8 7 6 5 4 3 2 1

A CIP catalogue record for this book is available from the
British Library.

Designed & typeset by Rebellion Publishing

Printed in the US

"If they existed, they would be here."
– *Enrico Fermi*

But they *are* here.
They're all around us.
They always have been.

Indigenes

Chapter One

THE FIRST TIME they caught me I thought that was it. Another disappearance, another name scrawled on the Monument to the Martyrs.

The name they would scrawl? Everyone calls me Dodge. I think that was wishful thinking on the nest-parents' part. They wanted me to grow up smart and wily, so they gave me that name. Living on the fringes just as they had, and their nest-parents before them, I'd dodge, I'd weave, I'd get by.

And it worked, or at least something did. I was always the kid who could outsmart just about anyone. I could just as soon run rings round a watcher-bound grunt as earn myself a slapped ear from a nest-parent for a wisecrack too many.

But still I nearly got caught, that first pid raid on my own.

JUST PAST MIDNIGHT, I dropped from a second floor window. Looming behind me: the great square block of the Processing and Monitoring facility. The street was empty, which was lucky. This was Cheapside, E District. Alien territory. Get caught here without the right credentials and I'd be disappeared for sure.

Knees still sore from the drop, I gathered myself in

9

the shadow of the P and M. Something moved in the gutter nearby. Too slow for a rat. Probably a livegrub, looking for something faecal and rotting to wrap itself around. I shuddered. I hated the things. I'd seen one latched onto Livia's little boy-pup only weeks before. She'd had to scald it off with boiling water. The pup had lasted a feverish, pain-filled week before the toxins took him.

Distracted. Why was I so easily distracted tonight? I knew I had to keep my smarts.

I stepped out into the light cast by the lightstrips on the walls. The night air was fresh, sweet with the treacly smell of a nearby pap unit where they processed all kinds of gunk the watchers called food. I knew people who ate that stuff. *People*. It made me retch just to think about it.

One of my old nest-sibs... I couldn't remember his given name, but we always called him Skids. We'd been close for the longest time. I saw him last winter, huddled under a torn-off sheet of tarp, wasted down to almost transparent skin stretched tight over his bones; a stick-man, barely able to move. He had become a wraith, one of the many who follow the off-worlders, the starsingers, mostly. Wraiths eat the aliens' food, even though it doesn't have the right nutrients and passes through largely undigested. It brings them closer to their gods, just as it wastes them away to skin and bone.

Skids had been in a pitiful state. Shaking from the cold and from whatever was wrong with his malnourished system, eyes glazed over and unseeing, hair thin and falling out in clumps. Skids was the same age as me, within days; we'd grown up together. Yet he looked like a man three times my age, or someone who'd been blasted with rads at a skystation.

I only recognised him by the starsinger tattoo I'd needled across his face when we were sibs.

He didn't recognise me at all. I don't think he even saw me.

Now, I shook myself, standing under the street lights in Cheapside E.

I was getting distracted again.

I realised it was the smell, the air loaded with something narcotic that was either a part of the pap or a by-product. Maybe that was what drew people like Skids...

Something was screwing with my senses, my head.

I remembered Sol and Ruth warning me of things like this. *Don't trust your senses when you're away from the Ipp. Don't trust anything. You're on alien territory, and that means everything is fucked.*

I moved on.

Two blocks later, I had squeezed myself into the gap between a ceramic wall and a sheet-iron fence, watching the checkpoint. The air was clearer here, and so was my head. I was able to gather myself and study my route.

This time of night the lone duty-grunt sat in its globular recharge pod, a man-sized shape part-visible through the vein-laced skin of the pod. Attached to the recharger like buds were twenty or so fist-sized sacs, some kind of parasite, their feathery gills fluttering in the slight breeze.

Beyond the pod: the wall.

It was high here, easily twice my height, and topped with a vicious-looking tangle of jagwire.

On this side: a largely industrial and administrative zone, mostly occupied by chlicks, watchers, headclouds and their assorted commensals, grunts

and slaves. On the far side: the Indigenous Peoples'
Preserve, the Ipp. Home.

I eyed the jagwire again. I could shin the wall easily
enough, but the wire would cut me to shreds as soon
as it sensed me. By the time anyone reached me I
would be mostly digested, and all that would remain
on top of the wall would be a slimy smear of what
used to be me.

I stepped out into the sulphur glow of the lightstrips.

There was no sign of movement from the pod until
I'd covered half the distance to the checkpoint, then it
quivered, and a rent appeared near the top, seeping a
rancid-smelling ichor.

The grunt's head appeared and the striated grey skin
told me this was an orphid, one of the slave races the
watchers used for policing and military duties.

"!¡caution | suppressed-attack | surprise¡!! Identify
yourself," it said, as it hauled the rest of its coiled body
out of the pod. It spoke a blend of my own language
and the emotion-laden rattles and sighs we call *click*.

Now standing over me at its full height, the orphid
was easily head and shoulders as tall as me again.

I couldn't speak for the sudden tightness in
my throat, instead giving an involuntary click of
"!¡bowel-freeing-terror¡!" In a moment of clarity I
realised there was something in the air again, clouding
my judgement, inducing a rising ball of panic. That
knowledge helped, and I found some kind of focus. I
wasn't going to let a dumb grunt with a brain the size
of one of my balls phreak me out.

The grunt's dun bodysuit was dry already. The
fabric looked silky-thin, but I knew those suits could
withstand close proximity grenade blasts and worse.
I'd known people who had tested that out.

The orphid's head rose without a neck from square shoulders, the slit of its mouth a narrow line drawn directly between a pair of red eyes. Clustered around the lower part of its face were more bulbous ticks, smaller versions of those attached to the recharge pod.

There was no way of reading the grunt's expression, but I knew already from that first click-response that the creature was on the point of shooting me on the spot.

"I..." I said, then tailed off. That panic in my chest again. This was it. The end. I'd come so close to home and the grunt was going to kill me.

This had been my first run, and would almost certainly be my last.

Then the grunt's head rocked from side to side and its eyes phased to green. "!¡*familiarity*¡! Dodge?"

Instantly, the panic eased as the orphid stopped exuding its terror-inducing phreak-vapours into the night air.

I stared. I had no idea how the thing had recognised me. Back in the Ipp, we used to come across grunt patrols all the time. They were usually a bit stand-offish, but sometimes we would chat with them, keep things friendly. Maybe that was the explanation: maybe I had met this grunt before. I started to nod, then–

"Dodge. !¡*compliance-breach indignation*¡! No transit approval."

Grunts, particularly watcher-bound orphids like this one, felt a very strict moral attachment to rules and duty. Nest-mother Sol had taught us that it was programmed into every cell in their bodies. If the rules said I shouldn't be there, then my presence was an outrage of high order, a disjoint in the universe that

13

had to be addressed. The grunt would feel that in its body as a physical wrong.

And it was pointing a gun at me now, some sleek chlick design with a wide muzzle, its stock plugged into a hub embedded in the alien's wrist.

I played dumb, my strong suit. It was my only suit, right then. "What? !¡confusion | surprise¡!" Lying in click takes a lot of practice; it's tough packing enough sincerity into a few taps and gasps.

I held my left arm up, palm towards the grunt, wrist exposed in the universal gesture of compliance. Standard procedure: the grunt was duty-bound to follow through. It flipped out a scanner and swept the device across my wrist.

"!¡puzzlement¡!"

The grunt looked at me, and then again at the scanner, then made another sweep.

"Dodge... !¡confusion | compliance | non-confrontation¡!"

"Dodge? I said. "!¡innocent confusion¡! Who's Dodge?"

I lowered my arm. The scan had read my pids, tiny personal identifier bugs running through my bloodstream. Just like click language, the pids never lie. Unless they've been stolen.

"!¡confusion | contradiction¡! Dodge?" The grunt stared at me. I could almost see written across the poor thing's face the inner battle between what the scanner and its own senses conveyed.

I did nothing for a breath, then another, and then the grunt stepped back. The scanner said I was licensed to be out and that I could pass. The protocols must be followed.

I walked through the checkpoint, safe. With a line of stolen pid-seed taped to my inner thigh.

* * *

THE IPP WAS home to me then, familiar territory. As soon as I passed through the checkpoint I felt the weight lifting, peeling back from me like a discarded skin. The Indigenous Peoples' Preserve was somewhere we could feel safe, where people lived alongside a rag-tag assortment of aliens who chose to live away from their designated zones for a variety of reasons.

There were no striplights here, but my eyes adjusted quickly. I felt like a fox prowling his territory. I felt something surging in my chest, building.

My first run outside the Ipp after curfew, and I had survived!

I turned onto Grape Street, expecting to find a ribald welcome from Hannie and the other hookers. Instead, my legs went from under me and suddenly I was winded, my head bagged in a fetid hessian sack, and I had the weight of at least one assailant pinning me to the ground.

Before I could even gather my breath I was hoisted over someone's shoulder. "!¡*alertness* | *silence*¡!"

I recognised the click, and knew immediately to stay quiet, and then blackness descended.

A SHORT TIME later I was naked, being sprayed by a hose with some kind of acrid-smelling liquid. I was cold and sore, and my inner thighs stung from where the stolen pid-seed had been ripped from my skin. I didn't know where I was, but it wasn't back at the nest.

At the other end of the hose was Divine, a muscular slab of a woman with spiky bleached hair and skin far paler than I'd seen on any other human.

To Divine's left stood nest-mother Sol, her arms folded, her eyes hard.

"Sloppy, Dodge," she said. "!¡*disappointment | reassessment*¡! Very sloppy."

I didn't know what to say. I still didn't understand how I'd gone from the buzz of a successful run to this.

"That grunt," she went on. "You thought it was a bit distracted, a bit stupid, eh? !¡*hostility | derision*¡! Is that what you thought, eh? Eh?"

I half-nodded, then stopped.

"It was wired," said Sol. "All the time you thought it was being slow, it was listening to the voices, watching the visual overlays, tasting the prompts from its bonded watcher. What did we tell you, Dodge, eh? !¡*chiding*¡! What did we tell you?"

Don't trust anything... don't get over-confident.

Another cold blast from Divine's hose caught me in the belly, making me gasp and ball up.

"You really wanted to lead them right back to the nest?"

There was no correct answer, so I held quiet and concentrated on not being sick from the cold and the fumes of the disinfectant in the water.

"How many buds were there?" demanded Sol. "Were you counting? Eh?"

Watch everything, count everything, look out for any change. You never know how they're going to get you. All you can do is stay on your toes. I knew all that. It had been drummed into me often enough. I thought hard. "Twenty-nine," I said. "!¡*embarrassment | shame*¡! On the pod. Another sixteen I could see on the orphid."

"And how many when you'd passed...?"

I didn't know. I hadn't checked. I'd still been tripping on the phreak vapours the grunt had been exuding.

"Just one bud," said Sol, more softly now. "It bursts as you go past. ¡*talking-to-child/imbecile*¡! Its spores latch onto you, stick to you, float in the air above you and follow you. One bud and you're labelled, traced, tracked..."

I slumped. I'd let my guard slip. My first raid out on my own and I'd nearly been caught, but worse, I'd nearly betrayed the whole nest.

I nodded towards Divine. "The disinfectant?" I asked. "That's got rid of them? Am I clean?"

Sol shook her head. "No," she said, "we already cleaned you up with a fumigant while you were unconscious. This is just to make you remember."

She nodded, and Divine blasted me once more, cold and hard, and I retched and heaved and vowed never to let my guard slip again.

Chapter Two

I LEARNED MY lesson well.

It was more than a year before I was caught a second time, and by then Sol had come to depend on me. I was sharp, I never let my attention lapse; every time I went out beyond the Ipp I learned something new, something we could use. I was the man.

But first, before we were caught again, there was a girl...

THE FIRST TIME I saw her was on the way to Precept Square. You know how it is. You're out and someone catches your eye. There's a glance, and then maybe another glance. She was definitely a two-glances kind of girl.

There on a corner, arguing with a sweet plantain vendor, she had an intensity that stood out, even from a distance. She was slight, probably only rising to my shoulders at most. She wore a ragged, grubby one-piece and knee-high combat boots. Her hair was honey-brown, cut in wedges, uneven bangs sweeping across eyes that were a vivid blue against her walnut skin.

I'm filling in the details, I know.

I couldn't see all that from the back of Vechko's wagon as we approached the square along one of the side-streets open for human traffic. At the time it was just a glance – slight, animated, gesturing; and then another – skin tone, hair, ass, boots.

Vechko was delivering ales to a beer tent on Precept South-West, and pretty soon he had pulled up the horses and we were hauling kegs off the wagon and rolling them round to the canopied holding area behind the tent.

Precept Square was thronged with the pre-curfew rush, mostly grunts and slaves, but with a scattering of indigenes out from the Ipps like us. After a time, Ruth, Divine and I paused from the keg-rolling to watch the world going by.

Out in the middle of the square, the crowd thickened around a boxing ring; humans, trogs and assorted aliens cheered and hollered as a brawny man with steel knuckle spikes flayed the flesh off a species I'd never seen before. Above the ring, a family flock of flitterjacks hung on the breeze to watch, and a scattering of sentinels hovered to record the action.

The human fighter's opponent seemed oblivious to its shredded body, the tattered flesh hanging in ribbons from its silver bones. It kept lashing out with skinny limbs, catching the man repeatedly in the gut and chin. There was blood in various shades of red everywhere.

"You should fight," Ruth told Divine, running a hand over the blonde woman's heavily-muscled upper arm.

"I do," said Divine, in a voice so low I could barely hear.

"I mean prize-fighting," said Ruth. "!¡*getting-aroused | flirting*¡! You'd be good."

I'd seen Divine fighting, more than once. On one phreak run, when we'd been couriering bootleg pharmaceuticals for some gang-boss out of a neighbouring Ipp Sol owed favours to, we'd been ambushed by three orphid grunts. Divine had taken them all out before the rest of us even had time to react: a kick rupturing one orphid's midriff, and a head-mash disposing of the other two. It had been over in seconds.

But Ruth meant something else: something sexy and glamorous, and potentially one of the more lucrative things someone from the Ipps could get into.

"You want me to spoil my looks? !¡*flattered* | *interested*¡!"

We stood and they flirted and my mind wandered back to the girl on the street corner with the honeyed hair who seemed to speak as much in gesture as in words and didn't seem to realise that she was on a thoroughfare forbidden to humans.

The clocktower chimed the fifth, and I clicked, "!¡*alert*¡!"

I dipped my head low and slipped away into the crowd. Out there, in the thick of it, I had never felt more lost, more anonymous. All around me there were grunts and commensals of many varieties, mostly orphids and craniates, but there were many others too. Some were obvious artificials, hard to tell if they were vehicle or machine or sentient mechanical; others were aliens with mechanical inserts, or mechanicals with biological inserts.

Almost immediately, I staggered up against a being shrouded in a flowing grey cloak. The feel of its body as we collided was like jelly with hard rods embedded in it; its eyes were grids of metal and crystal, set in rows around the crown of its fungus-scabbed head. It shrieked and shrilled at my clumsiness, the clicks I could decipher packed with violent outrage at my gall, before the thing was distracted, staggering into a pair of blob-headed craniates. Its balance was clearly upset, either by planet-side gravity or some phreak brew from one of the stalls, or a combination of the two.

I checked myself over, head swirling from the panicked phreaks exuded by the clumsy alien. There was no sign of any tracer deposited on me by the being, or by any of the others I had brushed against in the crowd. These days we had scanners to warn us of such things, devices I'd seen the grunts using and had subsequently found a supplier for. This development was one of the many reasons Sol had come to trust me after my inauspicious start.

Just then I saw Sol ahead of me, cutting past the crowd around the boxing ring, a white scarf wrapped like a turban around her bald head. She walked in a straight line, and I took an arc, and we converged at the transit station at the northern end of the square.

There were grunts here, armed with some kind of automatic gun plugged into their arms. Beyond them, in the foyer of the station, I could see chlicks and watchers and several species I didn't even have names for. The diversity, and the bustle and the barrage of talk and clicks and cries, of phreaks and other scents... it was all quite staggering, even now that I was more accustomed to the alien zones of the city.

There were no indigenes here. Transit was out of bounds for the likes of us.

Just then, a shrouded figure emerged from the station and I knew this was the sign. The figure was a chlick. From what I could see of its scarred, wrinkled face, it must be ancient, and chlicks could live for a very long time indeed. Its entourage of four, trailing a short distance behind, was human, though, and as they emerged from the station a visible wave of outrage passed through the alien crowd, accompanied by a jangling chorus of clicked "!¡*compliance-breach indignation*¡!" "!¡*outrage*¡!" "!¡*confrontation \ address-wrongdoing*¡!" "!¡*protocol-abuse anger*¡!"

I didn't have time to wonder how the chlick had brought the four humans this far. That wasn't any of my business. My concern was getting them out of here alive.

Divine was the first to move. I hadn't even noticed that she and Ruth had joined us. She slipped between two grunts, who were too busy exchanging indignant clicks to get to her in time. Almost immediately, she reached the first human and hugged him.

Sol was next through, then I spotted an opening and barged past an orphid that had been distracted by Divine's move.

I found my mark, the third of the refugee indigenes. I stopped before her and for a moment I thought she was going to run. Her brown eyes widened, her mouth opened and closed, her whole body flinched, and then she was in my embrace, hanging on tight as our bodies pressed and where skin touched skin – hands, arms, neck, face – there was a fizz of contact, exchange.

Then my body rocked back, as if a blast-wave had struck me. One of the craniate grunts had butted me in the ribs, knocking me down. It landed on top of me in a mad scrambling of scaly limbs. The wind had been driven from my lungs by the impact, and now the craniate's web was binding me so tight I could barely breathe in again.

We had all been caught.

Then I sensed the change in the sounds coming from the square. I managed to twist and see the grunts

23

fending off a larger crowd that had materialised from the rush-hour mass.

Suddenly the grunts were ignoring us as they fought back the crowd. I struggled with the webbing, and then the woman I had embraced was on her knees, peeling me free.

I stood, and the crowd broke through.

I locked hands briefly with the woman who had released me, then let go, and we both melted into the chaos.

THEY ROUNDED US up, of course.

The grunts may be protocol-bound, but they can be ruthlessly efficient, too. A short time later they had separated out the human protestors and had them all corralled in one corner of the square, contained behind a loop of twitching, impatient jagwire.

Not one of us had escaped: Sol, Divine, Ruth and the four refugee humans were all captive within the crowd of thirty or so. That was a blow: we had hoped that at least some would get away in the melee.

Just then, I spotted someone else who had been caught in the round-up. The girl.

She stood slightly alone, as if the crowd had parted a little around her. Her head was tilted to one side, and those eerily vivid blue eyes were striking in their blankness.

On the steps of the transit station, one of the grunts' superiors, a fiery-skinned chlick with decorative plastic studs and hooks pushed through holes in its face, stood flanked by two orphid grunts. She spoke in a language I recognised but could not follow, and the first of the human captives was hauled forward, his arm pulled upright and his wrist scanned.

"!¡*identity*¡! Stine Pastor 37, authorised all indigene and mixed zones," announced one of the grunts.

"!¡*frustration*¡!" clicked the chlick. Then: "!¡*regret*¡! Formal apologies for improper detention, Stine Pastor 37."

The grunts released the man and he brushed himself down. "I guess," he said. "!¡*indignation*¡! I was just going about my business when I got caught up in all this."

His name wasn't Stine Pastor at all. This man was a street cook I knew as Skinny Beans. I'd visited him earlier that day and subbed his pids for him with a new personal identity. He'd joked that he wanted the pids of a chef he knew who worked at a travel house at the skystation, but he'd had to take what we had available and he knew it.

The grunts stepped aside to let Skinny out through a gap in the jagwire corral, and another human was brought forward.

It was the woman I had targeted; the refugee.

I watched as they scanned her, my heart thumping.

"!¡*identity*¡!" clicked the grunt with the scanner. "West Strider 46, authorised all indigene and mixed zones."

"!¡*frustration | agitation*¡!" clicked the chlick commander, irritation showing as the first two detainees had credentials that gave them protection from punishment. Then, forcing propriety to reassert itself, the commander said, "!¡*regret*¡! Formal apologies for improper detention, West Strider 46."

My target walked free, and I was happy. All she had to do now was get to the meeting place and join up with those of us who escaped detention.

I allowed my attention to wander back to the strange girl. She was more alert now, but she still looked confused. Her eyes flitted from the chlick commander to the jagwire, to the people all around her, as if she might bolt for freedom at any moment. It was as if she had just woken up from a bad dream only to find that the dream was continuing around her.

That was when I was struck by a strong feeling that she could be in more trouble than any of us, caught up in a mass arrest that was nothing to do with her. We were all prepared for this, but she wasn't.

I edged through the crowd until I was within an arm's reach of her. Those eyes were a blue I'd never seen before, the whites the purest of white.

What happened next only took an instant, but it was one of those moments where time froze. One of those moments where everything changed, the world shifted, futures were determined.

I reached out and touched her bare arm.

I expected her to flinch, but she stayed calm, just her eyes flitting to fix on mine.

Her skin was cool, smooth, her flesh firm, the muscles hard in spite of how thin she was.

My scanner found nothing. Taped to my chest, it turned my skin into one continuous reading device. We touched, it read, it found nothing.

She had no pids. She was nobody.

Everyone had pids.

Was she wild, from beyond the Ipps? But if so, what was she doing here? Who was she? *What* was she?

She was nothing.

And if they found her, I had no idea what they would do.

All this in the briefest of instants.

At some level, I was in control of what happened next, but it was not a conscious thing. Earlier, I had met my target, we had touched, exchanged; where skin touched skin I had shunted stolen pids and she had taken on a new identity: West Strider 46. But now: I was empty, had been emptied. I had nothing to give. Except...

I'm not sure I even understood what was happening at that point, but I shunted, pushed, and there was a buzz, a fizz of contact, exchange.

Now she reacted. She gasped, blinked, looked away, withdrew her arm from my touch.

I felt dizzy, wasn't sure what had just taken place. The crowd shifted, and I returned my attention to the pierced commander, visibly antsy now, as she was forced to release another innocent human whose faked identity protected him from detention. The chlick knew there should not be so many of us with this status here in Precept Square, but was bound by protocol to abide by the rules.

A short time later, we were down to a dozen or so detainees. A grunt stepped down into the corral and I thought it was going to seize me, but instead it reached past and took the girl by the arm. I hadn't realised she had been so close behind me.

It led her to the station steps. When she didn't raise her arm to be scanned, the grunt grabbed her hand and jerked it skywards so sharply she winced. For an instant she struggled and then she slumped, surrendered, passively waiting for whatever fate she had in store.

Another grunt scanned her wrist, then turned to the commander and said, "¡¡identity¡! Reed Trader 12, authorised all indigene and mixed zones."

That flash, that fizz of exchange... Reed Trader was the identity I had assumed for the day: I'd shunted some of my own borrowed pids into the strange girl's bloodstream.

She looked around, and those blue eyes found me briefly.

I thought she was going to say something, do something, but instead she just stood there.

"!¡*regret*¡! Formal apologies for improper detention, Reed Trader 12."

The chlick was getting really pissy now. Its cheek pads were flushed red, its eyes swollen. When the girl remained standing there, the chlick flapped an arm, and shrieked, "!¡*anger* | *frustration* | *confusion*¡! Improper detention!"

"Move!" hissed Sol, from the front of the group of detainees.

The girl went. She shuffled away through the gap in the jagwire corral and disappeared into the thinning pre-curfew crowd.

They freed Sol and a woman I didn't know next, and then it was my turn.

The touch of the grunt's hand on my shoulder made me suddenly panic. I don't know if it was some kind of phreak transmitted in the touch, something in the air as the grunt came close, or simply that it felt wrong to have a powerful clawed grip on my shoulder.

I let the thing guide me forward through the crowd, up one step, then another, until I stood before the commander.

Close up, she was a daunting sight. Her skin was ribbed and deeply indented, its hue shading from vivid orange to dark umbers and browns. Some of the studs and hooks on her face barely pierced the rough skin, but others were buried deep. Her eyes were black, glassy, so that you could not tell where she looked, except that they flitted constantly, the skin around the sockets pulling and twitching as the eyes moved. She smelled of sulphur and old urine, so potently that I had to struggle not to gag.

I held my left arm up, exposing the inner wrist, and let one of the grunts scan me.

The grunt with the scanner twitched twice, clicking, "!¡*confusion error... confusion error*¡!" over and over. At a prompt from the chlick commander, the grunt calmed and said, "!¡*identity*¡! Reed Trader 12, authorised all indigene and mixed zones."

I stood quietly.

The commander leaned towards me, and it was all I could do not to let its aura of phreak-stink reduce me to a quivering, terrified wreck.

"!¡*suspicion | frustration*¡! This one does not look like Reed Trader 12," she said. She stabbed a scaly paw at my chest, striking me so hard that I staggered. "Reed Trader 12 was female."

I met the chlick's look.

Softly, I said, "I am Reed Trader 12. I was just going about my business when–"

The same scaly paw flashed across my vision and I staggered again, my face numb, my ears ringing, the metal taste of blood in my mouth.

The chlick commander barked an order and the grunt seized my arm and scanned my wrist again.

Just then, I remembered the first time I had been caught, that night at the checkpoint: the confusion in the grunt's face when my pids had contradicted its own recognition of me.

I looked at the chlick commander, its colour shifting to a more fiery pattern.

Protocol won. There was a flash of her arm again and I expected another blow, but instead she was gesturing, dismissing me.

A grunt pushed me roughly, and I almost staggered into the jagwire. That would have been a quick end for me and perhaps somehow an end that would have been acceptable in the aliens' strict moral framework: an accident, a twist of fate, not a deliberate act at all.

I caught myself, straightened, glanced back at the commander only to see her glassy black eyes fixed on me, turned away again. Calmly, I stepped through the gap in the corral and was free.

Chapter Three

I DIDN'T HEAD straight back to Cragside Ipp. I knew better than that.

I didn't head for Sol's meeting point, either; I'd done my bit already. I didn't even know where they were to meet, although I could guess: our nest-mother could be a bit predictable in her planning.

Instead, I went to the Swayne and walked along its embankment, choosing my route carefully to avoid the proscribed main streets. The river was wide here, as it twisted like a snake through the city. This stretch of bank had been raised and cut straight, though, no doubt by some alien settler for long-forgotten reasons that must have made sense at the time.

Chantran market stalls lined the embankment, and out in the water, families of tilelias skipped and played, flashing silver and black and filling the air with their wailing.

The sixth would strike soon, and then it would be a race to get back before curfew, but for now I was good to catch my breath.

Across the river, I could see a marina, all sleek speedboats and cruisers of alien design; the river was not human territory. Beyond that, a sprawl of buildings clung to the hills of the northern districts.

I had never been far above of the Swayne, had only once even been as far north as the skystation we normally only saw as occasional jet-streaks in the night sky. My world then was a small place consisting of Cragside Ipp, the neighbouring mixed zones and Ipps, and some of the commercial districts where stolen pids allowed us to move outside curfew.

Again, I felt like that fox prowling his territory, marking the boundaries.

Cragside was Sol's domain for now, and I hoped it would be for a long time. But maybe one day, when Sol stepped down... maybe when that came to pass, the Ipp would be mine. Maybe.

I came to a green area, where trees had been allowed to grow. Silvery lianas were draped across the branches, home to a million tiny silk nests alive with finger-thick dragonflies.

I thought of the girl.

Maybe I'd been thinking of her all along, just fooling myself that I was not. I don't think I yet understood how deeply she had insinuated herself.

She had no pids.

I'd never come across anyone without an identity before, and it was my business to deal in identities. We stole them, we faked them, we traded them. Each of us had unique pids added to our bloodstream at birth; if that didn't happen, for any reason, we had them added later. Every time we passed through a checkpoint we were scanned, and anyone without pids would be found out. The oldest child I had known without pids was caught out before her fifth birthday, and she had only lasted that long because her mother was simple and rarely ventured out beyond her clan nest.

I wondered where she could be from, this girl of about my age with the bluest of blue eyes.

I was intrigued. If she could get by this long without being caught, there must be some lessons to learn from her. It was a professional interest. A technical thing.

No more than that.

ONCE YOU HAVE pids in your blood you can change their identifying codes – with the help of some dodgy black-market kit – but you can never be free of them. So the first thing I did when I got back to the nest that evening was reimpose my originals, make myself Dodge again and not Reed Trader 12, whoever he might be. Elsewhere around the Ipp, all those with borrowed identities would be doing the same.

Somewhere in their systems, the chlicks would be evaluating what had happened in Precept Square that day, and it was a safe assumption that soon they would be rounding up some of those involved. I didn't want to be Reed Trader any longer than necessary.

The clan's main nest was known as Villa Virtue. It was a concrete block grafted on to the cliffs deep in the city's South-East 6 Indigenous People's Preserve, a district otherwise known as Cragside. Behind the walls, caverns were burrowed deep into the cliff, excavated generations ago.

I had spent all my life here.

As the sun sank in a bloody sky to the west and the bells tolled seventh and curfew, I sat on a parapet with my back against a moss-covered rock, my feet dangling over a sheer drop to the street below.

Down there, old Sully hauled his hand-cart over the cobbles, cursing and muttering at the sentinel hanging in the air above him, logging his late return. A dog snapped and played at his heels, waiting for a titbit to fall. Three nearly-men, heads cauled with glowing alien webbing, rushed in the other direction, momentarily snagging the attention of the sentinel.

I heard a commotion out on the terrace, then. Sol's voice, a mutter of clicks and spoken comments from the others. She had brought the refugees back from the meeting place.

I stood, balanced on the parapet, and threaded my way back round to the terrace. Time to purge their pids, time to switch identities and rewrite the stories told in their blood.

Sol greeted me with a wave of one hand. I thought she was going to make proper introductions, but instead she said, "Here he is. !¡*matter-of-fact*¡! The pids boy I was telling you about. He'll sort you all out in no time, eh?"

I reimposed their identities, allowing the scanner to tweak the algorithms coded into their blood so that their old IDs were now attached to the borrowed profiles of local residents with respectable trades and clan histories. I did not know where they had come from, but now, according to their pids, the four were Lucias and Pleasance Benchport, Marek Moon and Callo Hart, indigenes of the city of Laverne.

There was small talk, expressions of gratitude. Callo, the woman I had saved, thanked me with a hug, western-style, with a brushing of cheeks and a pressing of shoulders. The other three, two men and a woman, barely seemed to notice me other than when they subjected themselves to the pid amendment.

As I removed the pad from the last man's arm, Sol stood from the bench where she had been sitting. "Let's get to that safehouse," she said. And with another wave of the hand and a click of "!¡*dismissal*¡!" I was sent on my way.

I retreated to my precarious perch, and soon the five had gone, heading deep into the caves where they could pass through the Ipp without breaking curfew.

I liked to think of myself as Sol's right-hand man, but at times like this I couldn't help but be reminded that I was just a part of the network, a useful tool.

I did not know who these people were, or why we had risked arrest in order to secure their passage. I did not need to know. I just played my part.

But I was curious, and so I followed them.

IT WAS STUPID of me. A dumb, spur of the moment decision.

Why did I follow them?

I was angry, frustrated. I had helped set up that day's successful transfer of the four refugees from the transit station; I had masterminded the pid swap that had seen us all safely through. I had cleaned up afterwards, given the four of them clean pids. And not once did Sol tell me what was actually going on, why these four were so important.

No matter how much I liked to believe I was central to Sol's activities, I knew I was not. I felt excluded.

And so I followed.

They went deep into the nest, passing through a labyrinth of passageways and halls, some of them natural caves, others excavated by hand.

I knew I shouldn't be following.

As I passed down through the chambers I almost cut away to my own cell. Maybe, even then, I could have convinced myself that I was just going down there to sleep and not following anyone at all.

Deep in the caverns, the passageway was natural now, worn away through years of seeping water eating at the limestone. The ground was uneven, polished smooth, skimmed with a pearly lustre of fresh lime deposit. The way was lit at irregular intervals by feeble glow-bulbs pasted to the wall.

Ahead, Sol and the four newcomers betrayed themselves with the glow of a hand-held torch and the occasional distorted rumble of voices. They made no particular effort to conceal their passage.

I trailed at a safe distance, finding my way by touch and sound and memory as the passage became almost completely dark. I knew where they were going after only two or three branchings; I had travelled this way many times as a child, when Skids and Jemerie and I had spent long days and nights exploring.

So confident was I of their destination that I took an early exit. If I followed them all the way I would emerge in the main hall of Villa Mart Three and would be spotted easily.

Instead, I emerged through a cleft at the base of the crag on which the Villa had been built.

It was long after curfew and the street was deserted. In the light of the nearby buildings, cramped together along the lane as if once there had been more room for them than this, I could see no sign of patrols.

Sticking close to the crag to stop my body-heat being picked up by any hovering sentinels, I followed the street for a short distance to where the Villa's sheer wall rose, the building set deep into the rock. Where wall joined rock there were gaps, handholds, foot-spaces.

I climbed, as I had climbed here so often as a boy.

Villa Mart Three was four storeys high, culminating in a rooftop terrace far wider than that at Villa Virtue, with views out across much of the western part of the city. This villa was the clan's secondary nest, used largely for raising and schooling our children. It would be a good place for visitors to lie low for a while.

As I had anticipated, the five were on the terrace already. I heard them before I reached that level. I knew Sol would bring them out here for the spectacle of the night-time view over the rooftops of the Ipp and beyond to the alien zones, with their blazing skyscrapers and needle spires and gravity-defying mushroom towers. And beyond that, in the northern district of Constellation, the occasional flashes and lightning jags of the skystation.

I settled into a niche in the rock, just below the terrace's outer wall.

Sol's voice was the first I heard: "...pids will be good. The boy's good. !¡*reassurance | calming*¡! You'll be safe with us."

"!¡*agitation*¡! As safe as we were in Angiere?" said one of the men. That brought the conversation to a long pause. Angiere was a city to the west of Laverne, on the coast of the Great Sea. I had heard of it, but had never met anyone who had been there.

"!¡*sadness | loss*¡! No one is safe in war." That was my woman, the one I had saved and whose restored identity was Callo Hart 76.

War...

THE MONUMENT TO the Martyrs was tucked away in a side alley to the south of Precept Square.

By its nature, it was not a large or showy monument. If you did not know it was there, you would walk right by without noticing anything unusual.

Nightcut Alley was so narrow you could touch the buildings on either side, with your arms not even at full stretch. Usually, it was lined with trash cans and mounded rubbish from the taverns and pap-houses of Night Street, always waiting to be cleared but never, seemingly, clear. The buildings backed onto a straight-sided channel, filled with fast-flowing black water, and the Alley cut across the channel on a rickety wood-plank bridge, and the Monument to the Martyrs was tucked away below that bridge.

Here, on the far side, the channel cut into natural rock, and below the wooden span names had been carved, going back way beyond living memory. Names carved on names, carved on names.

Names of the Disappeared, names of the executed, names of those who had died in other ways at the hands of aliens.

Were they martyrs, though?

I never thought so. Maybe some of them.

Those of us who grew up in the Ipps, none of us were really rebels. We got by, we survived. Some of us took more risks than others. There were laws, of course, although the watchers had different laws to the chlicks, who had different laws to the starsingers and all the others. We had our own clan codes too, but they were quite apart from the rules of the aliens. Some of those laws we knew, but how could you ever understand the laws or moral protocols of sentient swarm-beings like the dragonflies of Clyd?

You couldn't, in short, and our only real law, underlying all the rest, was the law of survival. We did what we needed to get by.

We were not rebels, and our martyrs had no cause.

We commemorated them for the loss, and for the

knowledge that the next name on the Monument could be your own and, in a world like this, you might never even understand why.

We were not freedom fighters. There was no enemy. There was no war.

At least, not as far as I knew.

Chapter Four

"!¡*SADNESS* | *LOSS*¡! No one is safe in war," said Callo Hart.

Silent, I clung to my niche on the crag below the rooftop terrace.

There was another long pause, and I realised that the break in her voice had been because she had been holding back tears. I could picture the scene: she was crying now, quiet, restrained, just a line of tears from each eye picked out by the nightlights. Lucias and Pleasance were probably standing nearby, maybe her hand on his arm; Marek might be hesitating, unsure whether to go to her or not; and Sol would be staring out at the night skyline, ignoring the show of emotion, waiting for the conversation to move on. I wanted to look over the terrace wall, see the tableau, but I did not.

"!¡*curiosity* | *probing* | *fellow-feeling* | *sympathy*¡! Angiere?" prompted Sol eventually, her tones much softer than usual. I had got her wrong tonight: I had not expected her to show such sensitivity to the strangers.

"Gone," said Callo, simply.

One of the men took over, Marek I thought: "!¡*matter-of-fact*¡! The purges started about a year ago. At its onset, they sent swarms of tiny black flies, each the size of a pin-head..."

Into the pause, Sol said, "How do–" but was cut off as Marek regained his composure and continued.

"The destruction was instantaneous. One moment, a clan might be gathered to eat, the children still playing and yet to come to the table; the next, a black cloud would descend and the place would be stripped clean. The flies would devour cloth, wood, flesh, waste... Within seconds, all that remained would be bones and building stone, and then, as if the building suddenly realised it had no frame, the whole thing would collapse."

"!¡*probing*¡! And you're sure this wasn't a natural phenomenon, eh?"

"!¡*cold*¡! The purges were targeted," said Callo. "They were carefully engineered. !¡*stifled-emotion*¡! I don't know how these swarms were controlled, but they were. They would target one building and leave those all around it untouched. At first, the clans most active in the resistance were targeted, but later the attacks were more indiscriminate: any indigenous enclave could be hit. Even the trogs were targeted."

The trogs, the dead people. Human on the surface, but look into their eyes and you looked into an empty space. Like nearly-men, only less.

"The swarms were only the start," said one of the men. "Clan elders were seized. !¡*sadness*¡! Sometimes they would return after interrogation, but increasingly, when they did, they had been tortured..."

"What...?"

"Sometimes it was obvious from the physical injuries, but other times it was their minds that were wrecked. We don't know what happens in the torture chambers, but we do know that the watchers and their grunts understand how to tear a human mind apart."

"!¡*loss*¡! Often they didn't return at all," said Callo softly. "My blood-father... He was taken. He never had anything to do with the resistance, or even with the black market. He was a good man. But now he is gone. Disappeared."

Another pause. I looked out across the city. The northern horizon was lit up with mushroom towers and needle spires. Occasional pulses of light sprang from one tower to another for no apparent reason. It was another world over there. Another world, right on our doorstep.

"!¡*defensive*¡! We tried everything," said one of the men. "We had contacts in the emissaries, but they would not even acknowledge that Callo's father had ever existed, let alone that he had disappeared and that some of their goon squads might be responsible. We had grunts we'd turned by supplying drugs and satisfying their strange fetishes !¡*repulsion*¡! but when we asked, none of them would even admit to knowing anything.

"So that was when the resistance became real."

I shifted slightly in my niche. I thought of the Monument to the Martyrs. I knew kids who had gone up against the grunts, but it was more a rite of passage thing than an act of rebellion. Stones and taunts and running like mad. What was there to rebel against? This was how things were. Far better just to survive and make good. I never had been an idealist.

"!¡*strong | assertive*¡! We weren't rebelling against their presence," said Callo. "We were defending ourselves. Everything had been fine until they started encroaching, squeezing us, steadily eradicating us. If things had carried on, we would have been wiped out in no time."

She snorted at that.

A sudden dark blur flashed across my vision, and then hands seized my shoulders. The grip was strong, painful. I gasped and swallowed back a yelp of pain.

I felt my body pulling away from the niche, teetering.

My feet were still in contact with the rock-face... and then they were not.

I hung in mid-air, feet swinging, over a four-storey drop, held only by the powerful, painful grip on my shoulders.

I looked at my assailant, and Sol glowered back at me. She was a powerfully-built woman, but still, her strength surprised me. It felt as if her thumbs had gone right through the muscle of my shoulders and hooked themselves under the bone.

"!¡*controlled-anger*¡! Just give me one good reason why I'm still holding on to you," she said.

I don't know how, but I could *feel* that gulf of space beneath my dangling feet. "!¡*bowel-freeing fear*¡!" I clicked. "!¡*panic*¡!"

"!¡*calming*¡! Because you are his nest-mother and he is one of us," said Callo softly. She put a hand on Sol's arm and I saw the muscles twitch as if my nest-mother was about to release me into the void.

The moment seemed to draw itself out forever. I couldn't breathe: for fear, for anger with myself at betraying my position, for anger at even having followed them in the first place.

I had been such a fool!

Sol glared deep into my eyes and it was as if her look was digging into my soul in the same way her thumbs and fingers were gouging into my shoulders.

Then she turned at the waist, dragging me roughly over the terrace wall.

She dropped me in a heap, and my legs hurt from striking the wall, and my head clanged like a clocktower bell from hitting the ground, and I cursed and cursed at myself for having ended up in such a position.

I MUST HAVE blacked out, briefly, because the next thing I knew I was sitting on a wooden bench on the terrace, Callo pressing a wet cloth against my head with a click of "!¡*sympathy*¡!"

They must have scanned me, as Marek said, "!¡*business-like*¡! Your pid-boy is clean. No bugs. No tracers."

"!¡*reluctance*¡! That we know of," said Sol. It was true: our scanners were good, but we could never be entirely sure they were up-to-date with whatever new tech or biota had just come in at the skystation.

"!¡*aggression*¡! So, why did you follow us here?" demanded Sol. "Why were you spying on us?"

I met her look. "!¡*defensive*¡! I wanted to know what was going on," I said.

"!¡*anger | hierarchy-reinforcing*¡! That's not your business," she said, leaning so close to me that I swear I could feel the heat radiating from her flushed face.

"!¡*defensive | stubborn*¡! You had thirty or more people with false pids risking detention and worse today," I said. "None of us knew why. We just had to trust your judgement that it was worth it..."

"!¡*superiority*¡! You just said it. I am your nest-mother and you have to trust my judgement. !¡*indignation*¡! I don't have to defend my decisions to a nest-pup who believes he's above his station!"

A calming hand on Sol's arm from Callo again, distracting her, disrupting the outpouring of her anger.

"Perhaps we should be harnessing the boy's curiosity, not snuffing it out?" she said.

Sol glowered at her with a dismissive click from deep in her throat.

"!¡*calming*¡! It's not as if we have any great secrets," said Callo, her tone still soothing. Her voice was like a blanket, smothering any anger, impossible to resist. She was a woman with great wiles and depths, I realised. "Our only secret is that we survived Angiere."

Marek joined in, then: "!¡*sensible*¡! All the rest will emerge soon enough. If word of Angiere's destruction hasn't already reached here, then it will do so soon. We cannot be the only survivors of the city's final days."

Sol turned away with clicks of barely suppressed anger and frustration.

The moment was broken by a streak of light across the northern sky, stabbing down at the skystation, like a needle-straight bolt of lightning. Another arrival from the stars, reminding me again of the vastness of what was beyond. There was not just a whole world I had barely seen, but space, the stars, the cosmos. I was not even a speck of dust in the vastness of it all.

Sol took a swig of the spirits they had been drinking, and visibly calmed.

"We need to prepare," she said. "!¡*authority | resolve*¡! We need to be ready, without stirring up panic in the Ipp. Maybe Dodge can help, after all..."

I studied Sol closely. I had always looked up to her, but now she seemed right on the edge, unpredictable, volatile. I realised then that she was scared, and that did little to help settle my own nerves.

"!¡*cautious*¡! I heard some of what you were saying," I said. "Angiere. How can we prepare for that if they turn on Laverne?"

Sol looked down. "!¡*defeat* | *frustration*¡! I don't know," she said softly.

"We don't even know it's coming here," said the other woman, Pleasance. She was much quieter than the others, with a hesitant, nervy manner. "We don't know why they hit Angiere, we don't know what provoked it. We just don't know."

Her mate, Lucias, hugged her, squeezing her shoulders with his big hands.

I looked again to the north, the skystation, and remembered my earlier line of thinking. We were – all of us together – not even a dust speck on the face of the cosmos. Tiny. Insignificant. Things happened, on scales we couldn't even imagine. At best, we were no more than rats, cockroaches, cowering in our little niches, feeding on the scraps of the greater races. We didn't understand why suddenly someone was trying to stamp on us, or rather, why they had suddenly stamped on Angiere, and why should we? How could we?

"We don't know that it's *not* coming here, either," I said. "We might not know why, we might not know when or even whether, but" – I nodded towards Sol, my nest-mother – "it's what she said: all we can do is prepare, be ready to protect ourselves, or flee, or whatever it is that we'll end up doing. We might not be in control of events, but we can try to ride them, turn tragedy into opportunity. It's what we do. It's what we do *well*."

Callo was nodding. "You see?" she said to Sol. "Aren't you glad you didn't let him fall?"

LATER, THERE WERE just four of us, and then Marek and Sol retreated into the villa and I was left alone on the terrace with Callo.

We stood leaning on the enclosing wall, watching the city lights, the silence between us comfortable. It felt like we already had a bond, forged at the transit station in that brief exchange of pids.

"There." She pointed as another bolt of light split the sky, another arrival or departure at the skystation. In daylight you could see the 'station's towers and gantries, reaching for the stars, but the nightly lightshow was always more dramatic.

We had talked for a long time, so that now it would not be long before the eastern sky was afire with dawn. Slowly, I had built up a picture of what had happened at Angiere – the world beyond the city of Laverne was largely unknown to me, and this evening was one of the first times it had started to take form, like random tiles suddenly falling into place in a mosaic.

The most deadly strikes on Angiere had come from the sky, beam weapons burning entire blocks to glass, something I did not even know was possible. Squads of grunts had gone in too, snatching community leaders who may or may not have had some involvement in the opposition. The squads were a mix of orphids, craniates and chantras, overseen by watchers and chlicks.

When Marek had said this earlier, I'd interrupted. "!¡*confusion*¡! But today... at the transit station. You were with a chlick." I remembered the being's ancient features, remembered wondering how many generations of my own kind she-he must have lived through.

Marek had turned to me. "!¡*chiding*¡! There are good aliens," he said, "and bad. Just like there are good people and bad. Just because Saneth-ra is a chlick, it doesn't mean she-he's the same as the chlicks who led the raids on Westwalk and Seagreen in Angiere."

"Multiply that," Callo had added, echoing the line of my own thoughts earlier. "!¡*awe*¡! Up there. Good, bad, all shades of the rainbow in between. !¡*sadness*¡! Motivations that are neither good nor bad but something else entirely, and something else, and something else. It's hard to know what's in one chlick's head, let alone a million of them, a billion. Alien minds hold thoughts that we could never form, just as our minds hold thoughts that they could not shape."

"This is how it is," said Sol. "Aye, this is how it is."

So later, when the others had retired and it was just me and Callo pointing at the starship's sky-trail and being reminded again of the scale of things, I said, "Sometimes... !¡*tentative*¡! Sometimes I wonder how we hang on. Like cockroaches." Had I said this already earlier, or just thought it? "Why they let us survive at all..."

"'Let us'?" asked Callo, turning to me with a click of humour. I had not really paid much attention to her before. A woman maybe ten years my senior, she was a handspan shorter than me but gave the impression of being taller, something to do with the authority in her voice and manner. Her dark hair had a coppery tone to it, her eyes green, her skin a pale olive.

After a brief silence she continued. "They don't let us hang on, Dodge. That's not how it is. Whose planet do you think this is? Whose territory?"

"!¡*awkwardness | distraction | attraction*¡! I... Well..." Talking in click betrays much. It's hard to conceal your immediate responses and I was thrown by my sudden reassessment of this refugee from a destroyed city.

"!¡*humour | interest*¡! It's ours, Dodge. All of it. We are the indigenes. This is our home, and yet we are confined to Ipps and the wilderness."

I shrugged. I didn't know how to respond. As I say, I never was a one with high principles; I had no agenda, no manifesto other than to survive as comfortably as possible. I was no revolutionary.

"We shouldn't be hiding in the shadows, Dodge. We shouldn't be waiting for them to eradicate us, like they did in Angiere. Just think: what might we have been if we weren't over-run by aliens? What is our true potential? And why do they want to snuff it out now?"

Chapter Five

I DREAMED OF her that night. I dreamed of her soft authority and of how she could arouse herself to sudden intensity and passion, and of the fire that sometimes roared but always smouldered deep within her.

I dreamed of her kiss.

The night had ended shortly after that exchange. I looked into her eyes and realised that she was exhausted, kept awake only by the heat of her words and the tail end of the day's adrenalin. There were faint crow's feet radiating from the corners of her eyes, but otherwise her skin was flawless, a smooth olive tone that ran to dark pools beneath each eye.

"Thank you, Dodge," she said.

For a moment I wondered what she was thanking me for, and then I realised she was thanking me again for my role at the transit station, for getting her through that final barrier on her escape from the destruction of her home city.

I shrugged, then looked away with a click of awkwardness.

"You're special," she said. "!¡*sincere*¡! Do you realise that? Really special."

I felt like an awkward teenager then, out of my depth.

"!¡*dismissive*¡! No..."

She put a hand to my cheek, her touch soft, almost imperceptible.

Her lips pressed against mine, firm and cool, over in an instant. I flinched, surprised, and clicked, "!¡*fear | excitement*¡!"

I reached for her but she had turned, stepped away, and almost before I could react she was pausing at the entrance to the villa, dipping her head to me in parting, and then she was gone.

I could taste her on my lips still. I could close my eyes and feel the pressure of her mouth on mine.

I went down through the caverns and found my way to a sleeping chamber; for what little remained of the night, I slept on my rock shelf and dreamed of the woman from Angiere.

I WAS WOKEN by Immy, one of the pups I sometimes looked after at Villa Mart Three. Small hands on my shoulders, like pincers or birds' claws, shaking me vigorously. I woke, shards of dream slipping away, and saw Immy's sharp little face looming too close to mine.

"!¡*urgency | importance*¡! Mama Sol wants you," she shrilled.

"Huh? !¡*alarm*¡! What... what is it?" Visions flooded in of swarming black flies destroying everything in their wake, of beams from the sky that turned all below to molten glass.

"!¡*dismissive*¡! Has a job for you. Lazy Dodge, silly Dodge."

I found Sol in the main chamber, sharing a mug of tea with a man I vaguely knew as a street trader from the Pennysway Ipp.

Sol broke off from her conversation when I arrived, and said, "Got a job for you, boy." She produced a fold of paper, sealed with wax. "Run this over to the Loop. It's for Boss Frankhay. Only for his eyes, eh?"

A message. Running errands. I looked at it, took it, tucked it into the front pocket of my breeches. Was this punishment for my foolishness the night before? Was it some kind of test, to see how I would react? Was it the first step in preparing for the worst?

There was no way of telling. All I could do was run the message, do what I was told, trust that Sol was doing things right and not just trying to remind me of my place.

THE LOOP WAS to the west of our Ipp, just past the centre of the city. It was a hazardous journey at the best of times, a cut through territory that was truly alien, where you could never be sure of what you would encounter, what rules to follow, what risks there might be. But on this day, it was even worse: the tensions in the city had reached levels I had never before encountered.

I took a circuitous route out of the nest, hoping to bump into the visitors from Angiere, but I did not see them. Ruth and Divine were in the foreyard, drinking tea and making doe eyes at each other. I ignored their almost subliminal click exchanges. I didn't need to know.

Divine waved me over to join them, but I shook my head. "!¡*self-important*¡! Business to be taken care of."

They smirked into each other's faces, and for an instant I wondered how others saw me: heir apparent or messenger boy, figure of fun. My head was all over the place, I realised: up one moment, down the next. I wasn't usually so erratic.

I passed out of the Ipp with no trouble, through the checkpoint and into Cheapside E, the site of my first night run, when I had so nearly been caught and betrayed the whole nest with my sloppiness.

Soon, I was crossing the line into Central, a boundary marked by a humped bridge over a wide canal. The duty grunt scanned my wrist and peered into my face: my pids said I was me today, and cleared for all central zones outside the hours of curfew.

The grunt paused for far too long, and I realised it was communicating with someone or something that was not there: its superiors, or their security systems.

I kept my smarts, stayed calm. I didn't look around for escape routes, because I'd already done that as a matter of course, on approaching the checkpoint.

Eventually, the grunt clicked me through, with a big sigh of caustic gases that made my eyes sting.

Just off the bridge, I had to stop. My senses were being assaulted. I was dizzy and dazzled and my head was spinning. How to even begin to describe?

With the street, perhaps. Back in the Ipp, our main streets are surfaced with cobbles or flat slabs that crack within weeks of being laid. Side-streets are mud, packed with hard core that flattens itself over time. A bridge is a cobbled-together affair made mainly of wooden spans, with occasional sheets of metal or plastic salvaged from beyond the Ipp.

Out in the commercial districts, the streets are smooth with tar and fine grit that repairs and maintains itself; some are topped with a rubberised plastic, yielding to the footfall and repellent of water and other spillages. Even the side-streets and alleyways where humans are allowed to pass are smooth-surfaced and flawless.

Here, in Central, the roads were alive. Place your foot and the surface would arrange itself to your imprint; lift that foot and the surface gave you an extra push – wheeled vehicles got such a push from the road surfaces that they barely needed to propel themselves at all, or so I had been told.

All around, the buildings loomed above me. Buildings with mirrored fronts, moving images blending with what they reflected, so that it looked as if my inverted self was passing through a distorted, surreal landscape. Buildings that were all sharp angles and flat surfaces; buildings that were organically globular, jellied so that beings passed through apparently solid walls, absorbed into the bodies of the buildings. I did not know what was inside them; perhaps you passed through into air, like a normal building, or perhaps you remained in jelly or fluid as you conducted your business. Other buildings were covered in webbed silk nests that were alive with dragonflies and all varieties of flying creatures – the nests could have been the homes of sentient beings or they could have been the nests of parasites and vermin.

Looking up: the undersides of the mushroom towers were lit up with rhythmic traceries of light, all supported by implausibly slender central stalks. Flying vehicles darted and twisted; flying beings cut through the flow.

And all about, a seething, chaotic throng of bodies. Aliens of all varieties mixed with humans and trogs. The humans and nearly-men here were business-like, some of them half-mech, others cauled in alien webbing, controlled, not human at all.

The aliens walked on two legs, three, four or more; they floated on personal transports; they sat in self-contained personal environments, sealed off from the world. They strode, rolled, flitted, hopped, skittered, flew, ran... They travelled in all directions, yet appeared to know when to give way and when to plough on. They chattered, clicked, shrieked and yammered; they rumbled and groaned and whooped and roared. They smelled of urea and dung and decay, of perfumed flowers and sharp spices, of raw meat and chlorine.

There must be a billion cities like this on a million worlds. More. I couldn't grasp the scale of the universe, couldn't hold it in my head. Perhaps this was why we humans hid in our Ipps: we really were the hangers-on, unable to take the pace of being full members of such a diverse, galaxy-spanning community.

After that initial pause, I managed to gather myself and walk through it all, Sol's message in my pocket, my path never straight for all the beings barging through, cutting across, blocking my way with wings held wide to convert me to their cult or to recruit me for something I couldn't understand or to sell me phreaks, knick-knacks, philosophies or experiences. I tried to duck my head low and avoid betraying any kind of interest with even a glance, but still they harangued, still they confronted, still they yelled and touched and phreaked with my head as I tried to pass.

Armed grunts stood in clusters at every junction, watching, sniffing, tasting. I kept my head down, trying not to catch undue attention from them, too. There were orphids and dome-headed craniates, but also several varieties I didn't know. At least with the ones we knew, we had some idea of the trigger points, the rules and implicit understandings encoded in their behaviour.

Already on edge because of the grunts and the kaleidoscope of alienness all around me, I almost lost it at one point when I heard a buzzing and looked up, and a swarm of tiny black flies descended in a cloud around my face.

The previous night's account of the destruction of Angiere came back to me in a flash of panic, but the flies were just flies and I swatted them away. They left a citrus-scented vapour of panic in their wake, and for an instant my head was filled with terror again, and then it was gone, and I was just stumbling, disoriented, senses bejazzled by the bombardment of images and sounds and scents.

THE LOOP WAS an Ipp enclosed on three boundaries by a lazy bend of the Swayne, the great river that wound its way through our city. The Ipp could even be considered an island, as a canal had been cut across its land-locked neck, short-cutting the loop in the river.

I passed through the checkpoint more easily this time – the aliens cared more about those entering their own zones than leaving – and paused on a bridge over this canal. When I leaned on the railing, its surface yielded under my arms like jelly.

Swallows skimmed the water here, their backs flashing an iridescent oily blue as they emerged from the bridge's shadow.

The message in my pocket was like a stone weight. I wanted to open it, I wanted to know if Sol was just sending me on a pointless mission to punish me for my foolhardiness in following her and the four refugees from Angiere last night.

I resisted, and headed on into the Ipp.

The streets here were narrow, wood-framed buildings leaning together to cut out the sunlight. It felt as if I were entering a network of caves.

The ground floors of the buildings appeared to contain a mix of shops and offices, but it was hard to see much through their tiny bull's-eye glass windows, just people moving about or hunched over desks, lit in sepia tones by gaslight.

The street was eerily empty after the bustle of Central, just an old petticoated woman scrubbing at a wooden door, and a couple of rag-wrapped derelicts sharing a plastic tube of something noxious.

Sol's directions took me as far as the end of the narrow street.

I emerged on a square, dazzled by sunlight again. Three horses were tethered to a rail by a drinking trough in the centre of the square, shaded by a cluster of lime trees. On the far side, a row of hand-pulled stalls was lined up, selling pastries, fruit, drinks.

"!¡*hostility | warning*¡! Dunnat move, see?"

I froze.

It was a female voice. Young, I guessed. Street talk, made even harder to understand by her throaty Loop accent.

I heard footsteps as she circled round and into view. Coal-haired, mid-teens, skin as white as Divine's, whiter maybe. She was thin, but her face still carried the puppy fat of youth; her eyes were smudged dark with kohl, and her lips were blood red. She wore some kind of trashy black lace petticoat-skirt, and a ribbed bustiere that pushed her small breasts up as if they were being displayed on a meat rack. And resting casually across one arm she carried a pistol crossbow, its stock a polished rosy-brown wood with ivory and brass inlay, its string drawn, aimed vaguely at my lower midriff.

"!¡*threat | no-messing*¡! Ya biz?"

"!¡*calming* | *non-threatening*¡!" I clicked, struggling to keep the disdain from my response. "Yes," I went on. "I have business here. I'm from Cragside Ipp; South-East 6. Sent by Sol Virtue with a message for nest-father Frankhay. I's biz, see?"

She clicked something hard to decipher. Derision. Frustration. Aggression.

Then she clicked a rapid-fire sequence, and suddenly another of Frankhay's minders appeared from between two buildings to my left. This one was a year or two younger, barely into adolescence. It was hard to tell if it was male or female; he – or she – had the square jaw of a boy, but wore a similar outfit of black lace and knee-high leather boots.

The new arrival didn't carry a crossbow. Instead, the child had me in the sights of a wide-mouthed blunderbuss that looked big enough to stop a troop-carrier.

They marched me down a side-street and then on a twisting route that turned and doubled back several times, before finally ending up at an alehouse somewhere in the heart of the Loop.

The public bar was packed, the air heavy with the smells of sawdust, beer, phreaks and smoke. In one corner, a couple of benches had been pushed together as a makeshift stage upon which two slope-headed, almost-human aliens performed some kind of strange slapstick routine. It felt as if I'd stepped into another world; the Loop was like something out of Vechko's stories of history.

The one with the blunderbuss pushed ahead into a back room: another bar, quieter this time, with only a couple of lacy minders on the door and a small group playing cards at a long, uneven table by the wall.

"Nest-father, you have a visitor from Cragside," said the girl, dropping the street talk.

A man with collar-length white hair and a black brocade frock-coat turned slowly in his seat. This was probably meant to intimidate me, but to tell the truth I'd seen it all before. If you want intimidating, just come and visit Sol Virtue when she doesn't want to see you...

Sitting with his back to the entrance was show: a statement that he didn't need to worry about his safety here, didn't need to see who was coming.

I dipped my head and clicked softly in deference.

He turned fully now, and I saw that the frock-coat was secured with brass buttons, a pink silk shirt beneath with thick body hair tufting out at the neck. His brocade breeches were cut at the knee, just above a pair of high, strapped-up boots with a four-finger wedge heel.

"Cragside, is it?" he said, pulling at one bushy sideburn and peering at me through thick eye-glasses. "Don't hear much from Mother Virtue these days. What is it, lad?"

I reached for my pocket, and crossbow girl instantly adjusted her aim towards my head. At a brief wave of a finger from Frankhay, she relaxed and I was able to extract the sealed note from my pocket.

Frankhay took the fold of paper, opened it and handed it to a woman at his side to read. It seemed fitting that the nest-father of such a backward Ipp couldn't even read.

The woman whispered into his ear and he nodded.

"!¡*probing*¡! Sol says you know all about this," he said.

I nodded. At that stage I didn't know what it was that I was supposed to know all about, but if Sol said I did, then I'd go along with her. I clearly wasn't just a message-carrier, then.

"!¡*hierarchy*¡! So then, you going to tell me? Angiere. What happened at Angiere? It's gotta be big, or Sol Virtue wouldn't be asking for a pact 'tween Cragside and the Loop. Sol doesn't lower herself to make deals with the likes of us, 'less she's scared of something. That right, lad?"

"!¡*assertive*¡! She's not scared," I said, thinking fast. "She's just a good judge of a situation."

Frankhay shrugged and let it pass.

A ripple of applause and laughter came from the front bar.

I realised Frankhay was still waiting for me to tell him what I knew of the fall of Angiere, so I recounted the story told by Callo and her friends: the slow start, targeting individuals, followed by whole nests being targeted and then destruction of the entire city by beams from the sky.

Partway through, my attention started to wander. There were seventeen people here, not including me. Several were visibly armed with knives and bulbous-handled pistols; others were almost certainly less visibly armed, but deadly just the same. All wore a variant of the black lace that seemed to be some kind of uniform for Frankhay's nest, from discreet armbands to bustieres and what I now realised was a kilt, as worn by the blunderbuss kid.

That was when I saw her.

Sitting just beyond the main group, she had one knee drawn up so that her chin could rest on it. She wore a figure-hugging lace vest, leggings that looked as if they had been made from netting, and the same black knee-length boots she had worn the previous day at Precept Square.

It was the girl without pids, the girl with no identity. I must have faltered, because I realised Frankhay was suddenly leaning towards me, staring.

"The... !¡*embarrassed | confused*¡! The..."

"!¡*scathing | amused*¡! The beams?"

"...beams of light from the sky. From orbit, we think." It was important to emphasise the *we* rather than have this be just someone else's story I was recounting. "They burnt entire city blocks, first targeting resistance nests, but then becoming more and more indiscriminate. Everything they struck was destroyed, melted to glass."

All the time, she sat there, not really paying attention, just glancing across every so often. She didn't look as if she really belonged with this mob, but then yesterday she hadn't looked as if she belonged in Precept Square, either.

At one point I caught her eye, but she just looked right through me, not recognising me as the one who had saved her the day before.

"!¡*sceptical*¡! Sol thinks it's going to happen here like it did in Angiere? That it?"

I shook my head, and said, "She doesn't know. But it's possible, and if it does, then we need to be prepared."

"!¡*dismissive | sceptical*¡! And how can we defend ourselves against being melted like glass?" said the nest boss.

"We retreat to the caves. We hide." Frankhay was hard to argue with: what *could* we do? Would the beams penetrate even the caves, or might we really find shelter there?

Frankhay was shaking his head. "No, we're in good with the Green chlicks and the joeys," he said. "That's how we protect ourselves. We don't need Sol Virtue hiding behind our petticoats." He leaned towards me, and said, "Come here."

I approached, cautiously, and he beckoned me to lean forward, as if he was about to whisper in my ear.

Just then, with a click and a sliding, scraping sound, a dagger blade emerged from his wrist. Its tip came to rest on the underside of my chin, pricking at the skin like a needle.

I didn't flinch, didn't try to back off.

"!¡warning¡! You tell your nest-mama not to mess with us, you hear? You tell her thanks for the kindly message but no thanks, we're not having it. You got that?"

With the blade against my chin, I chose not to nod until I had straightened.

I backed off, turned, passed through to the public bar where someone on the impromptu stage was singing an old song about lost love, and then I was out on the street getting my bearings from a shaft of sunlight breaking between the buildings.

Chapter Six

LET ME TELL you about Hope.

Hope. A girl with no pids, no identity. A girl who was nobody.

Her story begins in darkness, with voices, a babble of voices...

SHE HAD THOUGHTS in her head, too. Knowledge. Language. Some degree of understanding.

She knew this was some kind of hospital, for instance. The people talking outside her door, the footsteps, the mechanical buzzing and humming, the smells of chemicals and old vegetables. The room: a bed with frames on either side, like a cage, to hold her in, tubes hanging from machines with electrical read-outs and dials and strange pulsing glows, the bland near-absence of colour, the lack of any kind of personality, life, soul...

Then, like a blast, a whirlwind, her head was full and booming and ringing like a million bells, so that she felt sick, felt that her skull must explode under the godsawful pressure.

Voices. Not bells, but voices. A million voices in her head, all run together into a single monstrous boom.

* * *

SHE HAD KNOWLEDGE.

Her name, for instance, was Hope. Hope of the Burren in full, although she did not know what or where the Burren might be. She liked it, though. It was a positive name, and it was one attached to a place or thing or clan. A name with optimism and connections was not a bad kind of name to have.

That day, in the hospital... The explosion of voices might only have lasted for an instant, but it left her shaking, nauseous, her skin slick with a cold, greasy sweat.

She did not know how long she had been there. In her head there was only an unconnected set of fragmentary images and sensations. The night-time smells of disinfectant and piss, all the more intense when lying in the semi-darkness of a room lit only by machine light. A doctor, a human one, with a nose like a blade and bushy black hair that grew in a fringe round a bald crown bulging with implanted hardware; leaning over her, speaking a language she did not know, prodding at her belly and running scanning devices across her chest and head. Another doctor with the puckered grey skin of a high-ranking chlick, leaning too close, green spit running in channels down its neck, staring at her with one glassy black eye and a pale one that looked as if it was made of polished chrome. The chlick's touch had been cold, rough, painful, too intimate and yet impersonal; she was like a slab of meat, a piece of furniture, a *nothing* to them.

She just wanted it gone, whatever it was that had blown up in her skull.

She didn't want to be special, which was what the chlick doctor said to her later that day. "Special, Hope." She-he clicked deep in her-his voicebox, but

Hope didn't know what the sound meant. "We will make everything all right." The chlick's voice rasped and wheezed, as if unaccustomed to speaking in this language that Hope understood.

HER ROOM: THE ceilings too high; the walls a sandy off-white, finished in some kind of wipe-clean plastic; the floor grey, with the same finish. The windows were tall and frosted and far too bright, and had horizontal bars running across them.

Her room. She did not think she had ever had a room before. But this room was more like a cell.

Was this a hospital, after all, then, or some other kind of place?

She slept, and dreamed vivid, too-colourful dreams of aliens and big machines with tubes and wires and scanning pads, dreams where everyone was shouting at her, yelling, leaning in close and bellowing. And she woke sheened in sweat, a knot of puke in her throat, her heart raging and racing like a heavy fish trapped in the cage of her ribs.

SHE HAD TO pull the tubes out of her arm before she could get out of that place.

Two needles, buried deep in the crook of her elbow, held in place by scabbed green gel. Tubes attached to the needles. Tubes that had made her feel better, calmer.

She wasn't calm now, though.

Outside, engines revved and sirens blared and wailed.

Inside, beings shouted and screamed and ran. She could see them through the frosted inner window of her room. Hear their panicked footfalls and cries.

This was why she had to get out.

She heard gunshots and the *zip* of beam weapons. She heard voices immediately outside her door, one hissing, scratching voice saying, "Where is she? Where *is* she?" and a snapping sound, a scream of pain, a thud as of something falling.

She yanked the needles from her arm, swung her legs, noting how skinny they were, wondering if they were even strong enough to support her weight. She could not remember the last time she had stood.

Her head felt as if it was still moving, even though she had halted, perched on the edge of the bed.

The floor, unexpectedly warm beneath her bare feet. It almost felt alive.

She stood, and breathed deeply to counter the dizzy rush and the blurring and blackening of her vision. The room was not so much spinning as bucking, trying to knock her off balance.

She took a step, another, another. She reached the door and edged it open. Outside her room she saw the back of a body-armoured grunt so tall its black-helmeted head nearly touched the ceiling. Beside it was a shorter officer, a chlick in a chain-weave bodysuit that clung to the uneven bulges of its asymmetrical body.

She stepped out into the corridor, all in that brief moment with their backs still turned towards her.

There was a trolley in the corridor and she caught herself, leaning on it for fear that her legs would buckle. It started to move and she had to stagger forward in order to remain upright. When she looked down she saw a small being wrapped in blankets, its head almost entirely obscured by a breathing mask full of steamy vapours.

A baby? Had she abducted a baby?

She didn't think so. On one arm it had touchpads grown in, ports and zip panels. She didn't think a baby would have such mods. Just a small being, then.

Pushing the trolley, she was ignored by the rushing, yelling troopers, but then the being in the trolley seemed to realise something was wrong, and started to shrill a crescendo of high-pitched clicks and claw at its wristpad.

She gave the trolley one last push and sidestepped through a door.

She was in a cupboard now.

More than just a cupboard. Some kind of storeroom. It had been ransacked already, with shelves pulled off walls, cabinets toppled, benches smashed.

She crawled under a leaning metal cabinet, shivering, sick, her arm icy and throbbing where the needles had been.

She pulled her knees up, rested her chin on them, hugged herself. Waited.

LONG AFTER THE corridors had gone quiet and the revving engines had departed and the sirens stilled, Hope pushed herself to her feet and went to the door.

Peering out into the corridor, she saw carnage everywhere. Windows smashed; doors hanging from hinges, panels caved in; trolleys tipped on their sides; pipes twisted and snapped off, hissing steam; cables dangling from the ceiling, occasionally crackling and flashing electric blue.

In the first room she checked, a young woman lay half out of her bed, her back at an impossible angle, a burnt hole like a black bowl scooped out of her chest and her head smashed bloodily against the floor. A wallscreen flashed jagged graphics and bleeped warnings, and a clear tube hung from a pump, drip-drip-dripping into a spreading milky pool on the floor.

In the next room, or cell, a man with an oddly square head lay on the floor, eyes staring into space, mouth half-open as if he was about to speak. His body was black and looked like it had been coated with tar. Then... Hope saw that the black surface was moving, and the man was not tarred but covered with tiny bugs, flies. They swarmed over his flesh, and into it, she realised, when she saw that the white lines across his chest were exposed ribs.

She looked again at the man's head, and saw that his eyes had turned, were fixed on her. His jaw twitched, as he tried to speak, but then a surge of black bugs moved up his neck, across the lower half of his face, and soon he was completely submerged.

Hope backed away into the corridor.

In the next room she saw a family of monkey-like fettorals, harmless and kindly beings, but these... all six of them had been beaten to death, their naked bodies pulped and flattened.

A short way along the corridor, she came across the trolley and the chittering midget she had abandoned earlier. The small being was clicking no more, its body sliced diagonally by some kind of weapon that had cauterised the wound as it passed. The creature smelled of burnt fish.

She felt dizzy, but snapped out of it when a tiny black fly buzzed in front of her eyes.

She backed away, then turned, ran, careering off trolleys and walls, stumbling over corpses, bare feet slapping and slithering on the wet floor, not knowing where she was going but only that she was going.

* * *

SHE FOUND HER way outside.

What she still took to be some kind of hospital was part of a complex of low, blocky buildings. The door she found opened onto a courtyard, where water ran through channels set into an austere paved surface.

She stepped out, and was instantly cold. Her thin t-shirt came to mid-thigh. She had no other clothes, no footwear.

Her bare arms goosebumped, and cold air stole up inside her top. Almost instantly, her feet went numb.

She felt exposed, and pulled the hem of her shirt down.

Cautious, she took a few half-running steps to the end of the building, where a low wall divided the courtyard from... as she approached, she saw a roadway beyond the wall, empty, save for an abandoned, burnt-out transporter.

She swung her legs over the low wall.

There was a body in the front of the transporter, possibly human, burnt beyond recognition. She moved on.

A short distance farther, she could see through a line of trees to an open grassed area, some kind of sports field. There, one last troopship was lifting, the air bent and hazed beneath its square, khaki bulk. In the distance, three more were already miniatures in the sky, heading out across a bay. The waves were edged with white in the stiff breeze that suddenly gusted off the sea and through the trees; they made her recall the white lines of the dead man's ribs, beneath the mass of flesh-eating bugs.

It felt like a slap, that rush of air, someone shaking her to her senses.

She felt something. A gut thing. A thing in the dark recesses of her mind. Elemental.

She started to run.

The chorus in her head came back and was almost enough to drive her to her knees, but instead she realised she could suppress it, with the pounding of her bare feet on uneven ground, the burning of muscle-pain in legs that could barely support her, the wheezing and gasping for breath in lungs that did not have the capacity for all the air she needed to suck down to feed her muscles, to fuel her escape.

Her throat burned. Her head was spinning. She reached a ridge of dunes and stumbled up them, battling through tough twists of sea grass and loose, shifting sand. At the top, her legs gave way and she fell, slid, slumped in a heap into a hollow before the next dune started to rise.

She heard a sound. Felt it. Didn't know what she did to sense it, but it was there, all around her, all through her.

Like a drone, too deep to hear.

Like a whine, too high-pitched to detect.

A vibration seizing her innards, turning solids to jelly, to liquid, to gas. To atoms.

A pressure, so intense she could barely breathe.

A heat.

The heat... the blast-wave swept across the dunes, so intense that the sea grass smouldered, charred, broke into sporadic flame. She felt her skin tightening with that sudden pressing heat, smelled hair starting to singe.

She could smell burning, and something else. Something acrid, clawing at her throat. Burnt plastics and rubber. Something chemical that made her eyes stream and her throat sting.

She cowered in her hollow, feeling as if the world was coming to an end.

WHEN SHE EMERGED, clambering up the dune to look back towards the hospital, darkness was beginning to settle. The sky was red and gold and it shimmered like the air beneath the alien troopship she had seen earlier.

The smell still hung in the air. Chemicals and burn.

The hospital was no longer there.

Instead, there was a plain of a dark glass, lit a deep maroon with reflections from the sky, smooth, like a lake on a breezeless day.

Chapter Seven

I WAS GLAD to get out of that bar, get away from Frankhay and his black lace goons. Glad to get away from that spring-loaded dagger blade embedded *inside* his wrist.

That was alien tech, a body mod like that. It made me wonder what else Frankhay had kept hidden.

And then I thought of another possible reason for Sol sending me on this mission, hopelessly under-informed and unprepared: she must have known Frankhay would turn down the offer of collaboration, so maybe she thought I would wind the gang-boss up so much I wouldn't get out alive, or at least I'd get enough of a beating to teach me a lesson about my place in the order of things.

I crossed the canal but then, even though the sixth had already rung, I chose not to take the direct route back through Central. I wanted to get back, but Central was just too risky. Too many aliens, too much chance of breaking some unwritten rule or code; too many armed grunts on street corners just waiting to leap into action. No law or protocol would protect an indigene from some trigger-happy orphid, wired up on combat-phreaks and paranoia.

I couldn't work out why, but the city felt different that evening. It may have been a direct result of our little drama on Precept Square the day before. It may have been somehow connected with what had happened in Angiere – a spread of tension, alien forces stirring up opposition and then squashing it, for whatever unfathomable reasons they might have. It may simply have been a change in me: now that I had heard Callo's story of destruction, I was more on edge, more ready to interpret an everyday grunt patrol as something sinister.

I queued for a ferry across the river. It cut the distance, but was still the longer way home, as I would need another ferry to cross again later. So close to curfew, you never knew when they might stop running, and there was the chance I would end up in a foreign Ipp for the night, huddled on the street like my old nest-sib Skids and his fellow homeless wraiths.

An orphid grunt scanned me before allowing me onto the ferry. Its buds were puffing out smoky vapours, putting everyone on edge.

From a nearby tree, a magpie chack-chack-chacked, as if taunting the grunt. Then the bird fell silent, and the grunt was re-holstering a beam-pistol.

The crossing took longer than it should have, as we waited in mid-river, held up by a fleet of big river barges lumbering past. Even this looked like something sinister, even though the barges were a common feature of the Swayne. Eventually, we landed in Satinbower, an Ipp I had only occasionally visited before, mostly back when gangs of adolescent nest-sibs from my home in Cragside would roam the city on the prowl for trouble and easy pickings.

It was an odd kind of Ipp, one that was both closely associated with the industries of the watchers and the precentians, and fiercely independent. Labour in the factories and production houses was made up of work gangs of trogs and nearly-men, organised by clan bosses who lived in alien-built terraces overlooking the waterfront. I remember, way back, there was a kid who tagged along with me and my sibs one day, who insisted his blood-father was in charge of it all: the aliens might think they owned the factories, but without the bosses they could do nothing, so it was the clan-fathers who really ran both this district *and* the aliens who owned it.

The kid was all mouth, and we'd beaten the crap out of him just for that. But still, Satinbower was different.

I pulled my coat tight around myself, dipped my head, and marched purposefully through the Ipp. I'd done my job, and I didn't need any more trouble. I just had to get home before seventh and curfew.

Satinbower had its own unique smell. It smelled clean. The place didn't stink of sewerage and decay and years of ruin. The buildings were mostly only two storeys high, their walls upright and squared off, made from neat bricks of clay and even plastic. The windows were wide, more like those in Central than the small bull's-eye glass used in most of the Ipps. And power cables ran through the streets, connecting up buildings that were clearly human businesses and nest-homes.

There was wealth here in Satinbower.

Maybe that kid had been right after all. Maybe humans did have the upper hand over their alien overlords in this Ipp.

Or maybe they *had*...

At this point I was still slow to understand what was happening, but my home city had turned dangerous since the four refugees had arrived from Angiere, even here in this chlick-pet human enclave of Satinbower.

The street I walked along was busy, one of the main thoroughfares that cut across the Ipp to where the river looped back around again. That was where I hoped to catch another ferry across, and then I would be almost back in Cragside Ipp. I walked fast, trying to make up for the delays on the first river crossing.

It was peculiar, being somewhere that was built with alien technologies, but was clearly an Ipp, full of indigenes, with only the occasional alien going about its business. The mix seemed all wrong.

Towards the next main junction, the crowd bunched up, and my progress slowed.

I tried to peer over the heads of those around me but couldn't see much, just another junction, a nondescript street cutting across this one at an angle.

Then the background drone of city noise grew louder and a dark green troopship swung round from behind a blocky grey building. It came to hang over the junction, its bulbous front tipped slightly down, like a bird of prey suspended on the breeze.

Then – no warning, nothing – beams of intense greenish-white light lanced out from the troopship and into the crowd.

I caught my breath, blinked, and the lines were still there, as if burned into my eyes in a vivid purple.

There was a pause, as if everyone was catching their breaths, absorbing what had happened. And then someone ahead of me screamed, then another, another.

The crowd surged back. Bodies and elbows and knees barged and dug and shoved. I caught an arm across my face, so hard that my ears rung and I tasted blood in my mouth.

I let myself be jostled along, following the flow like a piece of garbage floating in a storm river.

Keith Brooke

Behind me, I heard that sound again, the almost whispery sigh of the troopship's beam weapons. And more screams and shouting. The rumble of feet on the road surface. Breaking glass. The crunching thud as a roadside stall was tipped over under the weight of bodies.

I spotted a side-alley, little more than a crevice between buildings. I heaved my body through the crowd towards it, made it, was almost sick with exertion and terror. Shaking, I leaned against a smooth wall and tried to regain my composure.

Every time I closed my eyes, I saw those beams cutting through the crowd. Every time I breathed in, I smelled the odour of burning human meat. Every time I swallowed, that was the taste in my mouth.

My head was a mess of all kinds of things, as I followed that gap between buildings.

I tried to stay focused on keeping moving, sidestepping the heaped garbage and iron stairways, following the alley as it turned and ran parallel with the street, squeezed between the backs of two rows of tenements.

I thought of that big square building on the junction, and back to the days of roaming with my sibs. That kid with the swagger in his click. His blood the gang boss. That encounter had been somewhere near here, maybe even that building, which could be why it all seemed so familiar. Was that the clan nest?

The sounds... occasional screams and shouts. The sudden booming of engines as the troopship – or another troopship – swung overhead.

I was heading away from the junction. A few other people had found the alley too, and were running or striding in the same direction as me.

I came to a side-street, eerily quiet.

An older man hesitated in the mouth of the alley as I approached.

"!¡*cautious*¡! You think it's safe?" I asked him.

My accent or looks must have betrayed me as an outsider and the man's expression closed, turned hostile. I thought he was about to answer, but instead he clicked aggressively and spat phlegmy spittle right at me.

It fell short. I looked from it to him, said, "!¡*hostile*¡! Fuck you," and pushed past him into the street.

If everyone's first reaction – Frankhay's, this spitting man – was to close in, turn against anyone from another district, then Sol's plan to unite the clans would never work.

But now, Sol no longer looked as paranoid as she had done earlier.

I walked a wide loop, my nerves on edge, the whole city's nerves on edge. At one point, as my route took me up a slight rise, I looked back and saw a pair of troopships hanging over Satinbower Ipp, noses down, twitchy and heavy, occasional beams stabbing down to the streets below.

Smoke hung over Satinbower as seventh rang out across the city.

Curfew.

There would be no ferries now until morning. I was stranded in a foreign Ipp that was under assault from alien forces.

That was when it really sunk in. Fleeing the troopers had been a short-term thing, a survive-*now* thing. But now I had to get through the night, without being rounded up or summarily shot by slaughter-happy grunts.

I roamed the deserted streets until darkness fell. There was no lighting, apart from that which escaped the shuttered windows of the buildings I passed.

In the distance I could still hear the troopships, and occasionally I heard the electric whine of street vehicles – more grunts, I presumed, on a sweep for curfew-breakers. There would be many of us tonight, with so many caught up in the raid.

I clung to the shadows and alleyways, looking for shelter and finding none.

Coming to the river, I darted across the road and dropped down to the rocky shore. There, I almost trod on a dark shape which turned out to be a man bundled in rags.

He swore at me, but didn't move.

A little farther on was another, a bone-thin woman, almost certainly a wraith, or a recovering one.

I found a niche in the boulders and tried to settle for what was to be a long, cold night. If the clanless slept here, then either it was a safe spot overlooked by curfew checks or I would at least be part of a crowd when trouble kicked off.

I huddled up, wrapped my arms around myself and tried not to shiver.

"Frankhay said no. With a knife."

Sol shrugged. "!¡*resignation*¡! So where'd you get to last night, eh?"

I'd found her at one of our workshops in Cragside that converted one kind of pulp into another. I didn't know what for, only that there was money in it, and some degree of protection for the clan.

Now, we walked back towards the clan nest at Villa

Virtue. I was sore and tired from an uncomfortable, sleepless night. Right up until dawn and the end of curfew, troopships had swung over that riverside doss, and patrols had passed by on the road, but the search had always passed over the rocks without pause.

By morning, my body felt like it had frozen itself into position. Shuffling to the ferry, filthy and stubbled, I knew I must look like one of the dossers I'd shared the rocks with, and wondered if the boundary guards would even let me cross. But I had money in my pocket and my pids gave me authority to travel, and so I was allowed to pass.

Sol was watching me closely as we entered the nest and headed up to the roof terrace. "!¡*weary*¡! There was trouble in Satinbower," I told her.

Two of the refugees were there, I saw, and the chlick, Saneth. They sat at a table, with bowls of tea. I hadn't known that chlicks drank tea.

We went to join them, pulling up another bench. This was the first time I had been so close to a chlick and not been threatened.

"!¡*deferential*¡! Saneth-ra was telling us of the incident at Satinbower," said Sol, dipping her head as she added the deferential -ra to the chlick's name.

"!¡*factual reporting*¡! Forty-seven humans were seized by an orphid task-force commanded by watcher Hadeen factionaries." The chlick's voice was soft and whispery, like a breeze through dry leaves. Its grey-brown face was grooved deeply with folds and wrinkles, pocked and scarred and calloused by the passing years. I saw now that the chlick had a false eye, some kind of mod; it looked metallic, polished to a dull shine. The false eye moved independently of the real one, disconcertingly so. "!¡*probably reliable hearsay*¡!

The human nest-parents thus seized were long-standing favourites of watcher Nullist factionaries. Many mutual ties of finance, favour and manipulation."

Callo was nodding. "!¡*dread*¡! It's coming here," she said.

I thought of the night on the terrace at Villa Mart Three, the kiss. She hadn't even met my eye since my return.

"!¡*earnest*¡! It is," said Saneth. "!¡*directing-juniors*¡! You must protect your own. You must protect what you have that is special and sacred."

"!¡*hesitant*¡! I saw it all in Satinbower," I said. "They must have slaughtered hundreds in the crowd, and flattened whole blocks."

Saneth paused, and I realised she-he was consulting some data-source. "!¡*factual reporting*¡! Thirty-six humans were killed during the incident. One additional death by heart failure could not be directly attributed. One building was damaged. This was the Satinals' clan-nest on Red and Hythe."

"So I exaggerated..."

Saneth slowly turned that mod eye to face me. I felt as if the eye's tiny black pupil was drilling through me. I swallowed, chilled, even though I knew there was some kind of phreaking involved, subtle mood-shifters making me feel tiny and insignificant before the ancient, lauded one.

"!¡*admonishing junior scholar*¡! You must be required to consider this with due gravity," the chlick said slowly. "Those of your type in Angiere learned to do so. !¡*inappropriate humour*¡! There are better ways to learn than the way they learned."

"!¡*confrontation*¡! Why?" I asked. "Why are they doing this?"

It was Marek who answered. He seemed to be the leader of the four refugees, a tall man, with sharp bones and a trimmed line of dark beard down his jaw. "This is what we have been trying to establish," he said. "But with all due respect" – he nodded to the chlick – "how can we possibly know what is in the mind of an alien?"

"!¡*concurrence*¡!" clicked Saneth. "!¡*humouring junior*¡! Just as it is hard for one such as we to see what occupies the mental processes of the human variety." She-he said this like a man talking to a lesser being, to a dog or a goat.

"So why...?"

"!¡*authority*¡! As Marek says," said Callo. "It's almost impossible to understand. Saneth knows a little, but there are so many factions and species. We observe their actions, we see what they do, but we do not see why. They want to weed us out. They want to find some of us and kill the rest. It's like some kind of harvest."

"Others just appear to want to kill us," added Marek. "All of us, regardless of who or what we are. It is as if humankind is a pest to be eradicated, a nuisance. That's what ended up happening at Angiere."

"!¡*tentative*¡! Maybe they're scared of us," I said.

Marek barked a short laugh, but was silenced by an impatient slap-click from Saneth.

"!¡*encouraging junior scholar*¡! It is a possibility that they are scared of what you might become," the chlick said. "It is a possibility that they are scared that you may be special. Lauded-one Saneth-ra contains within both the she and the he; what potentials does the scholar pup Dodge and those who are like him hold within? It is a possibility that they fear that you may be what they could never be."

Chapter Eight

SPECIAL.

Let me tell you about special.

Hope was special. That girl with the honey-brown bangs and the look in her eye that would stop a man in his tracks with his heart racing and his mouth dry. The girl whose memories started with darkness and an explosion of voices in her head. The girl with no pids, no identity, nothing. The girl who had survived an attack that had turned a seaside hospital into a lake of melted black glass.

Hope.

THERE WAS A road leading away from the beach, and she walked along its blistered asphalt surface. The road was narrow as it cut through the dunes, away from a small parking and recharge area. On leaving the beach, the road was bounded by tall, dark hedges that kept the day's sun from her.

The night in the dunes had been cold and full of strange noises: birds piping on the beach and in the air above; the occasional drone of a troopship, its lights dancing over the sea; the whistling and drumming of the wind in her ears. None of it was enough to smother the voices in her head.

The road led to a larger highway, this one with traffic, and that scared her. Those who had attacked the hospital had departed in troopships, but what if there were others travelling by ground transport? Or road blocks to keep the curious away? In her institutional sleeveless shirt and bare feet, she must look like an escapee.

She did not want to be caught by the beings who had burned the hospital to glass.

On the highway, cars like translucent teardrops passed at great speed, while heavy goods transporters rumbled more slowly along the paired central tracks. In the near lane, occasional horse-drawn wagons passed. It was one of these that took her to the city, the old driver insisting that she ride with him because he was easily bored, and she had a nice voice for chatting and she would make the dull scenery so much more attractive.

She didn't say much, and in her tattered, grubby shirt she was hardly a pretty sight, but the man made her smile, and that was good, because she had not felt capable of smiling at all until he had stopped for her.

Tween was not quite an Indigenous Peoples' Preserve, but generally the aliens treated it like one, ignoring what went on there. It was a grey zone in the city of Angiere, a margin, a quarter where everyone turned a blind eye.

This suited Hope perfectly.

She slept in a little square of parkland that first night, one of the clanless, one of the unaffiliated. She was not the only one who slept there.

She had a blanket now, given to her by the old man who had brought her to the city on his wagon. He had great heaps of them in the back, neatly folded and rolled and secured with string ties. That was his trade, blankets. During an evening of wandering aimlessly from street to street, she had worn hers as a shawl, but at night it was large enough to wrap herself in, like a scratchy cocoon.

In the darkness, the voices were a constant murmur, the jostle and bustle of a crowd all trapped in her head.

The sound was almost soothing, like ocean waves, but that was even worse. She didn't like to be lulled by them.

She roamed through Tween the next morning. Early, there were wagons pulled up to shops and bars, delivering fresh supplies and taking away debris from the night before. The buildings were tall and narrow here, made of tiny clay bricks, and many of them painted with flowers and the sun and moon and stars, birds and people and all manner of strange beings.

She came to a bar, a corner-building with thick, distorting glass in its windows and a frontage of dark, varnished wood. As Hope passed, the door burst open and a woman staggered out, belching and giggling. She paused, straightened her almost non-existent wraparound skirt, gave Hope a big leery grin and staggered off along a side-street.

The door had stuck, half-open, and Hope peered into the gloom. There was pipe music and laughter and the overpowering smells of beer and smoke and heady, woozy phreaks.

She was not sure if these people had started drinking early today, or if they were still here from the night before.

A man in a skimpy vest, skinny as a straw, had one arm draped around an alien, or maybe another man with add-on alien parts – grafts, body-mods, growths. The thing turned to face the first man and Hope saw that it was a man, too, after all, the face human with pale features and a wisp of a moustache. He blew smoke into his partner's face, and then their mouths met, locked, ground together.

A woman walked across Hope's line of view. She wore only tiny black underwear, and her tattooed body was pierced so much that she jingled as she moved. Alien pods were attached down her spine, as if feeding on her, giving out little puffs of phreak as she moved and jangled and her tattoos swirled as if they were alive and her hair was snakes, writhing and twisting, and Hope realised that something had got to her, a vapour, a phreak, something had latched into her brain and... and...

"!¡*friendly*¡! You coming in?"

It was a man. Tall. Pale. He had big brown eyes and dark hair that ran down along his jaw in a neatly trimmed beard.

She glanced sideways, along the street where the belching, giggling woman had gone. She took a step backwards.

"!¡*friendly*¡! We don't bite," said the man. "!¡*humorous*¡! Well, you know..."

Hope relented. The man was doing friendly, like the old man on the wagon had done friendly earlier. That had worked out. She'd got a blanket out of that, now draped across her shoulders against the morning chill.

"Drink?"

In the bar now, the man held an arm as if to put it across her shoulders where the shawl was, to guide her, engulf her. Instead, he held his arm back, ushered her in.

She went to stand at the bar.

"I... I have nothing," she said. "Just a shirt." And the blanket.

"!¡*soothing*¡! So I see," said the man. Then: "Hey, Ubrey," to the bald man behind the bar. Ubrey was standing there, watching his left hand as it turned almost a full turn, then back the other way, over and over, over and over. There was something mechanical about it, and then Hope realised the barman had a prosthetic arm, and there was something wrong with it. At the other man's call, Ubrey straightened and let his arm drop, the broken hand still rotating back and forth.

"!¡*business-like*¡! Get the girl a drink, would you? Beer? And maybe a ham fold?"

Hope turned to him. "Thank you," she said.

The man already had a drink on the bar. He took a long draw at it and a line of froth stuck to his upper lip. "You looked lost," he said, leading Hope to a table in a dark corner. "And you're wearing an infirmary gown beneath that raggy blanket. !¡*curious*¡! I bet you have a story to tell."

"I don't know," she said. She did not know what her story was. Her head was full of a clamour of voices. That was her world, her story.

"!¡*cautious*¡! I know people," the man said carefully. "They tell me there was an infirmary, down the coast at a place called Anders Bars. A military place run by watchers. The kind of establishment they keep quiet and which never appears on maps. !¡*pressing*¡! The kind of place someone might escape from with only the clothes on her back and not much idea what was going on."

The voices in her head were like a hammer. She slumped forward, catching herself on the wooden table between her and the man who knew too much.

Her head was spinning, her mouth dry; when she looked up a woman was looming over her: the woman she'd seen before, all tattoos and piercings and breasts bulging out of a low-cut shelf bra. "Your food and your drink, my love," said the woman. "And if Marek here's bugging you, just tell me and I'll have his nuts on a dinner plate. Okay?" She smiled, tweaked Marek's ear, and returned to the bar.

"!¡*calming*¡! It's okay," said Marek. "Eat your food. I promise I won't keep bugging you. You can trust me, please. Eat."

She looked down, saw a napkin with a meat-filled fold of flat bread on it and a tall mug of beer.

She ate.

She could not remember the last time she had eaten. It must have been at the infirmary, she guessed.

"They burned it," she said, eventually. "Anders Bars. The infirmary. It's gone. Destroyed."

Marek nodded. "!¡*encouraging*¡! So we'd heard. It's not the first place they've wiped out, and it won't be the last. You want to know how I worked out you must have come from there?"

He was smiling, clicking reassuringly.

Hope just looked at him, as she chewed her ham fold.

"!¡*mildly disconcerted*¡! Your top," he said, gesturing with a hand. "It says 'ABI' on the collar. Anders Bars Infirmary. We really must find some new clothes for you."

Hope glanced down, saw the letters. She hadn't noticed them before, had not really had any cause to look at herself except to note the goosebumps on her arms the day before.

"I have no money," she said. This man might be doing friendly, but she knew that there were usually limits to friendly. She could not get new clothes without trading something.

He waggled his head from side to side. "!¡*reassuring*¡! I know some people," he said. "Some people who would like very much to hear your story. They will take care of you in return."

Trading. She understood trading. She would give and they would give in return. She could do that.

WITHIN A SHORT time, Hope had established herself in Tween. She paid attention to people, and here she learnt that this was something that most people did not do: they cared about themselves, their own needs, their own voice being heard. Hope listened. She responded. She fitted in.

One day she woke to Marek moving around the tiny room he had found for her. He wore only a tiny pair of under-shorts, enough to cover his bony arse and his pencil-thin cock.

This morning he wasn't doing friendly.

He didn't usually stop over, but last night there had been a disturbance in the Tween and he had shown up long after curfew, breathing raggedly and limping. She had gone to the window immediately to see if there was any sign that he had been followed. She knew to do this, although she did not know what it was that he did on nights like this when he was out with a shadowy group he called the Vanguard. There'd been lights over the Tween. Sentinels buzzing the rooftops with flashes and bolts of blue; a troopship hanging heavy in the air above the Citadel, white beams tracking movements in the streets.

"Trouble?" She rarely asked questions, but that night his excited demeanour had almost seemed to demand it of her.

"!¡*playing down*¡! There was a modicum of bother," he'd said, going to her water jug and splashing his face and head liberally with its contents. "A squad of orphids got involved, sniffing a bit too closely at the transit... We just managed to get our cargo on the shuttle before the party was rumbled."

Marek's cargo was people, refugees fleeing the watchers' clampdown, Angiere no longer safe for them. Since arriving here, she had heard of entire city blocks being destroyed by the watchers' beam weapons, and ever more draconian purges of any opposition.

The Vanguard would be regarded as opposition, providing safehouses and protection, spiriting people away ahead of the purges.

Marek brought with him danger.

That night, he had come up behind her at the window, turned her, and forced her head down on him, a fist tangled in her hair. She was thankful that he was over-excited and quick.

Just as she had realised when she first met Marek, there was a limit to friendly.

Later, lying beside him, she had watched the rapid rise and fall of his bare chest and thought he was asleep. He surprised her by saying, "!¡*musing*¡! I'm envious of them, you know. The refugees. The ones we help to escape this dying city. Envious."

She stayed quiet.

"They're on their way. Somewhere out there... somewhere there's a place. Harmony, we call it. A place where humankind are not beggars and scroungers living on the scraps left by the occupying aliens."

In her head, a sudden surge, a blabber of voices. She did not want to hear him talk this way, not if it did this to her head. She tried to turn, but he pinned her in place with an arm and a leg, his captive audience.

"!¡*domineering*¡! A place where we belong," he continued. "A place where people can be people, not scuttering rats in the gutter. That's where they're going, the people we saved tonight. That's where we belong. Harmony."

She couldn't breathe. It was like a belt tightened around her chest. *Harmony*. Just the word scared her. The voices in her head were like a clanging explosion. She remembered the dunes, the clamour then, and the way she had learnt to smother the bellowing chorus.

She breathed in, and concentrated on the air filling her lungs. Out, her rib cage sinking, emptying.

The clamour, subsiding. Dying away.

In the morning, the arrogant strut around the small room, Hope curled up on a sleep mat on the floor, a loose sheet twisted around her.

"!¡*agitated*¡! We cannot leave it long," he said. "!¡*dismayed*¡! The city... have you seen it? There are more blocks destroyed than still standing, more people sleeping on the streets than in the Ipps, perhaps even more killed than still surviving. I will be going soon. I cannot stay here."

She noted the *I*. The Vanguard would remove their own.

"Where would you go?"

"Laverne." Then in response to her blank look, he added, "!¡*patronising*¡! It's the region's major city, on the River Swayne to the east of here. Heavy alien populations, tight controls on the Ipps, but a good place to lose yourself."

It took him that long to realise how crass he was being, and to remember that friendly won him better favours than cruel. His face softened, he went to her on his knees, cupped her chin in his slender hand. He had stubble blurring the edges of his neatly trimmed beard, a few crusts of sleep in the corners of his eyes.

"!¡*sexual excitement*¡!" he clicked, but she had already seen. It wasn't friendly that turned him on, it was power. His grip tightened, fingers and thumb digging into her jaw. "!¡*domineering*¡! You think you should come along?"

She thought then that he would kiss her, but that was something he had never done and he did not do now. With a flash of frustrated anger, he cast her away like a piece of garbage, and her head hit the floor.

"You have to earn it, baby. You have to earn it."

SHE EARNED IT.

Marek was wrong: they clung on in the city of Angiere for another eighth before finally they fled.

Hope was not an inquisitive person. She preferred to fit into the background. But after that night, that morning, she became curious about what was happening in the city around her. She took to roaming Angiere whenever she could get free from working in the Flight of the Paradise, either behind the bar or on her back in one of the rentals above.

She was drawn to the harbour in particular. She liked the way the boats clanged and bobbed, the bustle of activity, of coming and going, the old, old buildings clustered shoulder to shoulder around the water, as if they had all been squeezed together to fit just one more in. She liked the big river barges that gathered here at the mouth of the River Swayne, their bulk making her think of them as floating buildings. She liked the smell of the sea, and the way the gulls lorded it over everyone, aliens and humans alike.

She was drawn to the parks, too. It was here that she learned the calming power of a tree that has lived for hundreds of years. The bulk of it, the solidity, the cooling shade of it.

She liked the crowded streets of the Ipps, clan territory where there was a sense of pulling together, of oneness, that was missing in the Tween where it was all just one big cosmopolitan mix of those who didn't fit elsewhere.

She didn't like that she had to pass through Westwalk and Seagreen to get to the places she liked.

Westwalk had been a thriving Ipp, she had learned. But now it was a burnt-out shell. What remained of the buildings had been cordoned off, and were only slept in by the clanless. Westwalk had been the first, she had been told. The first to be ruined like this, she supposed they meant.

Seagreen was the Ipp just to the north of the harbour district. Strictly speaking, she did not have to pass through Seagreen to reach the places she liked, but she was always drawn to it, since the day she had followed a side-street from the harbour, curious at the sense of open space at its far end.

The open space was not meant to be there. The open space had once been filled by buildings, or maybe the towering, ancient trees of parkland. But now, now it was glass. The Ipp had been destroyed, just as the infirmary had been destroyed. The ground was slick, translucent, moulded into weird globular flows, and it smelled of a strange kind of burning, almost chemical.

She did not like these parts of the city, but as her time in Angiere passed there were more and more of them.

ON THE DAY that Marek was to leave Angiere and Hope believed, without regret, that she had seen the last of him, a woman came to her room so early that not even the delivery wagons were out in the streets.

"!¡*urgency*¡! Come," the woman said, letting herself in without even the customary slap on the door. "I am Vanguard. We need to get you to safety. We need to get you out of this place."

Hope, sitting up on her mattress, looked at the dark-haired woman, whom she recognised as one of Marek's friends. She was called Callo.

"What?" Hope managed. "But... why?"

Callo leaned down to put a hand on Hope's arm. "!¡*reassurance*¡! Did you think we would leave you? Did that no-good arse Marek do nothing to reassure you of our intentions? !¡*frustration*¡!"

Hope allowed herself to be pulled to her feet, and she stood there dumbly as Callo cast around for clothes to dress her.

"We couldn't leave you, Hope. !¡*sincere | kind*¡! You're too valuable. What you have in your head is just too precious, too special. Do you understand?"

Chapter Nine

ON THE NIGHT the watchers and their grunt squad raided Cragside nest, I'd already had the biggest shock of my life. It really did seem to be one thing after another that evening.

I'D SPENT THE afternoon at a safehouse down where a spur of the Ipp sticks out into the River Swayne, forming a natural harbour, a place of transit where strange faces were never a surprise. This provided perfect cover for people-shipping. My job: swapping out pids for a bunch of travellers who had put in at the docks that morning. New identities. I didn't know what for, or where they had come from. I didn't know if they were rebels or just hustlers like we were, or if they were merely a group Sol owed a favour. I had learnt not to ask questions, but rather to observe and take in.

Back at the nest, there was a party stirring up. I'd forgotten all about Divine and Ruth's coming together. I came out onto the roof terrace, saw Divine and approached. She gave me a drunken grin and almost squeezed the last breath from my body in a big hug. Ruth gave me a tall mug of beer, and I drank half to the two of them and half to the gods of the river, which I knew Divine still had some kind of respect for. The next, I drank half to Divine and half to Ruth. And the next, well, I'm sure I found something at least vaguely appropriate to drink that one to as well.

At one point the three of us sat looking out over the city, towards the towers and gantries of the distant skystation. There was a starsphere hanging over it that day. Giant, shaped like a flattened melon, beams of light linking it to the skystation below.

"!¡*puzzled*¡! So... so how does the starsphere *hang* there?" I asked no one in particular.

"Wha's it matter, anyway?" said Divine, her words accompanied by a slur of drunken clicks. "Not's if you're ever going to get near one."

"!¡*indignant*¡! Don't want it falling on me, though, do I?"

Ruth and Divine chuckled, although I didn't think it was that funny. I was serious.

Divine raised her mug. "!¡*sincere*¡! And half to... to..."

I didn't catch the second half of her toast. Just then Sol arrived, accompanied by Marek and Callo. Marek had a hand on Callo's arm, possessive, controlling.

I remembered that night. The light touch of Callo's hand on my cheek, the press of her lips against mine – firm, cool, brief and then gone. I wondered what there was between the two of them.

I drank more beer, half to Ruth and Divine and half to the refugees whose skins we'd saved and were they even grateful, eh, were they grateful at all, but hell, we'll drink to them anyway. Ruth topped us up, and I lost track until much later.

Darkness had descended and the terrace was lit with wire-framed lanterns. I found myself standing with Sol, Marek, Callo, and Jersy and Madder, a couple of clan elders who had been my principal carers when I was small and rarely let me forget it now that I was not.

The talk was of the troubles in the city and Sol said, "!¡*anxious*¡! Think we'll go the way of Angiere, then, eh? Will it come to that?"

My head was clearer now, and I waited to see what Marek or Callo would say. It was Marek who spoke. "!¡*authority | hierarchy*¡! They want to wipe humankind out. Or, at least, some of them do. Some of them just want to crush any hint of opposition. But it's genocide we're really up against."

Sol nodded. "So it'll come here, then."

"!¡*frustration*¡! Look around you! It's here already..."

Callo caught my eye and gave me a kind of a smile. She moved around so that she was next to me.

"!¡*awkward*¡! I haven't seen much of you," I said. "Any of you."

"!¡*reassuring*¡! We've been busy," she said. "Forging new lives, making contacts around the city. And seeking someone. Someone we had, and then lost."

"!¡*eager | too-eager*¡! Can I help?" I asked. "I know the city well."

"!¡*humouring*¡! Later. Maybe later." Then: "Come." She gestured with a tilt of her head and we left the small group.

There was no hesitancy on her part. She took my hand, led me across the terrace and into the nest villa. We passed through tunnels and down stairs until we reached the room where she had been staying. It was sparsely furnished, with just a thin mattress and a wooden chair. Her few spare clothes were folded neatly on the floor.

I felt her hand on my cheek once again, that almost imperceptible touch.

"!¡*sexual arousal*¡! I…"

She silenced me with two fingers across my lips.

"I want you to see," she said. "!¡*reassuring*¡! I want you to understand."

She took her hand from my face and loosened the cord that held her wraparound silver gown together.

Beneath it, she wore nothing.

Her body was lean, the ribs prominent beneath small, high breasts. Her olive skin, in the low light, made her appear insubstantial, ethereal, a shadow among shadows. The black V of hair at her crotch was a pool of inky depths. She had a tracery of scars across her left hip and down over the thigh.

I reached for her, but she stilled me with a hand around my wrist.

She moved her other hand to her collarbone. She rested her hand there for a moment, then pressed. The fingers dimpled her flesh, hollowed it, penetrated it.

I stared.

Her grip on my wrist with her other hand was like stone.

She pulled at a fold of flesh and unpeeled her chest until half of her torso was exposed.

There was no blood, no mess. Beneath her skin were bundles of fibres, like muscles but white, like plastic, or the fibres I'd once seen exposed in the body of a wrecked car.

She released my hand, and I realised that the moment to flee had passed.

"!¡*calming* | *reassuring*¡! I wanted you to see," she said. "I wanted you to understand. !¡*intimate*¡! I've seen the way you look at me. I've even encouraged you, led you on, which I should not have done. But we are different, we are *other*. We are here to protect and serve. I am your guardian, Dodge. We did what we could in Angiere and now we are here. For you, Dodge. You and all those like you."

"But why?"

"!¡*patient | calming*¡! There are some who would wipe out what remains of humankind," she said. "What happened in Angiere has happened elsewhere. But there are others who feel different, who see in humankind a hope for a dying universe."

"'What remains of humankind'?"

"!¡*matter-of-fact*¡! Humankind is a rare and broken race," said the thing that was Callo. "But it has something. Something different. We will not let you be wiped out."

I put my hands to my own chest then, inside my vest, and I tried to bury fingers into flesh that would not yield, a seam that would not be found. I tried to tear myself apart to reveal a mass of muscle-like white fibres, but no, I would not be torn, my chest would not be opened.

I was whole, not assembled, constructed... whatever it was that had produced this woman before me, who stirred feelings deep inside me even now, when I knew she was, as she had said, *other*.

I went to her, then, that fold of flesh still hanging away from her torso.

I put a hand to her cheek.

She felt real. Her face felt like a real woman's face. The slight musk of her body scent smelled like that of a woman.

"!¡*confused | distracted*¡! I don't comprehend what you've just told me," I said. "I can't take it in. I can't hold it all in my head. But I will. I'll work it out. I'll deal with it. And then I'll work out just what it is that I should do next."

I backed away, turned, then paused in the doorway of her small room as she said, "!¡*impressed*¡! Remember, Dodge. There is a great deal at stake here. And not everything is as it seems."

I DIDN'T GO straight back to Ruth and Divine's party.

Instead, I took a detour and sat quietly, alone, in a common area. This hall had been used as a classroom when I was a pup. I remembered fooling about there with Skids and Pi and Jemerie while Vechko had lectured us about the importance of clan history.

I thought of Callo. There had always been something different about her, a spark, a sense of otherness. That was what had intrigued me, had drawn my mind back to her, attracted me.

But what was she?

Alien? Construct? Human with extreme mods? I was sure she had talked of her blood-father shortly after arriving here in Cragside. He had been one of the early victims of the purge in Angiere. So maybe she had been human once, at least.

Were all four of the refugees the same as Callo? All four, our not-quite-human guardians, come to protect us from what had happened in Angiere?

I remembered then something the chlick, Saneth, had said to me: just as a chlick carries within it the potential to be he, she, or both, the alien had asked me what potential I had within, what potential my kind might carry. Something in our hearts, something in our heads. *Something different*, Callo had said.

She had also vowed that they would not let humankind be wiped out. That was hardly reassuring after what had happened in Angiere, though...

I sat back on my low wooden bench, my back against the cool wall, and thought of all the times I had come to this hall as a pup. Times when my main concern had been how to stop Vechko or Lissy being quite so boring, or how to get into Pi or Carille's pants.

I stood, deciding that my problem right then was that I had become too sober. The solution to that was simple, and I headed up to the terrace in search of beer.

The raid was abrupt, like thunder out of a clear summer sky.

I was on the terrace arguing about the best route to Satinbower with Pi, a wide-eyed, big-breasted mouse of a girl. By this point in the evening my encounter with Callo was buried beneath a few more mugs of beer and the generous distractions offered by Pi.

We were laughing, leaning close, clicking soft subliminals at each other, all tease and flirt and come-on.

She smelled of beer and garlic and lilies. I wanted her, then, badly. I know it was a reaction to what had passed earlier between me and Callo. Pi was a diversion, a distraction from what was in my head, and a damned good one at that.

I leaned closer to hear what she had just said, a low drone smothering her words.

Then I paused, turned, and the bulbous head of a troopship was suddenly looming around the crag that formed the back of our nest's roof terrace.

I remembered the troopships at Satinbower. We had just been talking about it, me painting up my experience there when I had seen the Satinals' clan-nest being destroyed.

Beams of light lanced down from the troopship, transfixing us.

I felt unable even to move my muscles, but I knew that was not a real thing, just an effect of the sudden shock, the fear, a rabbit frozen by the beam of a torchlight.

Sol moved.

She spun, found Marek and Callo and rushed them to the back of the terrace. If she could get them into the caves they might be safe.

But I knew immediately that we wouldn't all be able to escape that way. The halls were narrow, the doorways few. A rush of people would block the passageway in no time.

The troopship swung round the crag and came to hang in the air above us. Door panels dematerialised along its flanks and spat out a stream of armour-suited grunts. They dropped to the terrace, their suits decelerating them an instant before landing. They started clicking and barking orders at us to stay still, to move over there, to stay calm, to say nothing, to stop rushing around!

A few shots from the grunts' beam-weapons were fired into the air, then someone – Ruth, I saw – started to object and was cuffed across the jaw by an orphid grunt. She went reeling into Divine's arms, her face a bloody mess.

Closer to where I was standing, a grey-bearded man – Maybry, I thought – was knocked from his feet by a barging grunt and lay groaning and sobbing.

Then a gun fired, and I realised someone, stupidly, had shot at the grunts.

This was going to get much worse, and quickly.

I bundled Pi over to the wall surrounding the terrace. The street below was deserted.

"Come on," I said, and swung a leg over the wall.

Pi hesitated, then joined me.

We paused partway down. Overhead, I could still hear the drone of the troopship and see its floodlights spilling out over the terrace.

Pi was breathing hard and shaking as she clung onto the crag. "!¡urgent | reassuring¡! It's okay," I told her. "They didn't see us. I know the way down from here. Used to climb here when I was a pup–"

"!¡exasperated¡! Fuck's sake, Dodge. It's not that. Just... just how high up are we?"

I hadn't considered that she might be scared of heights.

"!¡reassuring¡! It's okay," I said again. "Keep looking at where your hands are. We're on a kind of ledge. Just need to follow it round to the slope, and then we're not really climbing, it's just a steep hill, down to Jury's Gap." The Gap was one of the side-entrances into the cave system that ran through the craggy hills. We were almost there.

I started to move, but when I looked back, Pi was frozen in the same position, still shaking, muttering something under her breath.

"Come on," I hissed.

I could see Jury's Gap now, a dark slash in the crag just across and down a little from where we were.

I reached the end of the ledge, planted my feet on the steep slope of the crag, twisted to look behind me.

Pi hadn't moved.

Then a beam of light swung out and around from above, the troopship moving, searching for escapees. It locked on her almost immediately.

I looked at the Gap, so close, but I hesitated too long and another beam swung round and locked on me. Again, I felt my muscles seizing, and that made me wonder if maybe there *was* something more than just the psychological impact stopping me from moving.

A grunt on a floating pad came down and seized first Pi and then me and transported us back up to the terrace, where most of my clan had been rounded up in small groups.

WE WERE KEPT on the terrace for most of the night, huddled into little groups, penned in by jagwire. We weren't allowed to move around, not even allowed to sit. They scanned our pids almost immediately. Although Sol had returned to the terrace and been caught, all four of the refugees – or whatever they were – from Angiere had successfully escaped. Or at least, they had not been caught here on the roof terrace with the rest of us.

I worked my way among the twenty or so in my small group, trying to find out if anyone had picked up even a snippet of information about what was happening.

According to what I learned, this raid had been prompted by what had happened in Precept Square. The watchers had worked out who it was that had been responsible for the stolen pids we'd used to mask our identities, and those of the four refugees from Angiere.

Alternatively, this was all the fault of the four: they were not refugees, but spies, and they had led the watchers and their grunts here tonight. There had always been something odd about them. You could never trust an Angierean, after all.

Or maybe this was just another in an apparently random pattern of raids on clan-nests across the city. It was exactly what had happened in Angiere, and now it was happening here. The Satinals' clan-nest had been destroyed; we were lucky the troopship had not simply blasted us out of existence.

Or the watchers were hunting down rebel factions, humans who were organising opposition to the way we were treated, and somehow they had identified us in that category.

And then I heard a name. Reed Trader. They were looking for Reed Trader, and thought we were harbouring him. That was the identity I had used on that day in Precept Square, one of a batch of pids I had stolen from a lab in Cheapside the week before.

That made me glad I was always so thorough. We had wiped the stolen pids from our bodies that evening. I had been Reed Trader, but I was no more.

As I moved among the detainees, I tried to calm them. My sib, Jemerie, in particular, was fizzing with aggression, his clicks degenerating into a torrent of hate. He'd always been fiery, particularly when he'd had a drink.

I saw that look in his eye, put my hands on his arms, said, "!¡*calming | urgent | sib-bond*¡! Jemerie, Jemerie, you want to get burnt to a fucking cinder, Jemerie? !¡*calming | insistent | sib-bond*¡! That what you want, my old sib?"

For a moment I thought he was going to swing for me. Either that or just twist out of my grip and lunge at the nearest armour-suited grunt, regardless of any jagwire in his way.

Maybe he thought that too, just for a heartbeat, but then he saw that Divine was standing at my shoulder, arms loose at her sides, ready to stop him making a suicidal fool of himself and risking retribution for the rest of us when he did so.

He visibly calmed, rolled his shoulders, breathed deeply. Shrugged at me, and gave that old smile. "'S okay," he said. "!¡*apologetic*¡! I'm easy now, Dodge. I'm easy."

THEY TOOK SOL.

Our nest-mother was in a group by the main doorway back into the nest. They knew who she was. One of the watcher officers went to her, spoke a few words, and Sol slumped.

She looked defeated. Broken, like a street-fighter who's lost his last match on Precept Square. That, more than anything, made me believe that we would never win. We might hide, we might cower in the gutters and dark places, but they would hunt us down whenever they wanted.

A grunt took Sol's arm and tugged her away from her group. I watched as my nest-mother was led to a float-pad and lifted up into the troopship.

As the door panel closed around her, I wondered if we would ever see Sol again.

They took old Vechko next. He had been with Sol, in the group by the doorway. He went without resistance too, and then I realised they had probably been phreaked, all resistance knocked out of them by a vapour from the watcher officer or one of the nearby grunts.

One by one, they took each of our clan elders and floated them up to the troopship.

Much later, as the sun silvered the eastern skyline and birds started to sing from the trees up on the crag, a watcher officer came to my group.

This one had taken the form of a human, but it

was only a temporary arrangement. Watchers were colony beings, each body made up of hundreds of individual creatures, jelly-like polyps that could stick, merge, reconfigure at will. A watcher's body could consist of as little as a dozen polyps, as small as a mouse, or it could be a vast, sprawling mass of billions that covered a continent. A watcher could absorb mechanical and other biological inclusions into whatever form its collective body was currently taking. A watcher was never just a watcher, it was always more than it seemed.

This watcher was clad in an armoured body-suit. Its head rose from square shoulders on a slender neck. Its face took the form of a human face, a man's with a prominent brow-ridge and a square jaw. Its features were smooth, though: no mouth, no eyes, no nostrils in its perfectly formed nose.

I'd never seen a watcher so close before. Normally they remained aloof, leaving their grunts to do their dirty work on the ground.

It surveyed my group and then, with a puff of fear-inducing phreaks that turned my bowels to liquid, said, "!¡*threat | menace*¡! You have no leaders now." It had no mouth to talk with; I don't know where the words emanated from. Its voice was a rasp, with an oddly musical tone running through it, like two voices at once. The sound alone made me want to cry. "!¡*commanding*¡! Tell me: who are your leaders now?"

We looked at each other. We shuffled our feet.

And then I saw that Divine was staring at me. Jemerie, too. Ruth. Pursney and Pi. Most of them my age, or older than me, but...

All looking at me.

The watcher had turned its face towards me as well, now.

I don't know how it happened, but suddenly it was just the watcher and me, as if everyone else had taken a step back.

I straightened. I remembered trying to stop Jemerie making a suicidal fool of himself earlier and now I wondered exactly how I might avoid that fate too.

"!¡*threat | menace*¡! We know you have associated with fugitives," said the watcher.

I stared into its featureless face and it was as if it was reconfiguring itself all the time, nothing ever fixed. It was like watching water swirling, flowing, surging. I swallowed, struggling to overcome the phreaks that made me just want to fall to my knees and sob.

"!¡*persuasion | authority*¡! We know you have harboured Reed Trader. And we know he has smuggled people through transit, and for that he will be punished. We will find him. And when we do, we will punish all those who helped him."

I had no idea who Reed Trader was, but I hoped the watchers would find him soon. He had never been here, I didn't know him; they could have him, as far as I was concerned. If they found Reed Trader we would be in the clear.

I only felt a little guilty that it appeared the only reason they wanted Reed Trader was because we'd used his pids as cover at Precept Square.

"!¡*threat*¡! You will behave with subservience and praise us. You will control your people. You will stay in line. Do you understand? Because if it is that you do not, then we will punish *you* and your people will run out of ones foolish enough to be their leaders."

I nodded. Swallowed. And then, as the watcher turned to leave, I looked around at my people.

My people...

How exactly had this happened?

Chapter Ten

IT'S NOT THAT I had a problem with the idea of taking on a little more authority within the clan.

In principle it was fine.

In theory.

But just then wasn't exactly the best of times. The watchers had taken all of our clan elders. They'd warned us that they would return, and they would be looking to punish more of us. And all around, our city was falling apart under an onslaught we didn't understand.

Had my friends and sibs deferred to me because I was the best candidate, or simply because they didn't want to be stuck with it themselves?

EVEN AS PUPS, my nest-sibs had deferred to me, just as they did that dawn on the roof terrace. I'd known a bit about the world, I'd understood how to make things happen and could make them happen for other people too. Back when we'd roamed the city, a gang of adolescent hoodlums out for shits and giggles and easy pickings, we had never had a leader. It didn't work like that. We were blood.

But times when Jemerie had wanted to cruise the beer houses of Precept and Skids had wanted to bum around the phreak joints of Satinbower instead, I'd always been able to do the haggle thing: why one or the other when we could do both on Cunnet Street just off Precept? I'd stop them fighting, I'd break the tensions, I'd find solutions. Like I say, I knew a little about the world, I understood how to make things happen.

Others recognised this, too. Sol and the other clan-parents had learned to come to me when they were struggling to deal with issues with my sibs, like the time when Pi got pregnant and was fighting with Jemerie about it all, and when Jacandra and Carille had lost most of a summer trogging out on bootleg phreaks and snout.

And when Skids had started getting the night screams and scaring the sibs with stories of being snatched by the watchers...

That was when we'd started to lose him, and I'd played my part in that; oh, yes. I'd been the one who'd let him down. The one who betrayed him.

THE SCREAM WOKE me. High-pitched and loaded with sheer terror.

The sib cell was in darkness, a low-ceilinged dormitory deep in the caves at Villa Mart Three. Eight of us slept there back then, all adolescent male sibs born within a couple of years of each other.

Skids was next to me and it was his scream that woke us that night. We had thin horsehair mattresses on the rock floor and he was sitting upright, blanket twisted around his chubby, naked body.

The scream went on and on, long enough for my eyes to adjust to the dark and for me to see him clutching his head in both hands.

I scrambled to my knees and went to him, held him like a nest-mother holding a wailing newborn, clicking soothing clicks, trying to still him. The scream subsided into coughing sobs, and I was momentarily angry at his slobbering all over my chest before I started to get scared.

This wasn't just a bad dream. He was terrified.

I pulled at his blanket and it was wet.

"!¡*soothing | calming*¡! It's okay, bub," I crooned, wondering what exactly the fuck had invaded my best friend's dreams.

He calmed down, slowly, the sobs becoming deep, gasping breaths and clicks, becoming wheezy breathing, becoming normal.

"!¡*gently pressing*¡! What's up, Skids? What's up?"

He stared at me, eyes so wide I could see the whites all the way round. Then he shook his head. I didn't know if he was unable to speak or simply wouldn't, but it was clear that I wasn't going to get anywhere just then.

The next morning we went to Madder's class on street protocols and for a time it was as if nothing had happened in the night. We learned about orphids and chantras and the differences in intonation and phrasing in their click and body language, subtleties that could make the difference between a normal day and getting shot cold by a grunt for giving the wrong response.

Skids had been quiet, not his usual self. When Madder mentioned the watchers, he snapped his finger and thumb for attention. Madder paused to let him speak.

"!¡*belligerent*¡! The watchers," he said. "What do they want us for?"

Madder looked briefly thrown by his question, then said, "!¡*authority*¡! The watchers care about order. They don't want us to be a problem to them. They want us to be subservient and respectful."

"!¡*agitated*¡! No, no," said Skids. "!¡*insistent | confrontational*¡! What do they *want* us for? Why do they take us? Why do they take us away like that?"

I GOT HIM out of that situation. I could see he was close to the edge, close to breaking down, like he had in the night.

"!¡*calming | soothing | supporting*¡!" I clicked to him, softly.

I glanced at Madder and she gave a slight nod, recognising that Skids was having some kind of crisis. Understanding that I was the best one to sort things out. She cut the class short and Jemerie, Pi and I steered Skids up on to the roof terrace.

"!¡*stern*¡! So what is it?" I asked. "What's got to you?"

He barged past me, went to the edge of the terrace. For a moment I thought he was going to throw himself over the low surrounding wall, but he stopped and waved a hand instead. Gesturing to the north, towards the skystation, I realised.

"!¡*angry | frustrated*¡! Them," he said. "!¡*confused*¡! Don't you... Don't you remember?"

I glanced at Pi and Jemerie. None of us understood what was happening to our nest-sib, but it was awful seeing him like this. I didn't know what to say or do.

"Yesterday?" said Skids.

I shook my head. I still had no idea what he was talking about. "!¡*patient*¡! We went to Satinbower and Cheapside," I said. We'd spent the morning there, a gang of us, all adolescent showing off and flirting. I remembered Jemerie roof-running over an orphid phreak plant in Cheapside, a stupid risk he'd taken to impress Pi, but she hadn't even seen it. He could have been shot or jagwired and she was drinking bull spirits with Carille and Jacandra and totally oblivious. I remembered the dry midsummer heat and the dusty, shitty smell of the streets.

I didn't remember anything out of the ordinary. Not then, at least.

"¡*dismissive*¡! Sure we did," he said. I'd never seen him so agitated. "But what did we do in the afternoon...?"

I shrugged, said, "Nothing much. What do we ever do?"

He clammed up after that. Just sat himself on the wall, legs dangling into space, looking north towards the skystation, while somewhere in the back of my mind I kept coming back to his question: what *had* we done that afternoon?

IN THE EVENING, after we'd eaten, I found Skids in the earth closet puking his guts out.

I thought at first that this might explain his sudden erratic behaviour: all the result of a fever. But no, even while I was there, he buried his hand in his mouth, pushing a finger down his throat to make himself throw up again.

All that came out was phlegmy spittle. Judging by this, and the stink from the closet, he'd already emptied himself quite thoroughly.

I put an arm around his shoulders and guided him back out.

I sat him in a small communal space and said I was going to get water.

Instead, I went to Jersy and Madder's room, a level below. They were both there when I slapped the doorsheet and burst in. Jersy put a calming hand on my arm as I blurted out, "!¡*scared | concerned*¡! It's Skids. I don't know what's up with him but his head's all screwed up and I thought he was going to jump off the terrace this afternoon and now he's making himself puke his guts out, and..."

I ran out of steam, tears of frustration rolling down my cheeks.

Jersy hugged me. I was only a kid, still, and I knew that what was happening to Skids was bigger than I should have to deal with on my own. I needed help.

Jersy and Madder went to Skids and managed to calm him, but that night he woke screaming again. As I jerked awake, I saw him fingering his throat, retching.

"!¡*calming | concern*¡! What is it, Skids?" I asked. "Why are you doing this?"

He stared at me with those big eyes, whites showing all the way around the irises again. "!¡*scared*¡! They're in me, Dodge," he said. "Help me get them out."

SKIDS CALMED DOWN over the next few days, but was never the same again. He took to roaming alone rather than with the usual crowd of nest-sibs. He took to vanishing after lessons, or skipping them altogether, and turning up again in one of the nest villas well after curfew. He rarely even ate with us, if he ate at all: his adolescent chubbiness left him, and he became lean, gaunt even.

I saw him coming back a few times, sticking to the darkest parts of the street, always from the north. That was when I realised he had been visiting the skystation. And that was when I started to fear that we were losing him.

"!¡*concerned*¡! So what do we do about it?" Pi had asked, on the night we decided to save Skids for his own good. "He's lost it. Gone totally screwy-in-the-head mad. Do we just let that happen?"

I looked around at the small group. Jemerie, Carille, Jacandra and Ruth were also there. All were looking at me, as if somehow I had the answers.

"!¡*uncertain*¡! I don't know," I said. "Jersy and Madder have been keeping an eye on him. Sol, too."

"!¡*dismissive*¡! What they done for him? They hardly even seen him. He's never here," hissed Jemerie. "All they do is a piss in the stream. They done nothing. What're we going to do, Dodge?"

"Maybe we should make him stay," I said. "!¡*decisive*¡! Maybe we can knock some sense into him."

And with those words I ensured that my closest sib would be driven away for good.

We sprang the trap at Villa Mart Three when he came back one night, long after curfew. We jumped him just as he came in and bundled him into a storeroom in the caves deep in the heart of the nest.

I'd thought it would be easy, but he had a remarkable amount of fight in him for one who was now so thin.

"!¡*authority*¡! Come on," I hissed at him, as we finally barred the storeroom door shut and stood facing him. "We want to help you, Skids. We want to save you."

He stood there twitching, eyes flitting about, a trapped animal.

"!¡*seething*¡! It's all right for you. You don't have them *in* you..."

"What?" I asked. "What do you mean?"

"!¡*frustrated*¡! The watchers! They were there, all over me, crawling, slithering..."

I had never seen a watcher close to, but I knew how they were made up of slug-like polyps, independent beings that came together to form one body. I imagined them flowing over me, smothering me...

"!¡*intense trauma*¡! They crawled *into* me. I could feel them sliding down my throat. Into me. Everywhere. Some of them came out, but not all."

As he said this, he was clawing at his throat with hooked fingers, leaving red marks. I went to put a calming hand on his arm, but he flinched, jerked away, then backed off until he was against the wall. Slowly, he slid down until he was sitting with his knees hugged to his chest.

"They're still in me. I have to get them out."

We left him with food and water.

It had seemed a good idea at the time, but we hadn't worked out what would come next, if locking Skids up in a storeroom until he got better didn't work.

We kept him for that night and most of the next day, but when word of what we were doing somehow reached Sol, that was an end to it. She was furious, and she made sure we knew it. We were confined to the nest for twenty days, and I got an extra ten as ringleader.

By the time we were free, Skids had gone.

WE SEARCHED, OF course.

We went to all our usual haunts, but there was no sign of him. We spread our search farther afield, but no luck. At the end of the day, until long past curfew, I took to sitting on the roof terrace at Villa Mart

Three, watching out for that shuffling figure in the shadows, but nothing.

When the others lost interest, or belief, or both, I kept on. Skids was my sib, closer than any blood. There was a huge cavern in my life where he had once been. And beyond that, I feared for him. How could he cope out there on his own, his head screwed up with the madness that had taken him over? That, and his anger at us for our stupid attempts to save him from himself. I felt so guilty about that.

One day I went to the skystation.

In our wanderings we'd occasionally come close, but it was a long trek across the city from Cragside, and I'd never come this far north.

I remembered Skids returning late, always from the north. I remembered him sitting on the terrace wall, always looking towards the station. He had been obsessed with the aliens. One of the last things I had done for him had been to needle a scattering of star tattoos across his face, a starsinger thing.

The station was in Constellation, a district of warehouses and bars, doss-houses, sex clubs and alien buildings whose purpose was never clear.

I set off early that morning, and spent the middle part of the day hiking from street to street in Constellation, mind blown away by the barrage of *alien* and *new*. Everywhere I turned, ads leapt out, haranguing me: *Dodge, you need to try my phreak... Dodge, come with me to a place where... Dodge, try... Dodge, buy... Dodge... Dodge...*

Strange sounds swamped me: musics, speeches, shouting and squealing and screeching. Phreaks filled the air, leaving me dizzy and stupefied and horny and hyper. Armed grunts stood at every junction, and I desperately tried to remember my lessons about not misreading reactions, not sending out the wrong body signals. I was only a kid, and suddenly partway across my home city I was somewhere entirely alien to me.

"!¡*deferential*¡! Excuse me... my sib. I'm looking for my sib."

I asked so many times, of so many different species and artificials and witches'-brew hybrid oddities. I asked animated posters on the walls. I asked the interactive ads hanging in the air all around me. I asked in shops and bars where aliens phreaked and imbibed all manner of substances. I asked in sex clubs where humans and aliens sat and lay and pressed together in combinations that boggled my young and still relatively innocent mind.

I asked mostly humans and nearly-men, figuring that at least I would not offend with my body language and intonation.

Then: "You asked Wraith Pedre, have you?" said a woman wearing only body paint and feathers and ritual scars, standing outside a bar and trying to draw custom inside.

She nodded down the street and I saw a man I had previously avoided. He was skinny, wearing only a pair of frayed trousers, torn off just above the knee. His ribs looked like the rungs of a ladder, and his skin was a sickly grey. On his head there was a strange, jellied growth.

He was preaching, and that was why I had avoided him. I hadn't thought a mad preacher could help, and I didn't want to get snared into his routine. The gods meant nothing to me, other than they were sometimes a way to get what you wanted if you were dealing with someone who believed.

I thanked the woman and approached Wraith Pedre.
I had heard the term *wraith* a few times, but at that
stage I had little idea what it meant.

As I drew closer, I saw that the growth on the
man's head was some kind of alien, wrapped around
him, attached by suckers. A caul, I realised; a mental
parasite.

"!¡*deferential*¡! I'm looking for my sib," I said to the
man. "His name is Skids. I think he knows this district
well."

The man looked at me curiously, and I wondered
what was in his head, whether it was even his head
that shaped his actions and words, or if he had been
completely taken over by the caul.

"Have you asked the Lord of the Stars?" Pedre asked,
accompanied by a torrent of clicks I could not decipher.

I started to edge away. Madness. I did not want
madness just then.

Then he added, "The Singer. Have you asked the
Singer?"

He rambled a little longer, and I eventually gathered
there was a starsinger living in the sheer-fronted
building where Pedre preached.

A starsinger.

I had never seen a starsinger, didn't even know what
they looked like. They were ethereal, shrouded in
mystery, one of the most ancient races.

I hadn't known we had one living in our city.

With a wave of an emaciated hand, Wraith Pedre
guided me towards the entrance. It looked like no
more than a slit in a mirrored metal wall, but there
was some weird perspective shit going on with it and
when I drew near I realised it was open and I could
pass within...

...and I was on a hill, the ground falling away below me in grassy folds. The sky was a pale shade of lilac, and over to one side a fringe of strange dark trees pressed together, swaying in the breeze and talking to each other in clicks and sighs.

I looked back and saw the narrow black slit that must be the exit back to the street.

I started to panic and instantly my head was filled with song, an alien chorus without rhythm or tone but somehow intensely musical. I started to breathe more slowly again.

I heard giggling, chatter, coming from the trees, but I didn't think it was the trees, and then a group of small beings emerged. They looked like human children, naked and fleshy, with ringlets, pale skin and pink cheeks. It was the high feathery wings that made it clear they weren't human. Flapping, the six of them rose from the ground and came to swoop and circle around my head.

I'd been phreaked, I realised. None of this was real.

I closed my eyes and willed them gone, but when I looked they were still circling and swooping, chuckling as they flew.

I took a deep breath. "I'm looking for the Lord of the Stars."

The flyers said nothing.

I looked around. Rolling green landscape stretched in every direction, fading into a misty blur at a distance.

"¡¡*assertive*¡! I'm looking for the starsinger."

The flyers stopped, and hung motionless in the air all around me. With one booming voice, they said, "You are *in* the 'singer. We are the 'singer. We are reality. We make it. We sing the reality. You like it? We make it *big*..."

Disappointed. In my head, a voice. *Don't like it. Not real enough.*

I shook my head, trying to shake the voice out.

Don't like this real.

I looked up, saw dark brown clouds swirling across a sky that had been the lilac of a child's story, saw the tops of the trees whipping in a sudden wind.

"No..." I gasped. "It's... it's pretty."

The trees calmed, the clouds thinned.

Sing good. Sing strong. Sing harmony with joined voices of star sibs.

Then, more gently, one of the winged beings hanging over me said, "You can be safe here. Do you want to be safe here?" And, giggling, they resumed their flight.

I turned, and although I stopped it was as if I kept on turning.

I was dizzy. I stumbled. I dropped to my knees.

I heard voices, my head full of voices, singing and laughing and crooning soothingly, eerily.

I opened my eyes and I was up high, looking down. I could see the snaking twists of the river as it meandered through the city; the line of craggy hills that cut the city in two.

I needed to get out of this building, I realised. The phreaks were messing with my head. Already, the real world seemed far away. Worlds away. The starsinger's reality was so much more real.

I would be fine. I would not be harmed. I could relax. A crooning, singing voice, filling my skull.

I could stay here for as long as I liked.

I could. Easily. (And a part of my mind, buried deep, reminded me that if I ever emerged I would be wasted, drained of life, drained of *me*.) So easy.

But I wanted something. What was it that I wanted? Something important...

I want to remember.

No... I wanted Skids. I wanted to find my nest-sib.

I closed my eyes and he was in my head. Images, fragments from when we were growing up, as if they were being pulled from me.

I know that Wraith Skids is safe. I remember that he is living in Constellation. I see that he has taken the caul. I understand and accept that he has made this choice because it is a manifestation of that which is within. He has become a part of the greater real.

It was hard to imagine Skids with an alien caul wrapped around his head, attached to him by suckers and tendrils buried deep in his skull, feeding on his brainwaves as it fed him with phreaks. But it was what was within and I felt good about that.

I could stay here... I could join my nest-sib and become a part of the greater real too. My destiny lay in the greater real.

No... I would stay and I would be happy and I would starve until I was skin and bones. I would not do that. I did not have it within me to exist on phreaks and dreams alone.

I started to break free, started to see walls around me, an arched metal ceiling high above me.

I was lying on the floor. I must have collapsed.

I rolled over, rose to my hands and knees. I felt suddenly sick, and then my guts were heaving and I was staring down at a pool of vomit and in that pool of lumpy, mucousy green there was a... *thing*... It had a semi-transparent pink body, like a lump of jelly except there were organs within and a *sense* of something more about it.

I remembered Skids' night terror, his insistence later that something had happened, that watchers had slithered inside him. *I could feel them sliding down my throat. Into me. Everywhere. Some of them came out, but not all.*

The thing died before me. The watcher, if that was indeed what it was.

And that was when I started to remember.

IT CAME BACK in snatches. Dream images you cling onto as you wake. Memory flashes prompted by some vague connection. Fragments that you struggle to piece together.

And then you wish you hadn't.

That afternoon. We'd been roaming Cheapside and Satinbower all morning, but later... at the docks in Cheapside, smoking our own phreaks in a huddle on a piece of wasteland behind a sprawling warehouse. Jemerie and Jacandra were arguing, pushing each other about, squaring up chest to chest. It had started off as flirting and bravado, but the phreaks and bull spirits had shifted it into something else. Things were getting quite serious between the two of them.

Then a squad of grunts, rounding us up. Jemerie getting antsy with them until he was taken out with a spray of something that just turned him off like an electric light.

Me, objecting and at the same time wondering why I was always the first to open my mouth.

And then nothing.

Waking that evening in the sleep cell I shared with my sibs.

Nothing in between.

Another fragment: a silky mesh mask smothering my face. Bright lights. So bright they hurt. Senses muddled, heavy, phreaked. Voices babbling in my head, but no words I could understand.

Another: lying, still, calm. Surrounded by jelly. No air, but I did not need to breathe. And then the jelly moved and I realised it was not a mass of jelly but a mass of *jellies*, of jelly-like polyps... of watchers. Slithering over me, around me, probing every orifice, entering me, exploring, penetrating. I was impaled by them, immersed in them and them in me.

I WANTED TO find Skids still, but also I didn't. I wanted to tell him that I remembered now. I wanted to tell him I had been wrong, so badly wrong, but the starsinger's words still rang in my skull. *Wraith Skids is safe.*

I headed back to Cragside, exhausted, still trying to absorb what I had learned. I made it back just before seventh and curfew.

Back at Villa Mart Three I headed straight for the junior hall. I needed to tell the others. They had been there on that missing afternoon. We all had. Had the grunts taken us all? Did the others still have watchers in them? For that matter, did I? I'd vomited up one, but could there be more?

I bumped into Sol in the main lobby.

She took one look at me and steered me off onto a second floor balcony cut into the crag face.

"!¡*agitated*¡! The watchers took us," I said. "Skids was right. They took us and... and did things..."

Sol looked serious, and took a long time to answer. Finally, standing with her back to the panorama of the city beyond the balcony, she said, "I know.

!¡*earnest | sincere*¡! They do it to all of us, particularly the young."

"!¡*rising panic*¡! But why? They get inside us!"

"!¡*patient | calm*¡! Measuring, monitoring, testing... they're always testing us. They don't want us to stray. They want to keep us in line."

"What if they're still inside?"

"!¡*reassuring*¡! They always come out," said Sol. "We make sure of that."

"But why?"

"Why, eh? You want me to tell you what's in an alien's mind? It's hard enough to tell you what's in another person's mind. I don't know. We live with it, is what we do. Sometimes it goes wrong, as it did with Skids. Maybe he didn't pass one of their tests. Maybe he just happened to remember what he should have forgotten. Who knows, eh?"

Suddenly it was all I could do not to cry. I felt my lips trembling and a great knot of tension in my chest and throat.

Sol gathered me up, hugged me against her broad cushion of a chest, and somehow I managed to fight back the tears.

"!¡*comforting*¡! You're a good kid," said Sol. "You could lead this nest one day. There's a lot of me in the way you are. That's got to be good, eh?" She chuckled. "Come on. Time to eat."

As we walked up through the nest my head was full of questions, like had this happened to us before, and would it happen again, and what could the watchers possibly be looking for?

Now, with Sol captured and me somehow leading my nest, I thought back to that time when Sol had identified my leadership potential. How could she have thought such a thing? The only time I'd shown any kind of leadership it had been to lock Skids up in a storeroom and drive him away from us for good. Me, a leader? I couldn't see it, didn't want it.

Back then I had just fucked up the life of my closest sib. Now *everything* was at stake...

Chapter Eleven

CALLO RUSHED HOPE through the early morning streets of Angiere that morning, still clicking and tutting at Marek for having failed to prepare her.

The air smelled of chemicals and burning, and Hope knew there had been another strike, although she did not know where. It must have been nearby, and recent, from the smoke hanging in the air and the ominous drone of troopships somewhere over the rooftops. She wondered how much longer the Tween would remain standing.

As she walked alongside Callo, the streets woke up. Shutters banged open, babies cried, men and women shouted and laughed as they hauled bundles of clothing and other possessions out of doorways to stack in the streets.

Down by the banks of the Cut, the homeless were stirring among the trees where they had slept, some on the ground and others in rough platforms built into the branches. In the streets, there was more activity than was usual so early: wagons being loaded, family groups shuffling by on foot with their possessions slung across their backs. It looked as if the city was moving out.

Hope and Callo came to the commercial district just south of the harbour, a quarter Hope had always avoided in her wanderings. The atmosphere here was tense and hostile, and there were armed grunts guarding every junction and sentinel bots skimming along above the streets, constantly monitoring.

As they passed one building, Hope heard gunshots and the triumphant battle cry of an orphid grunt from within.

Eventually, Callo led Hope into a quiet alleyway on the fringe of the commercial district.

"!¡*caution*¡! I can't go any farther," said Callo. "I have to keep a low profile while I remain in Angiere."

Hope had thought Callo would be fleeing with her, not staying behind in what remained of the city.

"!¡*reassuring*¡! It's okay," Callo went on. "We're meeting a friend who will take care of you. !¡*matter-of-fact*¡! We've arranged passage for you away from Angiere. You'll travel on a transit to Laverne. Once there, you just need keep yourself safe. Mix with the trogs, sleep where the clanless sleep, do as they do. We'll follow soon. Go to Precept Square, just off the central commercial district, every midday and we'll find you again. !¡*pressing*¡! Do you understand?"

Hope nodded, because that was expected of her and she did things to keep people happy. At times like this, with Callo so strident, almost haranguing in her intensity, and what was another voice to add to those in her head?

The aliens took her by surprise, a chlick and a bulky four-legged creature she did not recognise, like some kind of pack animal but with strangely intelligent eyes, faceted and glistening black like an insect's.

The chlick was ancient, its stone-coloured skin ravaged with scars and folds. It stood almost as tall as Callo and its lower torso was encased in some kind of plastic shell. One of its eyes had been replaced with something mechanical.

"!¡*deference*¡! Saneth-ra," said Callo, dipping her head. "This is Hope."

Hope needed no introduction to the ancient chlick. She knew the being from Anders Bars Infirmary. That kind of thing sticks. She remembered the wires all over her body, too, the smothering masks, the phreaks that made her head feel as if it had been emptied and then the aftermath when the first thoughts that had returned were dark and twisted and filled with self-loathing and she had wanted to hurt herself, do harm, die.

The voices were a fever of sound. She clutched her skull, pressing at the temples, wanting it all to just *stop*.

"!¡*urgent | concerned*¡! Hope. Hope!" Then Callo turned to the chlick and said, "!¡*factual reporting*¡! She does this. Has blanks. I'm sorry. I know you need to–"

"!¡*admonishing junior scholar*¡! Human Hope is undergoing mental placement trauma. Senior scholar Saneth is cognisant of junior human's condition."

Hope stared. She understood that Saneth was familiar with her condition. At the infirmary, Saneth had tended to Hope, studying her, maybe causing whatever it was that was in her head.

"!¡*reassuring*¡!" Callo put a hand across Hope's shoulders and hugged her. "It's okay," she said softly. "Saneth is a friend. Trust us."

"!¡*matter-of-fact | dismissive*¡! The transit leaves imminently," said Saneth. "Junior human Hope must be prepared."

"Deep breath," said Callo with one last squeeze of Hope's shoulders.

Hope had been so focused on Saneth that she had paid little attention to the other alien, dismissing it as some kind of menial commensal species in the service of the chlick. It was bulky, about twice as broad as the already stocky chlick, and it was shaped like a massive dog, or a squared-off pony, with a great slab of a head and those glistening black eyes.

Now, the thing moved forward in an uncannily abrupt motion: one moment it was there, behind Saneth, and then it was... facing Hope, so close she could smell its briny breath.

It reared up on its hind legs.

Hope flinched, tried to turn, tried to take a step, but the thing came down on top of her in an instant, engulfing her in its mass.

Wet flesh surrounded her like a damp fist, and her chest was pressed tight so that she couldn't breathe.

"!¡*authoritative*¡! Now to transit," said Saneth, and Hope heard it clearly, and she saw the chlick before her in vision that was somehow both sharper than she had ever known and more granular, with colours doing strange things as they rippled across the chlick's skin in patterns she had not seen before with her own eyes.

The chlick turned and headed out of the alleyway towards the commercial district of Angiere, and Hope followed. Or the thing she was in followed.

She could not work it out.

She could not breathe. There was no way she should be able to see or hear. And yet... her senses were richer than ever; the world had greater definition than before, the colours more vivid.

And her head was quiet.

She knew this state would not last, and already she missed it in anticipation.

She followed Saneth through the tightly-packed crowds. There was an urgency here, where there had been a more resigned desperation in the refugees earlier in the Tween. She did not know if this was normal for this district or not, but she sensed that tensions were higher. There was an air of something about to happen, to change, a buzz in the atmosphere that again she realised was a heightened perception, something picked up by this commensal creature and which any mere human would have missed.

The transit station was a building made of sheer glass, half-mirrored so that only indistinct shapes moved within. Its walls sloped back at strange angles and gun-pods were grafted onto the walls beside every entrance, scanners turning, fixing, following as travellers passed within.

She followed Saneth, and scanners to either side locked onto them. With her enhanced vision, she saw every little twitch of the things, and she realised that they were alive in some way, sentiences devoted to their unceasing observations and analyses. Sentiences that lived only to watch, to monitor, to act. The air between the gunpods was buzzing with communication.

And then the scanners swung back and Saneth and the Hope-commensal were inside.

They passed through a vertical sheet of blue light which Hope somehow knew was another scanner. She relished the fizz in the air, tasting its blueness as they passed.

They pushed through crowds, the Hope-commensal clearing a path for Saneth, who now followed in her wake. They stepped straight into a small carriage, shaped like a bullet and resting on a cushion of air above a single line of track.

They were the only passengers in the small compartment.

Saneth settled on a jelly bench that shaped itself to her-him. The Hope-commensal just hunkered down on the floor, becoming instantly passive.

The bullet carriage started to move. Through the translucent walls, Hope could see buildings rushing past, then trees and fields.

She did not understand why she was getting this special treatment.

"!¡*informative | objective*¡! You are special," said Saneth. "You are all special. Each one lost is a crime against the Great All."

The chlick was inside her head, she realised. Or inside the commensal's head. She was struggling to see boundaries between her and her alien host now.

"!¡*approval for junior scholar*¡!"

She felt defeated. She had been trapped at the infirmary, but in Tween she had known some kind of freedom. Now... she was trapped again, and at the mercy of an alien who had kept her imprisoned at the infirmary. An alien who was working with the humans she had tried to trust. She was powerless. At Saneth's complete mercy.

"!¡*impatient | dismissive*¡! Concern yourself with your own value, not that of those you encounter."

She wished for the voices, the clamour. A screen of sound to block out the prying chlick.

There was a long silence.

Outside, the world passed by, a blur of fields and woods and small settlements.

It was true, for all that Saneth might be dismissive. She was powerless. Saneth was in control. Saneth could do whatever she-he wanted. Saneth was as a god to humankind.

"!¡*intrigued*¡! Life evolves," said Saneth. "Intelligence is emergent. It will always appear, given long enough. There are billions of inhabitable planets in the Great All, and there are billions of sentient species. With those numbers, ungraspable to your mind, for any species that has evolved and in which intelligence has emerged, it is improbable to the degree of near-impossible that many more have not emerged sooner. For every intelligent species, there must be multitudes more that evolved earlier in the history of the Great All."

Wishing for that wall of voices.

"!¡*patient*¡! Those that evolved earlier progressed farther. Intelligence so advanced as to be incomprehensible to even the next most advanced. Intelligence passing beyond a level that those in earlier stages can even see as intelligence.

"They would be, as you say, gods, scholar pup."

She felt frustrated. How could she even begin to understand a god?

"!¡*gently leading*¡! By riding the crests of the waves," said Saneth. "A pebble does not need to understand the dynamics of the ocean in order to skip across its surface."

Then what was the point? She felt frustrated. She didn't know how to argue, or how to draw a line under a debate.

"!¡*patient*¡! The gods understand the ocean," said Saneth. "The gods understand the pebble. The gods *understand*. But what do the gods do when there is nothing left to understand, scholar pup?"

She waited, but the chlick would say no more.

IN LAVERNE THEY emerged at the transit station on Precept Square, stepping out into harsh sunlight. The Square was a wide space, paved with wide slabs and surrounded by low, blocky buildings.

The Square was thronged with many different species, most of which Hope had never seen before. Hope remembered Marek telling her that Laverne was larger than Angiere, packed with aliens, more heavily militarised and with tight controls on the Ipps.

She found this new city heady, disorienting, confusing.

She followed Saneth down some wide steps to the Square, and then across to one of the low buildings. The smooth wall parted before them like thinning mist, and then flowed back to close behind them.

They were in a small chamber, sealed off from the outside world. The walls were a sheer off-white, without texture or features.

"¡*matter-of-fact*¡! This is a private location," said Saneth. She-he gestured with a gnarled hand and gave a rapid sequence of clicks.

Hope felt a sudden convulsion passing through her body, and then she was up on her rear legs, twisting, tearing, *pushing–*

and she was on her knees, catching herself on the floor with her hands, gasping, sobbing, head spinning. *Wet.*

Head-to-toe wet.

She looked around. The world was a duller place. More *muffled*. And in her head: a subdued murmur, growing louder.

Saneth indicated a canvas bag on the floor. "¡*terse*¡! There are clothes, some local money."

And then the chlick was gone through the wall, accompanied by the commensal who had been Hope's host for the journey.

Hope went to the bag, found a brown one-piece that had seen better days and a pair of battered knee-high boots. She stripped out of her wet things and used the bag to swab herself down. She stank of the commensal's juices and her mouth was full of a salty, pissy taste.

Dressed, she turned a full circle, surveying the blank walls of the small chamber.

Panic rose. Saneth had kept her at the infirmary and now...

She stepped towards what she thought was the outer wall. Nothing happened, and her heart began to pound harder, and then... it thinned, it dissipated, and she was able to step through.

The Square was a hubbub of noise and activity again. A welcome din, vying with the noise in her head.

SHE STAYED IN the vicinity of Precept Square for several days. There were food stalls around the fringes, with lots of pickings among the garbage.

She spent the nights cowering away from curfew patrols with the homeless, and returned to the Square every day, following Callo's instructions. She had nowhere else to go.

The streets radiating from the square were full of bars and clubs, and it made Hope think of Tween, back in Angiere. The mix was different here, though. There were far fewer humans, more aliens, more that was strange to Hope's eyes. She had felt at home with pierced Emerald, who had become something of a friend and guide. She had even felt comfortable with Marek and all his petty cruelties. She had understood those people, she had known how to get the right responses from them.

But here... she did not know what to make of a club where grey-skinned, bug-eyed aliens went to have their skin painfully flensed with metal graters, or where liquid was poured on a creature that was something like a slug on many legs, the liquid attracting a seething mass of bugs to eat the creature's flesh. She was strangely disturbed by the alien scabs that latched onto buildings and watched everything that passed with individual slow-moving eyes, colours flashing across their crusty surfaces. She did all she could to avoid the humans she came to know as nearly-men, the ones with dead emptiness in their eyes and alien growths on their bodies, with twitching faces and limbs and naked bodies covered in scars and filth and bruises.

She kept a low profile, sleeping among the soulless and homeless on a tract of wasteland where a block of buildings had been razed. That scared her, too. Had she come to another city that was being subjected to the same kind of assault as Angiere? Would there be an end to this, other than inevitable destruction?

The only fixed thing in her life was returning to Precept Square for the middle of each day. And so she was there the day that Saneth brought Marek, Callo and two others through the transit station, and that was what set her on the path to Reed Trader.

Chapter Twelve

IN THE MORNING we sat in the great hall, drinking tea and arguing over what had happened.

I was exhausted. I'd spent the night with the others, herded into small groups on the roof terrace, penned in by jagwire, forced to stand while we waited to see what the watchers and their grunts were going to do with us. But catching up on lost sleep now was out of the question. Tensions were running too high. We were agitated, angry, scared. We'd lost Sol, Vechko, Jersy, Madder and the other elders, all taken up in the troopship, maybe never to return.

And somehow, I was the new elder, the new clan-father even.

"!¡*authority*¡! Enough," I said. I hadn't shouted, but still my clicks and words cut through the din and everyone turned to look at me.

It was in that instant that I started to believe that maybe they had turned to me as leader because they had some kind of faith in me, rather than simply because no one else wanted it.

"!¡*reasoning*¡! It's no good sitting here arguing," I said. "We were caught unprepared last night. We can't let that happen again."

"Tell them about Angiere," said Divine.

She was right. Not everyone here knew the full story of the coastal city.

I nodded. "Sol was starting to prepare us," I said. "Trying to pull the clans together." I told them how raids like the one we had suffered last night had been only the start of things in Angiere.

"¡¡*sceptical*¡! But how do we know that's what's happening here?" said Jemerie. "Why should we even believe what those four ¡¡*condescending | dismissive | insulting*¡! tell us about a city none of us have ever even seen? They were here last night, but they managed to avoid getting taken, didn't they? Just what are they doing here?"

"¡¡*patient*¡! We don't have to believe a single word they tell us," I said. "But answer me this. Would it be worse to be prepared for an awful event that never occurs, or to be unprepared for one that does?"

Jemerie wanted to argue further, but Pi stopped him with a look and a slight shake of the head.

"How do we prepare?" she asked. "¡¡*scared*¡! What do we prepare ourselves for?"

"¡¡*patient reasoning*¡! Last night..." I said, "we were exposed. Everyone was out on the roof terrace together, just waiting to be rounded up. We can be sure we'll get raided again. We can't make it so easy for them next time they come."

"Everyone was out there, yes," said Jemerie. He was a thunderbolt waiting to strike, his body a coiled ball of energy; twitchy, muscles taut, eyes wide and staring. "But who managed to get away, eh? The four so-called refugees from Angiere! How convenient was that? Who set that up, eh?"

"¡¡*guilt*¡! It was Ruth and me... our coming together," said Divine. She was tending Ruth's bloodied face with a damp cloth, tenderly cleaning the dried wounds. "It was all our fault that the clan was so exposed."

"!¡*assertive*¡! But whose idea was it that we all party in the open air?" said Jemerie, returning to his theme.

"Mine," said Callo, appearing in the doorway.

Everyone turned to look.

"Sol said it was your coming together, Divine, and I said what a beautiful thing that was and that we should celebrate, not hide away. I thought it would be an affirmative gesture in difficult times, to celebrate what is good. !¡*guilty*¡! I'm sorry. I was wrong. It was no set-up. It was a misjudgement. No more."

Jemerie still wasn't satisfied. "!¡*aggressive | confrontational*¡!–"

"!¡*admonishing*¡! Sol got us away," Callo continued, cutting Jemerie off. "She heard the troopship, realised what was happening, and bundled us into the nest before we could do anything. There was no conspiracy, young man. There was just one good nest-mother who was quick-witted and salvaged what she could from the situation. If the watchers had found that you were harbouring us, it would have been so much worse."

"!¡*matter-of-fact*¡! So what do we do?" asked Divine. "How do we prepare?"

"!¡*calm | authoritative*¡! We spread ourselves out," I said. "We know they targeted particular clans in Angiere, and now it seems to be our turn. We should never all be in one place at the same time. We should move around so that there are no predictable patterns to our whereabouts. We should post watch at both nests, all day and all night. We have one big advantage: the caves. We can use those to get about and to escape, if only we get enough warning."

I paused, my head reeling.

"!¡*tentative*¡! We should continue Sol's planning," said Divine. "Contacting the other clans, giving them a chance to prepare too."

I nodded, even though my only attempt to do that had ended up with clan-father Frankhay's wrist-knife at my throat.

Callo nodded as she came over and sat with us. "!¡*sceptical | doubting*¡! All good," she said, her clicks denying her words. "You can, and should, be better prepared for a raid like last night's. But what will you do when they come with some weapon or creature, or both, that can chase you through the caves, something that can hunt you down? !¡*urgency | fear*¡! What will you do when they burn everything in this Ipp to glass? Will the caves protect you then? Will look-outs and escape routes save you?"

I glowered at her, willing her to stop.

It was bad enough that she was saying these things in front of everyone, when it had been all I could do to rouse them and stir their fighting spirits.

It was worse that she was merely echoing my own thoughts.

She met my look, challenging me to disagree.

I remembered the last time I had looked into those eyes... Callo peeling herself open, revealing her true nature, showing me that all was not as it appeared.

Who was she to be dispensing advice to us? What was she? She had said she was our protector, but could I believe that?

"!¡*frustrated*¡! So what do we do to prepare for a full-on onslaught?" I asked, adding, "!¡*harshly cutting*¡! What did you do in Angiere?"

"!¡*patient*¡! We moved people out," she said. "We identified those we needed to save and we started to move them out. We didn't move as many as we should have soon enough. When the last days came, it was all we could do just to escape ourselves. And even then !¡*deferential*¡! we needed help."

"!¡*shocked*¡! You're saying we should leave Laverne?" asked Pi. "But why? Why are they doing this?"

"The ones who don't want to wipe us out altogether?" said Callo. "Maybe they *want* us to sort ourselves out, sifting out the few with the will to survive from the dull masses, the trogs and the nearly-men. Maybe it's some kind of selection."

"If we want to survive, we have to earn it," I finished for her. "!¡*challenging*¡! But where do we go? You left Angiere, where they were hunting you down, and you came here, where they're hunting you down. Where is there that they won't be hunting us down?"

"Where did the others go?" asked Divine. "The ones you helped escape from Angiere. Did they come here?"

Callo shook her head. "!¡*tentative*¡! They headed east," she told us. "To a place called Harmony. A city where humans live as equals with others. A city where we don't subsist on the scraps of other cultures. A city of twisting spires, in the mountains a long way east of here – I don't know how far."

"!¡*disbelieving*¡! You're saying we should leave?" I asked. "Leave here for a city you've only heard rumour of?"

"!¡*patient*¡! If it reaches the point that we must leave Laverne," said Callo, "will you have a better alternative?"

WE STAYED AND discussed the options, and slowly the conversation wound down, all of us exhausted and angry and scared from the events of the night before.

After a while Callo rose and went to the water channel to refill her cup.

I followed her. There was a question I hadn't wanted to ask in front of the others. Jemerie had already been open in his hostility to, and suspicion of, the four refugees from Angiere. I didn't want to fuel his divisiveness.

"!¡*discreet*¡! Where are the others?" I asked her now. "Marek, Lucias, Pleasance? Where's the chlick who got you through transit and then pretty much vanished? Saneth – where's Saneth?"

"!¡*factual reporting*¡! They're out there," said Callo. She took a sip of her water, and then continued: "They're out there in the city, doing what I have been doing here. Preparing the ground. finding people who have that spark of difference, people who might just have the spirit to survive.

"!¡*trust-inspiring*¡! You know I'm different, Dodge. This is what I do. This is what *we* do."

I didn't ask the one remaining question.

Why should we trust you, Callo Hart? Why should we trust you when you pass as a human but are not, and when you appear to know far more than you ever let on?

SOL WAS RETURNED to us a few days later, just as the city was starting to tear itself apart for good.

I was sitting with Divine, Pi and Jemerie in a chamber just off the main hall in Villa Mart Three. Jemerie had come in with stories of fighting in Satinbower, some kind of attack against Satinal clan in retribution for their close relationship with the watchers.

Humans fighting humans. This was the way things were going. So much for Sol's plan to unite the clans: the pressures were setting us at each other's throats.

Just as Jemerie was telling us what had happened, one of the pups came in, a pony-tailed boy of about seven years. One of Jude's kids, I thought.

Big-eyed, he stood in the doorway, twitching from foot to foot as if unsure whether to say something or run. Then he caught Pi's eye and she gave him a reassuring click and he said, "Hey, people... Hey, people, have you seen the *city*?"

He wouldn't say any more, just scampered off into the depths of the nest, leaving us to make our way up to the terrace.

The afternoon sun was blinding after the dim light of the interior and it took a moment for my eyes to adjust as we walked across to the wall, where Ruth and a few others were gathered.

Ruth pointed as we approached but there was no need. Black smoke hung over the city to the west.

"!¡shock¡! Is that Satinbower?" asked Divine.

I nodded. Jemerie had just been telling us about Satinbower... the reprisals. An attack by a neighbouring clan, was what people were saying.

Through the smoke I could see troopships buzzing about and it wasn't clear if they were responsible or merely monitoring the situation.

I looked down at the ground. It was hard to believe this was happening.

Then I remembered my responsibility. I had to offer some kind of lead.

But, just as I opened my mouth to speak, not even knowing what words I might find to turn this situation around, there was a sudden loud drone, heavy engines, motion, and a troopship reared its bulbous head over the crag at the back of the terrace.

"!¡*urgency* | *command*¡! Cover, everyone. To the caves!"

We ran, and this time everyone reached the entrance to the caves in a moment. I hung back, the last to retreat. The troopship was dark green, smudged with black as if it had flown through fire. I wondered if it had come from the trouble in Satinbower, although it was hard to see why it would come here from there.

Three door panels dematerialised on the troopship's flank. Floating pads popped out, mounted by a handful of grunts. On the central pad, a chlick officer stood with Sol.

I stood facing them, my back to the cave entrance.

The pads floated down to the terrace and landed, just as another emerged from the troopship, this time bearing Jersy, Madder and Petro, accompanied by two more grunts.

I sensed movement behind me. Divine rested a hand on my shoulder, and it was as if her strength flowed into me.

We approached the little landing party.

Sol saw us, and looked instantly down at the ground. In that instant I saw a broken person; Sol, tall and strong and bullish, was now stooped, empty.

The chlick officer turned to leave, and before I could stop myself I stepped forward and said, "!¡*authority* | *command*¡! Hey!"

He-she paused, and turned towards me, twisting much farther than any human neck could twist.

"!¡*hostility* | *hierarchy*¡!" The grooves in his-her skin were moist, a sign of fight-readiness, we had been taught. Non-confrontational, I lowered my gaze away from the chlick's glassy black eyes.

"!¡*deferential*¡! There were others," I said. "Vechko. Meliss. Fairhead. Why have you not returned them, too?"

"!¡*dismissive | cruel*¡! They were weak," said the chlick, sending a pulse of fear-inducing phreaks in our direction. "Interrogation broke them."

The commander stepped onto a pad and retreated to the troopship with the grunts.

I turned to Sol. "!¡*kinship | respect*¡!" I clicked.

She just nodded, and we all turned to watch the troopship lift abruptly and swing back towards the north.

"!¡*respect*¡! Clan-mother," I said, dipping my head, and Divine echoed my clicks, my words.

Sol straightened, and suddenly the life returned to her empty eyes. "!¡*uncertainty*¡!" Then: "!¡*authority*¡! Right," she said. "So who's going to tell me what I've missed, then, eh?"

Chapter Thirteen

ON THE DAY the four refugees from Angiere arrived in Laverne, Hope was waiting in the crowd near the transit station, her regular haunt at that time of day. She had come here many times, but today, finally, she saw Saneth, and then following in the ancient chlick's wake, Marek, Callo and two others.

Just as Hope was trying to work out whether to approach them then or follow more discreetly, there was a disturbance in the crowd. A man and three women burst through – me, Sol, Divine and Ruth, although Hope didn't know us then.

Chaos ensued. Grunts descended, shots were fired, hovering sentinel bots swooped in; gun-pods swivelled, scanned, aimed.

Hope didn't understand what was happening. She thought we were attacking the four, at first. She didn't realise that we were saving their lives.

When the crowd surged, Hope was carried along. There were more shots. A sentinel swooped so close she thought it was going to hit her. The air fizzed with excitement and fear and a dizzying medley of phreaks. And the voices in her head were louder than the roar of the mob.

She dropped to her knees and was battered and buffeted by legs and booted feet and bodies surging around her. She felt dizzy, out of control.

When the mob was finally contained within a fence of twitching jagwire, Hope was among them. She stood a little apart, dazed. The voices in her head were roaring, as if angry with her at getting caught up in this.

She knew this must be the end for her.

She saw Marek and Callo, pretending that they were not together. She saw one of the others staring at her, a tall, skinny boy who was barely a man. That was how she saw me that first time, what she made of me. Not so flattering.

The first human was scanned and, reluctantly, released by the body-pierced chlick commander.

Second up was Callo. Hope swallowed and looked away. Of all of them, it was Callo who had shown her the most kindness. A grunt scanned Callo's wrist, there was a pause, and then the chlick said, "¡*frustration* | *regret*¡! Formal apologies for improper detention, West Strider 46."

They had done something clever, she realised, probably in that rush to embrace before the grunts intervened. They had done something to fool the security scanners. Hope was not slow to work things out.

She waited as more detainees were scanned and released one by one.

And then that boy, the skinny, staring one... *Me*. I touched her arm. She just looked, didn't understand what was going on, didn't comprehend my confusion when I realised she had no personal identifiers in her bloodstream.

She glanced down at my hand on her arm, the long fingers resting on her walnut skin. Then she felt a stab, a tingle of exchange, sensed something passing between us. The voices in her head surged, then calmed. She looked at me, trying to work out what had happened, what had triggered such a response.

When her turn came, she knew they had her.

She had managed to stay free for this long, but now...? She eyed the jagwire and considered throwing herself onto it, ending things then and there.

She let the grunt lead her to the steps, its gloved hand too tight on her arm.

She stood before the chlick commander and studied its pierced features, the rings and studs and bars driven through the folds in her face. She was much slighter than Saneth, and her skin had a fiery flush to it.

The chlick commander hissed something in a language Hope did not recognise. One of the grunts seized Hope's hand roughly and raised her arm to be scanned.

Hope gasped at a bolt of pain in her wrist where the grunt had squeezed and twisted her roughly. She tried to pull free, then realised it was pointless and slumped.

There were more hissed words and then the grunt with the scanner said, "!¡*identity*¡! Reed Trader 12, authorised all indigene and mixed zones."

Hope was confused. She was not Reed Trader 12. She knew that much. Then she remembered Callo's new name, West something.

She looked around and briefly found me in the crowd.

Then the chlick commander flapped an arm, irritated that Hope was still standing there. "!¡*anger | frustration | confusion*¡! Improper detention!" the chlick rasped.

Hope looked at her. The commander's cheeks were flushed a vivid red now and her eyes were bulging.

"Move!" hissed someone from nearby in the crowd.

Hope moved.

She dipped her head and left through a parting in the jagwire fence.

She had barely left the corral when she was confronted by a broad-bodied alien in a grey cloak. Its eyes were grids of metal and crystal, set in rows around a head that was crusted with some kind of scabby growth. It seemed agitated, excited, and she couldn't be sure whether that was its normal state or the result of too much phreaking.

"!¡*outrage* | *alarm* | *confused-distress*¡! You! That is not that is you!" it cried. Its shrill voice made its heavily accented words and clicks hard to understand.

Hope tried to sidestep past the creature, but even in its agitated state it was able to block her.

"!¡*etiquette breach*¡! You are not that is Reed Trader of 12. This is one that knows that one that is not you."

The voices rose as one, and for once the normal clamour coalesced as a single word: *Run!*

She ran.

The alien who knew she was not Reed Trader tried to block her again, but Hope careened off the body check and kept running, leaving the alien jabbering angrily in her wake.

Attracted by the disturbance, a sentinel swooped in and flew before her at just above head height, matching her pace, its three glistening eyes trained on her. She didn't know what it would do, whether these small hovering spheres were capable of anything more than just surveillance, and so she ran. When she came to an archway over a side-street that led away from the square, the sentinel crashed into the brickwork in a fizz of blue sparks.

Something fired at her then, leaving a black burn line on the wall nearby. The shot had come from the Square.

A couple of people just ahead of her had ducked down, shouting and pointing at the burn line.

Hope barged past them and sprinted the length of the side-street, other humans and menial aliens shying away from her, not wanting any of whatever grief she was carrying.

At the end of the narrow street she twisted again, took another turn into a short alleyway, and found herself in a yard piled high with garbage. She kept running, and used her momentum to clamber up the stacks of old plastic casings and over the containing wall, dropping down into another street.

Instantly, she gathered herself and slowed to a walk, her pace casual but swift, as if nothing had happened. Either she had thrown her followers or she had not, but either way, running would just attract more sentinels and the attention of any patrolling grunts.

All she could do was walk and hope and desperately keep an eye out for any sign of pursuit.

SHE HAD THROWN them.

All she knew to do was put distance between her and Precept Square, so she kept walking. Instinctively, she stuck to streets where there was a human presence. She did not know this city, but it seemed larger and more... *extreme*... than Angiere had been. The voices were quieter when she kept away from aliens, too.

She passed through a district where stone-built buildings huddled together, and it reminded her of the harbour quarter in Angiere. Human-built buildings, on a human scale. None of the strange materials and improbable angles and dimensions of alien constructions.

She considered finding somewhere in this district to stay for the night.

She still had the small purse Saneth had left her, its contents untouched. She did not know if it would contain enough to pay for a bed for the night. Up to now she had slept rough, but she felt exposed now, vulnerable. Where before four walls had felt like a prison, now they offered security, protection.

But there was something unsettling about this district. At first she had taken it for an Ipp, but now she realised that while humans worked here, they no longer lived here. Once a human district, now this was occupied territory.

When she went into a bar to ask the price of a room, there was not a single human customer. Most were chlicks, and most of these were wearing some form of military shell.

She backed out.

In the street, she was suddenly aware of the hovering sentinels, and the air of unease hanging over the humans as they hurried about. She had encountered districts like this back in Angiere. The humans here seemed like flat versions of the real thing: lifeless, no spark, no spirit. Marek had called them trogs and nearly-men.

Rounding a corner, she came to a wall where two men and a woman hung naked, impaled on a single spike each that pierced their backs and emerged through the chest.

Flies buzzed around the corpses, and a crow perched on the tip of one of the spikes, tilting forward precariously to pull at an open chest wound.

She hurried on.

*   *   *

SHE HAD TO pass through a checkpoint to get out of this district and enter what was clearly marked as an Ipp by the five-fingered hand sign at the junction.

An orphid grunt peeled itself out of its veiny recharge pod to challenge her. She remembered the orphids from Angiere. They were ruthlessly violent and showed no compassion. Emerald had said they were machines made of flesh and blood, not sentient beings at all. Whatever they were, this one stood across Hope's path, a gun dangling from one hand, its thin bodysuit drying almost instantly in the sun.

Turning its neckless head on her, it said, "!¡*caution* | *threat-but-boredom*¡! Halt. Identify."

The thing intimidated her, and the heady rush of phreaks exuded by the buds suckered onto its body made her want to turn and run. The thing was pumping hard, beating her up with its phreaks. At its shoulder, a sentinel hovered, and she wondered if this grunt knew already that she was a fugitive.

She raised an arm and the grunt waved a scanning wand past it. It paused, and she wondered if it was communicating somehow with the sentinel, or with others more remote.

"!¡*authority*¡! Identify, verbal."

She hesitated. Then, "Reed Trader 12," she said. That was the name they had given her at Precept Square. "I'm Reed Trader."

After another pause, the orphid turned away, the confrontation over. Hope watched the grunt's retreating figure as it hurried back to the comfort of its pod.

She passed through the checkpoint, and found herself in a densely populated Ipp. The buildings were high here, some of them reaching five or six storeys. She should have been content with this. She should have found something familiar, a bar or a club or a huddle of homeless, clanless street people.

But the sentinel had disturbed her. The way it had hung at the grunt's shoulder, the way it had watched her.

She still felt the need to put distance between her and the disturbance at Precept Square.

And that was her downfall.

THIS IPP WRAPPED itself round the great sweep of a wide river, and for a time it really did have the feel of the docks back at Angiere. There were even the same big river barges out in mid-channel. The district was dense but compact, and after a few blocks she came to a point where a canal cut away from the river.

A hunched bridge crossed the canal, but before she could traverse it she had to pass through another checkpoint. This one was controlled by a grunt of a species she had seen around this city but never anywhere else. Strangely humanoid, with a coating of short fur and long, looping ears. It was so tall it had to stoop to hear her when she identified herself again as Reed Trader 12. It scanned her wrist to confirm her identity, then waved her through.

Hope crossed the bridge and entered an Ipp where the narrow streets were lined with wood-framed buildings, so close together that little sunlight penetrated.

Partway along that first street, Hope heard a series of clicks from behind her.

She stopped, turned, and the first thing she saw was a pistol crossbow aimed at her chest. It was held by a girl of about Hope's age, maybe a little younger. Her too-white face was framed by straight black hair; her eyes were smudged black, her lips a blood-red rosebud. She was clad head to toe in a black lace one-piece, its lace dense in some places and wider than fishnet in others.

"!¡*hostility* | *warning*¡! Dunnat move, gel, ya see?"

Hope stared. She could barely make out a word of what the girl had just said. She knew not to move, though.

"!¡*hostility* | *demand*¡! Ya get name?"

It took a moment for Hope to work out that she was being asked to identify herself. "My name..." she said. "My name. It's Reed Trader."

At that, the girl with the crossbow smirked, and said, "She da one." She nodded along the street, in the direction Hope had been heading. "!¡*instruction*¡! Ya be going ahead, see? An' I be right here ahind ya."

CROSSBOW GIRL TOOK Hope to a bar a few blocks away. She marched her through to a door at the back, past a whole crowd of people dressed in various combinations of leather and lace. There were aliens here, too: a couple more of the tall ones like the checkpoint guard, hunched over and pointing and chittering at a small screen unrolled on a table between them; and in the far corner, cutting strange shapes in the air with a paddle-like hand, a smaller humanoid, with smooth metal arms and a mirrored strip for eyes.

The back stairs were narrow, dark. Hope went up, followed by the girl. Pausing on a landing, the girl gestured to a door. Hope went in, and a moment later, the door swung shut and she heard the click of it being locked behind her.

The small window was only large enough for two panes of bull's-eye glass, one above the other. Hope peered out at the street and the buildings opposite. She tried the door, but that just confirmed that it was locked.

She sat on the thin sleep mat, knees drawn up.

She closed her eyes and tried to block out the voices.

THE GIRL TOOK pity on Hope, in her tattered brown body-suit, and gave her a change of clothing. All that Hope retained was her knee-length boots. She must have stunk, she realised, as she peeled her clothes off and dumped them on the floor. She pulled on some skinny net leggings and a delicately patterned lace vest, all the time watched by crossbow girl.

When she was done, she was led out and down, out through the bar and on a convoluted route through more narrow, gloomy streets, the dusk light broken only intermittently by the yellow glow of gas lights.

They came to what she first took to be a long, low building but turned out to be a barge, just like those she had seen earlier on the great river, moored on another canal. Steps led on board, and guards with muscled arms like thighs stepped back to let the two through. Hope studied them as they passed. She didn't believe those two kilted men cradling blunderbuss rifles were all man: they were more – pumped up, greater than, enhanced.

They followed a narrow gangway along one side of the boat and came to an open deck. They paused, and crossbow girl said softly, "¡¡*sympathetic*¡! See da boss. No givin' da lip, see?"

The boss stood at the far end, leaning against a railing with his back to Hope. There were others there, too, but it was clear which one was the boss.

He was an imposing figure in black drainpipe trousers and a dark frock-coat that was covered with a lacy pattern. His hair seemed to glow an unnatural white.

He turned and smiled, stroking his bushy sideburns with a long forefinger.

"!¡*warm* | *welcoming*¡! So then," he said, "our guest. Welcome to the Loop. Welcome to my little domain. I trust that First Deputy Ashterhay has been taking care of your needs an' wishes. That the case, gel?"

Hope glanced back at her guard, who was now chatting with a kilted boy by a doorway leading belowdecks. She remained silent. She didn't trust this superficially friendly welcome for a moment.

The group gathered around the gang boss were clad in an array of lace, leather and brocade. They wore deathly white face make-up and carried an assortment of knives and pistols.

"!¡*businesslike*¡! So, then, you going to tell me who you are, gel?" asked the boss. "Just wandering in here like this. These are tendentious times. Tough times. Nobody should be just wandering about without a care, 'less they has a reason, gel. So who are you, and what's your business here?"

She met his look. "I'm Reed Trader 12," she told him. "I'm Reed Trader 12 and I don't have any business, here or anywhere else."

The sudden rush of voices in her head told her she'd got it wrong, long before she translated the wry smile on the gang boss's face into the cold threat that it was. The murmur of conversation in the small group around them fell silent and, glancing over her shoulder, Hope saw Ashterhay's pistol crossbow trained on her.

The gang boss's smile became a soft chuckle.

"!¡*mirth* | *menace*¡! How enchantin'!" he said. "You're Reed Trader, you say?"

Cautiously, she nodded.

"!¡*gentle amusement* | *menace*¡! Well then, just how funny is that then, gel? 'Cause you see, so am I. I'm Reed Trader, and someone's been playing fuck games with copies of my pids, and that hasn't left me rightly amused. See what I mean, gel? !¡*menace*¡! See what I mean?"

HE PUT AN arm out, inviting her closer, and Hope had no choice but to join him at the railing. The canal water looked oily black from up here, and a long way down. The height made her realise just how big this barge was; it had been hard to get a sense of its scale when they had approached through the narrow streets.

The gang boss, this other Reed Trader, put an arm across her shoulders. His hand was like a claw on her arm. He smelled of sandalwood and sweat.

"!¡*hierarchy*¡! My apologies," he said. "I didn't make any introductions, did I, gel? Let me make amends. See, I'm only sometimes known as Reed Trader. That's my given. That's what's in my pids. Most times I go by the name Frankhay, clan-father here in the Loop. You see all this?" He waved a hand, gesturing at the closely packed buildings of the Ipp. "It's mine. I've earned it. I've taken risks. I've won fights. I don't like it when someone screws with me and risks what I've gone out and earned. You see that, gel?"

The claw on her arm was cold, like a bird's talons. She looked at Frankhay and said, "I'm new here. I didn't know."

He chuckled.

"!¡*confiding*¡! I have dealings," he said. "That's what I do. I have friends and contacts. A few days ago a chlick partner of mine, h'she tells me his-'er nest-sibs had a lab where they'd been holding samples, pids from their contacts, that kind of thing. Only they'd been broken into and the samples stolen. And then today I get the heads up that I'm on a seek list, identified in some incident at Precept Square, a place I never go. It's really not a good thing to be on those kinds of lists, particularly not now when the city's being ripped apart all around us."

The arm, the claw. So tight.

"!¡*menace* | *hierarchy*¡! And then who should come a crossing the canal an' into the Loop but a young waif who tells the border goon she's Reed Trader, and when it scans her it finds that her pids confirm this?"

"I can't explain," she said softly.

He looked at her. "!¡*encouraging*¡! I really didn't think you could," he said. "But you could tell me, gel. You could tell me all about it an' see if *I* can do the explaining."

She told him.

She told him about being at Precept Square, about the rush of the crowd and how it had buffeted and battered her and left her feeling dizzy. She told him about being caught in the round-up, detained and imprisoned behind a fence of jagwire, which had grown around them the instant it was released from its pod by an orphid grunt.

She told him about the young man who was not much more than a boy, his touch, the fizz of something exchanged and how that must have been when it happened and now she felt an intense stab of guilt at betraying him because she had said too much already, and would only be forced to say more.

"!¡*intense*¡! Describe him," Frankhay told her, and she realised that her words might just have sentenced that young man to death when all he had done was save her.

"Taller than me, a little paler," she said. "Dark hair. Thin." Could have been almost anyone.

"!¡*insistent*¡! Who was he with? He can't have been working alone."

She looked at the dark surface of the canal. She wanted to lose herself in it. And all the time, in her head: voices. Insistent voices.

The claw. Tighter on her arm.

"There was a woman, I think." The one who had hissed at her to get going when her pids had given her the all clear and the chlick officer had started to get agitated. She had been one of the four who had rushed in to start with. "Tall, dark, strong. Bald, I think. She had a white scarf tied around her head, but there wasn't any hair poking out. I think they were together."

That was when Frankhay started to work it out. He didn't know me at all, had probably not even heard of me. But he knew Sol Virtue from old times.

MY VISIT TO the Loop the next day with Sol's message was about as bad as timing can get. I didn't know Frankhay's pids were among the stolen batch we used to cover our tracks that day in Precept Square. I didn't question why that lab had kept several batches of pids separately. I just took them.

Maybe there's no such thing as bad luck, though. Maybe that's just cover for sloppiness. I shouldn't have taken the easy pickings from that lab. I should have been sure of myself. I should have taken more trouble to find out whose pids we were using.

And above all, I shouldn't have wandered into the Loop with Sol's message alone and unprotected.

But I did, and Hope was there, the girl who had caught my eye the previous day, only now she was part of Frankhay's entourage. I wasn't to know that he had just brought her out of her locked room when he heard that his little crossbow-packer Ashterhay had captured me entering the Ipp. Hope looked like part of his set-up to me.

I wasn't to know that all the time I was trying to convince him to join an alliance to defend humankind against what had happened in Angiere, Frankhay was playing games, stringing me along in the knowledge that I was the messenger from a clan that had somehow set him up.

I wasn't to know that after he had drawn me in, held his wrist-knife to my throat and warned me and my clan to back the fuck off, after he had watched me make a hurried and grateful departure from that back-room of a bar in the heart of the Loop... that he would have one of his laced thugs bring Hope over to him and he would lean towards her, making her breathe his sweat and sandalwood scent, and say to her, "That him, gel? !¡*pointed threat*¡! Was that the one you saw in Precept Square?"

She didn't need to answer, didn't need to nod falteringly.

He knew.

Chapter Fourteen

I SHOULD HAVE known that seeing the girl again would mean trouble. The one from Precept Square. The one with the walnut skin and honey-brown bangs and double-take eyes. Seeing her in Cragside Ipp would definitely be trouble.

But all I knew was that she had some kind of a hold over me, some kind of connection from that moment when we touched, so briefly, and exchanged pids. Maybe before that.

On the day after Sol's return, the girl was hanging back in the shadows on the cobbled street at the foot of Villa Mart Three, dressed in the black lace of Frankhay's gang and looking as if she was about to take to her heels at any moment.

There was someone with her. A boy, a good couple of years younger. I recognised him from my visit to the Loop. He was wearing a black kilt, and he was carrying a blunderbuss.

And that was when I realised there was trouble brewing.

EARLIER THAT DAY, I'd gone out looking for Skids and nearly hadn't made it back alive.

"Skids," I'd told Pi and Jemerie, over flatbreads and tea that morning.

"!¡*dismissive*¡! Skids? You out of your head?" said Jemerie. "How's he going to help us against chlicks and their grunts, armed to the eyes with weapons we don't even understand, and all overseen by the watchers' supermind?"

Skids had always been the bright one. His mind made connections, deductions. He saw patterns. He understood.

Ever since we were pups, he had been drawn to anything alien, fascinated by them. Since leaving the nest, he had devoted himself to getting close to the starsingers. He had become a wraith. He was the one person I could think of who might be able to understand at least something of what the aliens were doing, what they were thinking.

"!¡*patient*¡! He might just have some insights," I said. "He might help us understand."

The last time I'd seen Skids, he'd been with the human wreckage on Riverside, a notorious area for dossers and street gangs. It wasn't a place to be after dark, or on your own at any time of the day. It was like a magnet for all that was broken in humankind.

Last time, I'd been with Ruth and Divine, heading back from Precept Square and avoiding the more direct route through a part of Central always heavy with intoxicated and hostile species: chlicks loaded with phreaks; flitterjacks hyper and violent on a narc they injected from venom sacs harvested from one of their domestic bugs; orphids, off-duty and leery on the contents of assorted pods stuck onto any exposed body part.

The aliens came to Riverside to beat up the human flotsam that ended up sleeping in the narrow strip of trees that flanked the river. It was as if it was some kind of sport for them. It was certainly not something forbidden by any of their codes of conduct or laws.

Skids had been huddled under a scrap of tarp, half-arsed protection against the drizzle. He'd been wasted, and his scalp bald save for a few tufts of hair, a sure sign that he'd been under the caul until recently, hosting an alien growth. The wraiths believed it brought them closer to their starsinger gods, gave them some kind of insight rather than being just another kind of brain-junk for an addict's easy hit.

On this morning, when we went searching for Skids and his alien insights, Riverside was quiet.

Unnaturally so.

I was there with Pi and Jemerie, who had come with me even though they both thought it was a dumb idea. "!¡*supportive*¡! You're just casting around for something to make you feel worthwhile," Pi had said on the way there. "Now Sol's back."

Maybe she was right. Sol still wasn't quite her old self, still in shock from what had been done to her in captivity, we thought. But she was Sol, and she was back, and suddenly I was in the background again.

The riverside park was deserted. We walked along the Straight, a street that ran along the raised bank of the Swayne. To our right, the river was the same as ever: wide and slow, a few boats and skimmers passing by, gulls hanging and twisting in the air. And to our left, the park: bare-trunked trees shading the ground with their heavily leafed crowns; thin grass skinning the hard mud ground; a few pigeons strutting and pecking.

There were signs of recent occupation. Occasional black patches and heaps of ash marked where fires had been. Blankets lay in irregular heaps.

The place had been abandoned in a hurry. No dossers would leave their trappings behind like this.

Jemerie put his arms out abruptly, stopping us in our tracks.

In the distance ahead of us was a line of grunts, most with their armour-suited backs to us.

We melted into the trees.

"!¡*alarm* | *fear*¡! What is it?" whispered Pi. "What are they doing up there?"

"!¡*authority*¡! Stay here," I said. And before Jemerie or Pi could object, I had slipped away from them.

I darted across the road and dropped to the rocks along the margin of the river. Moving over the boulders was slow, but it kept me out of sight.

When I reached a stone buttress that ran from the road down to the river, I edged up and peered over. I was much closer now. I could see the sunken faces of the people who had been rounded up. I could hear sobbing, smell the body odours, the sweat, the fear.

A grunt stood with its back to me, so close I could almost reach out and touch the shiny black carapace of its bodysuit. A little farther away, a woman said something and another grunt smashed the butt of its weapon into her face.

The sudden, unthinking violence shocked me, even then. I had seen destruction. I had heard so many stories. But seeing that... the woman lying crumpled, her jaw smashed into a shapeless mess, another woman struggling to drag her clear... I felt sick. I felt angry. I felt powerless.

Forcing my eyes to move away, not wanting to see what the grunt did as it went towards the woman for a follow-up, I looked farther along the Straight. There were vehicles there. Some kind of haulage truck, maybe ten or more of them. People were trudging up ramps into the backs of the trucks' long trailers.

I edged back down. I'd seen enough.

When I reached the rocks and turned, I saw that one of the skimmers had come in closer to the river bank. An angular speedboat, with arrays of eyes and scanners grown into its hull and gun-pods protruding from its deck at all angles. It had turned towards the bank, trained its eyes, its guns...

It was watching me, and I knew then that I had no hope.

Something knocked me out. I don't know what. All I know is that one moment I was standing on the rocks, realising I'd been caught, and the next I was on the road, on my back, my sight swimming and my head ringing and my entire body as sore as if I'd been stung by a million wasps.

"¡¡confused | disoriented¡!" Something struck me again. I don't even know if it was a physical blow. It was as if I was being beaten from the inside.

I clamped my head between my hands, as if that might somehow help.

A hand took my arm, yanking so hard that my whole body jerked off the ground.

In my bleary vision I saw an orphid grunt run a scanner over my wrist.

"¡¡reporting¡! Dodge Mercer 43, authorised central areas, subject to curfew." It released my arm and I fell to the ground in a pain-addled heap.

Another being leaned over me. As my vision cleared, I saw that it was a watcher in humanoid form. Clad in a bodysuit and hood, all that was visible of it was a featureless face moulded from translucent polyps.

In a voice that was like two voices, not quite in harmony, it said, "¡¡threat | menace | humour¡! You would not appear to be in charge any more." It sounded almost as if it were joking. And it knew me. It knew that I was the one nominated as clan elder by my fellows when Sol had been taken. It might even have been the same watcher that had commanded that operation, although I knew the concept of individuals did not apply to watchers. To an extent, it *was* the same watcher, in that it shared memories of that raid, and maybe even some of its constituent polyps had been there. It knew me in the way all watchers would know me: it had access to memories in which I featured.

So, this watcher reached down with one gloved hand, took a fistful of my hair and turned my head. Forced to peer along the Straight at the lines of dossers filing into the trailers, all I could think of was how uncanny it was for fingers that felt like jelly to have such a powerful grip.

"!¡*hierarchy*¡! We don't want you yet. You're not on the manifest. You get to live for a few more days, Dodge Mercer 43."

And then I was on my feet, jerked upright by that fistful of hair in the watcher's jelly-like hand.

"Go. Run." It kicked me in the backside, propelling me so hard I staggered and had to struggle not to fall. Somehow I kept going, half-running, half-walking, my head still spinning from whatever had knocked me out, slowly grasping the watcher's words. These people, lined up to enter the trailers, were not being transported anywhere. They were being slaughtered.

And our turn would come soon.

I JOINED Pi and Jemerie in the park, and as we worked our way back to Cragside I managed to blurt out a confused and broken account of what had happened.

When I told them about getting caught Pi hugged me. "!¡*reassurance* | *comfort*¡! You don't have to prove anything by doing things like that, Dodge. 'Kay? Taking stupid risks only makes you stupid. You get that?"

When I told them about the slaughter, they went quiet. Really, this was no worse than many of the stories Callo, Marek and the others had brought with them from Angiere, but... it was *here*, we'd *seen* it. We were part of it.

We made it back to Villa Mart Three, wary of every checkpoint, every grunt patrol. The drone of troopships over the city seemed to be everywhere, sometimes nearby, sometimes farther away, but always audible.

I'd gathered myself by then. I was back in control. Sol was on the terrace, a beer before her, a distant look in her eyes. Divine was talking to her, but I don't know how much she was taking in.

She hadn't said anything about what had happened to her when she had been taken away, but now she seemed half the woman she'd been before.

"!¡*urgent*¡! We have to do something," I told her. "!¡*calm* | *reasoning* | *factual-reporting*¡! We've just returned from Riverside. They're rounding people up – humans, nearly-men, trogs even. They're killing them. It's just like Callo said, just like Angiere."

Sol met my look, and for a moment there was a little of the old spirit there. "!¡*defiance*¡! But how can we fight them?" she asked. "How can we ever stop them? Do you have an answer? Eh, Dodge? Do you?"

I remembered what Callo had said about the city to the east, Harmony. A place where humankind lived as equals with all others. Was the only answer to go looking for somewhere better than this?

But all we had was the word of someone who was not one of us. Callo said she was here to help humankind, to watch over us and steer us. But was that a convincing enough basis for us to throw away everything we had?

I shook my head. "!¡*uncertain*¡! I don't know," I said. "I don't know what we should do, but now that I've seen what's happening, I know we have to do *something*."

GOING TO WAR with another clan was not what I had in mind.

I was sitting on the terrace wall, kicking my feet over a big drop, when I spotted the girl: Hope, as I would come to know her. She was down on the street, hanging back under the overhang of a building. It was hard to work out whether the kilted boy with the blunderbuss was with her or detaining her, but either way, to see one of Frankhay's militia out in Cragside, openly armed, was unheard of.

I couldn't work her out. On Precept Square she had appeared lost, confused. But then, only a day later, I had seen her with Frankhay's crowd in that bar on the Loop. What was Frankhay doing with people with no pids? What was he up to?

Down in the street, the boy gestured with his gun, and the girl crossed the street and was lost to view.

I turned my head to see who was still here. I opened my mouth to call to Sol and Divine, to warn them that something was happening but I wasn't quite sure what, and then something struck me and I was tumbling back onto the terrace, my head ringing from hitting the ground and the wind knocked from me, my limbs trapped in a tangle of lace-clad attacker.

I twisted, but a knife was at my throat. One wrong move and it would be my last.

I made sure it was the right move.

My attacker was a young man, his eyes a fierce black as his face hung over mine. I flexed my leg and then slammed it upwards. His legs were spread as he pinned me down, and my hard knee made contact with something soft.

He grunted and cried out and I twisted from beneath him, and was back on my feet with another kick to my attacker's midriff for good measure.

I looked around.

The terrace was overrun with Frankhay's mob. It looked as if the battle was going to be over before it had even started.

Chapter Fifteen

HOPE HAD PICKED up from her guard, Ashterhay, that
Reed Trader – or Frankhay, as Hope had now learned
to call him – was planning a raid on the nest of those
responsible for stealing his pids.

She was in her room above the bar, staring out of
the window to where she could see a distant sliver
of the Swayne. Ashterhay sat cross-legged, watching
her.

"What does he plan to do with me?" asked Hope.
"Frankhay. Why is he keeping me here like this?" She
had been stuck here for days now, with no indication
of what was to become of her. Her only company
had been Ashterhay and the other guard, a boy called
Jerra. And the voices in her head.

Ashterhay shrugged. "!¡*ambivalent*¡! He dinnat say.
Jerra an' me, we's thinkin' he wants to bring you in,
get you to stay. We's thinkin' he likes ya. Get that?"

Hope thought back. She remembered Marek liking
her too, back in Angiere. She hoped Frankhay wasn't
going to be the same.

Hope watched a wagon, heavily loaded with kegs,
trundle down the street below.

"!¡*reassuring*¡! I's a thinkin' he jus' busy, right now."
Ashterhay tilted her pistol crossbow up towards the
ceiling and grinned. "!¡*excited | arrogant | hierarchy*¡!

We's a gonna kick them Cragsiders' butts. Gonna show 'em as none gonna mess with the Loop!"

Hope thought of the man, the Cragsider, who had given her stolen pids in Precept Square. Just to save her skin. And still she had told Frankhay everything he wanted to know. This whole thing was her fault, but she didn't know what she could do about it.

"I know them," she said tentatively. "The Cragsiders. I could help you get in. Maybe that would convince Frankhay that I can be useful?"

SHE HADN'T KNOWN us at all, of course, other than that brief exchange in Precept Square. But she knew that Frankhay's revenge attack was wrong, and when she said to Ashterhay that she could help, the voices in her head subsided.

If she could be there, maybe she could make a difference.

Frankhay came for her at noon the next day. He opened the door and stood surveying her. He had replaced his brocaded frock-coat with a heavier leather jacket, and the heels of his wedge boots were lower.

He carried two long-muzzled pistols, suspended from loops on his hips. He was clearly prepared for action.

"!¡*musing*¡! Who are you, Hope Burren, with your foreign name and your pretending you don't know squat when you've got the eyes of someone who knows far too much?"

She looked at him. She didn't know what to say.

"!¡*business-like*¡! First Deputy Ashterhay tells me you can get us in, over at Cragside. That the truth, gel?"

She shrugged. "They know me," she said. "They're not going to turn me away."

Frankhay approached her, raised a hand and stroked her cheek with the ball of his fist. Hope remembered Frankhay threatening me with the dagger blade embedded in that wrist. She knew that at any moment the blade could flick out and slash her face, or stab right through and into her brain. She knew Frankhay's tender touch was loaded with threat.

"¡¡*business-like*¡! I'm going to keep you close, gel. You understand? I'm going to keep you real close. And if you mess with me..."

He smiled, and said nothing more.

HE KEPT HER real close.

They approached Cragside by boat, cutting along the river in four tugs that had been moored in the canal cutting by Frankhay's barge, and then following a small channel through as far as they could before covering the rest of the way on foot.

Hope hadn't expected the reinforcements.

Waiting for them on the checkpoint into Cragside was a squad of a dozen of the tall aliens with long ears she had first encountered when she had crossed into the Loop. At first she thought they were there to bar Frankhay's progress, but at a series of clicks from the nest-father, they fell into step.

Ashterhay met Hope's look and smiled. "¡¡*superior*¡! The joeys 're good," she said. "They's with us."

A short time later, Hope stood in a doorway at the foot of what Ash had told her was one of the Cragsiders' main nests. Jerra stood with her, his blunderbuss cradled in one arm. The street was quiet, and the occasional trogs who did pass hurried on when they saw Jerra and his gun.

Up above, there appeared to be some kind of parapet, and she could see someone sitting there, feet dangling into space.

Frankhay, in the shadows of the crag, gestured with a nod, and Jerra chaperoned Hope across to where he stood by a barred door.

"!¡*urgent*¡! So how's we get in, then, gel?"

She looked at the door. She shook her head. She didn't know.

The gang-boss took one step and the blade flashed from his wrist. He held Hope by a fistful of hair, his blade against her throat. "!¡*anger*¡! Just as well I didn't trust a single thing you said, then, isn't it, gel?"

He hurled her aside so that she landed on her knees against the cliff. "!¡*command*¡! Watch her, Jerra," he said. "And anyone comes out of this door, you take their head off with that big fucker of a gun you're carrying, you hear me?"

While this happened, the aliens called joeys had been opening out the discs wrapped around their bodies. Frankhay and his militia stood on these, and with a sudden fizzing sound were lifted into the air. The joeys went with them, on more discs or scrambling up the vertical crag with long, loping swings of their arms and legs.

From the ground, on her hands and knees, Hope craned her neck to follow their ascent...

...AND SUDDENLY, UP on the roof terrace, they were all around us, among us, jumping from floating discs like the float-pads I'd seen the aliens using on their previous raid. But these were no aliens. Or rather, they were, or at least some of them were. But most of the attackers were Frankhay's militia from the Loop.

I stood in a low crouch, my assailant doubled up on the ground, clutching his crushed balls.

I should have finished him off.

If I were a fighting man I would have snatched the knife he had dropped and stabbed him, or slashed at him, or whatever it is that a real fighting man would do with a knife and a compromised opponent. I'd know the correct angle so that I could stab upwards from below the ribs to pierce the heart. I'd know the feel of warm blood gushing down over my hand.

Instead, I looked around, struggling to understand what had happened. This nest should have been impregnable, and yet Frankhay's mob were all around us.

Divine had already taken out one of the tall alien joeys with a chair leg through its throat. The thing kept fighting, but it was steadily flagging as its wound seeped deep maroon fluids. As I watched, it lashed out one last time, and caught young Justice with a flailing arm. The boy went down, screaming from what had only been a glancing blow, and I realised there must have been some kind of venom in the alien's touch.

Justice spasmed, went stiff, and died.

Some of the attackers carried guns, but I realised I hadn't heard a single shot. They weren't using them, probably fearful that the sound of a gunfight might bring unwelcome attention from an alien grunt squad.

Sol was over by the nest entrance, only a few steps from relative safety in the caves. Nobody would be able to fight their way into the caves. I willed her to move, but she just stood there like a confused old woman.

I ran to my nest-mother just as Frankhay approached, striding through the battle as if that was not a long dagger that had just swept past his face, or that a club swinging down on someone else and nearly taking him with it.

Frankhay's pistols remained at his side, but the blade from his wrist jutted menacingly.

I stood between them.

"!¡*command* | *menace*¡! Move your skinny backside, pid-thief," said Frankhay. "I want Sol. We have business. I'll deal with you later, you hear?"

Slowly, I shook my head, but then events were taken out of my hands.

One of the joeys leaned down and swept me off my feet and out of the way. The thing was only a head and shoulders taller than me, but it was like being plucked from the ground by a giant.

Sol stepped forward. I didn't know what she was doing, but then it became clear that she didn't either.

"¡*confused*¡! Eh?" she said. "You, Franko? What's it you're wanting, then?"

Frankhay was poised, ready to lunge forward with his blade, but instead he paused. He had clearly expected some kind of fight, some effort to resist.

Not the bumbling, confused shell of a woman that Sol had become.

Frankhay looked at her, and then around at the fighting.

With a piercing whistle he called it all to a halt.

"!¡*disbelieving*¡! Sol?" he said softly. "What's happened to you, woman? What's happened?"

DOWN ON THE street, it was as if nothing was happening. Hope did not know what she had expected, but this silence was eerie.

At one point, a squad of four orphid grunts passed and Jerra melted into a side alley; if they'd seen him with his blunderbuss, they would have seized him instantly. Hope found herself alone. She could have left, then. She could have just wandered off, tailing the grunts and knowing that Jerra wouldn't dare try to stop her.

But she didn't.

She had brought this all on. She couldn't just flee.

The door opened and she stepped back. Jerra was instantly at her side, his blunderbuss trained on the opening as a figure emerged.

It was a man in knee-length black boots, a kilt and a lace vest. When he saw Jerra, he gestured.

Hope and Jerra followed the man up through the stairs and tunnels of the nest. The place felt ancient, carved into the crag, the walls a dimpled, polished marble. The steps were bowed in the middle, worn hollow by generations of feet.

In one long hall, a small group of Cragsiders huddled, guarded by a couple of lanky, stooped joeys. Up another flight of stairs, they emerged on an open area, a terrace, surrounded by a low retaining wall.

Small groups stood guarded by members of Frankhay's militia. The fighting must have been over in an instant, the Cragsiders subdued by numbers and surprise.

Jerra took her to join Frankhay, who stood with the bald woman Hope recognised from Precept Square: one of the four who had helped Marek and Callo get away, the one who had urged Hope to go when she had been cleared by the grunt with the scanner and hadn't known what to do. Standing to one side, in the casual embrace of one of the tall alien joeys, she saw me, the man she knew had saved her back at the Square.

And the voices in her head... they fell briefly silent. She met my look, and I saw the question in her expression, and then the voices were back and she looked away.

Frankhay turned to her. One of his long-nosed pistols hung loosely from his left hand, and he used the blade emerging from his right wrist to point and gesture.

Now, he stabbed the air towards Hope. "!¡*conversational*¡! Her," he said. "So tell me, Sol, if you can find a word in that addled head of yours. Tell me what little Hope of the Burren has to do with all this, eh? She wanders into the Loop pretending to be me, with pids given to her by your young thief here. She plays all innocence. She says she knows you all, but does she? She doesn't have a clue when we get here.

"!¡*threatening | demanding*¡! So tell me, Sol, my old nest-mother compatriot, who is she? What's she up to?"

He leaned in close to Sol's face, but the bald woman just stared back blankly.

"!¡*reasoning | patient*¡! And here's my real dilemma. I came here bent on revenge. Nobody fucks with my pids. Nobody gets me put on a seek list. Nobody messes with the Loop: we stand alone from the rest of you clans. We always have. You don't fuck with us."

The voices were getting louder, a roar, merging into a loud drone. Hope squeezed her eyes shut, trying to blank everything out.

"But look at you, Sol. Look at you!" He turned to me, and asked, "!¡*concern*¡! What happened to her, pid-thief?"

"!¡*matter-of-fact*¡! They took her and our other elders – a watcher and a squad of grunts. Returned them a few days later. Or, at least, those that survived the interrogations. She's been this way ever since."

"!¡calm¡! I'd heard rumours," said Frankhay. "So here I am looking for bloodshed and, I'll admit it, maybe the chance to inflict some serious damage on a rival clan, but... but fuck, I'm getting soft in my old age. Look at her. *Look* at her!"

A brief whistle broke the stalemate. Someone over by the edge of the terrace; one of Frankhay's mob.

Frankhay turned and went to look, and Hope and I followed.

A squad of about twenty grunts lined the street at the foot of the crag. Hope recognised the four orphids she had seen earlier, distinctive in their green body suits. They had returned with a squad of craniates and their chlick commander.

They all stood with blast rifles aimed upwards to where we were standing.

Had they followed Frankhay and his militia here to Cragside? Had they somehow picked up on the fighting and come to suppress it? Had someone betrayed Frankhay?

Whatever, they had the leaders of two clans trapped here, and they were clearly about to close in.

Chapter Sixteen

THE BLACK CLOUD came down almost immediately.

We were all distracted by the troopship that had come in to hover over the nearby rooftops. It hung heavily in the air, giving almost animal twitches every so often, gun-pods trained on the terrace.

A couple of the joeys stepped onto float-pads and tried to slip away. They skipped over the retaining wall and dropped down to roof level, heading for a side-street where they might lose themselves to view.

As I watched, needle-thin white lines connected the joeys to the troopship, and then they were gone, and the white lines were just a memory burned on the back of my eyes.

It was Hope who saw the cloud first of all, Hope who understood what it was. She had seen it before, back in that room at the Anders Bars Infirmary, the black swarm that ate everything it encountered.

To me it was just a dark smudge on the sky.

It hung a short distance beyond the troopship, a sooty thumbprint on the silvery grey clouds, a charcoal smear.

I saw Hope staring, and looked more closely as the smudge became a stain became a cloud in its own dark, smutty right.

Over us, cutting out the sun, emitting a high-pitched

whine that sounded like I had a swarm of mosquitos trapped inside my skull.

A tail of black flicked down from the cloud like a whip. It brushed past nest elder Jersy and he screamed and went down, clutching at his face. His mate Madder dropped to her knees at his side and tugged at his arm, as if trying to get his attention.

One hand on his face was down to white bones, almost instantly, and a seething black bracelet worked steadily up his arm, stripping the flesh.

His face... For an instant, his eyes still stared out of bony sockets, and then they were covered in a black film and then they too were gone, the sockets empty, and I could see the black mass sinking through into his skull.

I felt someone tugging at my arm. Hope. She pulled me away. We were too close. We staggered back as Madder sobbed and then was covered in black and then was a mass of white bones and disintegrating clothing, picked clean, collapsing onto the heap of bones that had been Jersy.

The swarm of bugs rose, re-merging with the black cloud overhead.

Hope was now pulling so hard she threatened to tug me off my feet if I didn't go with her. I needed no persuading now. We turned and ran towards the doorway.

All around, chaos was rapidly taking hold.

Some of the people just stood around, bemused by the sudden rush to flee. They hadn't been as close as Hope and me, and clearly hadn't seen enough to know that panic and mad escape were the only sensible options. Others had seen, and were running for the exit.

Already, I could see people cramming into the narrow doorway, too many to fit, like leaves plugging a storm drain. I grabbed Hope's arm and managed to stop her in her flight. We would never get through there.

"!¡*urgent*¡! This way," I hissed, nodding towards the far side of the terrace.

She looked at me, then past me and I followed her gaze. One of Frankhay's mob stood a short distance away, arms lashing wildly, a muffled, liquid groan emerging from his throat. His body was black, as if someone had dipped him in tar.

As he fell to his knees, I felt a sharp pin prick on my cheek.

I slapped at it and my hand came away with a smear of blood. I smacked again, rubbed, backing away from the mayhem, only stopping clawing at my face when Hope pulled my hand away, shaking her head, saying, "There's nothing, there's nothing. You hear? Nothing on your face."

We gave the dying man a wide berth, and found our way to the retaining wall. I swung my legs over so that I could stand on the small ledge of rocks on the outside.

Hope followed, clambering awkwardly after me. I started to climb down and across to the balcony, only a short distance away.

Feeling safer here, I stopped and turned to help Hope cross the last gap. She stumbled forward into my arms, and for a moment I held her and she clung on and it was the most human, most needed, thing in the world. Something real in the middle of nightmare, a moment of calm in the most violent of storms. And then we turned and Hope followed me into the heart of the nest.

Inside, it was eerily quiet.

The balcony opened onto a passageway that was the main route down from the terrace.

There, ahead, only slightly reassuring, I saw someone hurrying away. One of ours – no black lace or leathers or kilt – but I couldn't see who it was. If one had got out, then there must be others, surely...

"!¡*authority*¡! That way's out," I said to Hope, pointing to the right. "Go! Follow that person ahead – see?"

Then I turned the other way. I had to find out what was happening to my sibs.

I ran round a corner and up a few steps and emerged onto an open, low-ceilinged area.

I stopped. From here I could see up another flight of steps to the terrace. The doorway was packed solid with bodies, so dense that only a little light seeped in from outside. Some of the bodies had tumbled forward, down the steps. Some even still moved.

All were coated in seething, crawling black.

I backed away, and realised then that Hope had come with me.

I turned, and she just stood there staring.

She had a blemish on her left cheek. A mark. A small black patch, like a blob of tar.

"!¡*alarm | fear*¡!" I clicked.

I stepped towards her, hooked my fist into an open claw and scraped it down her cheek, feeling my nails raking through flesh, my fingers slick with blood.

The black lump burned like hot fat. It seethed in my grip, that small knot of bugs.

I hurled it away from me but some stuck and I felt them going to work on my hand, skin and flesh dissolving.

I dropped to my knees and ground my hand into the rock floor.

The bugs were tiny fleshy things. They squashed easily, bursting red with our blood inside them.

I looked up and now Hope was clawing at her cheek.

I ripped my shirt off, balled it over my fist and scrubbed at Hope's face, squashing the bugs into her flesh, rubbing them away. The shirt began to disintegrate as the bugs started to digest it, but it was enough to get rid of most of them, and Hope's clawing, rubbing hands removed the rest.

For the second time, we collapsed into each other's arms. Her face was a mess of blood, hers and mine, the flesh on one cheek shredded. As I held her, she wriggled a hand free and raked at her face again.

I clung on tight, trying to stop her from tearing herself to pieces, and suddenly she slumped and I thought she had fainted but her eyes were still wide, staring, lost. I didn't know at that time about the voices in her head, but they were a screaming cacophony just then, bellowing and shrill, and while she knew moving would calm them, she had no strength, and her legs were like drinking straws, and it was all she could do to hold herself upright against me, and all I could do to hold myself upright against the cold marble wall behind me.

We were snapped out of our shock by a sudden surge from the roof terrace steps as bodies shifted, settled, and a collection of bones that had once been a body, or bodies, fell clattering to the ground. As I watched, the mass of what had once been human shifted and fell, tumbling down into the open area where we stood. The bones shattered on impact with the hard ground, and a cloud of white dust rose into the air; a twisting, swirling mass, swarming with black flies, hungry for more.

Suddenly alive again, I pushed away from the wall, took Hope's hand in my wounded one and headed deep into the nest.

We passed through passageways worn smooth with use, through rough-walled caves, deep into the heart of the crags that ran through Cragside Ipp.

All the time, Hope clung to my hand, until finally I had to stop and prise it free and swap sides so that she could hold my undamaged one.

Later, we emerged in Villa Virtue, the clan's main nest. In the main communal area, people sat around in clusters. Sol sat with Divine and Ruth, staring into space while the two of them talked in a low mutter. A couple of black-laced members of Frankhay's militia sat at a bench, a teenaged boy tending to the girl's wounded arm, which was swollen and purple, with a big red welt on the forearm. I learned later that she had been accidentally stung by one of the joeys as it went down under a mass of bugs. Hope caught the wounded girl's eye and nodded, and now I finally had time to wonder what Hope's role had been in all of this. Was she with Frankhay? She was dressed like them, and I'd seen her with them when I'd gone on my mission to the Loop; she'd come here to Cragside with their attack. She didn't act like she was with them, though.

In all, there were sixteen of us, all survivors from Villa Mart Three.

I slumped down at a bench, just as Jemerie came over with a bowl of something. "!¡*control* | *authority*¡! Sit tight while I see to that injury," he told me. He swabbed at my hand with a cloth dipped into what turned out to be icy cold water infused with healing herbs.

I'd been lucky. When the blood and loose skin was cleaned away, my hand was just raw and sore. The bugs hadn't eaten me to the bone; my hand would recover. "!¡*shock*¡! What *were* those things?" I said softly.

"!¡*restrained anger*¡! Living weapons," said Divine, coming to stand by me. "Simple to breed, programmable so they can be set on specific targets. Note they didn't follow us through from the Mart: they must have had some kind of boundary programmed in so that they don't destroy everything. It's like Callo told us: exactly what happened in Angiere."

"They did worse in Angiere," said Hope, her voice small. "I... I was there. I saw it all."

Jemerie went to her then. She seemed to be in shock. And her face... The bugs had eaten away her left cheek, through to the jaw. No wonder her voice had sounded so weak! She could barely open her mouth to speak.

I looked around again.

It appeared that Hope and I had been the last to escape through the caves.

"!¡*shock*¡! Is this it?" I asked. "Is this all of us?"

That was when the Loop girl with the wounded arm spoke up. "!¡*cautious*¡! Some as got out on the pads," she said.

I recalled seeing the joeys trying to escape on the float-pads, most of them shot down by the troopship. "Did any get clear?" I asked.

The girl nodded. "!¡*reporting*¡! Frankhay did. I sees 'im out well clear. 'Im an' Buller was clear. Couple a joeys, too. Dunnat know as any else."

No one wanted to remain in the nest that night. Villa Mart Three was too fresh in our memories.

When it was suggested that we sleep in the strip of parkland by the river known as the Hangings, mine was the one voice of dissent. I remembered our search for Skids on Riverside, the grunts rounding up the homeless, trooping them into those trucks... While it made sense to get away from the nest, the streets of Laverne were unlikely to be any safer. I turned to Sol for support during the debate, but she was still in shock, staring and muttering and no use to anyone. Everyone else was for it, so I stopped arguing.

We sat around for a time before anyone made a move to leave. I think we were all in a state of shock. We had heard the stories of what had happened elsewhere, but Hope was the only one among us who had actually seen this kind of attack before. I think that up until that day, we had still believed that Angiere was a distant place and this could not possibly happen in Laverne.

I sat with Hope, while Jemerie applied a dressing to her ruined face.

"!¡*probing*¡! So what's your part in all this?" I asked her. "You turn up in Precept Square with no pids, you're there with Frankhay's mob at the Loop, you're part of their raid... What's going on? !¡*pressing*¡! Who *are* you?"

She looked at me, and after a time said, "You saved me. You made me Reed Trader. But... that's who Frankhay is: his real name is Reed Trader. He made me tell him what you did. You saved me, but I betrayed you. I had to come. I had to do something."

It all fell into place: the things Frankhay had said up on the roof terrace, his anger; suddenly there was a reason for his raid. I cursed my own sloppiness, then. I should have checked the background of the stolen pids before using them. Hope blamed herself, but it was my fault, not hers.

I squeezed her hand and said, "!¡*sympathy*¡! It's okay." Then I nodded towards the dressing on her face. "Does that hurt?"

She nodded. Her eyes were loaded with tears.

I closed my eyes briefly, and instantly flashed back to Villa Mart Three, the wall of bug-tarred, disintegrating bodies surging down the steps from the terrace. I felt sick, just thinking of what we had so narrowly escaped, and of what had happened to so many people I knew and loved.

As I say, I think we were all in shock then, each in our own particular mix of pain and fear and flashback and numbness.

WE WENT TO the Hangings as evening descended, and saw that someone had lit a fire. A small group huddled around it, fending off the chill of the late summer evening.

It took me a while to recognise one of them as Skids.

At first he was just another one of the dossers, a blanket pulled around his shoulders, his face buried in his knees. He could have been anybody.

We settled among the trees nearby, and none of the clanless around the fire looked up. I kept glancing across at them, partly curious, partly wary – we might seem like easy pickings to them, in our shocked, broken state.

After a time Skids raised his head. Maybe he recognised a voice; maybe he'd been lost in some reverie and had only just come back to awareness.

He glanced across at our group and I saw a scattering of stars tattooed across his gaunt face.

I gasped, finally recognising my old nest-sib. I'd been convinced he must have been rounded up and loaded into one of those trucks, long before now. I'd been convinced I'd never see him again.

He caught my eye, nodded. That was all.

Wary, I moved to sit by him. "!¡*tentative*¡! Skids," I said. Life hadn't treated him well. He was skinny and pale and lost-looking; his hair was long, but thin; his eyes were sunken into their sockets. But he was *Skids*.

"!¡*cautious*¡! I came looking for you," I said. "Before. I saw them rounding everyone up." I flashed back to the watcher holding my head by a fistful of hair, making me watch the homeless being trooped into the trucks. Laughing at me. "They were killing them all. I thought you–"

"I saw," said Skids simply. "I watched. I saw you there. I knew you would be back. The Singer of the Ways showed me your path."

I wondered then if the sickness apparent in his body was also a sickness in his head. There was something missing from the Skids I had once known. I did not consider the possibility that there was something *more*.

"!¡*patient | concerned*¡! We've been attacked," I told him. "Jersy and Madder were killed. Jacandra and Carille too. And Vechko, Meliss and Fairhead, before this. They raided the nest: watchers and their grunts."

Skids nodded as if he already knew, although maybe he was just agreeing, encouraging me to go on.

"This is it now." I spread my hands to indicate the small group of us. "We are what remains. They'll be back. The watchers. They did this in Angiere, and now they're doing it here."

"What will you do?" asked Skids.

I shrugged. "!¡*uncertain*¡! If we stay, they'll wipe us out," I said. "All we can do is leave." I remembered what Callo had once told me. "Maybe we'll go east. There's a place... Harmony. A place where we can be safe."

"You know how to get there?" asked Skids. "You think you can do it?"

I shrugged again. I didn't really see what alternative we had.

Then Skids surprised me. "I'm coming with you," he said. "Our paths align. This is how our way has been sung."

Chapter Seventeen

WE SPENT THE night underground, in the living, breathing guts of the city.

We'd been in the Hangings, the stretch of parkland by the river. I'd been reluctant to go there, but the others had argued we would be safer among the homeless. My fears were confirmed that night, when with a sudden, throbbing groan a troopship swung low over the trees.

We all looked around, not sure where to turn, and then Skids caught my eye, nodded towards the river and said, "!¡*reassuring*¡! Come. This way. Follow me."

I nodded and he moved away. I went after him. The others in my small group hesitated, then one by one followed.

Skids clambered over the low wall by the river, onto the rocks. With one more glance back at me, he nodded and then ducked into the rocks and vanished.

I climbed carefully over to where he had been. There was a gap between the rocks, an opening. Some kind of drainage pipe.

"Bring a torch," I called back to Jemerie; soon, the two of us squatted by that opening with a flaming torch lighting the way.

I ducked down and squeezed through the opening, the pipe's walls slick against me, their surface ribbed.

My feet were submerged in water and the air smelled of stagnant ditches and old latrines.

I took the torch from Jemerie and ventured further into the tunnel.

After its mouth, the drain opened out and soon I could stand upright. I looked more closely at the walls, then, and saw that its ribbed surface pulsed to an irregular beat.

I saw Skids, a dark shadow just ahead of me.

"!¡*hesitant | taken aback*¡! What *is* this?" I asked him.

"!¡*matter-of-fact*¡! The city's drainage system," he said.

"!¡*incredulous*¡! But... it's alive."

He nodded. "It is part of the All," he said. "!¡*gentle*¡! We can be safe down here for the night. We have the protection of the All here."

"!¡URGENT¡! WE HAVE to get out of Laverne," I said to the small group gathered around the fire. "We can't stay here, hiding in the guts of the city like this."

Skids had helped us build the fire in a chamber deep in the city's drains. The burning dispelled the bad air and the smoke was carried away through the network of tiny channels that branched off from our hiding place.

Where the fire burned into the surface of the chamber, amber liquid oozed out and scabbed over, healing the damage as fast as the fire could burn. Skids broke these scabs off and chewed on them, spitting out the husks when he was done. "!¡*matter-of-fact*¡! There aren't many nutrients," he had told us when he first did this, "but it stops you being hungry." Eventually I tried it, and he was right: the sweet juices released by chewing on the scab material deadened the hunger in my belly.

But this couldn't last: we could not survive like this for long. We had to get out of this city.

"!¡*frustrated*¡! But where?" said Divine. "We know this city. None of us knows what's beyond."

"Harmony," I said softly.

"!¡*harsh*¡!... is just a word," said Sol.

"It's more," said a voice from the shadows. Hope. "It's a place. A safe place. Sanctuary."

"!¡*harsh*¡! And you know that, eh?" said Sol. She was agitated tonight, rocking back and forth as she sat, as if she were about to erupt. "!¡*dismissive*¡! You've seen it, have you?"

Hope leaned forward so that her face was suddenly caught by the flickering light of the fire. I saw that she was crying. She put hands to the sides of her head. "It's in my head," she said. "The voices... Harmony means something to them."

I looked at her and thought she was mad, then. Had the bugs that had eaten half of her face pushed her over the mental precipice? Or had she been mad already?

"!¡*matter-of-fact*¡! Callo told me about Harmony," I said. "She..." I was on the verge of saying that she was different, *other*, but I pulled back. "She knows more. Where is she? Or the others from Angiere? We should make them tell us what they know."

SHE WAS IN Pennysway Ipp, with the others from Angiere, when a watcher-bound starsinger made it not real.

Skids and I saw it happen.

That night in the tunnels below the city, Sol told us that she had seen Marek that morning, and knew that the four were working over in Pennysway, trying to convince clan-mother Faithsway of what was unfolding in the city. "!¡wry¡! I think they've given up on me, eh?" said Sol, calmer than after her earlier agitation.

"!¡reporting¡! They said it was urgent," Divine added. "They said there were signs of things escalating in Pennysway, said they'd seen it go that way back in Angiere."

Pennysway was Cragside's neighbour to the west, the two Ipps separated by the craggy limestone ridge that divided the city from north to south.

Skids and I set out the next morning to find Callo and the others. As soon as I said I was going, my old nest-sib said he would accompany me. "!¡urgent¡! I want to know," he said. "I want to hear about Harmony."

I still didn't know what to make of him. In many ways he scared me. There was an intensity he had never had when he was younger, an earnestness. He reminded me of Pedre, the wraith I had encountered in Constellation district when I had looked for Skids the first time; there was a phreaked, mad-preacher look in his eyes. It unsettled me, and it jarred with the Skids I remembered.

Early the next morning we passed through Cragside, the streets deserted save for a few trogs and a roof-high buzzing of sentinels. Villa Mart Three had been burnt out and now there were black smudges around the windows and doors.

We hurried along the rutted streets, heads down, stunned into silence by the extent of damage to the Villa and the burnt shells of neighbouring buildings.

We followed a trail up over the crags, and as trees closed around us the atmosphere lifted. I started to breathe more freely, unaware until then of the tightness in my chest.

As we climbed the steep trail, I glanced across at Skids and, briefly, it was almost like old times.

I was kidding myself, I knew. My old sib was haggard, pale, his eyes sunken. His long hair grew in patches where a caul had been. It was not old times at all. Too much had happened to pull us onto diverging paths.

"!¡*hesitant | sincere*¡! I'm sorry, sib," I said, almost choking on my words.

He looked across at me. He didn't know what I was talking about.

"!¡*guilt | anguish*¡! For what we did. For how we treated you."

He looked ahead again, dismissing my words.

"We drove you away," I said. "!¡*anguished*¡! We thought we could force you to get better. We didn't understand what was happening to you."

"!¡*matter-of-fact*¡! That is the way our paths were sung," he said. "We sing together. We sing apart." Then he smiled, and the faraway look snapped out of his eyes. "I mean it's no biggy, see? It led me to the last four years of my life." He clapped me on the arm and then turned back to the trail, the conversation over.

Close to the top, we paused to look back.

Cragside was sporadically burning, a few blots of black smoke hanging in the still air. Across the river, Satinbower, too, lay under a heavy pall of smoke.

And yet, to the left, the jagged spires and mushroom towers of Central lay in full sunlight, the air crystal clear, flyers and transporters darting and hanging over the rooftops. It was like another world altogether. It was clearly only the Ipps that were being targeted.

We turned, cresting the ridge, and before us we saw Pennysway being torn out of existence.

The uncanniest thing, at first, was the silence.

Until we passed over the last ridge, there had been nothing to indicate what lay ahead. No smells of burning, no sounds of conflict or of hanging troopships orchestrating the action. Nothing.

Even the birds and the normally ever-present rasp of cicadas and crickets had fallen silent as we stood and tried to make sense of what lay before us.

It should have been a district where streets were laid out in a grid. Industrial units, mostly run by craniate work gangs, would mix with U-frame terraces of housing: instant buildings erected by the gangs in mere moments. Some of these would be occupied by the Sway clan, led by clan-mother Faith. The Sways were the closest clan to us, both geographically and socially, and I knew some of them reasonably well from occasional gatherings and shared festivals.

It wasn't, though.

The air above Pennysway shimmered like the hot air above an open fire. The light was unnaturally intense, bleaching the colour from everything.

And the buildings... all corners and edges that should have been sharp were blurred, indistinct. All detail was gone.

I found that my eyes would not rest anywhere. There was nothing for them to settle on, nowhere to focus.

It made me feel dizzy, as if I were about to fall.

It made me feel sick.

And in my head I heard a song, a raising of voices, a chorus that simultaneously jarred and harmonised.

I turned away and saw that Skids had fallen to his knees. Tears poured down his face and ran into the sparse stubble lining his jaw; his mouth was open as he breathed shallowly, almost panting.

At first I thought he was in some kind of religious ecstasy, but then he turned to me and I saw his pain.

I opened my mouth to speak, to ask him what was going on, for I was suddenly sure that he understood far more than me, but then Pennysway began to unhappen.

It started from the centre, an intensifying of that already unreal light, a leaching away of colour, of detail. Lines blurred and merged, colours faded together.

I had to look away. My brain couldn't make sense of what my eyes reported.

It spread.

The leaching, merging, blending.

And from the centre, Pennysway started to fold in on itself, to collapse, to cease existing.

"!¡*distress | disbelief*¡! It's being unsung," said Skids, softly.

He stood then, and turned his back on the infolding of Pennysway. Clutching at my arm, he tried to turn me too. "!¡*urgent*¡! Dodge," he said, "we have to go. We don't know where this will end."

But I was transfixed, glued to what I couldn't quite look at.

A big industrial block slipped into the ground; a U-frame terrace undid itself from one end to the other, like a sea serpent sinking below the water. Left behind was bare ground, dirt and rock and a thin green fuzz of vegetation.

Another block went. A building made up of three tall spires with platforms near the top. Another row of U-frames.

The undoing was creeping closer to the crags, and suddenly the sound of insects and birds shrilled all around us, screeches and clacks of alarm and whistles and trills. Birds threw themselves from the trees, all plummeting eastward, away from the unravelling.

I turned and ran with Skids.

Back across the ridge and down the rough trail, almost falling headlong as one or other of us lost footing, slipping on rubble and dry dirt. My breathing was ragged, painful; the muscles in my legs burned. I ran until taking another step was more painful than anything I had ever known, and then I kept on running.

We finally came to a halt where the trees ran out and the buildings of Cragside Ipp began.

I rested against a tree trunk, my breath rasping painfully. When I could move again, I turned to Skids and grabbed him by the shirt, wincing at the sudden pain in my damaged hand.

"!¡*intense | serious*¡! What was that?" I demanded. "What happened?"

He was scared. Very scared.

"!¡*shocked*¡! The 'singers," he said. "They can sing realities. They can make pockets of reality that are different from the reality around them."

I remembered my search for Skids when he had run away, years before. Wraith Pedre had directed me towards a starsinger. The Lord of the Stars, Pedre had called it. That building: I had gone inside and it was as if I had entered another world, another reality; the tumbling hills, the trees, the child-like flying beings. I had thought it was some kind of phreak, a hallucination fed by vapours and other trickery.

But now... I remembered the song in my head, an alien chorus without rhythm or tone but somehow still intensely musical.

"!¡*urgent*¡! The starsingers," I said. "What about the 'singers, Skids?"

"!¡*hesitancy* | *confusion*¡! It was as if... as if they were unsinging the reality of Pennysway," he said. "!¡*shock*¡! Unravelling the strands of world so that it stopped *being*."

I released him. His words were messing with my head, just as what I had seen had messed with my head.

I didn't know what to think.

I backed away from my old nest-sib, doubting his sanity, doubting my own.

I turned and started to climb the trail again.

Skids hung back for a moment, then followed.

I paused below the top. Everything seemed normal, everything seemed fine. A bird sang loudly from an oak tree. Crickets and cicadas shrilled. The sun beat down, strong now that the early morning chill had lifted.

At the top I could see westward to where Pennysway had been.

The ground was flat, bare, fuzzed with thin green. Other than that, no features. Nothing.

Pennysway was no more.

Pennysway was, if Skids was to be believed, unsung.

Chapter Eighteen

HOPE WAS USED to living in the present moment. Her past was a blur, her future uncertain.

Now should have been no different.

She woke in darkness, waiting for her eyes to adjust to the dim light from the dying embers of the fire. She was in the underground chamber, the living drainage channels through which the city regulated itself.

Now, she understood: the city was a living thing. A tree with a network of roots spreading under the ground. A fungus, a mass of fibres and tubes sprouting mushrooms above the surface.

She wondered, when a city like Angiere, and now Laverne, was destroyed above the surface, turned to lakes of frozen glass – did the city survive below ground? Would it regrow when the human pestilence had been wiped out? Was there, even now, a fresh, newly formed Angiere sprouting by the sea to the west? Sheets of blackened glass splitting, parting, as fledgling buildings pushed up from the soil below?

She rolled onto her side. Her neck ached, and the left side of her face felt numb, as if she had been sleeping on it awkwardly.

She raised a hand to her cheek, found the dressing the Cragsider Jemerie had applied, and remembered.

The previous day in the clan nest, it had felt as if her face was dissolving, and the pain had been almost unbearable. She remembered the old rug dealer who had taken her in his wagon to Angiere – because she made the view prettier, he had said. No one would say such a thing to her now.

She did not know how she felt about that yet. Her looks had got her by: work in bars and on her back above bars, Marek's attachment to her... Little things too. People are always more eager to help a pretty girl.

She sat, and saw that Sol was watching her.

The clan-mother was a big, strong woman, her skin like polished tree bark, her eyes dark pools.

"!¡*strong* | *restrained*¡! You're different," said Sol. "There's something going on with you I can't quite place..."

Hope didn't know what to say. She didn't want to be different. She wanted to get by. But she knew it wasn't normal to have no past. She couldn't change that, but she could start to think about the future, perhaps.

"You have to leave," Hope said, recalling the discussion around the fire last night. "We all do. I was in Angiere. I saw it happen, just like this. Clans wiped out. City blocks burned to glass. They won't ease off now that this has started."

Sol was shaking her head. "!¡*patient* | *hierarchy*¡! This is our home," she said. "This is what we know. This is our place. Pups like Dodge and Jemerie might dream of some place better, but that's all it is: dreams. The reality is that our only place is in the Ipps. !¡*firm*¡! We can't leave. It's how it is."

Hope was reminded then of grunts, locked into their protocols of what's right, what's allowed. "The rules are changing," she said. "They have to change." She put her hands to her head. "I feel it. I know it."

"!¡*sensitive*¡! What's in your head, kid? Eh?"

She looked at Sol. She didn't know what it was that was in her head, but she did know that the voices wouldn't quieten down while she remained in the city.

SHE WAS OUTSIDE watching the skimmers and boats on the Swayne when I returned from Pennysway with Skids. The river was wide, and its white-capped waves reminded her of the sea at Angiere. The buildings on the far side were like a child's toys, so little and far away.

She heard voices and turned, and there, gathered among the trees were Skids, me, Sol, Divine and a handful of others whose names she still hadn't mastered.

She saw that we were in some kind of shock, felt dizzy with a surge in her voices, clung to a rail for support.

Drifting closer, she picked up on me struggling to explain what we had witnessed in the neighbouring Ipp. "...blurring, folding in on itself, disappearing. !¡*anguished*¡! The whole Ipp! Just removed."

"!¡*shocked | awestruck*¡! Unsung," said Skids softly. "Realities realigned. Removed from the real."

"!¡*urgent*¡! You're saying the starsingers are behind this?" asked Sol.

Skids shook his head. "!¡*exasperated*¡! Not behind it," he said. "But it was a 'singer that did that. I heard it. I heard the song in my head."

By this time I'd had enough of my old nest-sib's addled semi-mystical rantings. I'd had it from him all the way back from Pennysway. Singing realities. *Un*singing an entire Ipp. We'd seen some kind of weapon in action.

Something new. And it scared the crap out of me. Just as I was about to say something, Hope put her hand, tentatively, on my arm.

She could see that I was agitated, antsy, about to pop. She could see the shock in my eyes.

And she sensed something more.

I looked at her and calmed instantly. Her broken face was a shock to me: so much had happened since the day before, and the dressing had slipped from my mind.

Reporting back to Sol fizzled out.

Hope stood there, trying to calm me, struggling to comprehend what we had just recounted. The aliens had found another way of wiping out an Ipp, of *undoing* it.

The voices in her head rose to a clamour at this, and she decided then that she really would leave this city. She did not have the ties that Sol did, the sense that this was her place. She realised that she feared the city more than she feared the unknown that lay beyond.

She led me away to the riverside, and for a time we simply stood and watched the river pass by.

She put a hand to her head and said, "You calm me."

"!¡*agitation | confusion ... calming*¡! You calm me, too," I replied, not yet comprehending what she really meant, but just knowing that she did, that her touch, her look, reached inside me in a way I had never experienced before.

"So..." I said to her. Small talk had always come easily to me. It was my thing. Until now, when my words seemed to have fled. "Hope. How... how's the...?" I gestured towards her face.

She shrugged, then said, "You saved me. Again." She remembered me clawing at her cheek, scooping the burning bugs out and hurling them away. She pointed at my bound hand. She knew that if I hadn't done what I had, even that small knot of bugs would have killed her.

"!¡*embarrassed | awkward*¡! It's my thing," I said. "Shall we walk?"

The Hangings seemed disturbingly normal that morning. The air had the freshness of late summer as it drifted into autumn. Swallows arced and swept low over the river; they wouldn't be here for much longer. Clydian dragonflies buzzed and swooped. Suddenly, what I had witnessed at Pennysway seemed very distant.

"I'm leaving," said Hope. "No one will survive this."

"!¡*sad*¡! We all need to leave," I agreed. "Sol will come round to it eventually. She has to. !¡*practical*¡! What we have to do is work out how we will do it, and where to go."

"Would they stop us if we just went?"

I shrugged. "!¡*uncertain*¡! The city has no walls. There are checkpoints on every road, though. And our pids... none of us are approved for more than Ipps and mixed zones, out of curfew."

She raised an eyebrow. "You do clever things with pids, though, don't you?"

I shook my head. "Not that clever," I said. "Humans don't have that kind of clearance; there are no pids for us to steal that would let us out."

Just then, a buggy came along the road and we ducked for cover behind the low river wall. The vehicle was a transparent bubble, sitting on a square base, and was occupied by a lone chlick.

I straightened, put a reassuring hand down towards Hope, who still cowered behind the wall.

"!¡*calming*¡! It's okay," I told her. "It's Saneth."

Hope looked up at me. She still wasn't reassured. She had reasons not to trust the aged chlick. She remembered Saneth from Anders Bars Infirmary.

Slowly, she stood and looked across.

Saneth stepped out of the buggy and then, from behind the chlick, a grey-green body appeared. It was a commensal, much like the one that had engulfed Hope and protected her on the journey from Angiere. It was a beast I'd seen occasionally around the city, but I had no name for it. I couldn't quite see how it had fitted into the buggy, but then it surprised me by unfolding, making coughing sounds and then convulsing, vomiting a human, a man, into the dirt.

The man settled on all fours, looked up, then wiped at the slime across his face. It was Marek, one of the four from Angiere. We had thought them all killed in the destruction of Pennysway.

Hope and I climbed over the wall and approached them, just as Sol and Divine emerged from the trees.

They were already talking by the time we reached them.

"...was there," said Marek, close to sobbing. "!¡*anguished*¡! I was with Callo, Lucias, Pleasance, Mother Faith."

"!¡*urgent*¡! Where?" said Sol. "!¡*authority*¡! What happened?"

"!¡*shocked*¡! Pennysway Ipp," said Marek. "It... they're gone..."

"!¡*factual reporting*¡! The emissaries from Angiere were in Pennysway Ipp when it was that the singer of the stars unsung the All," said Saneth, in a whispery voice. The chlick's false eye swivelled independently, taking in the gathering of humans one by one. "Junior emissary Marek survived the unsinging."

Hope put her hand on the small of my back, a reassuring, solid presence. Before me I saw the alien and the small huddle of humans, but in my head I saw Pennysway undoing itself and I remembered the deathly silence all around.

"!¡*shit-scared*¡! What happened there?" I said. "How close were you?"

Marek was on his feet now, rubbing at his face and head with hands and forearms to clean the alien goo away.

He peered at me, and then at Hope, as if surprised to see her here. I realised then that there was some kind of history between the two of them, something more than either had yet revealed.

"!¡*brave-faced*¡! I was too close," said Marek. "We all were. Right in the thick of it. Mother Faith had put us up at the Keep, their main nest."

I knew the Keep well as the site of the annual winter solstice festival; a square, brick-built building that dominated Pennysway. Childhood memories of all the parties shared with Sway clan were, for me, always set against childhood nightmares featuring that dark, looming building.

"!¡*disbelief* | *shock*¡! We were in a hall, sharing bread and grape-juice to start the day. The light changed. All around us. The walls seemed to get thinner, translucent."

"!¡*factual reporting*¡! I was warned," said Saneth. "But too late. !¡*surmise*¡! The timing would appear to have been a thing that was deliberate. !¡*factual reporting*¡! I sounded an alarm, but humans exhibit poor discipline and comprehension of alert phases. Management of a crisis dictates priorities under circumstances such as these."

"!¡*tired*¡! She-he fled," explained Marek. "!¡*emotional* | *struggling*¡! I realised something serious was hitting us. I remember Angiere burning. Melting. !¡*ashamed*¡! I did what Saneth did. I fled. It was a free-for-all, a rush for the street.

"I got out. There was Saneth-ra and the sidedog commensal and the light was getting brighter and everything was getting less clear, less *distinct*..."

"!¡*uncertain*¡! The sidedog folded itself over me... I think it protected me somehow. I don't know how we got out. I just remember looking back and seeing that Pennysway was gone."

"!¡*factual reporting*¡! It was unsung," said Saneth. "!¡*indignant* | *outraged*¡! Somehow the Hadeen watchers have coerced a starsinger into redefining that part of the city. A rogue starsinger is a dangerous thing indeed."

"What happened to the others?" asked Sol.

"!¡*factual reporting*¡! They were unsung," said Saneth. "I came away with junior emissary Marek. We left Pennysway Ipp just before it ceased. Reports account for four members of Sway clan who were outside the Ipp and therefore survived. All others, including clan guests Callo Hart, Lucias Benchport and Pleasance Benchport, are no longer real."

I looked at Sol. Dead. Saneth meant that they were all dead.

I wondered if our nest-mother was now beginning to accept that we would have to leave all this behind, depart the city and strike out for a new start elsewhere.

I didn't have time to ask her then, or later, for that was when we heard the first rumble of the approaching death trucks.

We stopped talking to listen, and then we saw them, two long wagons that twisted like snakes around corners, approaching along the riverside highway at a little more than walking pace. A swarm of sentinels flew above the wagons and as they approached the Hangings they peeled off and buzzed through the trees, surveying the territory, spotting us, identifying us, targeting us for the watchers and their squadrons of grunts who followed on foot in the wake of the wagons.

Chapter Nineteen

I STOOD BEHIND a tree that forked at head height, its trunk shielding my body as I peered through the split to where the first death truck had pulled up.

I held Hope close, her slim body tight against mine. I had expected her to be trembling, had expected her to be on the edge of panic – the same panic that I kept desperately bottled up in my own head. Instead, she seemed calm, curious, strong. I found her strength seeping through me, helping me to focus.

The second truck went past and kept going, leaving the first to disgorge its occupants: a squad of about twenty grunts, led by a faceless, human-form watcher commander. They knew we were here. They'd come for us.

I looked around, trying to assess the options for escape. The trees provided cover, but beyond were buildings with only a few gateways and alleys; as soon as anyone fled, the grunts would find it easy to cut them off.

Staying in the Hangings and sneaking through the trees was an option, but progress would be slow and the grunts could easily outpace us along the road and intercept us.

The river cut off any other escape route.

And all the time, as I looked around and weighed up the options, a sentinel hung a short distance over our heads, monitoring.

"!¡*seeking attention*¡!"

I glanced across. Skids was hiding behind a tree nearby, clicking softly for my attention. He nodded, said, "!¡*urgent*¡! The drains. If we can get to the drains we can lose them there."

There was no other way out.

The only route to the drainage tunnels was from the river bank, but that would involve crossing the highway in full view.

Just then, Saneth emerged from beyond the truck where her-his buggy had been. Immediately, a knot of sentinels clustered over the chlick's head. "!¡*consternation | confusion*¡! I..." Saneth said. "I don't understand what it is that is happening here. !¡*hierarchy | sneering*¡! Ah, a watcher of the Hadeen persuasion. Good, good. Clear the way for me, lower-denomination-being. You understand? I wish to pass through, but you hinder me."

Saneth waved contemptuously with both hands at the watcher commander, the gestures reinforced by a string of patronising, dismissive clicks.

The watcher raised a hand and pointed at Saneth, and immediately four grunts trained beam-guns on the chlick. It was impossible to see anything in the alien's featureless face.

"!¡*amused | dismissive*¡! How quaint!" said Saneth. "!¡*commanding*¡! Allow me to pass, body of collected slugs."

The watcher snapped its hand up, back at the wrist, and the grunts fired, beams of blue light stabbing at where Saneth had been.

But the chlick was no longer there.

Hope squeezed my arm and nodded to where Saneth now stood by the riverside wall.

The grunts aimed again, but their watcher commander appeared to halt them, redirect them – with a gesture, a thought, a command I couldn't detect... As one, the grunts swung left to where Divine, Skids, Ruth and some of the others were scampering across the road towards the river.

Divine was first to the wall; she swung over, squatted among the boulders and reached back to help Ruth, but she was too late. As Ruth reached the wall and swung a leg over, her foot caught and she stumbled. A blue needle-beam swept across her. The top half of her body fell to the ground as her legs and lower torso twisted and bucked and fell against the wall.

Divine cried out, turned on the aliens and then ducked down as more blue beams swept the rocks.

Skids was there, and over, and hunkering down, dodging the beams. Jemerie too, and Pi.

I looked, but it was too far for Hope and me, and I had spotted what was happening under cover of Saneth's diversion too late. We wouldn't have a chance.

Then, with a cry of rage, Sol advanced on the watcher. "!¡*outrage*¡! What are you doing, killing my people?" she cried.

Hope and I edged through the trees as, ahead of us, Marek hurdled the wall and landed among the rocks.

Sol got close enough to strike the startled watcher in its blank face. Her big fist sank into the thing's head and then pulled free with a sucking sound audible even from where Hope and I hid in the trees.

The watcher pulled back with a fluid movement, like a ripple of its entire body. Then the snout of a weapon emerged from the watcher's wrist and fired into Sol's face.

Sol staggered back and half-turned. There was a hole right through from her face to the back of her head, wide enough that I could see daylight through it.

And then she turned back to face the watcher.

"!¡*authority*¡! Enough!" she cried, and I didn't know how she could when she must surely be dead already. "These are my people!"

She struck the watcher again, and her hand passed through the thing's head as if through water.

The watcher fired again. A hole opened up in Sol's chest. The next shot sliced her arm so that the flesh hung off it, black skin flayed away from bunched off-white fibres. Like those Callo had revealed when she had wanted to show me that she was not one of us, but rather there for us, for our kind... a *guardian*, she had called herself.

Sol looked down at her arm and tried to swing it, but it was useless to her now.

She threw herself at the watcher, and I managed to tear my gaze away for long enough to see that some of the grunts had closed in, so that even with the distraction Sol offered we would have no chance of reaching the river and the safety of the tunnels.

"Here," hissed Hope. "Now. Duck down."

Saneth's commensal, the sidedog, had crept towards us through the trees, and now Hope gestured at it, using the command she had seen Saneth use back in Angiere.

The commensal folded back on itself and Hope pulled me into its embrace as it plunged down on top of us, around us, engulfing us in that wet, fleshy interior. Instantly, my chest was squeezed so hard I couldn't breathe and then I realised I didn't have to breathe, didn't want to breathe, surrounded as I was by the sidedog's bulk. I could feel Hope against me, tangled with me, I could sense her, feel the shape of her presence.

For a moment I was lost, as the oneness with Hope and with the commensal swept over me, and then I realised that I could see and I could hear and I could smell. All my senses were sharper, more specific, than my dulled human senses had ever been.

And there before me, I watched and heard and smelled my clan-mother, who was not a human at all, but rather a guardian like Callo, being burned and sliced and dismantled by the watcher commander.

I wanted to go to her. I wanted to run from her, from the she that was not a she but an *it*. I wanted to throw myself at the watcher, stop it from slicing, slicing, slicing and revealing my clan-mother to be not what I had believed, turning her to slabs of meat and skin and mechanical components.

I could not do any of that. I was absorbed, contained within the commensal sidedog. Its body – our body – turned away from the destruction. In that single movement, our pin-sharp vision took in the grunts: watching their commander, checking the trees, watching us as we turned away...

I felt an urge to relax, and realised that the urge had been pushed towards me by Hope.

The body we were in was struggling to move, and I understood that this was because I was resisting, focused on what was happening to Sol.

I relaxed and the body moved more freely, swung away from the carnage, started to run in a shambling four-legged movement that felt natural, right.

I heard movements behind, the sound of a grunt raising its beam-gun. The brief pause that followed as it took aim, and then we dropped and rolled, and I saw a needle-beam burn blue through the air above.

It was as if the world had slowed down, our enhanced perception giving us just that little bit more time to react.

Something burned into our back and we gave a high-pitched yelp of pain, smelling the burning of our own flesh.

We paused to look back and saw Saneth speeding away in her-his buggy while the grunts and their watcher commander all turned their attention on our escape.

We reached the wall and simply lifted our legs and flowed over it with no break in our stride.

Another beam stung our hind quarters and now Hope was sending calming waves both to me and to our host.

The rocks slowed us, but soon we had dropped to water level.

We paused. Divine was waiting in the opening of the drainage duct, but we realised now that we would never squeeze through that gap in our current form.

I remembered the sidedog spewing out Marek and how it had taken him long moments to gather himself, orient himself, find his senses.

We did not have that much time.

Already, grunts were advancing across the road, and out on the river two skimmers were swooping in towards us.

Divine raised a fist in defiance and mouthed, "Martyrs," and then she was gone and the drainage duct was only a dark slit between piled boulders.

We turned, stepped into the river's dark waters and instantly plunged down. The water was dark and piercingly cold.

It tasted of mud, and its chill spread rapidly through our shared body.

Submerged, we flailed, lost all orientation.

We pulled our legs up, tucked our head in and only then did a sense of direction return as we dropped to the river bed.

The current took us and rolled us along. Occasionally we got lodged in rocks or mud or weed, and we would push with a leg to break free.

We rolled and tumbled and bounced along the river bed, going with the current, a ball of icy flesh, the three of us.

And then I started to sense Hope. It was more than just the awareness I had initially felt. She was a shape, a form whose boundaries met my own, overlapped my own, merged.

She was a presence, and within that presence I heard voices.

A constant babble of voices. Distant, subdued, their words impossible to distinguish. It was like Pennysway being unsung: just as the Ipp's lines had blurred and lost detail, so these voices were blurred, indistinct.

They came from Hope, that much was clear. She had mentioned her voices before, and now I knew what she meant. This would drive anyone mad.

EVENTUALLY, WE STARTED to fight the current, clinging to the rocks of the river bed and hauling ourselves up onto dry land.

We emerged from the river among the abandoned market stalls of Riverside. Normally a place full of bustle and cries, colour and movement, now the area was deserted. All around us, my home city really was dying.

The sidedog stood on a small grassy area and tipped back, and Hope and I unfolded from its interior. The thing stood there for a moment longer, and then turned and trotted away and was soon gone.

Hope and I lay on the grass, slick with the alien's juices. I rubbed at my face and Hope at hers. Her dressing had come away, and the left side of her face was healed now, smooth scar tissue covering the area where the wound had been. It was almost as if the sidedog had tried to fix her when it returned her to the world.

I looked down at my damaged hand and it too was smooth, the scars blending in with the surrounding skin.

I took my shirt off to dry in the sun and Hope did the same. Her body was skinny, her ribs clearly delineated, her breasts small, dark-nippled.

I dragged my eyes away, closed them.

And saw Sol being sliced apart by the faceless watcher.

A soft touch, fingertips, on my cheek. Smoothing away tears.

I opened my eyes and Hope was withdrawing her hand, studying me closely.

"!¡*confused* | *anguished*¡! Sol," I said. "Did you see what happened to Sol? Did you see... what was inside?"

Hope gave a simple nod.

"!¡*confused*¡! What *was* that? What was she?"

"That's not what a person looks like inside," said Hope. "I've never seen anything like it. Not even at the infirmary."

"!¡*hesitant*¡! I have," I told her. "Callo. One of the four from Angiere – she came with Marek and Saneth." And she was dead now, too. *Unsung*, as Saneth had put it.

Hope stared. "I didn't know," she said. "And the others? Is Marek... not one of us?"

"!¡*uncertain | confused*¡! I don't know," I said. "Callo: she told me that everything is not as it seems. I think she was telling me that she knew about Sol. She said she was a guardian, here to protect us. That's what Sol did, too. Even at the end."

I was crying again, even as I worked things through in my mind. Sol: she, or it, or whatever she was, had protected us to the last, but now she was gone.

Hope reached for me, pulled me close, let me sob. Skin against skin, we were one again, as we had been in the commensal sidedog, boundaries dissolving.

Eventually, my sobbing subsided and we just held each other.

"Did they get out?"

Slowly, I eased my embrace. I could smell burning now, a chemical burning. It was faint, distant, carried on the soft breeze that followed the river. Another part of the city, dying.

"!¡*hesitant*¡! I don't know," I said. "!¡*optimistic | untrue*¡! Probably. !¡*factual reporting*¡! I saw Skids, Jemerie, Pi and Marek all cross the road safely and reach the rocks. When we reached the river they had gone." No bodies, is what I meant but couldn't quite say. "I saw Divine in one of the tunnels."

"And they would be safe in the tunnels?"

I dipped my head, pressing my forehead hard against my knees. "!¡*anguished*¡! The tunnels drain the city," I said. "!¡*doubting*¡! If they can just find their way through the network, they'll be okay."

She nodded.

"!¡*reassuring | positive*¡! We'll find them," I said. "And then we'll work out how to get out of this city. There's nothing left for us here."

Chapter Twenty

For Hope, our escape from the Hangings in the sidedog commensal had offered strange respite. She had gone from cowering in the trees as we witnessed the carnage, with no way out and the voices in her head clamouring and wailing, to... release, quiet.

Just as last time, when the sidedog enfolded her, the voices in her head softened to a murmur and then stilled. All she was aware of was me, and the commensal, the three of us sharing a single body, our beings blending, mixing and remixing, just as I had felt the blending and mixing. And as she pushed her voices out, I had sensed them, shared them. For that short time, as we bounced along the bottom of the great river, we were one, different elements of a single being.

And when we emerged, I was a little bit Hope, and Hope was a little bit me.

Lying on the grass in the sun, she had wanted to hold me long before we fell into each other's embrace. She knew the comfort it offered, the touch of another body.

We talked of Sol, and Hope was not shocked by the clan-mother's nature. She had not known Sol well enough to see her as a person. To her, Sol was an intimidating figure, fierce protector of the clan; she was little more than another part of the backdrop of a strange new city.

But Callo... Callo had helped her escape from Angiere. Callo had shown her human kindness. In their few brief encounters, Callo had given Hope a model for what it was to be human.

And yet she was not.

"And the others? Is Marek... not one of us?" She remembered his taste and smell. She remembered the touch of his wiry body; he had so much hardness about him, in his body and in the way he was with people.

Was he man, or was he other?

"I HEAR VOICES," Hope told me, after a silence in which we lay side by side, our arms touching. "In my head, voices."

She turned her head towards me and I nodded.

"!¡*reassuring*¡! I know. You've said. And... I heard them."

She knew what I meant immediately, had suspected it, had wondered where the voices went when she had pushed them away. "They scare me. I hate them. I don't want them."

I turned to her, put an arm across her, aware again of her semi-nakedness against me. She sensed this and gently pushed my arm away. We sat again, hugging our knees. I reached for our shirts, dry now, and handed Hope hers.

I pulled mine over my head, and as Hope covered herself, I said, "!¡*earnest*¡! Maybe you should try listening to them, rather than shutting them out. Maybe they have something to tell you."

"HOW WILL WE find them?" Hope asked later. "Where will they go? Where will they be?"

She hadn't believed my assurances that we would find the others again. To her, there was just the two of us now, but she knew I had to convince myself of that too before we could move on. She remembered exploring in the night we had spent underground, venturing away from the fire and following the drainage ducts deeper into the city, away from the river. The ducts had grown narrower the deeper she went. It was possible she had chosen a bad route, and that the main ducts would remain high and broad, but her experience didn't encourage her to believe that.

"!¡*positive*¡! We'll find them at the Monument to the Martyrs," I told her. "It's tucked away to the west of Central, by a bridge over a storm channel. That's where we need to go."

Hope nodded, but she had a faraway look in her eye. The voices had risen, a swell of noise. She tried to listen to them, but couldn't. There were no words, not even any recognisable syllables.

"Where are we now?" she asked.

"!¡*matter-of-fact*¡! We're at the west end of Riverside," I told her. "It's a trading zone, non-residential. The smoke across the river is coming from Satinbower Ipp. Farther west is the Loop – that's where Frankhay and his mob come from. South, beyond those buildings, is Central. Back east along the river is the Hangings, Cragside. What's left of it."

She turned to me. "You go. Go to the Monument to the Martyrs. Find whoever else has survived."

"!¡*confused* | *alarmed*¡! What will you do?"

"I'll join you there," she said. Remembering her arrangements to meet up with Callo and the others when they came to Laverne, she added, "Be there at midday every day. I'll find you."

I moved onto my knees, facing her. "!¡urgent¡! No," I said. "We can't split up now. Why would we do that? Come with me to find the others, and then we'll work out how to get out of this city. !¡insistent¡! We need to stick together!"

She shook her head.

"No. I'll find you later. I know what to do. I'm listening to the voices, like you told me to."

SHE INSISTED, AND there was nothing I could say to persuade her otherwise. She listened to the directions I gave her for finding the Monument to the Martyrs, and patiently answered my questions until I was convinced she knew how to find it. She wouldn't tell me what she was doing. She must have known I would argue. Frankhay and his mob had attacked us at Cragside, and they had made it clear that they didn't want to have anything to do with the other clans, even as the city was demolished all around us.

And now she wanted to go to him.

As soon as the thought had occurred to her, the voices had lulled, faded into a background murmur.

She must go to Frankhay.

As I walked away into the industrial zone that backed onto Riverside, she started to doubt. I was leaving her alone in this dying city. Would she see me again?

She waited until I was gone, then headed west.

As she approached the Loop, the city came back to life a little, with aliens and trogs in the streets, and flyers buzzing around the rooftops. She passed through a small area where dome-shaped buildings clustered and bat-like creatures flew about, entering and leaving the buildings through slots around the apex of each dome. She did not know if they were aliens or not, or if they were a threat. It seemed almost shocking that in these pockets of the city normal life could continue, regardless of what was happening elsewhere.

She stuck to the alleyways where possible, fearful of being challenged, not knowing if her pids allowed her passage on main streets in this zone or not. Even before the city had started to fall, Laverne had been so much more hostile to humans than Angiere had been.

She couldn't help but feel that what was happening was personal. The watchers – the Hadeen, Saneth had called them – were systematically wiping out all that was human. She – and me, Divine, Jemerie and the others – were being hunted down, and she could see no end to it.

Beyond the bat domes there was a cliff-like building, square and long, not much more than a wall with windows. She passed through an archway in its base and came to the canal. A small bridge crossed it, and on the far side there was a checkpoint guarded by two of the tall aliens they called joeys.

She knew that some joeys had allied themselves with Frankhay and had joined him on the Cragside raid, but she had no way of telling whether these guards belonged to him or were from a different faction.

She hesitated briefly, but could think of no other way to enter the Loop.

She crossed the bridge and the joeys ignored her. They stood facing each other, almost touching, as if they were staring each other out. Some kind of argument, perhaps. She did not know. She hurried on past them and found herself on a narrow street, with half-timbered buildings huddling in on either side.

She didn't know where she was heading, only that the voices had stayed in the background since she had chosen this course of action.

Last time she had come here, the checkpoint guard had sent word ahead, and she had been stopped by Ashterhay and Jerra by the time she had reached the end of the first street. This time, she doubted the guards had even noticed her pass.

She came to a small square she thought she recognised. Apricot trees and vegetables grew within an enclosing fence of black iron railings.

She turned left and took the first exit from the square. She knew, at least, that she needed to stay near to the canal.

At the end of the next street, she saw that she was in the right area. A spur of the canal left the main body here, spanned by a narrow humped bridge.

She crossed, and there was the bar where Frankhay held his council, and where Hope had been kept prisoner in an upstairs room.

She managed to get all the way to the door before a sudden jag of pain ripped through her shoulder and she looked down and saw a crossbow bolt protruding from her collarbone, blood spreading fast and scarlet across her shirt. And then she looked up again and saw a face at an open window, a sickly white face fringed with dark hair, a movement of the body as a pistol crossbow was withdrawn, dropped with a clatter, a cry. A swirling rush of darkness, starting in the fringes of her vision and then spreading, spiralling inwards.

And then... nothing.

Chapter Twenty-One

I HEARD IT. I heard the voices crying out. And there was nothing I could do.

When I had left Hope in Riverside, I had felt powerless. There was no shifting her, no getting her to explain what she was planning. All I could do was hope that she would survive, hope that she would find us again at the Monument to the Martyrs.

The direct route to the Monument was through Central and Precept Square, but I wasn't happy with that. It was a risky enough route at the best of times, travelling through the most alien part of the city, and the most hostile to humankind. With things as they were now, I didn't believe I would pass through even the first of the checkpoints, let alone get through Central where there were checkpoints on pretty much every block. Instead, I headed back through the city towards the southern fringe of Cragside; from there I would be able to follow the ridge of limestone crags south, looping behind Central, until I reached the densely-packed district of pap-houses, bars, gambling dens and brothels known as Cunnet.

As soon as I was away from Riverside, the city seemed disturbingly normal. There were a few more checkpoints, but the grunts waved me through after the usual quick scan of my pids; there was the occasional drone of a distant troopship, the occasional whizz and rush of a passing military flyer, low over the rooftops, but nothing more than that. I passed through Grape West, another of the trading districts that gathered around the fringes of Central, and the streets seemed just as busy as normal. Off-duty grunts huddled around recharge pods, phreaking and play-fighting. Chantras and headclouds filled the open bars, drinking and melding and playing games involving hooded heads and strange body movements, the action taking place in some virtual world, or so Vechko had once explained.

I stopped by one of the bars and looked in. A screen divided it in two, and the smaller section away from the door and windows bore the five-fingered hand sign to indicate that humans could drink there. Save for a pair of wired-up orphids, the place was deserted, and that reminded me that normal for orphids and chlicks and chantras did not necessarily mean normal for us.

I hurried away, not so fast that I'd draw the attention of any grunts or sentinels in the vicinity, but still as fast as I could manage.

I cut through an alley I had used many times in the past, an unofficial route that took me behind the main street and through an industrial block to the jagwire boundary of my home Ipp, Cragside.

But the jagwire was down, and it took me a moment to comprehend what my eyes were telling me: beyond where the jagwire should have been, Cragside was no longer there.

Cragside had been unsung.

Before me stretched land covered with a fuzz of new green growth. The soil was dark, as if mixed with ash. The landscape rose and fell in gentle folds like a rucked blanket until the great crags rose up, denuded of trees, their gnarled faces and corners smoothed to a marble sheen.

I turned, and saw the familiar view of Grape West that formed a buffer between Cragside and Central. It was a view I knew well. Clan Virtue did much of its trading in this zone, a place where clans and gangs and various factions of aliens could mix freely. There were times when I had almost lived in the dives and dens of Grape West.

I turned again and Cragside was still gone.

Now that I had come this far, I had to go on. I had to pass through the area that had been my home Ipp in order to hit the trail that would take me down to Precept.

I stuck to the fringe, walking close to where the jagwire boundary had once been. Apart from anything else, out in the open I was completely exposed, an anomaly. The sentinels would be on me in no time.

The soil was loose and tindery. In places, embryonic seedling trees had sprouted. The air smelled like a summer street after rain.

It was all unnaturally natural.

And then, when I looked back at the rest of Laverne from within what had been Cragside, I found that my eyes wouldn't focus. The detail was gone, the sharp lines of reality blurring.

For a heart-pounding instant I thought the rest of the city was being unsung, and I didn't know what to do.

I blinked, rubbed at my eyes, and the city came back.

Struggling not to lose myself in blind panic, I ran to the former boundary, crossed into the city, and everything was normal once more.

I stayed in the city proper for as long as I could, only crossing into Cragside when I had to. I felt sick, just walking there.

I reached the first rise of the crags. Again, this should be familiar terrain, but the trees had gone and the rocks had been remoulded.

I climbed the incline and eventually found a shelf in the rocks where the trail had once been.

I followed it round the crag face, deeply disturbed by the smoothed rocks and the lack of birds and insects and other creatures. This landscape was newborn, unravaged, unlived-in.

Soon I was clear of my old home Ipp. It felt much better to walk with trees around me, with birdsong in the air and the whine of crickets from the bushes and undergrowth. It felt much better to look back across the city to Central and beyond, and not have it all blurring out of reality.

I came to a fallen tree and sat there for a time, soaking up the sounds and smells of the normal, the familiar.

We had to leave.

If I hadn't really believed it before, I knew now that there was nothing for us here in what was left of Laverne.

We had to gather ourselves and leave. No alternative remained.

I straightened, about to push myself up from where I sat, and that was when I heard the voices in my head, a sudden clamour, so loud and *sharp* that I reeled, fell sideways, retched into the dusty dirt of the trail.

I looked down and saw red spreading across my shirt from a hole in my shoulder. I felt the pain, burning and intense, as if someone had tried to rip my arm out of its socket.

I felt blackness, numbness, nothing.

Some time later, I came round, opened my eyes. Grit was stuck in the side of my face, stinging.

I sat up, reached for my shoulder, and there was nothing. No pain. No blood.

It was fine.

In my head: silence.

It was Hope, I knew. Something had happened to her.

I listened hard, but my head was empty.

Whatever connection had linked the two of us, it was now gone.

I had never felt more alone.

I CAME DOWN from the crags by a back trail that led into Cunnet.

The trail led through a cluster of pap plants and packing houses onto Nightcut Alley, which led down to the storm channel and onto Night Street, one of the district's main thoroughfares.

I entered Cunnet with a knot of dread in my gut, my head full of Hope's innocent observations about how unlikely it was that anyone would have survived by fleeing through the drainage ducts at Riverside.

I had seen Divine in there; I knew others had reached the rocks, and had seen nothing to indicate that they had been caught or killed. They must have made it underground.

But could they really have passed any distance through the channels? And was there any way out, other than the openings by the river?

As I walked, I convinced myself that the grunts would have gone after them and caught them easily. Again, I felt alone, and I wondered why I had allowed Hope to abandon me. I remembered the intensity of the pain, the vision of blood spreading, the rush of voices in my head. Whatever had happened to her... would it have happened if we had stayed together?

I remembered that moment when we had held each other and I had suddenly been aware of her skin against mine. She had sensed it, had pushed me away.

Had something changed between us, then? Was that the moment when she had decided to turn me away?

I had responded to her just as I would to any half-naked girl in my arms, but... Hope was different. I realised then that my feelings for her were something more, something complicated that I had never known before, and then I realised that all this was futile, going round and round in my head when I had felt her pain, heard the roar of voices, seen her blood.

Futile, when I had somehow witnessed Hope's death.

Where the Alley reached the storm channel I paused. There was a plank bridge here, held together by rope and wooden pegs. It looked rickety, but I had seen horses haul wagons across this bridge and knew it to be stronger than it appeared.

Below, the channel cut a deep cleft through the rocks. The water was slow here, sluggish. I could see dust and dead leaves stuck to its surface, flies flitting across it.

By the bridge there was a gap. I stepped through, and found the rough footholds that took me down the rocks to the channel.

Here, below the bridge, generations of humans had etched names. Names of the lost, the taken and never returned, names of the martyred. After scraping at some of the moss and algae, I found the familiar shape of Bard Mercer, perhaps a blood of mine. Nobody had recognised the name when I had asked about it years before, and the etching was almost smoothed away beyond recognition. As always, I felt humbled by the Monument. How many generations back was Bard? The only stories of our clan, of our past, were those handed down by storytellers like Vechko. The specifics, the lives of people like Bard Mercer, were gone forever.

I pressed a finger to the letters, aware that even my touch was hastening the loss of the etched name.

There were other names there, some I recognised and had known in life. Way back, when Skids had fled Cragside and taken up life with the wraiths of Constellation, Pi and I had come here and chiselled his name into the rock, believing him lost forever. The name was there, still, the letters clumsy and rough and twice as big as any of the others, lined up crookedly along a fold in the rock.

That was when I saw that new names had been added, not carved but written in ink. It wouldn't last, but it was better than nothing at all. And when I saw the names, I knew that someone had made it out of the drainage channels of Riverside.

The new names were Sol Virtue, Ruth Laty, Jacandra One, Carille One, Jersy Waters, Madder Rue, Vechko Mercer... the list went on. My surge of relief upon realising that someone had been here since the escape from Riverside was tempered by the shock at seeing so many names, the reality of our loss.

I sat, with my back against the etched names and my feet dangling over the turgid water, and waited.

EVERY TIME I heard voices, footfalls, the roll of a wagon's wheels, I started, my heart racing, ready to rush to my sibs, ready to flee.

During that day, traffic along Nightcut Alley was sparse. From my hiding place in the shadows, I peered up and saw trogs rushing about their business, commensals and slave species carrying great loads, or hauling carts. One wagon was so heavy I watched the bridge bow under the load, and I tensed to leap out of the way should the wood start to splinter.

There was no one I recognised, and as the night began to draw in I started to think about moving, wondering where I should be when curfew kicked in.

And then there was a noise, the scuffing of feet on the footholds down from the Alley.

Divine.

In the dim twilight, her pale skin almost glowed, her white hair matted, the spikes clumped in uneven tufts.

She saw me, paused, and then took a single big stride towards me and was in my arms, sobbing.

Divine never cried. Divine was the strongest person I knew. She had once taken out three orphid grunts on her own. She had stood strong through everything that had happened recently. Divine never showed weakness.

But only that morning she had watched her lover Ruth sliced in half by the needle-beam of an orphid gun.

I knew then that it was Divine who had written the new names into the Monument to the Martyrs.

I wondered if she was the only survivor.

I held her, let her sob.

I didn't know what to do. I'd dealt with some shit in recent times, but Divine sobbing her heart out and squeezing me so tight I could barely breathe was just about the most painful thing of all.

*　　*　　*

SHE HAD BROUGHT tools. A lump hammer and three chisels of various sizes and shapes. By the light of a stubby tallow candle, we went over the inked names on the Monument of the Martyrs with chisel and hammer.

As we worked, we exchanged faltering words, slowly catching up with what had happened.

I learned that when Divine and the others had fled into the ducts, they had been faced with a choice – hide, or escape through the ducts? There were nine of them. Gathered there with Divine in the broad duct chamber, where we had slept the night before, were Jemerie, Pi, Marek, Skids, Herald and Fray, and two children, Tuck and Immy. For a moment there, Divine had been on the verge of losing it. The only light was that reflected in from the entrance, making the pulsing of the walls' ribs even more pronounced. It was as if they had been swallowed by some giant beast. She had felt hot, she had felt choked with panic, and in her head was a barrage of images: the look on Ruth's face as the needle-beam had sliced through her, a mix of shock and disbelief; the way Ruth's torso had slid down the cut and then snagged and tumbled; the cross-section of her body, cauterised by the beam, spine and guts and pelvic girdle cut clean through. Images that filled her head then, and had stayed with her all day and would be with her forever.

She chipped at the names on the Monument to the Martyrs with controlled precision. This was her penance for surviving, her tribute to the fallen. I'm not sure she wanted my help at all, but she didn't try to stop me.

The small band of survivors stayed together, following the main channel deep into the city until finally it grew too narrow for them to pass.

They sent Tuck ahead. He was small and fearless, used to climbing the crags and exploring the caves that ran through them. They didn't let him go far, though, for fear that he would get lost in tunnels no one else could penetrate.

They tried other branches, always fearful that each time they headed back they would be confronted by grunts following them from Riverside.

Finally, Tuck found a way out. Divine had been with him, following behind as he wriggled through a slick, pulsing duct, when suddenly he had vanished. She'd forced herself forward, her head emerging from an opening, partway up the wall of a storm duct. Tuck had been in the shallow water below, on his knees, winded and dazed from the fall.

Divine had followed, and landed in the water. If her broad shoulders would pass through that opening, then so too would the rest of their party.

The storm duct had been in Grape West, and they had chosen to come here, to the Monument of the Martyrs, directly through the fringe of Central, rather than by the roundabout route I had taken.

I told her what had become of Cragside, and we were silent for a time after that. Divine hadn't been aware. She didn't know what it was like to see the place where you had grown up simply wiped out of existence. She only had my words, not nearly enough for her to fully comprehend.

"!¡*sensitive*¡! What happened to Hope?" asked Divine, after a time, as she chipped at the last of the names and I rested my sore hand and wrist. "I saw what that chlick's sidedog did to get the two of you out. Never seen anything like it."

"!¡*anguished*¡! We have to wait for her," I said.

"...but?"

"!¡*grieving* | *loss*¡! When we were in that thing, the sidedog," I said. "Something happened. I saw the world as the sidedog did. And as Hope did. I heard what was in her head. Everything merged while we were in there."

"And?"

"!¡*grief*¡! I left her behind in Riverside. She had something she needed to do. She said she'd join us here, which is why we have to wait. But later... later I heard the voices from inside her head again, as if we have some kind of bond, a bridge between us. I felt pain in my chest, my shoulder... I saw blood there. Something's happened to her, Divine. Something bad."

Divine looked at me in the light of the stubby tallow candle, pausing from her work. "!¡*tender*¡! We have to give her a chance, bub." She put her hands on my shoulders, then, and added, "!¡*firm*¡! But when we're done giving her a chance, we're going to have to shift ourselves pretty damned quickly before this whole fucking place gets unsung around us, you get that?"

I nodded. I got that.

I didn't know how long we could wait for Hope.

WE SPENT THE night in a warehouse in south Cunnet.

We were a morose group, each lost in our own thoughts. Only Herald and Pi found distraction, sitting with the two pups, talking to them, reassuring them, telling stories and singing songs to lull them.

Marek sat apart. He had always been aloof, but now... Now I couldn't help but watch him, study him for signs of difference. He had come here with

Callo and had been close to Sol. He was cold, he was distant, he was different.

I kept my peace. No one else knew about Callo, and none of us had spoken about Sol, although I had not been alone in witnessing our nest-mother's confrontation with the watcher commander.

At some point I slept, because I woke stiff and sore and cold, lying awkwardly against a metal wall. The pain in my shoulders reminded me of the pain I had felt the day before, and the rush of voices that had accompanied it.

I woke sharply at that memory. I had to look for her. But then I remembered that I had arranged to be at the Monument, to wait for her, at midday every day. The morning was still young and I had no need to hurry.

I went there, regardless, and Divine accompanied me.

We each had our reasons.

Divine tended to the new names on the Monument, working quietly at etching them deeper.

I sat and waited, my feet swinging over the water.

I felt powerless.

All I could do was be here, wait, hope that she would be okay.

As it turned out, I did not have long to wait.

That first day as the sun crept higher in the sky, approaching midday, I heard a sound and saw a slim form clambering down the footholds in the rock, knee-length boots leading the way.

My heart surged and then my hopes were dashed, as the small figure stepped down onto the rock shelf and turned to face us. White face, rosebud mouth, ragged black hair... It was the Loop girl, one of Frankhay's black-lace mob.

"!¡*wary | scared | defensive*¡! Dunnat do anyt', see?" she said in her low, throaty tone. "I's a message, see?"

"!¡*distrustful | aggressive*¡! A message?" I said. "Why's Frankhay sending messages now? He didn't want anything to do with us."

"!¡*factual reporting*¡! Innat Frankhay," she said. "I's a message outa da gel. Da Hope, see? I's a message outa Hope."

THE GIRL FROM the Loop introduced herself as First Deputy Ashterhay. She said she'd come from the Loop. Said Hope had given her the directions, and said to be here at midday.

She said she'd shot Hope through the shoulder.

"!¡*defensive | wary*¡! Innat my bad," she rushed to add, holding her hands palms-up, as if to fend me off. "!¡*factual reporting*¡! I's a guardin' duty. Da Loop. Everynat' edgy. Crazy. Is a gangs a trogs even, comin' an' stealin'. I sees 'er an' I's on edge, ya see? !¡*defensive*¡! An 'as to be quick, see? I sees 'er an' I fires an' den it's da' I *sees* 'er 'an I 'members who as she is."

"!¡*brusque*¡! She dead?" asked Divine, always to the point.

Ash shook her head. "!¡*factual reporting*¡! Na'," she said. "Is sore as! She's a strong'n."

"!¡*intimidating*¡! So you come all this way just to tell us you shot her but didn't quite kill her?" said Divine. "!¡*menacing*¡! How fucking touching."

The stone chisel hung casually from one of Divine's hands, and it was clear it could be right through Ash's heart in an instant.

Ash was shaking her head. "Na," she said. "!¡*eager*¡! I comin' 'ere 'cause Hope tells as to. I comin' 'ere 'cause as Hope has a plan for as how we can get outa dis city, ya see?"

"!¡*menacing*¡! And what's that plan, then?" I demanded.

"!¡*eager*¡! As you an' 'ow many else as survivin', ya come with me, ya see?" said Ash. "Ya come with me to da Loop, an' we's all leave Laverne together, see?"

My head was swirling with possibilities. How had Ash known where to find us? What must they have done to Hope in order to extract that information? Why would they even bother? Didn't they have bigger battles to fight now? And what if this dough-faced kid was actually telling the truth?

"!¡*gentle menace*¡! Why should we believe you?" I said.

"!¡*derisive outburst | tension-release*¡! Why as ya trust me?" she said. "Why as the fuck ya wouldn't? Why'd I come all over 'ere to tell ya what I tell ya if 'n it didn't matter? Why'd I come an' tell ya I shot da gel, eh?"

I looked at her. I didn't have an answer.

"Ya comin' den?" she asked. "Ya comin' or ya stayin' here in a city that ain't gonna be, any more? Eh?"

Chapter Twenty-Two

THEY TOOK HOPE into the old bar where Frankhay occasionally held office and laid her out on a long bench.

She felt sick with the pain from her shoulder. Every time they moved her it felt as if her arm was being torn slowly from its socket. She wanted to black out, but couldn't. Wanted the pain to go, wanted the voices to recede. Instead, she drifted in and out of consciousness.

Frankhay loomed close and said something, but his words ran together. Others gathered around, heads low. Someone prodded at her shoulder and pain stabbed through her body. A short time later, there was a voice, the girl, Ash, growling at the people around Hope, driving them away. A tearing of fabric, exposing the wound. Something cold and wet against her flesh.

A sharp tug. Agony.

And Ash held the crossbow bolt up to the light; satisfied that it was not broken, she tossed it to one side. More cold and wet against the wound, and then a bandage bound tightly around her shoulder.

Finally, more words. "!¡*distraught*¡! I's sorry," said Ash. "Dinnat see as you..."

Hope put a hand on Ash's arm to stop her.

* * *

"!¡*BRUSQUE* | *INTIMIDATING*¡! So what is it you're doing here, then, gel?" demanded Frankhay. They were upstairs, on a long balcony that looked over a canal towards the huddled buildings of the Loop. Frankhay stood with his back to her, peering back across his shoulder.

Hope sat on a bench, her back to the wall. "I need to get out of this city," she told him. "I think you do, too. I think we should do it together." Beyond Frankhay, grey clouds hung over the city, a permanent feature in recent days.

"!¡*amused*¡! And what about your Cragsider friends, eh?"

"Them, too. We all need to get out of here, before we're wiped out."

She was taking a big risk, she knew, but she was starting to feel strong again, and the calming of the voices in her head encouraged her.

She looked at Frankhay, and remembered Sol. He was a clan-parent, just as she had been. Was he like Sol, then? A being that looked and talked like a human but was not?

She did not know, and she did not really care.

Sol had loved her clan; she had lain down her life – or her existence, at least – to protect her people. Hope had seen enough of Frankhay to trust that he would do the same for his own, regardless of his true nature.

"!¡*exasperation*¡! If we was to make our departure, why should we be taking the Cragsiders too?" Frankhay demanded. "Mother Sol and her pid-stealing street-crooks aren't exactly my top choice of company these days."

"Sol's dead," Hope told him, and his jaw sagged instantly. "They came for us in the Hangings. Sol tried to protect us, but... the watcher killed her."

"!¡*dismay*¡! Well, fuck. We go back some, Sol an' me. Hard to think she's gone..."

He looked down, and now all Hope could see of him was his back. "She did it for her people," she said. "She did it so they'd have a chance to survive and get out."

"!¡*mild irritation*¡! Get out? And how do you plan to get us all out, eh?" asked Frankhay, turning to face her, leaning with his backside against the balustrade. "If you don't have the pids, then there's no crossing the checkpoints around the city, gel. The way things are, they'd as soon shoot you as turn you back."

Hope shook her head.

"!¡*irritated | intrigued*¡! So, what is it? What's your grand plan, then?"

"I think we can get out," she said. "I think *you* can get us out."

IT WAS THE next day that Ash found us at the Monument to the Martyrs. Hope was recovering well from her wound, but Frankhay wouldn't let her go. Ash knew the city and would find us far more quickly and safely than Hope could ever do.

By late in the afternoon, Frankhay was getting restless. Now that he had decided on a course of action, he didn't want any delay.

Hope stood with the kilted boy Jerra on the raised rear deck of the great barge Frankhay used as his main clan-nest in the Loop. With his chubby-faced androgyny and his big fuck-off blunderbuss, Jerra was difficult to gauge at first impression, but he had always shown Hope kindness, even when he had been one of her guards.

"!¡*curious*¡! You think as we'll get out?" he said now. He waved at the piles of supplies gathered in the street below. "You think innat we stand a chance?"

"You think we'd stand a chance if we don't do anything?" Hope asked.

Jerra shrugged. "!¡*uncertain*¡! They haven't much touched the Loop yet."

"They only need to touch it once," said Hope.

From the rear deck, Hope could see forward to the three canvas-roofed cargo holds of the barge and the small foredeck. Here, and on the streets to either side of the narrow canal, members of the Hay clan busied themselves with preparations for departure. "The joeys?" asked Hope, indicating the dozen or so tall aliens helping with stowing supplies. "Are they coming?"

"!¡*uncertain*¡! I don't know. They work with us sometimes. Depends if Father Frankhay pays them enough. Maybe, I guess."

Just then, there was a disturbance at one of the nearby side-streets: guns raised, a staccato jabber of voices, a couple of joeys rising on float-pads to survey the scene.

A small group. Hope recognised me first, then Divine and Ashterhay.

It was a sorry-looking bunch. Six adult Cragsiders, plus Marek and the wraith Skids, and a couple of children. Were they all that had survived from Mother Sol's clan? Hope had convinced Frankhay that the Cragsiders would be useful collaborators, but we hardly looked the part.

Hope went down to meet us as fast as she could manage, every movement sending grinding pain through her wounded shoulder. By the time she reached us, Frankhay was already there, grilling us about what we had seen. Divine told him about their escape through the drainage ducts, and Frankhay said, "!¡*impressed | mild surprise*¡! You were riding your luck there. The pipes'd as soon suck you up as spit you out."

I told him about Cragside.

"!¡*shocked disbelief*¡! Gone..." I concluded. "It's as if it was never there."

"Unsung," Skids added. "The starsinger recast the real so that it never was."

"!¡*decisive authority*¡! We have to go," said Frankhay. "No way as we can take on a rogue 'singer." He turned to me, then. "!¡*matter-of-fact | no-arguing*¡! You an' yours wanna tag along, then tag along. Call it paying back old debts to Mother Sol, boy. You hear? Only one thing. You or any of yours cause trouble, an' I'll have your balls. Fair?"

I nodded, happy to defer to the clan-father.

When he was satisfied, Frankhay turned back towards the canal. "!¡*commanding*¡! Right," he said. "I reckon it's about time we made a move."

FRANKHAY'S BARGE WAS on a spur of canal so narrow that you could climb from the street onto one side of the boat and down onto the next street off the other. It took two tugs to set it in motion, one pulling and the other pushing.

The small gathering on the foredeck gave a cheer when the barge started to move. Up until that point Hope had doubted her plan would work, but once they were under way, edging along the canal, she started to believe.

The barge hadn't moved in generations. Frankhay had never known it to have been anywhere but lodged in this spur of canal; he had even suggested that it might be bedded in mud and immovable.

Around them now, night was settling, the city

253

streets lit by strip lights and the glow from open windows.

Occasional knots of beings stopped to watch the strange vessel pass, but none seemed to consider the boat's passage remarkable. It was a large barge on a small canal, that was all.

The first bridge nearly stopped them; the second reunited them with another survivor.

At the first crossing, the lead tug passed under, but when the barge approached it became clear that the wooden bridge was too low and there was going to be a collision. Hope and the rest of the party on the foredeck fled back along the sides of the barge.

The foredeck passed under the bridge with a handspan to spare, and then the raised bulwark of the first cargo hold rammed the wooden construction. The barge juddered, and there came sounds of cracking and splitting as the bridge rose and came apart, collapsing in a slew of beams and boards.

Hope threw herself into the second cargo hold, its tarpaulin roof shielding her from falling debris. In the dim evening light, she could see another dozen or so cowering there. In all, the barge must hold no more than forty or fifty, mostly from Frankhay's clan.

Eventually, she convinced herself that they were still moving and not sinking. She looked out, and that was when she saw the sidedog lumbering along the street running by the canal. She couldn't be sure, but it looked very like the one that had travelled with Saneth and saved her twice.

She emerged from the hold, clambering awkwardly over the bulwark, struggling with her bound shoulder. She called for attention, but nobody noticed.

She found Jerra, and said, "Look! See, we have to let

that" – she didn't know what it was called – "we have to let that thing onto the barge. It's... it's a friend."

Jerra just looked at her, clearly not understanding why she seemed so worked up.

She found me, and pointed, and I saw it and understood. The sidedog was running alongside us now, but the canal was wider here and the gap was too far to jump. That was when I realised that I had no idea how we would ever slow the barge down.

I looked around, wondering what to do, and when I looked ahead I saw the second bridge approaching. "!¡urgent¡! Ahead: there's another bridge!" Then, to the sidedog, I called, "Run! To the bridge!"

The commensal gave no indication of having heard me, but gradually it speeded up and got ahead of us. When we hit the bridge, the beast jumped, curled into a ball and landed on the tarpaulin covering the rear cargo hold.

The bridge collapsed on us, as the first one had, and we continued on our relentless journey.

Hope went to the sidedog, where it stood shivering on the rear deck. She put a hand on its head and it was cold and there were fresh wounds on its flesh. She wondered what had happened to the ancient chlick, and marvelled that there were so few survivors already.

THE BARGE HELD together until we were almost clear of the city.

The first sign of problems hit just after we passed through the water gate between the main Loop canal and the River Swayne. Slowly, the barge caught the current and swung round behind the lead tug, facing upriver. But by then it had picked up momentum and it kept swinging until it was facing across the river, back the way it had come. Now, out near the middle of the river, the current hit the barge and high waves broke over us.

It was dark now, and this far out the light was a thin silver, spilling over from the city. Hope and I cowered in a cargo hold, powerless to do anything. Others hurried about on the deck, although it wasn't clear what they were doing either.

The barge swung around again and this time managed to stay facing the current.

Now that the barge's course had stabilised, I had time to start worrying about how we would get out of the city. A barge crewed by humans, out in full view. We had timed it so that we had darkness on our side, but even so...

When Frankhay had raised this objection with Hope earlier, she had managed to convince him. "I've watched the river," she said. "There are always river barges. There were at Angiere and there are here in Laverne. Some of them are crewed with trogs and other slave races. If most of us hide in the cargo holds, we'll look just like any other river barge."

That was all we had. It had seemed a reasonable risk when we had discussed it, but now, out in the open, we felt incredibly exposed.

For a time, we made slow progress up the river, and I studied every other vessel that came close to us, just waiting to be found out. To the north, we could see the beams and flashes of the skystation and eventually, to the south, we saw the dark fringe of trees in the Hangings.

Beyond, the crags bulked dark against the night sky. Cragside was marked here by a complete absence of light. No street lamps, no buildings with lights flooding out. Nothing.

Lost in thought, my head full of memories of my

unsung home, I came back to the present with Hope tugging at my arm and saying, "Look! Look! Here..."

My first thought was that we had been spotted by a skimmer or a sentinel, but then I looked more closely at Hope.

She was pointing down at her feet, and I realised my boots were in water. Looking up, it suddenly became clear that Frankhay's barge was sitting lower in the river.

"The barge," she said. "It's sinking."

I don't know if it was colliding with the two bridges that did it, or if the barge was simply not river-worthy after sitting for so long in that narrow canal in the Loop, but whatever it was, the barge was not only sinking, but starting to break apart.

I took Hope's hand and we climbed up onto the narrow deck that ran the length of either flank of the barge.

The deck should have been level, but it was tipped sideways, as if the barge was splitting apart along its length. We clambered back to the rear deck and joined a small cluster around the second tug.

One by one, we clambered on board until the tug was sitting so low that it seemed it, too, would sink.

By this time, the lead tug had come back and some of us climbed onto it.

When everyone was off the barge, the two tugs eased away, and in the dim light from the city we watched the dark bulk of the barge sit lower and lower in the water until the river closed over it and it was gone.

And so the thirty-seven of us, crammed onto two small tugs, crept through the night up the river and clear of the city we had called home.

Heading into foreign territory, unsure and scared

and knowing only that we couldn't go back. All of us were aliens, now.

Exogenes

Chapter Twenty-Three

WE TRAVELLED FOR the rest of the night and most of the following day, struggling upriver in two tugs so over-laden with people that their gas engines could barely overcome the current. People spread themselves across the cabin roof of the tug I was on, or clung to the sides. Every so often, water lapped over the gunwales and into the boat.

We could not go on like this for much longer, and when the engine cut out late on the first afternoon, it was clear we would have to find some other means of transport.

We had been passing through a landscape that alternated neatly-manicured, robot-tended farmland with dark, tangled wildwood.

I had never seen anything like it. The trees of the Hangings and the crags were nothing to the towering behemoths of this forest, a variety I did not recognise; the darkness beneath the canopy was like night, even in the middle of the day.

The farmland was neatly ordered, wheeled robot workers straddling the rows, each bushy, unidentifiable plant uniform in height, spread, colour.

We made camp in the woodland clearing on the bank of the river where our broken-down tug had come to shore, nudged and steered by its partner.

Sitting around a roaring fire, we debated what to do next.

"!¡*hierarchy*¡! So what now? Where do we go from here? We can't all fit on one boat. We've seen plenty of farmland hereabouts, though. Plenty of easy pickings. I say we find a place to settle, build ourselves a new Laverne." That was Herald. Middle-aged and short of sight, he'd barely done a day's physical labour in his life. He clearly saw himself as our new leader, and was trying to establish himself in that role.

I knew he was wrong, but didn't feel up for the fight. Right now we needed to get some food and rest, not rush into big decisions.

Frankhay took up the argument instead. "!¡*hierarchy | dismissive*¡! Do you not think it a tad rude to hitch along with the Hays and then start telling us what it is we should do?" he asked. His voice was smooth like a concealed knife. It was exactly the tone he had used with me on my visit to the Loop, when he had leaned close, spoken softly, and pressed a blade against my throat.

The tension was broken by a soft moan from the sidedog commensal. It had been standing in the shadows, close to where Hope sat. I wondered then if it was unwell, or was finally suffering from the injuries it had picked up – I remembered the burning sting of beam weapons striking our flesh when Hope and I had ridden within it.

Then the sidedog gave a big shudder and another gurgling moan and I realised what was happening. It lifted its front legs, folding itself backwards.

A head emerged from its fleshy internal folds and then the sidedog heaved and expelled a wet, squirming mass onto the ground. The thing it had ejected twisted, straightened, stood: a chlick. Everyone backed away, except for Jerra, who now had his blunderbuss trained on the alien. Then I recognised the gnarled grey skin and the false, staring eye. I stepped forward into the line of fire, and said, "!¡calm authority¡! No. It's okay. It's Saneth. We know this one." I surprised myself at how grateful I was that the ancient chlick had made it.

Saneth stood before me and gave an almost imperceptible dip of the upper body. "!¡admiring junior scholar¡! Such turbulent times," she-he said, addressing me. "The sidedog is like an armoured suit for one such as we in these circumstances, but it is that it is !¡great humour¡! an unbecoming and status-lowering mode of being."

The chlick turned, taking in the rest of the gathered humans, and said, "!¡superior | matter-of-fact¡! We emerged both because sitting within was unbecoming and because we wished to make the observation that it is that this is not the most propitious place in which to wish to make settlement."

I wasn't sure if she-he referred to settling on a course of action or actually choosing to settle. Saneth's words seemed a bit garbled, but then perhaps the double-meaning was intentional.

Frankhay turned on Saneth. "!¡authority | menace¡! We sent you out of the Loop," he said. "And if you go over-asserting yourselves we'll do just the same again. You hear?"

I turned away, frustrated that we had descended to fighting and territory-grabbing so quickly.

I went to sit with Hope and she gave a quick smile as I lowered myself beside her. I didn't know what to make of her. I found myself drawn to her just as I found myself puzzled by her. She seemed other, she seemed more, she seemed... I thought that maybe it was just a sex thing. When we settled to sleep she snuggled in against me; I responded and she moved slightly, aware and neither encouraging nor discouraging.

I wrapped an arm around her and drifted, exhaustion taking me swiftly.

HOPE DIDN'T SLEEP. She lay in my arms, grateful for the protection, aware of every softening of my body as I slipped into sleep. Aware of the sounds of the forest, the insect chirps and clicks and whines, the hoots and cries, some distant, some nearby. Aware of the people, the tensions between them, the way the Cragside survivors formed a knot a little apart from the Hays, the way Marek, separate from the others, kept casting proprietorial glances in her direction.

Aware of the voices clamouring in her head.

Listen to the voices.

There was something about this that wasn't right.

Over by the river bank, Saneth stood with the sidedog. She wondered if the alien was struggling to settle or whether she-he needed sleep at all.

She looked around at the forest, lit in dark tangles by the glow of the dying fire. Trunks stood sentinel, branches intertwined. Nothing else grew among the trees, just as each carefully manicured farm strip had contained just one variety, all else eradicated by the patrolling bots.

And then she realised what it was that was bothering her. Should the wilds be ordered like this? Were these wildwoods at all, or rather just another carefully maintained form of agricultural plot?

She disentangled herself from my protective arm and sat up.

The fire... just a few glowing embers, now. The fine moss of the clearing: it looked as if it had spread around the fire, reclaiming burnt ground. Healing over.

Skids lay nearby, deep in a bed of moss, moss which had not been so deep and lush when we had found the clearing, moss that had started to wrap around his arms and legs, to creep up over his scalp, so that he appeared to be half-buried, or emerging from some primeval swamp, floating to the mossy surface.

Hope tugged at my arm and then scrambled over on hands and knees to Skids, pulling at his clothes until he woke with a start. He tried to sit and couldn't, held back by the fine mesh of roots, a spongy blanket smothering and restraining him.

He tried again, and this time managed to pull himself upright.

By now, I was up and on my knees, only vaguely aware that I'd had to pull myself clear of the ground, my sleep-addled brain still struggling to understand what was happening.

"Look!" said Hope, waving her hand at the clearing. "The ground. The moss..."

I did, and I saw, and without yet understanding, as Hope did, that this clearing and this forest were just a different form of managed, protected land – *hostile* land. That the clearing was attacking us, and that we must learn not to trust anything in this new world we had entered.

WE LOST NO one, although if Hope had not alerted us when she did I wondered how much longer it would have been before we were trapped, absorbed, the clearing healed over as if we had never been there. It was an invaluable reminder that we should never allow ourselves to become complacent.

We made our escape on the one functioning tug, but that only lasted until a short time after dawn when its engine failed and we drifted back to shore.

We kept moving, our only goal to keep heading away from Laverne. From that point on we were on foot, following tracks that led through field and forest, for there was no alternative. It was hard not to watch every step, for fear that your foot would stick to the ground, start to sink, be taken over. It was hard not to study everything around us, the trees looming as if ready to lean over and smother us, the bots tending the farm strips apparently oblivious, but were they monitoring, reporting back, or might they lash out at us as pests to be eradicated from the neat order of the tended landscape? In the city we knew to watch for sentinels and grunts, but here – here everything was new and potentially hostile.

"You knew something like that would happen," I said to Saneth as we walked. To our left, a dark wall of forest; to our right, neat rows of vines with the occasional glints of tiny bots crawling over them, through them. "You emerged from the sidedog to warn us."

The chlick kept staring ahead, only its false eye swivelling to look at me. "!¡*lecturing junior scholar*¡! Many crops are bred with a strong imperative to self-repair," she-he said. "That includes eradication of pest species and competitors. Out here, any plant may be laced with poisons, any animal may be hostile – engineered to be so, bred to be so, it may even be the sentient owner; any bot may be a dumb servitor or a deadly defender of its territory. Even the bugs can be deadly."

"!¡*challenging*¡! You didn't exactly try very hard to warn us, back in that clearing."

"!¡*superior*¡! It was awareness of risk that was identified," she-he said. "A lesson has been learned with greater efficacy than if it had merely been taught. You will adapt more rapidly now."

Skids caught us then. "!¡*earnest*¡! But what if we want to learn from the lauded scholar?" he asked.

"!¡*amused | chiding*¡! You are not learning from lauded-one already?"

A short time later, we came to a fork in the track. A little ahead of the rest of the group, we paused. "!¡*deferential*¡! Which way?" I asked.

"!¡*toying*¡! Which way to where?"

"!¡*assertive*¡! Harmony," I said. "Which way to Harmony?"

Frankhay, Hope and a couple of the others caught us then.

"!¡*challenging*¡! So which way?" he asked, repeating my own question. "You know where we are, Saneth-ra" – I noted that for all his brusqueness, Frankhay still added the honorific to the chlick's name – "you have maps in your head, you can tap into a web of data that none of *us* can see. Which way is safe, wire-head?"

"!¡*mocking*¡! It is that you want safe?" asked Saneth. "Or is it destiny you would prefer?"

"!¡*irritated*¡! A place where the ground doesn't up and try to swallow you whole in the middle of the night would do me, for now," said Frankhay.

"!¡*provocative*¡! Scholar pup wants Harmony," said Saneth, indicating me with a swivel of the eye.

Frankhay glanced at me. "!¡*condescending*¡! A thief *and* a dreamer," he said. He made no secret of not trusting me, of holding my pid-stealing past against me.

I could live with that. I preferred that he was open in his hostility; better that than keep it hidden.

"Which way?" he asked again, and Saneth indicated the left-hand fork of the track.

"!¡*curious*¡! So what do you know of Harmony?" I asked Frankhay, as we resumed our journey.

"!¡*stand-offish | relaxing*¡! It's like the bogeyman and the river gods," said Frankhay. "A thing of stories. Something we tell each other to keep hope alive. A human place where we can be safe and free."

"!¡*amused | provocative*¡! You do not believe in the bogeyman, and the gods of the river?" asked Saneth.

Frankhay stared at the chlick. "!¡*intense*¡! Maybe I do," he said in a low voice. "Maybe I believe in them all."

"!¡*toying*¡! So what is it to be, Clan-father Frankhay? Safety or destiny?"

That question... It would be with us throughout our journey, and in the end it would be what tore us apart.

Chapter Twenty-Four

STILL TO RESOLVE the question of whether we were seeking some safe haven or if we really were in search of Harmony, our days fell into something of a routine.

Every evening, we made camp somewhere just off the track, doing all we could to assure ourselves that it was likely to be safe. Sometimes Saneth would advise, but other times she-he would remain aloof, leaving us to make our own choices and learn our lessons. We always posted look-outs, a curious kind of guarding where we were as much watching the ground and the vegetation as we were watching for intruders.

And during the day we walked. We didn't really know where we walked, although some of us were quick to learn rudimentary navigation skills, so that we knew we were heading steadily east. If Frankhay was to believed, Saneth was the one who knew most: if the chlick was hooked into the aliens' communications networks, then she-he must know where we were, and where we were heading. Even without a hook-up, the chlick's knowledge of geography must be far greater than that of anyone else in our party.

Marek was another who almost certainly knew more than he let on. He had already made the journey from Angiere to Laverne, and I knew little about him: he could easily have travelled farther afield in the past.

When it came down to it, I didn't even know *what* he was. Was he a guardian like Callo and Sol had been? Some kind of artificial being in human form? It made sense that he was, or at least might be, and if that was the case, then what knowledge did he carry in his head? Might he even have access to the networks? I did not know, and I trusted him about as far as I trusted Saneth, which wasn't very far at all.

Summer was drawing to a close as we made this journey. This blessed us with crops we could pilfer along the way, always being careful to guard against over-zealous bots – young Tuck lost a finger to one bot, but it could have been far worse. The late-summer abundance reminded us also that soon there would be no easy pickings, and we would have a winter to survive.

With every day that passed, the question of where we were going and how we would live grew more pressing. A split was growing steadily within our number. Some – notably Saneth, Skids and Marek – held firm to the vision of a place called Harmony, where humankind could be free and equal. Others just wanted to find some quiet corner of the landscape where we could settle and hope to be overlooked.

I was unsure. Harmony seemed such a tease: a mirage held just out of reach, a seductive rumour that we might pursue and never find. But the alternative? First Angiere and now Laverne. Someone wanted rid of our kind; a watcher faction called the Hadeen, according to some. We did not know who these Hadeen were, and we did not know why they wanted us gone. Realistically, we would probably never know these things, we were just tiny players in a vast, unfathomable game.

But what we did know was that if our pursuers wanted to wipe us out they would seek us, find us, destroy us. No question.

So: pursue a sliver of a dream, or hole up somewhere as securely as possible?

One night I took watch with Frankhay. At first I thought he had fixed it so he would have one more opportunity to intimidate me, this having become something of a sport for him on our travels. It wasn't until much later that I could reflect on this period and see it as one of growing mutual respect. Between us, we had the leadership of our ragged group. He was the natural leader of the Hays, their clan-father; and our small band seemed to turn to me, just as the clan had back in Cragside, when the watchers had taken our elders. Taking every opportunity to harry me showed Frankhay's awareness of that; it was his attempt to assert authority over someone who was fast becoming his equal.

That night I was on my guard, wary of being alone with him. He was still an exotic creature, a flamboyant man, full of bragging and posturing. He had a cold edge to him, and I felt that he was perhaps the most dangerous man I had ever encountered.

That night, we were camped out in a hollow scooped out of a scarp of limestone hills that reminded me of Cragside. The woods here were ancient and mixed; they looked genuinely wild, without the monoculture, the sterility, the glint and scuttle of bots, the absence of scrub and waste matter we had come to expect. Still, we could not relax too far. Even in the wilds, there were dangers.

We had come across ag-bots that appeared to have gone feral, tending little plots viciously with no apparent cause or reason, just programmed routine and behavioural patterns.

We had come across great fleshy plant-traps, bulging and pink and covered in bristles that glistened in the sunlight. The first we found was a curiosity, as was the second. The third had the half-digested carcass of a young deer impaled on its bristles, and as we passed, the deer turned its head to us and emitted a piercing screech unlike anything I'd ever heard.

I wondered how long it had been there, and how long the thing would keep it alive as it slowly absorbed the deer into itself.

And I wondered if we would have suffered a similar fate if we had been just a little slower on that first night in the wilds, when the forest clearing had tried to absorb us.

We passed through a tract of forest that was the scene of some form of biological battle, the trees skinned over with jelly-like scabs. An alien growth, a disease... none of us knew. Here, there was no bird or insect life and the air smelled of rotting flesh. We hurried through, and for a long time after were fearful that these rancid growths would break out on us, too.

BUT FRANKHAY... FRANKHAY, nest-father of the Hay clan, lord of the Ipp known as the Loop, a man clearly not averse to dealing with aliens and yet fiercely independent even of the other human clans of Laverne.

He sat on a rock, examining a long-snouted handgun in the light of the near-full moon.

I had just completed a tour of the camp, checking for *anything* – anything changed, anything different, anything that might turn out to be a new kind of threat we hadn't encountered before and so hadn't known to check for. Laverne seemed so far away, so long ago.

Frankhay looked up, nodded, shuffled aside to make room.

I sat, and in the sharp, silvery light, an autumn chill adding a bite to the air, I saw Frankhay differently. Ask me any time before how old he was and I'd have said maybe forty years, his hair turned prematurely white or perhaps even deliberately bleached. Ask me that night, as he turned to me and the lines on his face were etched deep by the moonlight and his eyes just looked *tired*, and I couldn't have said.

Frankhay looked old. Frail, even. Had he always been this way, or had the journey done this to him?

"!¡*authoritative*¡! We talk tomorrow," he said. "All of us. We need to have it out, purge the wound."

I nodded. It was time for that debate. Settle somewhere for the winter or continue to seek Harmony? Seeing Frankhay that night, I wondered if he had the strength to resist the challenge of Herald or one of the others, the strength to continue leading. It was only then that I really appreciated how much I relied on him as a leader.

"!¡*supportive*¡! We need to," I agreed. "There are too many grumbles. People have such short memories."

"Shortness of memory's not such a bad thing, sometimes," said Frankhay. "It can help you focus on the now and what's ahead."

"!¡*musing*¡! We need to hang onto the past, too," I said.

"Aye, but not cling to it, boy. What's now is what matters."

I peered at him. "What *is* now?"

"!¡*pensive*¡! Now's about holding it together," said Frankhay. "Now's about us being the only survivors of our kind that we know of. That's one almighty responsibility, boy."

For a while we shared silence. Then, "!¡*hesitant*¡! You know about the guardians?" I asked. "Callo. Sol..."

Frankhay remained silent, and so I continued.

"!¡*confused*¡! Sol was never the same after the watchers took her. It was as if they'd broken her. Or replaced her... When she died: she was a guardian like Callo, some kind of engineered being in human shape. I saw her insides. I still don't know if that was the same Sol or if it was a substitute they sent back after taking our real clan-mother."

"!¡*suppressed emotion*¡! It was Sol," Frankhay said, in a strained voice.

I stared at him.

"Sol was always that way," he said. "A guardian. But it didn't make her any less of a person. It didn't make her without feelings, or the capacity to love."

And so I learned of the true nature of my clan-mother, from the man who had loved her and discovered her secrets and then lost her.

REED TRADER GREW up on the streets of Laverne. By his own admission, he was at best a rough diamond, a boy with a fast wit and a faster temper and a determination never to come off worst in anything. His carefully applied brutality and his sharp judgement of when to push an advantage home and when to appear to yield lifted him through the ranks of the street gangs until, by the age of fifteen, he led the Hays, a mob renowned for its viciousness and efficiency. They were the only human gang that dared run the hookers and drug rings in Central and Precept, usually the preserve of craniates or joeys, or one of the few other species that dared go up against the watchers.

His rise was secured when a pack of joeys found him in the backroom of a bar just off Precept Square one day. Almost as soon as they cornered him, they had him up against a wall, his feet off the ground, suspended by the wrists so that he was face-to-face with the leading alien, a scrawny, ceiling-high male with loose jowls and an all-over covering of grey bristle.

They were poised to spike him, poisoned talons at the ready, and Reed knew he had to come up with something. "!¡*hierarchy* | *authoritative*¡! Give me an Ipp," he said, in a low, strong voice. He met the lead joey's yellowed eyes and he knew that this alien would either finish him now or would own him for years to come until Reed eventually worked out how to turn tables and own the silver-stubbled bastard creature himself.

The joey spat a staticky rattle and a moment later a translator panel on the wall said, "!¡*aggressive* | *offended*¡! Explain, shit-comb."

"!¡*calm* | *commanding*¡! Put me down and I'll explain," he said, and when the lead joey chattered and the two joeys suspending Reed by the wrists let him drop, he knew that he had started the process of owning the fuckers.

There was a rough part of the city, rougher than most of the rest. Most of its docks and riverside warehouses were derelict, most of the buildings were squats occupied by junkies and other deadbeats of any number of species. Just about its only redeeming feature was that you were never more than a block away from the river, which wrapped around the newly-formed Ipp in a great sweep which became known as the Loop.

Granted a new identity and protected by the joey gang that had nearly killed him, Frankhay became head of a newly-forged clan just as comfortable working with alien crimelords as with the other human clans of the city.

But still, back then, he made the effort, and it was at his first Council of the city elders that he met a young elder of the Virtue clan from Cragside Ipp, a striking, athletic woman with a shaved head and a confrontational attitude that was almost a match for his own. That was when he met Sol Virtue, and almost immediately he was besotted.

There was something Frankhay didn't like about his fellow clan leaders from the outset. Something in their manner. He was quick to work out that it was the way they all liked things just the way they were. Each clan had its own preserve, each had its scams and trades and working arrangements, and none of them wanted that to change.

A new clan, a new Ipp, a clan-father with attitude and the balls to back it up... Frankhay scared them. And he *wanted* to scare them. He wanted to rattle their cozy routine. He had risen from nowhere, he had shown that the strong could forge a better existence for themselves and their followers.

The corollary of that was that the weak might not do so well.

"!¡musing¡! At least, I *thought* they were scared of me," said Frankhay. "That was before I really understood how things were. Before I understood that they were scared *for* me."

He went to that first Council prepared for hostility and on the look-out for opportunity. Sol was there in support of her clan-father, Levi, but it was clear that one day she would attend the gatherings in her own right. Frankhay saw something different in her. She didn't seem scared of him. She even seemed happy to talk to him, curious about his new clan grown from the street gangs.

On the first night of the council, she and Frankhay slipped away from the stuffy spirit-drinking elders and found a corner in the human section of an ale-house on a side-street in Pennysway, the Ipp where the Council was being held. They drank beer and swapped stories late into the night.

Sol impressed Frankhay with her grasp of how the city worked, and how the clans fitted in; she had many valuable lessons to teach someone who had risen so quickly from such an unusual background.

Frankhay impressed Sol with his rough charm and his willingness to overturn any established rules or precedents if that was what best served the interests of his people. He explained that his clan's dress code was a badge, a public statement that his clan were willing to be different. Until that night, he hadn't really thought of it in those terms; he just dressed how he liked to dress.

That night they made a pact. While Frankhay would ally himself with no-one, he vowed that his clan would never turn against the Virtues. Sol, likewise, swore that her clan would never turn against the Hays.

"!¡*wry*¡! That lasted for years," said Frankhay, "until you stole my pids and set the watchers on me. It was the Virtues who turned first."

They sealed the pact by spending the night together in a room above that bar. "!¡*nostalgic | regretful*¡! I should have known," said Frankhay. "How could I not have known I was fucking a machine, for the sake of the gods? Eh, lad? She went at it with some or other passion, I tell you. Never known anything like it, before or since. You don't want to be hearin' about how your old clan-mother screwed? Ha!"

"¡*intrigued*¡! When did you find out?" I asked. "How?" Frankhay was still toying with the handgun. He dipped his head and now I saw the glint of a tear on his craggy cheek.

"¡*factual reporting*¡! My second Council," said Frankhay. "A quarter later. Deepest winter I'd known, with brown snow ploughed high by the main streets, side-streets and alleys blocked in with snow frozen solid, so as you entered buildings through upper floor windows. Blocks of ice in the river. When it thawed, there were bodies of frozen street kids poppin' out all over. 'Minded me it wasn't far since I'd've been one of them."

After that first Council, Frankhay and Sol had kept up a distant relationship, meeting in the bars of Precept and Riverside. Neutral territory. Just friends, drinking and screwing at any opportunity.

Frankhay felt sick in his gut with the longing, the need. "¡*deep anguish*¡! That's the only time," he said softly. "The only time I've ever let myself feel like that for snatch."

Frankhay's second Council meeting took place in Cragside. He felt more the part this time, more established. He didn't care if the other elders shunned him or tried to put him in his place. He encouraged it. He never wanted to be like them. For a time he got lost in the facings-off and showmanship of it all, so that when Clan-father Levi Virtue was killed by a deranged flitterjack, he was caught completely off-guard.

They were gathered on a rooftop terrace with a view to the skystation to the north. Just chat. He couldn't remember what it was about, just some minor elders jockeying for position.

The flitterjack flew in around a corner of crag with a whine and a buzz and an iridescent flickering of gauzy wings, and it took a glance and then a second take for Frankhay to spot the egg sac hanging heavy from the thing's belly. He cried out an alarm, a warning. The flits were fine almost all the time, but when they were heavy with egg they were hypersensitive, picking up on signals that on their own world must mean something – a colour, a movement, a sound...

The thing swung around and the clan elders threw themselves away from it, but Levi Virtue was too slow, too distracted, and he noticed too late. The flitterjack's jaws scythed through Levi's midriff, slicing him in two right where he stood.

Frankhay's first thought was, *By the gods, but now I'll be fucking a clan-mother*, and his second was... shock.

There was no blood, no gore. He had seen people killed brutally many times, and always there was spouting blood, guts spilling out, torn flesh.

Levi just snapped. His insides were neatly ordered, what looked like fibres and plastics and flesh that could have been bread dough. Even as Frankhay watched, a film spread over the wound, as if it could somehow heal such a major injury. But Levi's body was in two halves and it was beyond repair, and Frankhay realised he was standing in disbelief while the flitterjack swung round for another go.

He looked around, and in that brief check to see how he could get to safety he was still able to see that none of the other elders seemed surprised at what they saw.

There was a whine, a buzz, starting to shift pitch and grow louder.

A hand on Frankhay's arm, the grip strong like metal, and he looked up and met Sol's eyes, and for the first time he actually felt fear. "!¡urgent¡! Down!" she hissed, dragging him to the ground, and the flit swung by again, its long, sword-like jaws screeching against the stone ground where Frankhay had stood a moment earlier.

They tumbled down the steps to safety within the clan-nest, and Frankhay caught himself, squatting, peering around like a wild animal.

"!¡CALM¡! THEY WERE all like that," he told me. "The elders. All but me, as I'd come to have my clan by different means. I ran. Never went to another Council again."

After that day, Frankhay set himself to trying to understand what he had seen. "The guardians," he said, "they've been there forever, setting their stall to protect us, nurture us. I think I've been waiting for all this to happen all of my life: if we have guardians set to protect us, then what are they to protect us *from*? Some serious shit, I'm thinkin'."

"!¡puzzled¡! What are they?"

"!¡uncertain¡! Who knows? Back then, I set myself and my clan apart. We did things differently, separately. But the guardians have never done us any harm, so maybe I should have trusted them, eh, boy? Back then I thought they were scared of me, but they weren't, they were just working out how to fit me into their scheme of things. But I wouldn't have it."

"!¡*gently pressing*¡! What did Sol do?"

"!¡*bitter regret*¡! She acted like a love-sick pup. She came after me, came to the Loop, sent messengers. I only ever saw her one more time."

She begged him. There, in the street by the barge he had made his home, her arms spread wide, beseeching. To Frankhay, then, it was a charade, a show, an act just the same as fucking like animals all through the night had been an act to draw him in. She was a machine, a construct, not human.

She could not love him, as she said she loved him.

She could not feel the feelings she claimed. It was a routine, a sham.

She could not love him, and he most certainly did not love her.

"!¡*remorse*¡! I turned her away," he told me. "I didn't believe that she cared for me and I convinced myself that if I had really cared for anybody it had been a version of her I held in my head, not the real thing."

Frankhay was pointing the handgun at me. Casually. Almost accidentally. But nonetheless, the pistol's single dark eye stared at me.

"!¡*menace*¡! I ain't ever told anyone all of this," said Frankhay. "An' I don't know why I've gone and got so maudlin tonight. Just one thing, okay?"

I nodded.

"Don't ever be repeatin' this, you hear, boy? 'Cause if you do an' you manage to convince anyone else that old Frankhay's a moonstruck gawp then that might jus' be the last thing you ever convince anybody. That clear, boy?"

I understood him now. Frankhay, terror-inspiring hard man of the Loop. He was about as much front as me. In many ways we were two of a kind.

I think he actually *liked* me.

* * *

THE NEXT DAY we had a meeting, all of us gathered around that hollow.

It was time for some decisions, time to work out what it was that we were really going to do, now that we had escaped from Laverne.

Chapter Twenty-Five

OUR CHOICES WERE stark.

We could find a place to settle and try to become self-sufficient.

We could try to find a community to join.

Or we could continue on our quest for a city of which we only knew by rumour, and that maybe none of us really believed existed.

THE NIGHT HAD passéd, Frankhay and I lapsing into a surprisingly easy silence and then standing down when Divine and a young Hay called Idle took over. I found Hope and curled myself around her, in an uncomfortably asexual way, aware of her body and her easy welcome of this intimacy, but equally aware of the lack of privacy and that I did not really know where her feelings lay.

I woke, damp and cold from the night's dew, alone. Hope, as was her way, had extricated herself from my embrace and gone to sit on the rock where I had sat in the night with Frankhay, losing herself in the view.

I joined her. No words.

The land spread out before us. Down below, the river wound through the countryside, silver in the early morning sunlight. Woods and fields slotted together.

Scattered thinly were a few warehouse-like buildings, and some small, clustered settlements. All were alien constructs: improbable architectures, clean lines and sharp angles, bulbous growths that emerged from the ground like pox, a single sharp spire with a coil of silver at its tip.

Back to the west, Laverne was lost somewhere in the haze of the horizon. I wondered if the city still stood, or if all was melted to glass, or unsung.

"¡¡*intimate*¡! Are you thinking of where we've been, or where we're going?" I asked, leaning close to Hope. The scarring on her face had healed to a pink layer now, a little shiny, distorted. The wound on my hand had healed similarly.

"I'm not," she said. "I'm thinking of where we are." And with that she tipped her head and kissed me tenderly on the jaw.

I wanted to put my arm around her like I did at night, but held back. I had no idea why I was so nervous around Hope, so tentative. I'd had my fair share of girls over the years. I had my lines, my moves. But Hope wasn't a girl for lines and moves and maybe that was why I was left frustrated and confused in her presence.

Behind us, our ragged band stirred, gathering meagre belongings together, bundling blankets, tending to the four children and one mewling baby that travelled with us.

"¡¡*commanding | over-stretching*¡! Gather round all," called Herald. He was puffed up with self-importance. Leaving Laverne had given him something he had never had back in the city, but in my opinion he was no better for it. He had always been a nail in the butt as far as I was concerned. "Clan-father Frankhay has called Council. Gather round."

Frankhay had told me he would do this. You either let opposition grow or you tackle it full face, and Frankhay was never one to dodge a fight.

We gathered round, a subdued group, and I wondered how we had reached such a low ebb without me really noticing.

Frankhay was right. We needed to tackle this now. We needed to know what our purpose was.

"!¡PATIENT¡! I'VE BEEN investigating our surrounds," said Herald. "I've detailed people to explore this area."

We'd been talking forever, it seemed, the morning sun now high in the sky. There was still no giving of ground by either faction. What surprised me was the extent to which Herald had established himself as the leader of those who wished to settle. I remembered Frankhay, frail and vulnerable in the night, and wondered for the first time if his moment had passed.

I'd had little to do with Herald back at Cragside, but away from the city it was as if he had come to life, found purpose. "!¡*factual reporting*¡! It's been two days since we passed through cultivated land, three since we passed a settlement of more than a few farm buildings. We're as far as we've ever been from settled territory. The land here is fertile. It's ours for the taking. We have a vantage point here, so that we can see whatever's coming. This is the perfect place for us to establish a new community, one new clan."

"!¡*doubting*¡! We need food," said one of the Hays, an older man in a kilt and a leather jacket with one arm hanging loose. "Had you remembered that?"

"There's fish in the river," said Herald. "And as I say, the ground is rich. There are fruit and nuts in the forest. Wild game. We have people among us who've worked in the pap-houses. We know how to prepare and preserve food."

"!¡*frustrated*¡! But we have no supplies," said Jerra. "It's madness. We can't just live off the bushes all winter!"

"!¡*patient*¡! That's why we put down our roots now, build up stores before winter settles in," said Herald. "Aimlessly wandering through the countryside isn't going to get us through the winter any better, after all."

When Herald spoke, there was always a rumble of agreement, a nodding of heads. The few who argued against him were more passionate, frustrated, but they were a definite minority. The longer this went on, the more convinced I became that the decision would be that we should settle and try to eke out our survival from the land.

I looked down at my soft hands, pale in the morning light. On the streets of the city I was tough, smart; I'd back myself against anyone, not only to survive but to emerge on top.

But out here? Out here it was blustery mediocre people like Herald who were better equipped. This was not a future I relished.

Earlier, another of the Hays elders had spoken in favour of finding a community to join. We had many talents among us, she had argued. Surely some small settlement would see the value in taking a band of humans in, exchanging our skills and effort for food and shelter? No-one had really believed her. Why would any community take in nearly forty vagrants? Some of us had valuable skills, yes, but we were a lot of mouths to feed, a lot of bodies to accommodate.

Forging our own settlement seemed more sensible,

and a number of Frankhay's clan were falling in behind Herald. We had survived by foraging and gathering as we travelled, so surely we could do even better if we stayed in one place? Supplementing living off the land locally with foraging raids farther afield, we might just see out the winter to a point where we would be able to start cultivating the land ourselves.

It seemed the obvious solution, but to me such a choice was as good as giving up. Did anyone really believe we would be safe out here from the Hadeen watchers, or whoever else wanted to wipe out our kind?

"!¡*hesitant*¡! What about Harmony?" I asked. "We could be safe there."

"!¡*dismissive*¡! What makes you think we'd be safe there?" asked Herald, shaking his head. "What makes you even sure that it exists?"

"!¡*tired | frustrated*¡! Oh, Harmony exists," said Marek, joining the debate for the first time. For days he had kept himself aloof from the rest of us, as if unsure where to fit in, unsure whether he even wanted to fit in.

"!¡*factual reporting*¡! The people I was with in Angiere, the Vanguard. We smuggled people out before the end. That was what we did. We sent people on the road to Harmony."

"!¡*confrontational*¡! You sent them to a fantasy," said Herald. "You sent them to a place you dreamed of, not one that exists!"

Marek shook his head. "!¡*tired*¡! No," he said. "We sent them home."

There was silence, then, a silence I eventually broke by asking Marek, "!¡*disbelief | excited*¡! You're from Harmony...?"

He shook his head. "!¡*factual reporting*¡! No," he answered. "I'm just a poet and keeper of histories from the district of Seagreen in Angiere. But the others, those I travelled with... Callo, Lucias, Pleasance... they came to Angiere from Harmony, and recruited people like me. Harmony is real."

I stared at Marek. He was a cagy one, keeping everything guarded. Just how much more had he chosen not to reveal?

Herald waved a hand in dismissal. "!¡*contemptuous*¡! Hearsay," he said. "You're telling us you know someone who claimed to come from Harmony and that's enough to justify us marching onwards until winter hits, and we run out of food, and one by one we start to drop. No one has yet convinced me that Harmony is real. No one has yet convinced me that such a city would welcome us. And no one has yet convinced me that even if it did, we would be safe there."

"!¡*admonishing junior scholar*¡! Harmony is safe because Harmony is sung to be so," said Saneth, in her-his whispery voice. Saneth stood with Hope, a little apart from the gathering, perched partway up the rear slope of the hollow. Sitting was not a position that seemed to suit chlicks.

"'Sung'?" asked Frankhay, finally joining the debate.

"!¡*patient | lecturing*¡! Sung," said Saneth. "Sung because their starsinger sings that it is so."

Until that point, Harmony had been a dream for me, a desperate hope that there might be somewhere better. Saneth's words changed that. Saneth's words gave the dream substance, rationale.

"!¡*excited*¡! They have a 'singer?" I asked.

Saneth inclined the upper part of her-his body in the chlick equivalent of a nod.

A human city, but one protected by a starsinger! I glanced across at Skids and knew that he, too, was sold. Even if we chose to settle here, I knew then that Skids would continue the journey; alone, if necessary.

Until now, Divine had remained silent, but now she joined in. "!¡*sceptical*¡! It was a 'singer that unsung Cragside," she said. "So now you're saying we look for a place run by one?"

"!¡*impatient*¡! Not run by one," said Marek. "*Protected* by one. !¡*controlled*¡! Harmony is a human city," he continued. "Run by people like us."

He stood now, and walked to the centre of the gathering. "!¡*passionate*¡! Look at you," he said, spreading his arms as if to embrace his audience. "Look at us all! This is our world, yet we're squeezed into reservations, segregated, abused. We have no history, no sense of who we are. We live in the cracks and model ourselves on our alien masters. We live in nests, in clans. We talk in a language that's a mixed up soup of a dozen alien languages. We have no history other than that we exist in the spaces afforded us by the dominant races. How much of what we are is truly human, and how much imported, copied, second-hand mimicry?

"Harmony is a place for us to learn to be human. It's a place where other humans are already being human."

"!¡*approving*¡! Harmony is a place where you can find your story," said Saneth. "Humankind has more story than any other species. Humankind has spark, has difference. Around us: the All is known, completely known; we ancient races... our stories have been told and retold. You must find *your* story. That is Harmony."

"!¡*pressing*¡! Where is it?" I asked. "If we choose to seek Harmony, to continue on our journey... how do we find it? Marek: you've been sending people to Harmony. What instructions did you give them? What directions?"

Marek stood before us, thin as a stick and his neatly trimmed beard grown more full on our journey. "!¡*hesitant*¡! To the east of Angiere," he said. "To the east of Laverne."

Click language gives it all away. Click language is from the heart, a spontaneous, hard to control thing. Click language betrays. Marek's hesitation said it all: he did not know where Harmony was. He did not know the way.

"!¡*faltering | exposed*¡! It's a city," he continued. "An ancient city, dominated by ten towers. A city of spires and blocks, much of it ruined over time, but with the core kept in good repair by its current occupants. A city set in the mountains to the east—"

"!¡*derisory | triumphant*¡! So you're telling us we are heading for a city that is... *somewhere*?" demanded Herald. "That's the best you can do? A city set in the mountains. I see no mountains! Does anyone see any mountains?"

"!¡*calm | reasoning*¡! If we see no mountains, then clearly we haven't travelled far enough to the east," I said.

"!¡*hostile*¡! Or it could just mean that you're pursuing a myth."

I turned to Saneth, and said, "!¡*respectful*¡! Lauded one... you've been leading us on this journey. Where do we go now? How much longer will it be? How far is it to the mountains? What do the maps in your head tell you? What's in the wires?"

Saneth swivelled that false eye to look at me and dipped her-his upper body.

And suddenly I knew that we had lost.

"!¡*deference to junior scholar*¡! We are old," said Saneth. "Very old. !¡*defiant*¡! But we know what is true, and we know that Harmony is the one place where your kind can find its destiny."

"!¡*pressing*¡! Where *is* it?" I asked.

Saneth's eye swivelled downwards. "!¡*factual reporting*¡! It is set among a band of mountains variously called in your terms the White Mountains or the Snake Belt or the Curl, after their colour or the shape they make on a map."

"!¡*pressing*¡! So how do we get there...?" I asked.

"!¡*timid | deferential*¡! It is to the east..."

Saneth didn't know.

"!¡*loss of status*¡! This lauded one is old," said the chlick. "This lauded one is weak. This lauded one is dying." Saneth reached for her-his false eye, plucked it from its socket and held it high, as if surveying the gathering. "Without this we are blind. Our senses fail us. This one has no maps in our head. This one has no links to the All, no means of locating and orienting and directing, guided from beyond. All that this one has is in memories and learning, and in that alone this one has the knowledge that we must seek Harmony."

Saneth's voice had dwindled to a whisper. "This lauded one is weak," she-he concluded. "This lauded one is what you see and no more."

A silence followed as we absorbed this.

A silence broken by Herald. "!¡*triumphal | contemptuous*¡! So here we are," he said. "Seeking a city we have no proof even exists, a city of rumour, a city of desperate fantasy. Guided by a creature who does not even know the way... Can anyone really argue in favour of blindly following this course? Can any of you even–"

"I know the way."

Herald fell silent.

The voice: small, hesitant. Up the slope, where Saneth stood, now Hope stood too. She looked like a frightened animal, about to bolt.

"I know the way," she said again. "To Harmony. I've seen it. A city of ten towers, four of them coiled like whirlygig seeds. A spaceship hanging above it. A beam of light from the ship to the tallest of the towers. The rest of the city is blocks of buildings – three, four, five storeys high – some with smaller spires and towers. Much of the city is abandoned, in ruins.

"Beyond the city there are mountains, white in the sun. And a river runs down from the mountains and through the city, its banks cut in straight lines. It is the river that runs through Laverne and meets the sea at Angiere. Harmony is where the river runs down from the mountains. To find Harmony, we follow the river."

Chapter Twenty-Six

HOPE. SHE HAD so much in her head, and she was only now coming to know it.

She had found herself on this journey, with this strange array of people, and all that she knew, all that she really knew in her heart, was that Harmony was a place she needed to be. The city's name was like a prayer, like a drug. It calmed the chorus of voices in her head. It gave her peace. She knew that the city was real, and she knew that it was good.

And so she had walked by day and slept in my arms at night, and she had slipped out of my embrace every morning to watch the sun rise in the east, the direction we were headed in.

She did not know what to make of me, other than knowing that my presence also calmed the voices, and so must be a good thing. I did not press myself upon her, as Marek and others had done. As Marek would still like to do: she saw his looks, and she understood the barely-masked messages behind his words whenever he spoke to her. She found me gentle and funny, two things I would never have have seen in myself. She was at her most peaceful with my arms around her at night.

There was one night, as we passed from cultivated, managed landscape into the wild lands that brought us to our debating place, when I was on watch and she had slept alone, as was her way, a little apart from the others, belonging to neither the Hays nor the Virtues.

Her head was singing, alive, and she could not settle, so instead she lay on her back on the stony ground and stared at the stars. Each one of them, she knew, had planets like Earth, and on these planets there were beings capable of lying on the ground and staring at the stars and wondering at the scale of it all. Even as she watched, a spark of light traced across the sky. A starship, or a satellite, or some other alien artefact.

She heard a scuff of a foot in the dirt nearby and then Marek was by her, squatting on his haunches, one hand resting on the ground to support him.

With his other he reached out, ran a finger down her jaw, her neck, hooking it into the top of her leather tunic. His fingernail was sharp against her skin.

She tried to move, but his finger kept her in place.

She did not want this. It made her head swirl and fill with angry voices. He had fucked her enough times in Angiere for it not to be a shock to her that he wanted to do it now, but she did not want it, did not want him.

"No," she said, but he ignored her, freeing the top two buttons of her top, sliding a hand inside to squeeze her breast so hard that she gasped.

On his knees now, with his other hand he fumbled at his trousers, loosened them, and she watched as he grew hard.

She shifted, and took his slender dick in her hand.

With her other hand she reached down to her waist, to her belt, to where she kept her knife.

She held him tight and she held her knife to him so that he felt its hard edge, and she felt him suddenly go soft.

"!¡*panic* | *fear*¡! No..." he said, and the roar of voices in her head fell silent and she thought that they wanted her to cut, but she didn't. She let go, and Marek scrambled away on all fours and then up on his feet, and the next day he walked as far away from her as possible, and she wondered if that was it, done, or if this was only the start of something.

It was a time to confront demons for Hope, and one of her demons spoke in a soft whispery voice and had grey-green skin that hung in folds and ruts, etched with age. One of her demons was the ancient, one-eyed chlick she had first encountered at the Anders Bars Infirmary.

She had thought the chlick to be some kind of doctor, or scientist, visiting her, prodding and poking at her with strange implements, doing things with lights and jelly pads and wires that did things inside her head, filled her with colour and sound and scent.

That morning... the morning after the night when she had come close to cutting Marek's penis from his scrawny body, she walked with Saneth, and she confronted the ancient chlick, asking, "What were you doing there? At the hospital near Angiere? Why did you keep me in a locked room and do those things to me? Why did you put the voices into my head?"

The chlick's false eye turned to her. "!¡*teaching junior scholar*¡! This lauded one did not put voices into the scholar pup's head," she-he said. "This lauded one knew of the scholar pup's nature and was impelled by our nature of being to learn more."

"You imprisoned me."

"!¡*factual reporting*¡! This lauded one did not !¡*ambiguous*¡! imprison the scholar pup," said Saneth, before adding: "This lauded one chose not to release the scholar pup. Such judgements are made."

They passed along a narrow trail, a pair of parallel ruts cut into the ground by the passage of wheeled vehicles, although that must be an occasional thing, judging by how overgrown the trail was. To either side, trees stood stark, their trunks bare where they emerged from the undergrowth, with no leaves until the canopy, some distance above them.

Hope didn't like the woods. She felt exposed. She hugged herself, her skin goosebumping. She knew the chlick could talk rings round her if it chose to, and so she fell silent for a while.

"You said my 'nature'," she tried, after a time. "What's in my head... is that what you mean?"

"!¡approval of junior scholar¡! What is it that is in the scholar pup's head?"

Hope took time to think. *Voices* was the obvious answer, but was that what the chlick wanted her to say? "A presence," she said, finally. "Presences. Always there, but when they rise up it feels like I'm being crowded out of my own head and I might get lost. Sometimes quiet, sometimes so loud it hurts worse than anything I've ever felt. Sometimes they guide me. When I try to listen to them, like Dodge told me to. Steering me. Helping me decide what to do and where to go. That's what's in my head. That's what it feels like."

"!¡approving¡! Inside the head of the scholar pup is another world," said Saneth. "!¡factual reporting | awed¡! Inside the head of the scholar pup is the essence of your kind, the *essences*. Everything that it is to be human. Your brain is like a connection to the Great All, a connection to the sum total of your kind, but that connection is to something within. !¡*frustrated* | *inarticulate*¡! The essence of the scholar pup's kind is held within. Within the pup's mind."

Hope stared at the wrinkled alien. "People in my head?" she said, struggling to grasp what she was being told. "You put lots of people in my head?"

"!¡*disappointed* | *frustrated*¡! Not people," said Saneth. "A species. All that is your kind. And no, this lauded one did not put them there, this lauded one merely studied what it is that the scholar pup is."

"What am I?" asked Hope. "What did you find when you kept me imprisoned... when you did not set me free and studied me instead?"

"!¡*struggling to articulate*¡! In your head there is the summation of your kind," said the chlick. "In your head there is the distilled essence of your kind. It is where your kind's story has been told. In your head there is the spark of another world, an All for your kind. That is what this lauded one found. That is what has been sung in your head."

SHE WALKED, AND she tried to let it all sink in, tried to understand. She carried humankind in her head. Little wonder that it felt crowded. Little wonder that they sometimes drowned out what it was that was *her*.

This was what had been sung in her head. Did Saneth mean that a starsinger had done this to her? She knew that Skids had spent time with a starsinger in Laverne, and so later that day she fell into stride alongside him.

He nodded to her, but remained silent.

The trail climbed now into another bank of craggy hills. Scrubby heathland grew to either side, and the scent of wild thyme was heady in the early autumn sun.

"Tell me about the starsingers," she said, after a time. "Tell me about the realities they sing."

Skids still bore the scars and bald patches from where he had worn the caul, an alien symbiont that allowed those who became wraiths to commune with the starsingers. His brooding dark eyes fixed on her, as if measuring her, assessing her.

"¡*struggling*¡! Remember looking back on Laverne from a distance?" he said.

She did. There was one point on their journey where they had stopped on a rise and looked back. She nodded.

"A hazy blur," said Skids. "You could see a few buildings, but most ran together. A few towers in Central and the skystation gantries were all the detail you could really make out. Well... closer up, you'd see more: individual buildings, details on those buildings – windows, roofs, doors, spires, guttering, murals. Even closer up and you'd see bricks and building stones, woodwork. Closer up: the heads of nails, the joins where blocks have been glued, a black stain from leaking gutters, a line of house martin nests beneath the eaves.

"That's what it's like. We see starsingers as if we see them from a distance. We see a vague outline of what they are. Starsingers are ancient. We can't even begin to conceive of what they are, or how they think or operate. Those words don't even apply. They don't *think* or *do*."

She regretted asking. She almost left it alone, then. But she needed to know. Had a starsinger sung the voices in her head?

"Do they notice us?" she asked. "Are they aware of our existence? Do they... experiment with us?"

"!¡*struggling to articulate*¡! They can be very aware of us," said Skids. "They grant us the caul. They seek to know us, from the inside. They are oblivious to most races, but there is something in us that they crave. !¡*frustration*¡! Ach, there aren't the words. The 'singers don't 'seek' or 'crave'. Those words only describe what the starsingers do like a city seen from a distance. Wear the caul and you'd see how clumsy words are, how they limit our understanding to what we can describe, rather than what we can *perceive*. Words do not describe the All, they constrict it."

"The starsingers sing realities?" Hope prompted.

Skids nodded. "!¡*factual reporting*¡! They recast reality around themselves," he said. "That's how they can travel across the All: they recast reality so they are *here* rather than *there*."

She considered the chorus in her head. Saneth said it had been sung. What might the starsingers want with her? She put a hand to her temple and said, "I think... I think they've done something to me. In my head. Saneth said something had been sung in my head."

Skids fixed her with those intense eyes again. "!¡*sincere*¡! The starsingers have touched us all," he said. "But remember: a starsinger is a single entity, never a 'they'. The 'singers stay apart from each other. They are solitary beings. It's far too dangerous for them to come together, too much of a toll on the All, with all those pulls on reality in close proximity."

"The voices," she said. "The voices in my head. Can they be *un*sung?"

"!¡*factual reporting*¡! Anything can be," said Skids. "You just have to learn how to make it so."

* * *

TWO NIGHTS LATER, Hope settled to sleep alone as I took first watch again, this time with Frankhay.

We were camped out in the hollow where we would later discuss our options.

Now wary of sleeping alone, Hope settled close to where Saneth and the commensal sidedog stood. Before doing so, she checked where Marek was, and was relieved to see him lying with a small group of Hays.

She curled into a ball and lay for a time with her eyes open. Saneth was washing, or oiling, her-his body with fistfuls of some secretion from a belly-gland. The stuff smelled of something citrus. Sour lemons, she decided.

She closed her eyes and thought of drinks with chunks of lemon in them, back in Angiere. It seemed to calm the voices, which was a good thing.

She thought of roaming the streets in Angiere, exploring. She thought of the dockside bustle, the impatient screeching of the gulls. She thought of Emerald, who had got her jobs serving in bars and tried to persuade her to get parts of her body pierced that should never have sharp metal pushed through them.

She stirred to arms coiling around her, a body pressed gently against her, and the night was suddenly cold and the body warm, and she recognised the touch, knew it was me, shifted so that we fitted like twined honeysuckle.

She slumbered again, woke, and my arm was still around her, a hand on her ribs, half-cupping her right breast. She knew my hesitancy around her signified something, some kind of bond. She knew I wanted her, but sensed also that I wanted more than anyone else had ever had from her.

This made her feel something in return, but she didn't know what it was. Something in her belly, which could easily have been a sex thing. Some kind of feeling of responsibility, too, an awareness that she could easily do harm.

She didn't think that this was what I was feeling though, and because of this she felt inadequate, less than human, because she couldn't reciprocate whatever it was that I felt.

She was confused, and her head, usually calmed by my presence, was loud, cacophonous. She knew she would not sleep again this night.

Carefully, she eased herself out of my embrace, sat with her knees pulled up, watched me sleeping for a while.

She peered around in the darkness, saw two Hays – Buller and May – standing guard a short distance downslope from the hollow. Marek lay motionless in the group he had joined for the night. Saneth stood nearby, still: maybe asleep, maybe not.

She went to sit on a flat rock that gave her a view out across the plain. Whenever the moon broke through the clouds, the land was lit with a thin wash of silver. Occasional lights pricked the view, some moving, all distant. Back to where Laverne lay in the west, a yellow glow spilled across the sky and occasional flashes and beams from the skystation jittered like a dry lightning storm.

The voices, the jam-packed essence of our kind... they were a murmur now, almost soothing, the distant, muffled breaking of waves on a beach. Which made her think of Anders Bars and her escape to the dunes by the sea just as the infirmary was burnt to glass, which made her think again of the hospital, the endless days in that room, the wires and lights and smells... Was that where they'd put the voices into her head, or had she arrived there already like this, captured for study by Saneth and her-his colleagues?

She breathed deep and held it, trying to smother the rising chorus.

She watched the sky lighten and detail begin to etch itself across the land, and as she did so she became aware of me behind her, pausing, and then coming to join her. We sat in silence for a time and then I spoke and she answered and she leaned towards me and kissed me softly on the jaw because in that moment she understood that maybe the gnawing uncertainty in her belly whenever she was with me was exactly what I was feeling, and so maybe she *could* reciprocate, maybe she *was* whole, maybe this was a normal thing to be feeling.

She watched me closely as I hesitated and allowed some indefinable moment to pass, she allowed herself a moment of frustrated anger with me when I did not turn and take her in my arms and then... people stirring, starting to gather their things, and the moment really had slipped away.

HERALD CALLED THEM together to debate what to do next, and for most of it Hope sat on the fringe, letting the words wash over her, just another chorus of voices.

She was surprised when Marek spoke more passionately than most, but when he talked of justice and equality she remembered the rough touch of his hand and the way he had treated her back in Angiere.

But he did not know how to find Harmony. All he knew was that it was a city dominated by ten towers, set in the mountains. And Saneth did not know either, Saneth who suddenly seemed weak and frail and who said she-he was dying and had no way to help them.

"I know the way," Hope said into the silence after Herald had finished his crowing. She had seen it in a dream, in dreams that were only now coming back to her, the returning memory keyed by Marek's description. The towers: six of them square and blocky, the remaining four twisting helices. Much of the city abandoned, in ruins. The white mountains beyond; the river channelled through straight-edged cuts.

What she did not tell them, because she did not want to put them off from continuing the journey and because it made the voices shrill in her head, was what else she saw in her dreams, the dreams that had only just come back to her now and which she realised had been disturbing her sleep for nights on end.

What she did not tell them was that the giant starship that hung over the city, connected to the towers by a beam of harsh light, was another angel of destruction, needle beams stabbing down, burning, destroying, melting the city to glass as, one by one, the towers slumped, folded in on themselves, lost all form and collapsed.

Harmony would be no refuge.

Harmony was another stopping place on the way to somewhere better, and one they must be careful not to stay in for too long.

Chapter Twenty-Seven

WITH THE WEIGHT of numbers behind Herald, and the fact that only one of us claimed to have any idea at all how to find Harmony – and that one was a girl who most regarded as flaky at best and who admitted she only knew from a dream – the outcome was inevitable.

But I was still surprised when it was Frankhay who finally swung the debate behind the settlers.

"!¡*menacing*¡! We have a simple choice," he said, and instantly the gathering fell silent around him. "We stay here, learn how to survive a winter and then build a community, hoping all the time that the watchers don't come after us an' destroy it like as they did Angiere and Laverne."

Herald opened his mouth to speak but Frankhay silenced him with a pointing finger and a glare. "Or we head east looking for a city we don't know exists with directions from a stranger's dreams."

This time he silenced me, as I tried to butt in.

"!¡*authority*¡! It's a choice 'tween the safe bet and, quite literally, hope," he concluded.

I looked around the gathering, and I knew where the consensus lay.

"!¡*hierarchy*¡! The choice is simple," said the clan-father. "If we carry on travelling into the winter, we have no guarantee of food. Every night we'll be riskin' everything on the chance of findin' shelter. It'd be a fool of a clan-father to lead his people into that when they could be staying in one place, learning their surroundings good and proper instead of learning and re-learning everywhere they go."

"!¡*dismay*¡! You're saying we stay?" I asked, disappointed in him. I thought we'd bonded, I thought he believed in finding a better place.

"!¡*decisive*¡! No," he said. He waved at the gathering. "I say *they* stay. This is a good spot, best we've found. The whole lot of us movin' on don't stand much chance, but if most stay here they do, an' a smaller party carryin' on to find Harmony stands a better chance of success too. An' if we find it, we can easy send back for the rest. *That's* what I'm saying."

WE STAYED ANOTHER day, helping to build shelters, saying our one-sided farewells: those who were leaving convinced that this would be a temporary separation, those who remained convinced that the two groups would never see each other again.

Frankhay made a show of leaving Ashterhay in charge of his clan. "!¡*authority*¡! Them as say you're too young, well, they'd best remember what it was like for me," he said to a small gathering round a fire that evening. "I was much younger when I founded the clan an' we took over the Loop. Age ain't nobody's business. It's what's in your head and in your heart that matters. Ash, you're like blood to me, but that's not anything to do with it. You're the one that's most like me in your head and your heart: that's what's made my mind up."

Frankhay had been sure to include Herald in the gathering while he handed the clan to Ash, and Herald clearly didn't know what to do. On the one hand, he was party to the handover of power, but on the other, well, the power wasn't being handed to *him*.

There would be trouble there, I felt sure. Frankhay must know it, and so must Ash.

I tried to put it from my mind, though. I could do nothing other than forewarn the Cragsiders we left behind.

Herald would stay, of course, and Fray too – a woman of similar age who had grown closer to him on the journey here. Back in Laverne, she had looked after the smaller children at Villa Mart Three, and now she had adopted the role of carer for the two pups from our clan who had survived, Tuck and Immy.

Hope and I were clearly going to seek Harmony. Skids was coming. He had always supported seeing the journey through, and mention of a starsinger protecting Harmony only gave him extra reason. Saneth was coming along, and Marek, too, the most passionate advocate of continuing the journey. Divine was torn; she did not think it was a good idea, but her loyalties lay with me as nominal clan-father of what remained of our people.

That only left Jemerie and Pi from the surviving Cragsiders. I needed to talk to them to determine their thinking.

I had to wait until later in the evening to learn what they thought, when we were splitting into smaller groups, organising ourselves and settling for the night. That was when the two of them found me, unusually hesitant, Pi gesturing at Jemerie with her head as if to say, *Go on, do it.*

"!¡curious¡! What is it?" I asked, tired and confused, thinking now wasn't the time for more complications, and that they should just be clear about their decision, whatever that may be.

"!¡*hesitant | uncertain*¡! I've got something to tell you," said Jemerie. "Something important."

"!¡*SUPPORTIVE*¡! YOU'RE STAYING?" I asked them. "That's good. Some sanity to go against Herald. That's fine, really. I think it's right that most should stay and only a small party continue the search for Harmony."

It saddened me to be parting from two of my oldest friends, but I was determined it would only be a temporary thing. If we found Harmony, then we would send back for the rest to join us; and if we didn't, then we would reach a point where we gave up looking and would return here.

"!¡*hesitant*¡! That's not it," said Jemerie. "We *are* staying, but that's not what I wanted to tell you. It's Hope."

I peered at him, then looked around to see where Hope was. After a moment or two I found her, sitting near to Saneth, knees drawn up to her chest. She looked alone, lost even. I remembered the gentle touch of her lips when she kissed me, all the nights we had shared.

"!¡*cautious*¡! Hope? What about her?"

"!¡*firm*¡! She's not like us," said Pi. "You need to know before you follow her to gods know where."

"!¡*defensive | confused*¡! What do you mean?"

"!¡*factual reporting*¡! Like Sol," said Jemerie. "When Sol was killed and cut open and we saw what she was like inside – not all blood and mess like we are. Not human. It made sense when I saw that."

"What did? What made sense?"

"!¡*factual reporting*¡! Back at Villa Mart Three," said Jemerie. "When the watchers attacked and only a few of us escaped... those bugs. The flesh-eating bugs. You got them on your hand. Hope got them on her face and I dressed it. Her face: it wasn't blood and muscle like one of us. !¡*revulsion*¡! It was fibres like plastic. It was like what was inside Sol when she was sliced open."

The guardians... Like Sol, like Callo.

Hope was a guardian.

Chapter Twenty-Eight

I STOOD ALONE and looked across at Hope. She sat by Saneth, waiting for me to join her for the night. Her honeyed skin looked almost orange in the glow of the fire.

I remembered the touch of that skin, of her lips.

How had I not known? How had I not realised?

I walked down the track, away from the hollow where we had found shelter and where a community would be built. The moon lit my way, just enough light not to stumble and trip over the uneven ground and the tangles of undergrowth.

Hope... not human. A guardian.

I felt as if someone had bound my chest tightly, so that I had to fight for every breath. My heart beat hard and fast. Around me: dark trees, the woods a deep black; the occasional sounds of night creatures, insects, an owl screeching, something scuffling in the bushes. The air felt heavy, as if rain was almost upon us.

I thought back to that day in Villa Mart Three. Frankhay's raid, the fighting over almost before it had started. The stand-off when Frankhay had realised what a broken, hollow shell Sol had become. The smudge on the sky that became a cloud, became a whining, seething mass as it descended.

It was Jersy who had gone down first. A tail had whipped down from the black cloud, flicked his cheek, and almost instantly his face had been eaten to bone, the hand that he had raised to his face stripped white...

Hope had pulled at me. She had known what was happening before anyone. She knew we had to flee. She had seen this before in Angiere.

The mad rush to escape, the mass of bodies plugging the doorway from the roof terrace, the two of us escaping across the crag. Seeing that mass of bodies from inside the nest, the seething mass of black, the harsh white of bone, bodies dissolving, bodies disintegrating.

The blemish on Hope's cheek. A tiny black mark like a blob of tar. The feel of my fingers scraping at her face to get the flesh-eating bugs off her.

There had been blood, but had it been hers or just mine?

She had held her hands to her damaged face, as if holding it together, or covering it from view.

Had the bugs eaten at her more slowly? If she had been real flesh and blood would she have survived?

She had kept her wound covered all the way out, until Jemerie had dressed it. Since the attack, I had only seen it covered, or healed over with new scar tissue.

Hope, a guardian, an artificial. I knew it to be true.

SOME TIME LATER I returned to the camping ground, exchanging a few words with Ash and another of the young Hays on guard duty. No one stirred as I threaded my way through the scattered bodies.

I saw that Hope was still awake, still sitting with her knees drawn up tight. Watching me, waiting.

I found a space where bracken had been trampled flat. Jemerie and Pi slept tangled there, and nearby were the dark-clad bodies of three members of Frankhay's clan.

I lay down, put my hands behind my head and stared at the stars.

She watched me still. She was confused then, didn't understand why I had gone off on my own, didn't understand why I had settled away from her now that I was back. She wanted the contact, wanted to be held. She did not know what had changed. She started to wonder if she had misjudged everything. Kissing me, as the previous night had shaded to morning, had seemed the right thing to do. But I hadn't responded, and now I kept my distance.

Now, the feelings she thought I'd held for her... that was what she felt for me.

Now, watching me from across the clearing, she didn't want to sleep at all, if it was not tangled with me.

And I lay there, and ignored her, because I still couldn't understand how she had so misled me about her true nature, and I didn't know what she was doing here or what she wanted, or whether we could even trust her directions to Harmony.

THE NEXT DAY broke grey and damp, a steady drizzle falling. Looking out from our vantage point, we could see little of the land before everything merged to grey.

Frankhay walked ahead with Hope; the clan-father was giving too many directions – "This way! No, this way!" – and trying to be jolly.

I hung back and found myself walking with Saneth, the chlick opting to ride on the back of the sidedog as a man might ride a horse. It looked a precarious arrangement, top-heavy, and the chlick's false eye swivelled repeatedly in what I took to be fear.

Nothing would improve my mood, it seemed.

We were splitting up, which now seemed such a bad idea to me. We were looking for a city that none of us even knew to exist, led by an artificial who had received directions in some half-arsed vision. And the rain was the kind that seemed like nothing but soaked you in an instant and made every item of clothing rub, and somehow you could feel hot and cold and clammy all at once.

"!¡*dejected | hopeless*¡! What is she?" I asked eventually, shaping the words almost before I had had the thought. "Saneth-ra, tell me. What *is* Hope? She's not one of us, she's not human. I know that much. But she sounds human, she feels human, she acts like one of us."

I remembered the feel of her body so intensely, then; it was as if I had jumped back in time to a point where we lay together and the world was distant. I remembered the feel of her lips on my jaw. "!¡*fighting for control*¡! But she isn't, is she?" I said. "She isn't one of us at all..."

"!¡*provocative*¡! She is you," Saneth said. "She is all of you. The scholar pup says Hope is not human, but some might conclude that she is more truly human than any of the rest of you."

The path climbed the hill and now the trees gave way to rocky outcrops and thickets of stumpy pine, barely taller than we were.

I wiped the rain from my brow. "!¡*stubborn*¡! She is not like us," I said. "She's an artificial. How can we trust her?"

"!¡*disappointed | leading-on*¡! Hope is herself," said Saneth, turning to look at me and wobbling precariously on her-his mount. "In her head she is a human like any other one of you. But Hope is also more than this. We each of us have many natures, many potentials. Within this lauded-one there is the potential for *she* and *he,* and such potentials mix with chemical and electrical impulses and patterns beyond mere human comprehension to make the rich and superior complex that is Saneth-ra ad-Pelastrum."

That last was a form of name extension I had heard before: a label that changed as the carrier's state changed. "You're right," I said. "I can never know you, truly. But so you can never know me. All we have are the words to bridge the gap."

"!¡*approval of junior scholar*¡! And so, can you even know another of your kind, with only words to reach across?"

Saneth was using my words against me, and suddenly I didn't know what I was arguing. "!¡*stubborn*¡! She's not like us," I persisted. "She is not of my kind."

"!¡*patient*¡! She is more," repeated the chlick. "Hope is one who carries within her head something that is special. She carries the All of humankind, a bridge to a condensate... a gathering together, a summing up. She is what it is to be human."

"!¡*confused*¡! But how? She's artificial. She can't be more human than a human!"

"!¡*patient explaining to junior scholar*¡! She is the result of a watcher experiment," said the ancient chlick.

"!¡*surprise*¡! The watchers? But–"

"!¡*admonishing*¡! The watchers are not all the watchers who would eradicate the kind that is human. The watchers are more than merely the Hadeen."

I tried to make sense of this with what I understood of the watchers from the lessons of Vechko and others.

The watchers were small creatures that came together, communal symbionts that formed the bodies we saw. Each watcher, whether it took the form of a humanoid or some other creature, was a colony; each such colony was part of a greater mass. They were hive creatures that could come together physically in various forms, while mentally they formed a continuum, a single, shared consensus. That was what we understood of the watchers.

"!¡*deferential*¡! The watchers are as one," I said, carefully. "So how can there be factions and divisions? How can there be the Hadeen who want us dead, and these others who experiment with us, who do things like... like *Hope*?"

"!¡*patient*¡! Watchers are as you say. But within, there are currents, non-uniformity. Nodes of difference form clusters, form differentiation. Some watchers have been sung to be different."

"!¡*alert*¡! 'Sung'...?"

"!¡*approving*¡! All reality has been sung, watchers included," said Saneth. "How else could it be?"

"!¡*doubting | disturbed*¡! So this has been sung? *I've* been sung...?"

"!¡*lecturing junior scholar*¡! If life emerges on one planet, then it is a universal truth that life must emerge elsewhere. And if life emerges in two places then it is so improbable for it to only emerge in two places in the Great All that it must emerge elsewhere, and elsewhere, and elsewhere. Everywhere, in all abundance and variety."

I nodded. I had never thought of it in those terms, but the chlick's reasoning made sense.

"Where life emerges, competition so emerges, and successful variants out-compete the weak, and life evolves. Sentience emerges, and if sentience emerges once from this developmental race, by the same reasoning, so it is that it will emerge more than once. Everywhere.

"The Great All is fecund with life and with intelligent life. For every intelligent species there will be species which evolved much earlier, and their sentience and knowledge will be so far greater that they would appear as gods."

Saneth's false eye swivelled forward and then across to fix me. "!¡*arrogant | superior*¡! Just as the chlick appear as gods to humankind," she-he said, "so there are others that are as gods to us. Gods so far advanced as to have conquered all of space, understood it, *known* it. Sentience is everywhere and knows all, and is dying. Once all is known, what more purpose can there be?"

My head was racing. I didn't know. I didn't know what more there could be than knowing everything. My own horizons stretched little beyond mere survival.

"!¡*hesitant*¡! I don't know," I said. "What is it like when all is known?"

"!¡*approving*¡! Everything. Every last detail is known, plotted, measured. All of reality is sung."

"Everything?" I peered around in the murk. We were approaching the crest of the hill now. I thought of Cragside, unsung. Re-sung to something other than what it had been.

The starsingers... Was Saneth telling me that the species so ancient, so far advanced that they should be regarded as gods even by the gods themselves... this race of super-gods was the starsingers?

Chapter Twenty-Nine

HOPE AND FRANKHAY were the first to reach the top of the ridge of hills. On that first day after our group of survivors split, the clan-father had done his best to keep everyone's spirits up, but soon had fallen to silence.

Hope's head was full of the night she had spent alone, distraught that by pressing herself upon me she had pushed me away rather than brought me closer.

Walking was hard, her clothes damp and heavy, her limbs tired from lack of sleep.

"Well," said Frankhay, sucking air across his teeth in a half-click of disappointment. "!¡*resigned*¡! I don't see me no mountains, then..."

The landscape tumbled before the two of them, mostly wooded, broken by a few cleared areas and the meandering snake of the river. It was like this until the distant grey land merged with the grey of the horizon.

No mountains. No city of ten spires.

AS WE DESCENDED from the hill, the trail petered out until we were just walking through the forest. We plotted a course from the sun, as we had learned to do, maintaining a straight eastward course rather than following the meandering path of the Swayne.

We would meet the river again before long, and save several days' travelling by doing this.

The going was tough, but Hope found that she coped more easily than some of the others. Frankhay, in particular, struggled. He didn't complain, but soon he stopped talking, concentrating on catching his breath, wincing at the aches and pains in his body as he crossed the uneven ground.

Skids, too, was struggling. We had already travelled a great distance from Laverne and his wiry frame carried no spare reserves. Now, he had the shaky walk of an addict or someone with a serious illness.

It did not bode well. We had not seen our destination from the top of the hill, so we clearly had a considerable distance still to travel.

Hope watched the ground just ahead of her footfalls, each step smooth, fluid. It was as if she could walk forever.

THE FIRST NIGHT, we made camp in not so much a clearing as a slight thinning of the trees. Bracken grew here in great clumps, and we could trample this down into a layer that broke the hard ground a little.

Jerra and Divine set off immediately to hunt birds. Since leaving Laverne, they had grown adept at hunting with slingshots, crossbow bolts and gunshot being too valuable commodities to expend in this way. Their hauls of small songbirds had been invaluable.

With Saneth, Frankhay and Skids sore and exhausted from the day's walk, that left me, Marek and Hope to forage for food. Like Divine and Jerra, we had found little on our journey.

Pickings were thin on the ground that evening. We found a few clumps of nettles we could boil down to make bitter tea, and a few pine cones which might yield seeds.

Fungi taunted us with their abundance. Bulbous, gaudy growths on fallen trees, dainty parasols thrusting from the ground, great dusty spheres, wrinkled folds of yellow and brown holding tiny pools of water and dead insects... The only wild fungi I had ever eaten were the little white-cap mushrooms that grew in Laverne's parks, delicate and nutty, and the small brown, thin-stalked phreak-caps that made you see strange colours and lights and distortions of the world around you.

"!¡*impatient*¡! We should try them," said Marek, pointing to a brown fungal slab growing at head-height from a tree. "Look: something's taken a chunk out of that one. It must be edible. That one alone's a meal for at least three of us!"

"!¡*cautious | irritated*¡! We have no way of knowing if any of them are poisonous or not," I said. "All we know is that *some* are. If you want to try some then go ahead, but I'm not touching them."

Marek clicked derisively and sliced at the growth with his knife. The thing oozed grey-blue juices and he backed away, wiping his blade on his backside.

Hope kept her distance, wandering through the trees, occasionally stooping to scrape at the leaf-mould with her knife, or turn a small log with the toe of her boot. I wondered if this mattered to her, if she even needed to eat at all or was merely going through the motions, continuing her masquerade as real flesh and blood.

Back in the clearing, someone had started a fire, but we had little but a few seeds and leaves to cook on it, and not even much water to boil them in.

The night was cold and I longed for some shared body warmth. Skids was shivering, and the two of us huddled close. I dreamed that Hope had joined us in the night and that she was real, but when I woke and peered around the near pitch-dark camp, she was still lying alone a short distance away.

When I woke next, with a thin light spreading through the trees, there was a stiffness to the bracken, a sharp chill in the air, and I realised that there had been the first delicate frost of the coming winter.

HOPE BARELY SLEPT that night. The bracken was scratchy, the ground seemed so much harder than it had on other nights, and she was intensely aware of the scale of the forest around us. She had seen it from the crest of the hill, trees covering every fold of the land, the dark green of pines, the golds and browns and greens of the oaks and chestnuts and beech. Trees as far as she could see, before the drizzly sky merged with the forest to form an indistinct horizon.

When she did sleep, though, she dreamed of the spired city. Lit by a shaft of sunlight, with ragged black crows circling around the towers, and forest spreading right up to the buildings like the waves of a dark sea.

And in her head, the voices of all humankind sang loud, sang high, sang exultant.

WE WALKED, HUNGRY and cold and in ever lower spirits.

In the forest, it was hard even to be sure we were sticking to the right course, but whenever we paused to rest, if there was sunlight enough breaking through the trees, Marek did a thing with a stick poked into the ground, where he plotted the line its shadow took as the sun moved and each time found east again.

"!¡*factual reporting*¡! We had some training back in Angiere," he explained to Hope. "We had to pass it on to those we smuggled out. Some basic survival skills."

Hope turned away. She felt uncomfortable with Marek trying to make conversation. She did not know how to respond. Sometimes she felt as if, rather than having her head crammed with something extra, there was something missing from within her, some element that others took for granted, an understanding of how to connect.

When Jerra killed a crow, we debated cooking it now or waiting.

"!¡*disdainful*¡! Look at it," snapped Marek. "A scrap of feathers and bones. Not even a mouthful between us. We carry on, we gather as we walk, we try the fruit of the forest" – he meant the fungi we had not dared try until now – "we wait until we have a meal and won't just be fighting over scraps."

Nobody liked what he said, or the way that he said it, but we gathered ourselves together and resumed the journey.

By the middle of the day we had another crow, some chestnuts and a bunch of skinny mushrooms that looked like the kind we might once have found on a market stall in the city. Despite these riches, the meal was sparse, a thin stew cooked in water from the stagnant pools in the bed of what must be a stream in the rainy season.

Resuming the march, I became aware of how the food had at least warmed me against the sudden chill of the air. I loosened my jacket, and then my shirt.

By the time the sun hung low in the sky and we

were starting to look for somewhere to settle for the night, I knew we had made a stupid mistake. Eating anything without being sure that it was safe... Bad water, meat from birds that looked emaciated and pestilent – why had they sat so low in the trees, just waiting to be shot? – Marek's innocent-looking fungi...

It may have been any or all of these that struck us down.

Divine had already vanished into the trees for a time, catching us up with her face pale as a cloud and black shadows etched beneath her eyes.

We had come to a patch of woodland where a tree had fallen and shafts of sunlight spilled through when the first cramp gripped my belly. "!¡*non-committal*¡! Here's as good as any," I said. It had been a long day. I just wanted to stop.

Pain stabbed and I clutched at my abdomen. Then I was throwing up and there were fibres of green nettle and dock in my puke and the pain in my belly was more intense than anything I'd ever felt before.

We stopped there, Divine already off among the trees emptying herself from both ends, Frankhay vomiting, Jerra squatting and letting rip a jet of brown liquid from beneath his kilt, and everyone else exchanging looks, wondering who would be next.

I dropped to my knees and retched again and again, someone holding my shoulders to support me. Skids. Speaking to me, trying to distract me from the pain and the burning in my throat and the heat. And then he let go, turned away, and threw up, just as I felt my guts cramping and I fumbled with my trousers and lay on my side on the ground, emptying myself.

More hands on me, turning me. Small hands,

walnut-brown, surprisingly strong, firm.

Hope.

I didn't want her touching me, tending me. Not now. Not ever. Didn't want her wiping at my soiled body with bunches of leaves. Didn't want her trying to get me comfortable.

Didn't want any of it.

NIGHT-TIME, AND MY symptoms had retreated to stomach cramps and a fever. A fever cooled by a light hand on my forehead.

I shifted, withdrawing from Hope's touch.

She didn't appear to have been ill at all, but then that made sense because, despite what Saneth might say about her humanity, she was not one of us.

Even then, I was aware of the irony. If she had been human, I would have longed for her not to suffer this sickness, but now I wanted her to suffer, resented her for not sharing in this curse that had befallen us.

I rolled onto my back and winced at the pain in my gut.

She put a hand out and I batted it away angrily.

"!¡*hostile*¡! Get away from me," I hissed. In the dim light from the remains of a fire someone had lit I saw the shock on Hope's face, but I didn't care.

"But..." she said, and then stopped.

"!¡*angry | confrontational*¡! Look at you," I said. "Here we are, heaving our guts out, and you just sit there, untouched. You're not *like* us. You're not human. Why should you care? Why should you care about any of us?"

She stared at me, and suddenly it was as if I had

just slapped a baby.

I dipped my head, struck by another wave of nausea, and when I looked up again she had risen to her feet and turned away, leaving me to wallow in my filth and heat and resentment.

Chapter Thirty

HOPE HAD WATCHED curiously as one by one we fell ill, leaving only her and Saneth untouched. She expected at any time to be taken with the illness, but she was not.

She remained well, and it reinforced her feeling that there was something missing.

She was an incomplete woman, and that was why I did not return her feelings.

She knew enough to boil the water she collected from puddles on the ground and in the joints of trees. Under Saneth's direction, she used Marek's sparker to get a fire going, and then collected water and boiled it in the fold-out bucket we carried.

She tended to me and the others, feeding us cooled, boiled water, mopping us with handfuls of leaves, trying to soothe and make us as comfortable as possible.

She saw us through the worst of it, and in return I vented my anger.

"YOU'RE NOT *LIKE* us. You're not human. Why should you care? Why should you care about any of us?"

She stared at me in the gloom, clutching the hand I had swatted away.

Not human.

It was what she had feared. She wasn't like the rest of us. She was less than human, something missing, just a vessel carrying the awful raucous mob of voices in her head.

She wasn't human, and I had seen that, and that was why I didn't want her.

She stood, turned away, left me in my self-pity and anger. Walked off into the forest, alone, thinking she might walk forever, leave us all behind, but then she became aware of hot tears sliding down her face, and in that moment she felt weak and very human indeed, and she sank to her haunches and sobbed.

Why did she care? Why *should* she care about any of this?

She went back to the encampment, and there was Marek, sitting up against a tree, watching her. She went to him, kneeled, reached an arm across his chest.

His skin was cold and clammy and he reeked of vomit, but he welcomed her touch, returned it, and this made her feel just a little bit human again.

THE NEXT DAY we were fit for little more than sitting around and waiting to get less ill.

Saneth took Divine's slingshot and vanished into the forest, returning some time later with three pigeons and a tiny warbler. Hope and Marek gathered nettles and grass; anything that could be boiled into a broth.

None of us felt like eating and no one wanted to trust the food, fearful of what our previous meal had done to us, but we forced some down anyway.

The broth gave me strength, and I was able to stand and walk a short distance. Divine had been hit harder than anyone, but she was strong and soon back on her feet.

"!¡*tired*¡! How much more?" I asked late that afternoon, as we gathered around the fire. We were a sorry-looking bunch, huddled and thin, bags under our eyes and carrying a general air of gloom. "How far is it to Harmony?"

We all turned to Hope.

"I don't know," she said. "I don't have a map in my head. I don't have a way to measure. All I know is what I have seen, and that is if we follow the river to the mountains that's where we'll find Harmony."

Travelling through forest like this, we had no way of knowing. We had to trust that Marek's readings had kept us heading east, and that we would meet the river again at some point. But we had no way of knowing where we were. We could see such a short distance through the trees – for all we knew the mountains might be close, or they might still be too distant even to see.

We had only belief to keep us going, and the dream vision of a woman who was not human.

"!¡*resigned*¡! We should consider going back," I said. "Finding the others. Settling down. Look at us..."

Frankhay didn't seem surprised by my proposal. I might even have pre-empted his own thoughts, judging by his lack of reaction.

But it was Divine who was the first to speak against. She stared at me, then said, "!¡*surprised*¡! How can you say that? We've barely left them behind. We can't turn back now, not until we've had a proper stab at finding Harmony."

Most of the others looked uncertain, but then Skids added, "!¡*determined*¡! Divine's right. You turn back now, then we're splitting again. I'm not going back. A city protected by a starsinger... That's got to be worth all this, or what's the point?"

AFTER A MORE peaceful night we set out again, our pace slow.

I walked with Divine. She was strong at first, energised by the resumption of our journey, and I started to feel positive again for the first time in days.

Partway through the morning, the forest started to change, with fewer and fewer deciduous trees and more conifers. This made the under-forest gloomier, which hardly helped our mood, but I remembered learning somewhere that conifers were the dominant trees of the uplands and I started to get excited. The land even started to climb, and for a time I fooled myself that we were approaching the mountains, or at least a viewpoint from which we might finally see them.

And then the land sloped downwards and we entered a block of oak trees, their yellowed leaves littering the ground. That made me smile at my own foolish, easy optimism, and then I realised that I really was feeling better now: stronger, more able to face whatever was to come. My wobble the previous day seemed so distant, as if it was something that had happened to another person.

That was when I noticed that Divine was struggling to keep up and I had to check my pace.

She had gone pale, and the skin around her eyes had a touch of yellow to it. Her breathing, too, was ragged, shallow.

"!¡*falsely up-beat*¡! Thought we were hitting the mountains back there," I said. "Then we headed downhill again. Must be getting close, though, eh?"

It was as if I hadn't spoken. Her eyes were fixed straight ahead, determined.

"!¡*concerned*¡! You okay, Div?"

Nothing.

I waved a hand in front of her face. "!¡*assertive | concerned*¡! I said, are you okay? Divine?"

She glanced at me then, and smiled. "!¡*exhausted*¡! Course I am."

Divine had never been one of the old gang. A couple of years older than me, she'd always stood out, her disciplined aggression making her one of Sol's most valued supporters. But even though we'd never really mixed, we'd been close. Being singled out by Sol was something we had in common, and then when she hooked up with my old friend Ruth we'd finally started to get closer.

I realised I'd barely spoken to her since Ruth's death, other than practical matters. We were a team, Divine and me; we made things work. Sometimes, though, that got in the way of the important stuff.

It was only a short time after all this ran through my head and I resolved to make up the lost time with Divine that she paused, put her hands on her knees as if about to cough, then fell to the ground.

I went to her, not realising that it was anything more than exhaustion at first.

She lay face down in the mosaic of fading golden oak leaves.

I kneeled, took her head in my hands, turned it so that she could breathe, and then realised that it was futile as she had already stopped doing so.

331

Her skin was white, her eyes wide open, staring into some unknown distance. A smear of mucusy red vomit was spread around her mouth and down one side of her chin.

I rocked back on my heels, and looked around at the others as they caught us up.

Divine was dead.

Chapter Thirty-One

WE CAME TO the river again some days later.

Hope's first realisation that something different lay ahead was a change in the light, a thinning of the trees.

She was walking with Marek, letting his words wash over her. He was assuring her again that he would be a man of substance in Harmony. As part of the Vanguard, he had helped people escape from Angiere and Laverne, and he knew they had all been directed towards Harmony. When our group arrived, Marek would be recognised and lauded for the part he'd played in saving so many. It was an account he had given many times already, and Hope did not discourage him, for his words meant that he was aware of her, which meant that at least in some small way she mattered to him, and so she felt significant, not dismissed and belittled. My rejection had cut her deeply, reinforcing the doubts and insecurities that already loomed over her.

And up ahead, a thinning, a brightening. An edge to the forest.

Hope and Marek hurried their pace to catch up with me, Frankhay and Saneth. We had come to pause at the last of the trees.

It was the river, which meant we were still heading in the right direction, but it was not the actual edge of the forest, after all, and there was no city before us, nestling among the mountains. Hope felt the gnawing of hunger in her stomach again.

The river was far narrower here, although still a good distance across. Parts of it were clearly shallower than the great river of Laverne, with white rapids spuming over a rocky stretch at the far side.

We were clearly much closer to its source, and when Hope and Marek came to the bank she peered eastward along the river, following the cleft it cut through the forest.

There was no city, though, no mountains. Soon, the river swept northwards and the trees cut the line of vision.

We made camp there, on the bank of the river. It was not long after the middle of the day, but we were starving and exhausted. It was not a decision we discussed; we simply did not move on.

Hope went alone into the trees, gathering grubs from the leafmould and skewering them on long pine needles, a source of food she had discovered a couple of days before. None of us liked it, but it was one of the things that had kept us going.

After a time she brought her wriggling harvest back to the encampment, keeping none for herself.

She did not know what it was like to be us; all she knew was her own experience. But hunger hurt, and it was a pain that she knew we all felt. The pain was another thing that she used to convince herself that she was more like us than she was not, despite what Saneth had told her, despite the things I had said in my feverish anger.

WE DINED WELL that night.

During the afternoon, Jerra brought down a duck over the water. He had to swim to retrieve it, and emerged shivering, sitting by the fire to warm himself even as the bird roasted on a spit. Marek found a stand of chestnut trees, the ground beneath them littered with nuts in their spiky jackets. Dandelions, nettles and dock made for another bitter broth to accompany the grubs, duck and chestnuts. It was the fullest meal we had managed to put together since leaving Laverne.

For what remained of the day we gathered more chestnuts, and boiled dandelion roots to make them easier to chew on when we resumed our journey the next day.

"¡¡hesitant¡! What if we dunnat find it, though?" asked Jerra. "What if it innat there?"

Hope fixed him with a stare. "I've seen the city," she said, and she had, again, the night before when we had lain in a clearing and the first light snow had fallen, hard crystals of white. "It can't be far. The river at Harmony isn't much narrower than this."

I still didn't feel safe to trust her vision, even though Saneth explained that it was the voices in her head, the shared experience of countless humans that she channelled.

But I did allow her words to give me a shred of hope to cling to. There were no mountains yet, but maybe soon, maybe soon we would find the city sung into safety by its resident starsinger.

WE FOLLOWED THE river.

Days before, from the vantage point of the hills where we had left the others, we had been able to plot a straight eastward route that would bring us back to the river eventually, which it had. But now we had no such advantage. Heading in a straight line east might take us away from the river forever.

And so we found a route through the forest that always kept the river to our left, following every curve and meander. We must have almost doubled back on ourselves many times as the river wound its way through the land, but we had no real alternative.

The days grew noticeably shorter, the grey winter clouds holding back the light of morning and bringing in dusk ever sooner. Snow fell, and hung heavy in the canopy, with only a few clumps making it to ground level.

The cold bit hard. Walking gave us some warmth, and at night we slept in a huddle of bodies by whatever paltry fire we managed to light.

Saneth appeared to suffer the cold more than the rest of us. At night, the chlick even deigned to join the huddled bodies, and I often woke pressed against the alien's rutted, leathery skin. The chlick didn't appear to have a shiver reflex, and in the cold her-his body felt like chilled clay beneath that tough hide.

I wondered why Saneth didn't ride more in the sidedog, for rest and warmth. The chlick didn't even mount it like a horse any more, as she-he had earlier on the journey. Then one morning we woke to a smell like roast gammon and when I turned towards the fire, rubbing at my eyes, I saw Saneth there, working at a thin slab of meat with a knife, another slab suspended over the fire's embers on a spit.

"¡¡*surprise*¡! The sidedog...?" I asked, joining the chlick and recognising the commensal's furred skin.

Saneth tipped forward slightly, a nod.

"But..."

"¡*factual reporting*¡! The beast died. ¡¡*bitter loss*¡! The beast was inadequately adapted to the conditions. !¡*regret*¡! Lauded scholar must walk always, now. Lauded scholar now has no companion of lofty intellect." The eye swivelled. "Lauded scholar experiences !¡*grieving*¡! loss."

The sidedog smelled of bacon, but tasted like shit. I swallowed as much as I could and it filled a cavity in my gut, but some time later that day the beast's meat had passed through me in part-chewed lumps, clearly undigested.

I recalled the human wraiths of Laverne who had eaten from the pap-houses in the belief that alien foods brought them closer to their gods, even though such food could not be broken down in the human body. I wondered if some of that food was sidedog meat.

It WAS LATER that day that I first noticed changes in the forest, and at first I put it down to the alien meat cramping my stomach.

The pain in my gut was sharp, and it made me think of the day when we had been brought down by sickness. My first selfish thought was that I had been struck down by it again and that I was going to be sick and I might die. And my second thought was of Divine, my lost friend, a thought laced with guilt as I realised my own selfishness had come first.

Emptying my bowels helped with the pain, just getting that undigested alien meat out of my body.

I walked with Frankhay, and he kept giving me sidelong glances, and I wondered just how sick I looked. He was unsettling me, doing things to my head, making me paranoid.

I stumbled, my foot catching on the rocky ground, and Frankhay reached out to grab my arm, stop me from falling.

"!¡*authority*¡! Steady, boy," he said. Then: "So you'd be feelin' it too, then, would you?"

I looked at him and wondered what he meant. I understood then that he had been watching me to see if I had picked up on something he had noticed.

I shook my head. I hadn't felt anything. I didn't know what he was talking about.

Above us, the trees went on forever. Their trunks were wider than any I'd seen, as broad as buildings; the canopy was so far above us that there was a layer of mist hanging below it.

The ground: rocks and pine needles and fallen branches; a few wispy ferns and marestails.

Our breath: misting as we breathed, the mist freezing, crystallising and falling in a tiny sparkling shower.

Looking up, I felt dizzy.

I had no idea where the river was, or when we had left it behind. Even the morning seemed long ago, waking to Saneth roasting her-his friend... which made me giggle, and Frankhay looked at me strangely, and then I realised what the clan-father had meant when he said *So you'd be feelin' it too, then, would you?* A strangeness in the air, a distortion of perceptions...

A phreak.

Something was playing with our senses.

I thought it was the meat. Had Frankhay eaten the sidedog meat, too? Had it done things to our heads as well as to our guts? Was that the real reason why the wraiths ate alien food that otherwise did them no good at all?

I turned to Frankhay again, and kept turning, because I couldn't see him, he'd vanished, and so had all the trees. Instead I was in a park, on grass, in sunlight, swirls of alien dragonflies with bodies the size of my forearm in the air around my head, and sparkling crystals like coloured snow hanging in the air. Children laughing, singing a song, a chanting song, its words indistinct, its tune haunting, hypnotic, building and jarring and swelling to fill the air.

Staggering forward, someone – Frankhay! – grabbing at my arm but unable to support me, so that I landed on my knees, my shins scraping against bare rock, the smell of fallen pine needles suddenly up close, in my face.

The forest.

Just the forest.

Pine trees, fallen needles on the rocky ground, my breath ragged and catching in my chest. Frankhay saying, "!¡*alarm* | *empathy*¡! You okay, boy?"

My guts: more the memory of pain than pain itself. My head: swirling, confused; struggling to make sense of what had just happened.

"!¡*perturbed*¡! Hnh," I click-grunted. "Yes, I think so. Just lost my footing. I'm good. All good."

I clambered to my feet, brushed the needles from my legs and hands, and started to walk.

The forest was just normal forest again, and my head was my own. I was okay. Or going mad. Or falling sick.

I carried on walking.

Chapter Thirty-Two

THE RIVER WAS much narrower now, cutting a deep course through land that was steadily climbing.

We were coming towards the mountains, I was sure of it. The forest had changed, the land was rising, even the air had a different feel, a different taste.

We still could not see anything beyond the trees, though.

The forest phreaked again as we climbed a steep incline.

The trees were thinner here, and a dusting of snow covered the rocks. Looking back, we could see across the tops of the trees and onwards over the forest canopy, a rolling sea of deepest green, going on forever into the distance.

Ahead of us were just rocks and trees, climbing sharply, and somewhere the roar of the river.

And a great wall.

A wall so high I could not see the top. A wall of mottled shades of brown and grey.

Swelling suddenly, a chorus filled the air, like the children before but this time more jarring, more discordant, cutting right through me.

To my left, Frankhay had stopped in his tracks, eyes wide, mouth partly open.

"!¡gut-wrenching terror¡! It's... that's..."

He pointed.

I took a few steps closer, peered at the wall, and the mottles of brown resolved themselves one by one. A face. A torso. Legs sticking out, arms flailing.

I stepped closer, closer, shocked and drawn.

The wall was a barrier of human flesh, of bodies welded together, still living, still moving as if struggling to break free. Legs, arms, bellies, genitals, chests, faces... knots of dark hair, on heads and crotches and chests.

And they were crying, and wailing, sobbing, groaning, mumbling, shouting, all adding up to an almighty chorus. I remembered riding the commensal sidedog in Laverne, escaping the watchers, sharing the space with Hope, her head in mine and mine in hers and hearing that chorus. This was what it must be like to be her. All of the time.

I looked around for her, and she was a short distance down the rocky slope, on her knees with her head in her hands.

I looked up and there were crows, rising and landing, rising and landing, pecking at bare flesh, cackling and cawing, and the flesh was red as well as brown and there was an edge of pain to the wailing and crying.

Closer to the wall, Saneth and Skids stood, talking animatedly. Skids was waving and gesturing, more energised than I had seen him since we were pups together in Cragside.

"¡¡*shocked*¡! What is it?" I gasped, struggling up the slope to stand with them. "What's happening?"

Skids turned and his eyes were alight.

"¡¡*excited*¡! It's the 'singer!" he said. "It senses us. It's reshaping the world around us. We must be close.... We must be close to Harmony!"

I peered at the bodies, writhing and twisting, struggling to break free. A man's dark eyes stared back at me, beseeching. He opened his mouth and wriggling white maggots spilled out. By his side a woman wailed, her jaws locked open, her throat deep, red, reverberating with her cry.

"¡*uncertain*¡! It doesn't exactly seem to be welcoming us," I said.

"¡*impatient*¡! Come on," said Skids. "Follow me."

And with that he turned, approached the wall, pushed his hands forward into a seam where bodies joined, as if parting curtains, and plunged in.

HOPE KNEW THERE was something wrong. She could feel it long before the forest started to twist and reform itself around them. She felt it as a force, pulling at the shapes inside her head.

She walked with Saneth as their path started to climb. The old chlick was slow now, panting in the cold air.

The forest was a tangle of trunks like bundles of wire, slender, twisting around each other, a nightmare tangle from which she felt she might never escape, might never want to escape.

Soon she was alone, Saneth and the others lost in the convolutions of the wildwood. She pushed on, until the gaps between the trunks were barely enough to let her pass. Finally she could progress no further. The space between the tangled trunks had reduced to the size and shape of her body, as if it were a cast made from clay. She could stay here forever, a baby in an artificial womb.

She pulled back.

She'd stopped breathing for a moment there, stopped wanting to breathe.

Her momentum tipped her over backwards and she landed on her butt on the hard ground. The jarring pain through her spine shattered the illusion around her.

She rolled over and found herself on her knees at the foot of a rocky slope which emerged from the forest. The others were ahead of her, standing before a vast wall made of writhing, flailing, human bodies.

The wall... the bodies... they were calling, singing, crying.

To her.

The chorus drowned out the voices in her head, replaced them with a massed presence that threatened to swamp her.

She didn't know what to do.

She wanted to turn and run. She wanted this desperately.

She wanted to block out the chorus, but even with her hands jammed hard over her ears, the awful sound rang through her.

She rocked back on her heels and looked up at the towering wall. If anything, it reached higher now, more densely packed with bodies and body parts.

She saw the birds then, the wild, ragged crows, swirling in flocks around the human cliff-face, landing on people's heads and shoulders, pecking at soft, exposed parts.

She saw a face with one eye gouged out, a crow tugging at the wound, flapping to retain balance. She saw a pair of crows scrabbling for purchase on the thickly matted hair of one man's chest, one bird slithering down, tangling its claws in the thicker hair at the man's groin where it merged with the top of a woman's head.

She saw a baby, crying with a needle-sharp wail. A woman with dark, rotting teeth. Another woman, breasts raked by a bird's claws, blood streaming down her torso to her swollen, pregnant belly. A man, his face a wild tangle of grey beard, matted with drool and puke, eyes glazed and staring.

She saw each of them.

She heard each of them.

She felt their presences inside her skull. Crowding, jostling, pressing.

She grabbed her head in her hands again, and realised she was wailing as if she were part of the wall.

"!¡COMFORTING | INTRIGUED¡! SCHOLAR pup, scholar pup."

A rough hand rested on her back. She turned her head a little, and saw Saneth leaning over her, touching her, trying to soothe her. A cool presence, a quiet one.

"!¡*gently persuasive*¡! Scholar pup, we must go. The others have left us behind."

The chlick's false eye swivelled, and Hope looked up the hill to the wall and saw that they were alone now, just the two of them at the foot of the awful wall.

"What is it?" she gasped. "It's in my head. It's everywhere. I... I can't take it!"

"!¡*factual reporting*¡! It is a defensive mechanism. A barrier. A wall. It is a reshaping of the reality of this locale."

"It's not real?"

"!¡*patiently explaining to junior scholar*¡! It is real. It is reality. It is just a different reality from the one that would normally occupy this locale. It is a barrier that has been sung in response to our intrusion."

"Intrusion?"

"!¡*encouraging junior scholar*¡! We have reached Harmony. The protective starsinger has detected our presence and does not yet know that we are friendly. Yet also it does not know that we are *not* friendly. Caught in this dilemma, it tries to scare us off without doing any physical harm. The 'singer takes its responsibilities seriously. This is all perfectly safe. Consider it an amusement, a distraction, if you will."

Hope looked at the wall, the tangled, torn bodies. The chorus of wails still smothered her senses.

An *amusement?*

"What is it?" she asked. "Where did it come from?"

Saneth's eye swivelled from the wall back to Hope. "!¡*amused | patronising*¡! 'Where did it come from?'" she-he asked. "It came from you, Hope Burren. All that is this came from you."

SHE STOOD BEFORE the wall, so close that if she were inclined she could reach out and touch the cheek of the woman before her, the woman wedged into a mass of flesh. The woman stared back at her from large, dark eyes. A man's hairy buttocks sat on her shoulder; a slender arm emerged from behind her ribs; a child's hand clung to hers, but the rest of the child was lost in the mass of flesh.

"From me?" asked Hope. "All of this?"

Saneth inclined her-his body. "!¡*approval of junior scholar*¡! The starsinger of Harmony reached out. It sensed our approach. It explored us, seeking to find our weaknesses. To tempt us or scare us into turning away. It tried different things that it found in the minds of those it penetrated, but finally it settled on that which was the most powerful among our group. !¡*indignant | affronted*¡! It settled on *you*, Hope Burren. It found what was in your head and made it newly real."

Hope stared at the woman in the wall. Somehow it was less horrific if she concentrated on the one rather than the many. The voices in her head, cast into reality. This was what it was like.

"The bridge in your head that connects you to the condensate of all that is human, the thing that you think of as your *voices*," said the ancient chlick. "That is what the 'singer found. !¡*affronted*¡! The lauded one considers that the chlick's mental defences defeated the 'singer, or why would it cast a wall of human voices when it could have all the richness from within the lauded one? !¡*disingenuous*¡! The lauded one is proud to have withstood the great singer of the All's attentions in such a manner as this."

Hope filtered out the chlick's defence of her-his dented pride. The voices in her head had quietened. They really were close to Harmony.

"How do we get there?" she said, interrupting Saneth's rambling. "Where are the others?"

"!¡*approval of junior scholar*¡! They passed within," said Saneth, indicating the wall with a hooked hand. "The pup that is Skids has a confidence in the ways of the 'singers. He saw through what this is and realised that one in possession of a boldness and willingness to act would gain passage."

"What did he do?" She was starting to get frustrated with the chlick's roundabout ways.

"!¡*approving*¡! He led the way. !¡*encouraging*¡! Go ahead. Push through."

Hope took a step forward. She avoided the bit where the woman clung to the missing child's hand and chose the other side, where the bare skin of the woman's side butted against an ill-defined slab of flesh that could have been torso, or a fold of large thigh.

She reached out.

The flesh was warm to her touch and slick with sweat. It reminded her of encounters in the rooms above the bars of Tween, back in Angiere, a sense of urgency and need. It reminded her of a hand on the arm or back, a touch, a squeeze, an intimacy giving reassurance and bonding. It reminded her of all things human, and she realised that this was exactly what it was, this mass of flesh and need and passion and anger: it was all things human.

The flesh yielded, parted, in response to her touch.

Without giving herself time to reconsider, she plunged forward.

The wall folded around her, and it was like being in the sidedog again, a wet enfolding, a moment of panic as she realised she couldn't breathe, followed by the understanding that she did not have to breathe. The voices in her head fell silent, as the voices around her rose in a wild clamour.

She pushed on, but it was like the forest again, that first recasting of realities as the trees had closed in, twisting and tangling and steadily constricting the space until there was only a Hope-sized niche and she could move no more.

She could stay here. Become part of the wall, part of the mass of humanity. She could never trouble herself again with people like me, like Marek, with our demands on her, our expectations, our judgement.

She could... just... stop... moving.

But something pulled her back from the brink of giving in, something spoke to her, sang to her.

Wrong as this whole thing was, the mass of bodies, the wailing and crying and distress... underlying it all was a sense that something more than this was wrong. A discord in the reality that was being sung.

She pushed, but it was like being smothered in a mass of warm clay. Nothing gave.

She tried to twist, to wriggle an arm or a leg free, to engineer some kind of space to move in, but all around her the skin pressed, the raw, open flesh smothered, the hair tangled across her face, in her nose, in her mouth...

She could not move.

She had become a part of the wall.

She began to drift.

I SAVED HER, again.

In Hope's mind, as her body started to meld with those around her, she drifted back to Precept Square, remembering.

Remembering lingering on the fringes, and then seeing that Callo and Marek were there, getting caught up in the general round-up of humans in the Square.

Penned in by jagwire, realising that when her turn came, the grunts would find that she had no right to be there, and she would be seized, interrogated, punished, returned to a hospital like the one that had been destroyed so they could carry on doing to her whatever it was that they had been doing to her.

Someone, me, a lanky young man edging through the crowd towards her, looking her in the eye, a moment of sudden bonding, and then I reached out, touched her gently on the arm. Confusion in my look, and then a jolt, a fizz where skin met skin, and I had shared my pids with her, given her a blood-deep identity that would be enough to get her past the grunt's scan, get her out, stop them from seizing her.

On impulse, with a transitory moment's insight, I had saved her.

And now, she felt that discord, that sense of something wrong, that sense that this real was not *her* real, was not the real she had discovered where a stranger could impulsively save your life. This real was different, it was *other*, and that realisation was enough to bring her back to herself. She focused, found a sense of her own body again, her boundaries, the bundle of sensations that defined who she was, where she stopped.

And she knew that she cared, and that she was not a person to give up like this.

She remembered in the forest, the twisting trees enfolding her.

She straightened, pushed, and felt a yielding, a parting. Able to wriggle and twist now, she worked herself loose and pushed, pushed, pushed, and then she was breaking free, staggering forward, and the mass of human bodies was gone from around her, nowhere.

She was on her hands and knees, gasping for breath. The others were there: me, Skids, Marek, Jerra and Frankhay. A moment later, Saneth was at her side, materialised from nothing, false eye swivelling.

She looked ahead, and that was when she saw Harmony, just as she had seen it in her dreams.

Chapter Thirty-Three

WE EMERGED FROM that hellish wall, one by one.

When I popped out, Skids was sitting cross-legged on a rock, as if he had been waiting for a long time. He smiled and dipped his head in greeting as I struggled for breath, my hands and knees on bare, hard rock and my head full of swirling memories of raw meat enfolding me, hair and skin up against me, a wailing chorus of voices all around.

We were on a craggy hilltop. I peered back over my shoulder but there was no wall, just a landscape of dark, gently folding forest.

Ahead, the river cut a gouge through more trees, the water lashed white by the rocks that occasionally broke the surface. I tracked its course, slowly taking in the broader view.

And there, in the distance, like a dream: a city, nestling in the snow-capped mountains, lit by a shaft of sunlight. At its centre was a cluster of towers, great twisting spires that dominated the city.

It was exactly as Hope had described it from her dream.

The city of spires.

We had found Harmony.

* * *

WE HAD TO make camp in the forest again, and it was late the following day before we finally approached the city.

The forest thinned here, on the rocky ground of the foothills, and as we approached it was as if the trees were peeling away to either side to afford us a view of our destination.

The first buildings we encountered were widely-spaced, built to a human scale and only rising two storeys at most. They were constructed from the local blue-grey stone, and had long since fallen into disrepair. None had roofs or doors or windows, and many of the walls had collapsed. Twisted, gnarled pine trees grew through the ruins, and great clumps of grey and orange lichen formed broad scabs on the walls and ground.

A stone road followed the straightened course of the river through this abandoned hinterland.

Now that we were entering the city, the towers dominated everything. Some had straight walls, squared corners and neat rows of windows, like some of the blocks in Pennysway and Cheapside. Others twisted and curved in organic, asymmetrical formations. Most striking were the five towers that thrust high above them, twisting improbably like some great ribbon coiled around itself. Occasionally, the ribbon showed gaps, as if eaten away, or never completed; here, a skeletal framework of slender ribs was revealed.

It was impossible to see how such apparently flimsy structures could support themselves. They were clearly of alien construction, and at that I briefly panicked, wondering if this was Harmony after all, or if it were some alien settlement waiting to entrap us.

I looked around our small group. Skids knew, a mad grin plastered across his features; Hope knew, too, from the determined set of her jaw.

This really was Harmony.

We had made it.

WHEN WE REACHED the second great wall, Marek assumed control.

It first appeared as a shimmering barrier, a play of light mostly hidden by the buildings through which we passed.

As we drew closer, it became clear that the shimmering light was another wall. Semi-transparent: beyond it, I could see more buildings, and people moving about. The buildings beyond the barrier looked more complete; this was the living part of the city.

The spires loomed above us, staggering in their scale. From this perspective it would be easy to believe that they ascended all the way to the stars.

We stopped before the wall.

Currents of light passed through it, separating and recombining, distorting what could be seen of the city within.

I opened my mouth to ask Saneth how we should proceed, but before I could speak a face appeared in the wall before us, and then a body.

The figure bulged outwards, as if a man was pressing against a stretchable membrane, pulling the flow of light and colour around his form.

"Identify yourself," said the man.

Marek stepped forward, and said, "!¡*authority*¡! I am Marek Moon, poet and historian from the city of Angiere, agent of the Vanguard, friend of Callo Hart.

I have sent many refugees here to Harmony. They will vouch for me. I bring more refugees, this time from the city of Laverne. The persecution continues, and we ask for sanctuary."

The figure in the wall froze, and I wondered then if it was a real person or a projection from the city's guardian starsinger.

Then the figure dissolved and the barrier of light thinned, giving ever more substance to the city within, until finally, there was a gap, an archway.

Marek stepped forward, passed through, and one by one we followed.

Two men and two women, dressed in heavy trousers and furs, stood a short distance from the barrier, waiting to greet us.

Marek appeared to recognise them. He opened his arms wide, and gasped, "!¡*recognition | delight*¡! Mazar! Alya! You made it. What a delight!"

A tall man with near-black skin and a full beard grinned in response. "Marek," he said in a deep voice. "The poet who never pens a line of verse. Good to see you!"

Marek laughed. "!¡*warm*¡! Poetry is in the head and heart," he said. "Tell me, Mazar: how many are here? How many made it?"

"We are a good number," said the tall man. "Many from Angiere, but we are gathered from all about. You are the first from Laverne."

"!¡*hierarchy*¡! And maybe the last," said Frankhay, stepping forward. "I'm Frankhay, clan-father of the Hays. And this here is Saneth, a chlick but a friend; and Dodge, Hope, Skids and Jerra."

"This is all of you?" asked a woman. She was tall, like Mazar, with long, chestnut hair and pale, almond skin.

Frankhay nodded. I almost spoke up, but then decided it might be wise not to mention those we had left behind in the hills. We did not want these people to feel swamped by our sudden arrival.

Then Jerra spoke, unexpectedly for one normally so quiet. "!¡hesitant | impassioned¡! Do you have any food?" he asked, and I realised he was close to tears, a flood-barrier about to break. "Any *real* food? We's been eating grubs an' weeds an' shit, an' my belly hurts to fuck..."

WE ENTERED THE ground-level atrium of one of the great spires, through a wall that dissolved upon our approach.

Alien technology.

I looked at Skids and he grinned. Alya inclined her head towards us and said, "This is an ancient city, its creators long since gone. Much of what they left behind still functions. It is a smart city, an intelligent city."

"!¡eager¡! And how much of it functions because it's sung to be so?" asked Skids.

Alya smiled, but didn't reply. Already, I was sensing a continuation of the barriers, an air of reserve about the residents of Harmony. Then I stopped myself: I had just spent the longest time in the close, claustrophobic company of a handful of people. We had been privy to every aspect of each others' lives, seen each other puking and shitting and washing, seen the highs and lows. There had been nothing hidden. Now, back in civilised company, just about anything would seem reserved in comparison.

I smiled back at Alya, and wondered just how filthy and uncouth we must appear to these people.

Inside the building, we passed through a foyer of some kind of exotic polished stone, all cream and pink swirls. Strange grooves and symbols appeared across walls and floor; I knew from the few glimpses I'd had into alien buildings in Laverne that these markings indicated functions, concealed openings, phreak zones, areas that could reconfigure at some ineffable signal or command.

The inner area was an atrium, like a small park. Our four hosts shed their furs, stripping down to light leggings; for the rest of us, it was a strange thing to suddenly feel warmth on our skin and not a sharp chill through our thin clothing.

Alya had dark tattoos that twisted and swirled around her belly and breasts. I tried not to stare, but inevitably my eyes were drawn.

It felt like a dream. A vast, heady dream. The warmth, the exotic landscape of ferny trees and sweet-scented creepers within the building; the gold and blue birds darting amongst the foliage and occasionally pausing to hover in a rainbow-coloured blur; the massive butterflies, jerking and twitching through the air as if tugged by invisible wires; the intense, erotic Alya and her swirling tattoos, and a sensuality that grabs you like only a dream can grab you...

Someone was talking, and I jerked myself back to awareness. Frankhay. Something about the trees, the heat. "!¡embarrassed¡! Hnh, yes," I replied. "It's like another world, isn't it? After the snow and cold outside."

He looked at me oddly, and then I wondered if there was more than just the shock of a changed environment affecting me. I remembered the markings in the foyer and wondered if this building was phreaking us, giving us this sense of dreaminess.

I didn't care.

I felt a loosening of muscles I had not felt in the longest time. As if I was being lifted up and no longer had to support myself.

We sat on a grassy slope and allowed our hosts to ply us with slices of roast meat, salad leaves and even fresh fruit.

It was not until we were seated that I looked up.

The atrium extended upwards as far as I could see, and the twisted ribbon building wrapped around it. This must be one of the tall, helical spires we had seen from afar. Daylight seeped in through the gaps in the outer layers, but not enough to explain the brightness and warmth. It was a dizzying sight, something only an alien could build.

Our hosts wanted to know of the world, and so we took our turns to tell them, and gradually the barriers of reserve fell away. Marek spoke of the final exodus from Angiere; I spoke of Laverne, and of the unsinging of Cragside; Frankhay told them of our escape on his barge.

In their turn, Mazar and Alya, and their two friends, Kedra and Faith, told us of their city.

"We are blessed with the protection of the Singer of the City," said Alya, and I was lost in her eyes in an instant. "All this" – she gestured at the atrium with a hand, and I saw that she had long red nails, like elegantly crafted claws – "is sung to be."

Mazar leaned towards her and continued, "If it were not sung, this great helix would be a shell, just another ruin left by those who created our city."

"But it is sung," continued Alya, and I was struck by their eagerness, by how novel it must be for them to receive visitors from beyond the city. "It is sung and so we are able to live this life."

That was when I recognised this place. I had been somewhere very similar back when I had searched for Skids. I had gone to Constellation, the district where the skystation was to be found, and a wraith had shown me to a building where a 'singer had taken up residence. The grassy slope, the idyllic parkland. Then, a group of small humanoids, like chubby pale children but with high feathery wings, had appeared. Looking around now, I half-expected to see them again, but there was only a butterfly, wobbling in mid-air on gaudy wings.

It was as if this was a stock reality, something a starsinger knew to conjure up because it pressed the right human buttons, made us feel secure, lifted our spirits; an idyll for our kind.

Food and warmth were a combination impossible to argue with.

Mazar and Alya showed us to a row of chambers that opened off from the atrium. There were enough for each of us to have a room, but without consultation we drifted into the largest of the spaces, even Saneth, who had become somewhat distant since our arrival in Harmony.

I dropped to my haunches, then sat, and immediately the floor reformed itself around me, soft like a pit of feathers.

I lay.

I OPENED MY eyes and knew that some considerable time had passed.

And then I sensed the body against mine and I saw that it was Hope, her honeyed hair close to my face, her back and arse curved into me.

I didn't know if this was deliberate on her part, or if, settling close together, we had just drifted into this familiar position in our slumbers.

I moved, and she turned her head.

"!¡*sincere*¡! I'm sorry," I said, although until the words tumbled out, I had not realised that I was. "!¡*self-pity | self-hate*¡! I was scared. I learnt that you were different. I backed away."

There was a silence, then Hope said, "I thought it was me you hated, not you."

This surprised me. I had never heard Hope use click; I didn't think she understood it. And yet she had picked up on the self-loathing in my clicks.

"!¡*struggling to articulate*¡! I didn't hate you," I said. "I didn't *understand* you."

"You have to understand me?"

We fell silent again, and I closed my eyes, and when I opened them again she had edged away from my embrace and I saw that Marek had a hand on her hip, and he was staring at me, and I wondered how long he had watched me as I slept.

Chapter Thirty-Four

"!¡*AUTHORITY*¡! I SAY we send for them," said Marek.

All seven of us sat on a slope in the atrium, and all around us small groups of Harmony's citizens sat and played and talked and laughed.

We had been in Harmony for several days now. Long enough for the blisters and sores of the long hike to be easing; long enough for our stomachs to have lost that constant empty growl.

It was hard to believe that the people of Harmony could live like this, such an easy, comfortable existence, such a complete contrast to the lives we knew. The city's 'singer provided everything.

Our hosts' numbers were hard to estimate. In this spire alone there were hundreds, and we had barely set foot in the rest of the city. Alya and Mazar and the others were welcoming; they had no reason not to be, living in such abundance. They wanted to share all this with us, and their bond with Marek made them all the more attentive. And now he thought it was time to share this further.

"We have been here long enough," he went on. "!¡*persuasive*¡! Every day we stay here without sending word back is another day when your friends and clan-folk are eking out a miserable, cold existence, battling with the elements, scratching for food... They could be dying of starvation, disease, cold. How can you live with that knowledge?"

"!¡*hierarchy*¡! We haven't been here long enough to be sure," said Frankhay. "How do we know it's as good as it seems, eh?"

Marek waved a hand. "!¡*dismissive*¡! Ask your full belly, old man. Then ask your conscience."

"!¡*hierarchy*¡! And what's going to become of us if we stay cosseted like this? Full belly ain't everything."

Jerra spoke up, then. "Full belly dunnat do any of them any harm, does it?"

Frankhay stared at the boy in surprise. "!¡*aggressive*¡! You talk against your clan-father, lad? !¡*dismissive*¡! You leave the talking to the grown-ups, you hear?"

Jerra stood, and he leaned over Frankhay. Suddenly the clan-father looked old and frail in the shadow of the looming, menacing youth. Jerra bunched a fist and held it before Frankhay's face.

"!¡*scared | threatening | violent*¡! You're not my clan-father," he hissed. "Remember? You gave that to Ash. !¡*erratic*¡! Right now you's just an old man. You's got no right tellin' us this place ain't what you want it to be. No right!"

The boy's arm flexed as if he was going to strike Frankhay, but instead he straightened, turned, and strode away down the slope.

I turned back to look at Frankhay, then looked away again, quickly. His face had darkened, his eyes bulged and he was trembling with anger.

"!¡*authority*¡! So we send for them," said Marek, ignoring Frankhay's opposition and the fact that most of us hadn't yet voiced an opinion.

"!¡*curious | probing*¡! Is it that you have a plan of action?" asked Saneth.

Marek turned to the chlick. "!¡*matter-of-fact*¡! We know the way. We can send supplies for the journey. We need someone resourceful and good at following the lie of the land. !¡*decisive*¡! I say we send Dodge."

I stared at him. Was this really just a ruse to get rid of me? Mere jealousy of the time I had spent with Hope again recently?

"!¡*confrontational*¡! We can't just send one person alone," I said. "How about you come with me?"

Marek opened his mouth to answer, but now it was Hope's turn to step in and rescue me.

"We can't stay here," she said. "We can't stay in Harmony, no matter how safe it might seem."

Now all eyes turned on Hope.

"In my dreams," she said, her voice getting small and shaky under scrutiny. "A vast alien ship hangs above the city... a beam comes down, and the city is destroyed, it lies in ruins. We can't stay here. We can't bring everyone here when it's going to be destroyed."

HOPE HAD DREAMED again, since arriving at the city. She wished that it could only be a dream, but she did not believe it to be so.

Before we had arrived in Harmony, she had dreamed of the city, and it had been exactly as she had seen. So why should she doubt the rest of that dream now?

All the time we were there, she had lived in fear that now would be the time when destruction would come, and their great escape from Angiere and Laverne would have been in vain. The image of the city lying in ruins beneath the vast starship was one that stayed with her constantly.

"!¡*dismissive* | *confrontational*¡! How can you know?" demanded Marek.

She shook her head. She had no answer that could convince him.

"!¡*teasing* | *factual reporting*¡! All is known," said Saneth. "That is the problem with the Great All. Knowing and mapping and plotting the All is not hard for a superior race. !¡*patronising*¡! This can be difficult for a junior, underdeveloped race to comprehend. !¡*musing*¡! When all is known, the All is a uniform and flat place."

"!¡*puzzled*¡! You're saying Hope is of a superior race?" I asked.

"!¡*disappointment for junior scholar*¡! Hope is as human as you are. This is a thing that you know. But Hope channels the All in her head. She channels the voices of your kind. She is a conduit to the ones who know."

Hope stood, dizzy from the roar of voices in her head, which forevermore would be associated with images of the wall of people.

She backed away.

She was trying. She had been trying to make them see.

Tears streaming, she turned and ran, and didn't stop until she was out of sight.

IN HER TIME in Harmony, Hope took some comfort in walking, just as she had in Angiere and Laverne. Exploring her surroundings, seeing where people went and what they did. Escape and observation. It was a reflex thing, for someone who did not fit in.

When she fled that discussion, and when she had calmed herself by watching the flow of water in a sparkling stream for a while, she walked from one side of the atrium park to the other. All was open grass, rich green trees, water running in small streams or gathered in lily-covered pools.

In the centre, she paused and looked up.

Dizzied by the perspective, she sat, then lay, and above her the inner spirals of the helical tower were hypnotic.

Eventually, she got up and continued her exploration.

There was a foyer in the far corner, much like the one we had entered by, although she did not think it was the same one. The far wall was a pearly white. She approached the wall and the surface started to ripple, to thin, to separate.

She stepped forward, through, out.

Outside was white.

Instantly, the cold bit through her thin clothing. A fierce wind swirled and swept through the city, driving frozen snow that pelted her skin, stinging and bruising where it struck. And in her head, the voices were wailing, screaming at her.

The buildings all about were in ruins, windows empty, walls crumbling. Snow piled high in deep drifts.

She looked at her skin, and the healthy brown tone now shaded to blue, and she felt sick with the cold.

Peering back up at the great tower, she saw that it too was a ruined shell. Large areas of its skin hung in tatters, revealing girders and fibres beneath. The tower only extended a few storeys before the walls ended in ruins, the whole building a ragged stump.

This was exactly how it had been in her dreams, only... only it was already in ruins. Her dream must have shown her what had already passed, not what was to come.

She almost fell to her knees, but somehow, instead, managed to keep her strength and stagger back towards the wall. Before her, it rippled, thinned, separated, and she staggered through, collapsing on all fours and throwing up with the shock of the warmth on her chilled body.

Out there... in here... which was reality and which was not? Or could they both be real? Her head swirled and she retched again, then slumped, losing consciousness.

She was only out for a short time, but that was long enough for her to be found by a passing citizen, for word to get back to Alya, who found me and brought me to where Hope lay in a reclining seat by a small stream.

Her eyes flitted all about, checking everything, looking for gaps, flaws.

As soon as she saw me, she said, "We have to leave. We can't stay here. It's not safe. But..."

"!¡gentle¡! But what?"

She glanced at Alya, and then back at me. "I've been out," she said. "Outside. It's colder than it ever was, and the wind is fierce, and we wouldn't last at all before we were frozen solid. We have to leave, but we can't, and then when I looked back at the tower and the voices in my head were screaming I saw it in ruins. It was a vision, just like my dream, a vision of what is to come!"

I glanced at Alya, who reached out, put a hand on Hope's bare arm, and said, "Everything is fine. You're safe here. Our safety is sung by the Singer of the City."

"But how do you know the 'singer will always protect you?" demanded Hope. "What will you do if it doesn't?"

* * *

HOPE WAS NOT the only one who saw that there were gaps in the song that protected this strange and magical city.

That night, while Hope was sleeping, Skids and I slipped away from the rest of the group. Hope's story had disturbed me, but more than anything it was the look of fear in her eyes that made me want to find out more.

All around the ground floor of the tower, rooms opened off into the flanks of the building, much like the chambers where we had been spending our nights. In some of these, citizens had made their homes, and as Skids and I passed, they smiled and greeted us and invited us to join them.

As we walked, we talked, and it was as if we hadn't spent years apart. "!¡*fervent*¡! It's like a dream," Skids said at one point, as we entered another glossy foyer. "A city where we have protection, a 'singer devoting an aspect of its All just to us. This place would be nothing without the 'singer, it'd be the ruins Hope saw – the ruins this city used to be. No watchers will get to us here. Not while we have the protection of the Singer of the City."

"!¡*concerned*¡! But how do we ensure that?" I asked. "Surely we're insignificant to a starsinger. So how do we ensure that this protection will last?"

"!¡*factual reporting*¡! You don't make a 'singer do anything," said Skids. "But the 'singers have an interest in us, a strand of their collective All that's dedicated to our well-being. We are significant."

"!¡*argumentative*¡! A starsinger unsung parts of Laverne," I reminded Skids. "A starsinger unsung

Cragside... So either they're not all dedicated to our well-being, or somehow someone *did* make a starsinger do that."

We met a citizen Alya had introduced as Lori. She was short and dark, with the whitest teeth I'd ever seen. She kissed us both on the cheek in greeting and asked how we were settling in, then invited us to drink and sing with her family that evening, if we were around.

As we walked away from her, Skids said, "Did you notice anything other than her tits?"

I laughed and said, "¡¡intrigued¡! Yes, I did. I saw it." I'd seen the marks on others too, the tell-tale signs of the wraith. Lori and some of the others had been under the caul recently. It was hardly a surprise that the citizens of Harmony chose to commune with their 'singer in this way.

"¡¡craving¡! It's been a long time," said Skids, and I wondered just how addictive it was. The caul was an alien symbiont: wear it across your skull and it joins you to the All, but also there's a chemical exchange, a linkage. Wraiths were caul junkies, and my sib still had the need.

We came to another wall with symbols on it, great slashes and curves in a subtly different shade of pearly grey from that of the wall itself. I had always thought these symbols signified function, but I'd been told they were abstract, a kind of art that didn't look like anything real.

When Skids put a hand against the wall, the surface shimmered and thinned, and I realised that this was another opening. He had been here before.

We passed through, and were in a sloping passageway that corkscrewed steeply down to some lower level. The light was dimmer here, emanating from a soft glow in the walls.

I glanced at Skids and was disturbed by the sudden intensity in his look.

As we descended, the air chilled and the light levels dropped. After two complete turns of the ramp we came to an open area. There was a sense of vast space, but it was impossible to see more than a short distance ahead in the gloom.

Skids put a hand on my arm, and I felt that he was trembling. It might only be the chill, I told myself, but I was spooked now, too.

"!¡*concerned | passionate*¡! Can you hear?" asked Skids, his voice little more than a whisper.

I strained. I held my breath. I heard my heart pounding. I heard our movements, a shuffle of feet, a rustle of clothing. A shift in the air, perhaps.

"Hear what?"

"!¡*frustration*¡! When we were in the wall. The voices. The presence of people all around, closing in, crushing."

I remembered my face pressed into flesh, not knowing what flesh it was, and feeling that my mind was the same, pressed hard up against other minds, other presences, not knowing who or what they were, being smothered by them. Every night since then I had experienced nightmares of being trapped in the wall, and I knew that must be what it was like for Hope all of the time, with the voices, the presences, crammed into her head.

I nodded, but then realised Skids probably couldn't see in the gloom, so I clicked, "!¡*agreement*¡!"

"!¡*anguish*¡! It's like that," said Skids. "Can you feel it? A presence. Trapped..."

I couldn't feel anything. I reached for Skids' hand and said, "!¡*reassuring*¡! Come on. Let's get out of here."

We turned and headed back up the passageway.

As we left, I felt a sudden stabbing in my head, like a pain, but a pain I had never known before. A twisting pressure, a spike of emotion, a piercing sensation. And I knew then what Skids had meant.

A presence. A sense of being trapped. Like all the voices in that nightmare wall, all condensed down to a single voice, a child's voice, trapped and alone.

ANOTHER TIME, AN afternoon when I had been sitting by a lily-covered pool, watching the water beetles skittering about on its surface, musing on Frankhay's question: what will become of us if we idle our lives away like this, provided for, not driven to learn and explore and survive? What kind of existence would that be?

Hope found me.

I smiled, still surprised at the lift in my chest when I saw her, when not so long ago I had been appalled by her.

She sat with me.

"!¡*teasing*¡! Marek let you go?"

She glared. She had told me about him, about his possessiveness, about being with him in Angiere, and that explained why he acted so jealously now.

"No one lets me go anywhere," she snapped, and then I was struck again by something in her, in the way she spoke, and I decided to ask her.

"!¡*curious*¡! I've never heard you use click," I said. "When you speak. I know you understand it, but it's just not something you do."

She thought about it.

"I... I didn't realise. It's just how I speak."

"!¡*factual*¡! Click's not a language," I said. "It's a gut thing. It says what you're feeling. It's *really* hard to fake or mislead someone with click. If you don't click, you don't expose yourself."

"It's not deliberate!" said Hope, eyes suddenly wide, loaded with tears. "I'm not trying to hide..."

"!¡*calm | reassuring*¡! I know. So why?"

"Maybe I never learnt..."

I nodded, then added, "And maybe it's a defence, a barrier. Something that protects you from revealing your true nature."

She looked at me. Up until that point I hadn't even been sure that she knew that she was so different, that in the purely physical sense she was not one of us.

"!¡*reassuring | tender*¡! It's okay. It's okay."

That was when I put my hands to her head, tipped her face back, and kissed her, softly, tenderly.

Our first kiss seemed so long ago, sitting on the rock by our encampment that time, as night shaded into morning and Hope had kissed me on the jaw and I had been too shocked, too surprised by my own reactions, too fucking dumb, to react.

So much had happened since then.

So now we kissed and it was a first time, all over again.

WE SAT, MY arm behind her, knuckles resting on the soft ground, the pad of my hand against the gentle swell of her butt.

"If I spoke click..." said Hope, resting her head on my shoulder. "You'd know that this is what I want, what I've wanted. You'd have known it all along."

"!¡*struggling to articulate*¡! I didn't know this was what I wanted," I told her. "Or I did, but I was scared. Scared by what's in your head. Scared by what's in mine, by my reactions, by my stupid pig-headedness."

"Why did you ask? Why did you ask now, about the way I speak?"

I straightened, and turned to face her.

"!¡*teasing out a truth*¡! Click exposes you," I said again. "It opens you up, lays you bare before the world. It betrays you."

I looked around, at the lilies, the water-beetles, at the lush green foliage of the trees, the twisting trumpet vines hanging heavy with rich blue flowers. A bird called from the trees, a fluting trill.

"!¡*musing*¡! They don't use click here," I said. "The citizens of Harmony. Have you noticed? No click."

"I hadn't really noticed," said Hope.

"!¡*matter-of-fact*¡! It's not obvious," I said. "We take it for granted. But when you do notice it, it really stands out. And when you do, you can't help but wonder that if they're that scared of betraying themselves, then what is it that they're scared to reveal? What are they hiding?"

Chapter Thirty-Five

SKIDS TOLD ME later that Frankhay and Jerra had been arguing again, earlier that afternoon, which explained the heavy atmosphere and sullen, angry looks when Hope and I returned to the open area by our shared dorm.

At first I thought it was just Marek, glowering at the two of us, but by the time I realised there was something more it was too late.

Saneth and Frankhay were standing together, deep in conversation. The ancient chlick seemed reinvigorated in the warmth of Harmony. I wasn't sure whether to join them or not, but as I hesitated, the chlick inclined towards me and said, "¡¡*demonstrating to foolish junior scholar*¡! Here is one who is young and yet does not have a head that is consumed with resentment."

Frankhay glared at me, and I wondered what I had done wrong, then realised that it was something else, and nothing to do with me.

"¡¡*frustrated*¡! Will none of you listen?" the clan-father demanded. "He's changed. Jerra's different now. He's not the boy he was on our journey. He's got delusions of power. He sees an opportunity to take me out and establish himself as a... I don't know. I don't know what he wants, but he's turned against me. It's like he says: he thinks I'm tryin' to persuade everyone

373

not to trust this place, when all I'm doin' is trying to make the right judgements."

"!¡*angry* | *confrontational*¡! But you are," hissed Jerra, appearing from a gap in the bushes, a part-concealed path. I wondered how long he'd been listening in.

Frankhay rounded on him, jabbing the air with a finger. "!¡*hierarchy* | *angry*¡! You need to remember where your place is," he snapped. "You need to not get above yourself."

Frankhay had kept tight control of the command structures of the Hay clan back in Laverne. It was shocking to see this unravelling so dramatically before us now.

Jerra stepped forward, so that Frankhay's pointing finger was almost touching his forehead, and suddenly this made the older man look comical, a fool.

Jerra looked strong, menacing. He laughed at Frankhay; just a chuckle, but it carried more meaning than any words, any click.

"!¡*victorious*¡! Accept it, old man," he said. "Your time has passed. We've found a safe place to stay. We'll bring the others. We don't need you any more."

There was a click, not from Frankhay's throat but from his wrist.

It was a sound I'd heard close-up before, the sound made when the blade concealed within Frankhay's wrist flicked out, stabbed forward.

The dagger blade emerged, a flash of metal, and entered Jerra's forehead.

The boy slumped, and Frankhay staggered forward, suddenly taking Jerra's weight on the blade. It was too much for him to support, and Jerra fell to his knees, and the blade slid out, slick and red.

Still on his knees, Jerra looked puzzled more than anything else. A small red spot marked the centre of his forehead. As I watched, the spot swelled, budded, and then a line of blood tracked down the bridge of his nose and over his mouth and chin.

He tipped back onto his heels, then splayed and fell backwards, dead.

Frankhay dropped to his knees, sobbing, and it wasn't clear whether the stab had been a deliberate impulse or an accident.

Saneth stood to one side, false eye swivelling constantly, taking everything in.

Then the old alien stepped towards Jerra's fallen form, and stooped.

The boy's eyes were wide open, staring.

Saneth reached towards Jerra's face and I thought the chlick was going to close the boy's eyes, but instead, with a jerk of one clawed finger, Saneth flipped at something.

I couldn't see what it was, but then Saneth repeated the action, and a transparent blob peeled away from Jerra's eye.

The thing landed on the short grass, and then flattened to a disk, a membrane spread thin, and appeared to dissolve into the grass.

Saneth's eye swivelled around the gathering. "¡¡*factual reporting*¡! It was a watcher. The boy played host to a watcher."

INSTINCTIVELY, WE EDGED away from Jerra, and from the patch of grass where the watcher had disappeared.

Then Marek burst forward, dropped to his knees, and started scraping at the ground.

I reached for him and hauled him back, and the two of us fell, exhausted, on the ground nearby, me holding Marek by the shoulders, both of us breathing raggedly.

Marek grunted.

I looked up, and saw Frankhay standing over us, one boot placed hard on Marek's chest. The clan-father leaned forward, elbow on the knee of that leg, the blade still protruding from his wrist, red with Jerra's blood.

"¡*controlled menace*¡! So," said Frankhay, "you gonna tell us what exactly it was you were just tryin' to do? Eh?"

I hadn't really thought about it. Had he been trying to catch the thing? Kill it? I looked from Frankhay to Marek and back again, and then I scrambled to my knees, keeping a firm grip on one of Marek's shoulders, keeping him pinned to the ground.

"¡*vicious*¡! You got one of 'em, too, have you?" asked Frankhay. He leaned closer to Marek now, and a tear fell, hit the blade, and ran red down to the tip.

Frankhay had killed one of his own.

He had thought it a simple clash for power, but we now knew that the boy had been carrying a watcher, looking through his eyes, controlling him.

Which was worse? Killing Jerra in straight confrontation, or killing him by mistake?

Marek's body bucked, but we had him held firmly.

"¡*menace*¡! You got one, too, eh? We gonna have to cut it out?"

Frankhay pointed the blade at Marek's left eye, so close that his captive stopped trying to break free for fear of impaling himself.

Marek started to sob. "¡*terror*¡! No. I haven't got one. They promised me, but I haven't got one."

"¡*surprised | outraged*¡! 'They'?" I asked. "Who? Why?"

"!¡*scared* | *pleading*¡! Mazar. Alya. The watchers here aren't Hadeen. They want to protect us. Carry a watcher and you're safe. We all need that. But I don't have one!"

"!¡*matter-of-fact*¡! The hosting of a non-Hadeen watcher did not afford Jerra much protection," observed Saneth. "!¡*leading junior scholar*¡! Did you consider that the offer of protection may be dishonest, and that the non-Hadeen watchers are more concerned with taking control of the host?"

"!¡*despair*¡! They promised me," said Marek, in a cracked, broken voice.

"!¡*brutal*¡! Why should we believe him?" said Frankhay. "If the watchers are controlling these people like this, then how do we know it's not jus' a watcher makin' him say that?"

I realised then that I believed Marek, regardless of the logic behind Frankhay's words. All it had taken to control Marek was a promise to sway him, an offer of a privileged position the rest of us did not have, an offer of power. He was weak enough, ambitious enough, to leap at an offer like that.

But Frankhay was demanding proof.

Saneth intervened. The chlick leaned over Marek and fixed him with a stare from her-his artificial eye.

"!¡*factual reporting*¡! This one's eyes are clear," said Saneth. "He hosts no watcher over his eyes, as Jerra did. There is no indication of interference that this lauded one can detect."

"!¡*uncertain*¡! What about inside?" I asked. I remembered that time, years before, when Skids had taken to making himself vomit, and we had thought him mad. But then after we had driven him to flee, I had puked up my own watcher from within, and I had understood his distress.

"!¡*matter-of-fact*¡! There is no indication," said Saneth.

Frankhay moved his wrist-dagger down until its tip was pressing hard against the skin beneath Marek's chin.

One false move on either part and Marek would be dead.

"!¡*menacing*¡! Which still leaves us a pretty dilemma," said Frankhay. "You may not be carryin' a watcher, but that's not because you didn't want to. A shit-poor traitor's still a fuckin' traitor."

I saw the muscles in his arm flex, and Marek winced.

I relaxed my grip on Marek's shoulder, then, and instead put a hand on Frankhay's wrist.

"!¡*calming*¡! Come on," I said. "Leave it."

I moved back, and rose to my feet. Now, looking down at Frankhay as he leaned low over his captive, I met the clan-father's eyes again and saw that the moment had passed.

I looked at Marek and didn't know whether there was gratitude or resentment in his eyes.

And then, crashing through the trees with a bulbous purple caul wrapped around his head, came Skids, groaning and mumbling in words that could not be distinguished, drool trailing from his mouth and his eyes staring mad.

I STOPPED HIM, took him in my arms, smothering him with a jabber of soothing, calming clicks.

"!¡*concern | alarm*¡! What is it?" I asked. "What's happened, sib?"

He stared at me, then jerked free, stumbled, sprawled on his knees.

Frankhay went to him, flipped him onto his back and started tugging at the caul.

Hope clawed at the clan-father, trying to stop him. "No! If you pull it off you'll kill him!"

Frankhay eased back.

"!¡*calming*¡! What is it, Skids? What happened?"

My old sib peered up at us, his hands wrapped protectively around his cauled head. "!¡*shocked | outraged*¡! Their 'singer," he said. "The Singer of the City... It's not their guardian. It's their *prisoner*!"

Chapter Thirty-Six

SKIDS HAD RECOGNISED the marks of cauls on the heads of the citizens of Harmony.

He had gone under the caul back in Laverne. He had been hooked on the symbiotic relationship with the caul, almost so hooked he had never emerged, the fate of so many wraiths. He had learned moderation just in time, though, had learned to balance the highs of communion against the need to survive in the physical realm.

But the pull would always be there, a chemical pull in his blood that never died.

That day, he had followed Alya to a room that was not her home, and there he had seen a tank containing a colony of growing cauls.

When she had gone, he broke into the room – another of the skills he had learned in his time living on the streets of Constellation – opened the tank and took a caul for himself.

He would commune with the Singer of the City. He would find that ethereal high once again.

Barricading himself into a room off one of the foyers, he took the caul and draped it over his head. Instantly, he felt the suckers binding, the needle-like tendrils prising holes in his skin, the sudden rush as the caul entered him, infusing his blood with its phreaked excretions.

A starsinger's presence should flood your senses. It should burst into your perception in full chorus, swamping your senses with the All, a single, snapshot explosion of all that is within the 'singer's demesne.

The human mind cannot grasp this.

The human mind can only perceive a minuscule fraction of what it is to be a starsinger.

To the starsinger the All is known, but a human can only know that it is known.

The caul is a bridge between what the human mind can know and what it can know to be known, and it does this in a perception-blowing mind-fuck of a brain-chemical rush that shatters most who come to know it.

The presence of Harmony's starsinger when Skids donned the caul was a mere whimper, a presence smothered by a layer of... Skids didn't know what. Something had deadened the 'singer. Something had confined it.

"!¡*distraught*¡! Do you remember that voice, Dodge? Down in the level below ground. That was it, the 'singer, trying to get through to us."

"!¡*struggling to grasp*¡! What's happened to it?" I asked. "Why is the 'singer like this?"

"!¡*indignant*¡! It's trapped. Imprisoned. Somehow they've controlled it, the people here. Somehow they've got it contained, and they're using its powers to keep this bubble reality going to protect them."

"!¡*factual reporting*¡! Not them," I told Skids. "The citizens of Harmony are being controlled by watchers."

"If a starsinger can create realities," said Hope in a quiet voice, "how do they control a starsinger?"

I had been wondering the same thing.

Saneth stepped forward and commanded our attention. "!¡*teaching junior scholar*¡! If the real can be unsung," the chlick said, "then so, too, can the known be unknown. The starsinger can only sing the known."

"!¡*earnest*¡! What doesn't it know?" I asked.

"!¡*factual reporting*¡! You," said Saneth. "All of you. Humankind carries a spark of difference to all that is known. A latecomer, a novelty. The 'singers suppress you, but they are a guardian race, they would do you no harm. But you are unknown, unpredictable. You stop the song of the All."

The chlick turned to Hope, then. "!¡*non-confrontational | gentle*¡! You are an experiment, Hope Burren. The Hadeen watchers would eradicate the unknowable in order to preserve an order in the All; the non-Hadeen would use the unknowable to control the known. Condense a mass of humankind, the spirit, the soul even, and it is as a weapon against those who rely on all being known."

"!¡*understanding*¡! The starsingers," I said. "A weapon against the 'singers."

"!¡*approving*¡! You, Hope Burren, are a bridge to that condensate. In your head you carry a non-Hadeen watcher, a benign morph whose only function is to act as that bridge, channel those presences."

I saw the wave of revulsion that passed around our small group when Saneth said Hope carried a watcher, saw the reflex movement of Frankhay's dagger arm.

"It's me?" said Hope. "I'm the one imprisoning the starsinger?"

"!¡*matter-of-fact*¡! Not you," said Saneth. "But one, or many, like you. You are not the first experiment of this nature."

"!¡*practical*¡! How do we free the starsinger?" I asked.

Saneth paused, and then finally answered. "!¡*bearing an unpopular truth*¡! The starsinger will be freed when the condensate of humankind is destroyed. If there is no condensate then those of the nature of Hope Burren cannot channel it and contain the 'singer."

Chapter Thirty-Seven

"!¡*TENTATIVE* | *MUSING*¡! So what is this mass of humanity?" I asked. "The condensate. Is it *us*? Are you telling us the only way we can free the starsinger is by destroying humankind?"

"!¡*disappointment for junior scholar* | *frustrated*¡! If it were humankind, that is what I would call it and not something else," chided Saneth. "!¡*instructing junior scholar*¡! The condensate is the essence of you. It is all of you.

"Humankind is a novelty, a new race which emerged long after all was known, all colonised, all niches filled. There was no space for a new sentience to emerge, and yet humankind evolved to fill the gaps."

I looked around our small group, and wondered how much longer our kind would have.

"!¡*matter-of-fact*¡! While the Hadeen-watchers would wipe you out as an affront to the order of the All, the non-Hadeen have been harvesting you, mapping and indexing and organising you."

"!¡*impatient*¡! To use as a threat against the starsingers," said Skids. "To control them. But how? How have they done this?"

"!¡*instructing junior scholar*¡! It is in your blood," said Saneth. "They read you, map you, capture the essence of what it is to be human."

I understood. I knew what Saneth was leading up to.

"!¡*dawning comprehension*¡! Our pids," I said. "That's how they capture us!"

"!¡*approval for junior scholar*¡! That is the mechanism."

"So how do we destroy it?" I asked. "The condensate. Where is it?"

Saneth paused, before finally saying, "!¡*difficult truth*¡! It is in the All. It runs through the All. It is..." – another pause – "!¡*frustration | struggle to articulate*¡! Your language does not have an adequate concept even to allude. How to eradicate something that is embedded in the fabric of the All...?"

THAT NIGHT WE reverted to the ways of the journey.

We settled together in the largest of the rooms allocated to us, and posted guards through the night. Suddenly this paradise felt like a prison.

The citizens of Harmony had left us alone that evening. This was not unusual, but still it felt as if they knew that we knew. Every small detail cranked up our paranoia.

I managed to doze a little, and then it was my turn to take watch.

I found my way to the room's arched doorway carefully, even though I knew the others weren't sleeping either.

Outside, the atrium was lit by a soft glow from high up in the spire. Trees clumped in dark blobs, a few flowers picked out as if luminescent. Frogs piped from the waterways and bats flitted through the shadows. It was like the most peaceful of summer evenings.

Frankhay sat a short distance away on the grass.

There was something about his pose that looked awkward, and I approached tentatively.

Closer to, I saw that he sat with elbows on knees, one hand supporting his chin. The hand with the dagger blade.

I rushed to him, dropped to my knees, reached out...

The whites of Frankhay's eyes flashed as they turned to me.

He dropped his hand, said nothing, and I settled back on my heels, calming myself.

After a time, Frankhay said, "!¡*grieving*¡! I raised him. Him and Ash. Lots of the kids in the Hays were orphans, street kids. We took 'em in, fed and washed and schooled 'em. I was close to 'em all, but those two... I didn't favour 'em because they were like me, none of that crap. I favoured 'em because they could have been so much better."

He waved his hand and there was that soft click and the blade emerged.

"!¡*angry | regret*¡! An' what good does it do 'em?" he went on. "I leave Ash in the middle of a fuckin' great forest, with that shit-head Herald up against her, an' I let Jerra get infected with watchers and then kill him because I think he's turned against me."

He jabbed the blade at his neck so hard it drew blood. "!¡*anguished*¡! This is what I deserve, but it's too good, too easy. I need to do something right, lad, d'you hear me? I need to make amends."

I nodded.

"!¡*determined*¡! We'll free the trapped human spirits," I said. "The condensate. And that will free the starsinger." For I'd realised that the condensate wasn't just some facsimile of our kind, a human mind-map: it was far more than that. Hope had been experiencing the condensate's anguish in her head, the chorus of voices; I had felt it when I rode with her in Saneth's commensal and our minds had touched; we had all felt it when we fought our way through that abominable wall of flesh.

All of our kind was trapped, just as the starsinger was.

And I had just worked out how we might free them.

LATE IN THE night, just as the light in the atrium was beginning to lift, Hope and I stood with Saneth by a pool fringed with hanging trees.

"!¡*tentative*¡! You say the way to free the starsinger is to destroy the condensate," I said, and Saneth inclined her-his body in agreement. "It's the condensate that is the problem for the starsingers – throwing together the boiled-down essence of humankind in the fabric of the All to undermine them, stifling them with the unknown."

"!¡*approving*¡!"

"Yet the condensate..." I went on. "Hope feels it, all the time. I've felt it. It's real. It's not just a copy of what we are – it's more than that. We can't just destroy something so... so *human*."

I saw from the look on Hope's face, as I spoke, that this was true.

Saneth turned to Hope, and said, "!¡*gentle*¡! Would you have the voices stilled?"

Hope looked from the chlick to me, and back again. "I... I always wanted them to be gone. I'd have given anything to have them sucked out of my head. I still would. But Dodge is right. The voices aren't in my head,

I'm hearing them from elsewhere, from the condensate. I would never *kill* them just for a quiet head!"

"!¡intrigued¡! So what does the scholar pup propose?" asked Saneth.

"!¡bold¡! Well," I said, "what if we could put them somewhere else instead?"

EVEN THEN, IT was hard to think badly of Harmony.

We knew it was a reality conjured up by an imprisoned starsinger, one tortured and smothered with a blanket of the unknown. We knew that Harmony's citizens had been taken over, good people like Mazar and Alya who Marek had known in Angiere, now infested with alien watchers.

And yet... the air smelled sweet, the light was pure, the trees rich and green, the flowers vivid. We were surrounded by the calls of birds and frogs. Butterflies and slender damselflies flopped and darted. Fish flashed bronze and silver in the waterways.

It was Hope who first realised we were being observed, that morning.

We sat in the open by our dorm rooms, discussing what lay ahead. Hope sat slightly apart, knees drawn up to her chin. The voices in her head were a low murmur, a susurrus. She was not scared. She was not daunted.

And then she saw a pattern in the screen of leaves and vines just across the pool: eyes, the line of a nose, a mouth. And as the image emerged, it could not be unseen.

One of the citizens was hiding in the bushes.

As soon as she had seen one, she saw others. She wondered how long they might have been there, whether they were always loitering in the undergrowth, observing, whether they had done that ever since Hope's group had arrived.

She caught my eye, gestured with a nod of the head, and it was a moment before the pattern resolved for me, too, and I saw the observers.

"!¡*alert*¡! We have company," I said, and conversation tailed off.

Alya emerged from the trees. Small and slim, wearing only a short wraparound skirt, her bare skin a swirl of tattoos. She smiled, and around her Mazar and about a dozen others emerged from the trees.

"!¡*controlled aggression*¡! Okay," said Frankhay, coming to stand with me as I rose to my feet. "So what do we do now?"

We could fight, but Frankhay didn't need to point out that defeating the human host didn't defeat the watchers they carried.

"!¡*authority | alert*¡! Hope, Skids," I hissed. Then, addressing Frankhay, I said, "!¡*deferential*¡! What can you do to buy us time? Any ideas?"

Alya still stood a short distance away, smiling. As I looked at her, her eyes appeared to bulge and it was as if the watchers were taunting us, showing themselves to us, no longer any need to hide.

"!¡*commanding*¡! Go now," said Saneth. "Frankhay? Marek? We will do what is necessary."

With that, the old chlick stepped towards Alya and the others. Frankhay and Marek stood shoulder to shoulder with the ancient chlick. "!¡*taunting*¡! When you play with the unknown you can never really know," she-he said.

I edged back with Hope and Skids to the fringe of the atrium where our rooms were. We had to get to the starsinger. We had to put a stop to this.

"!¡*urgent*¡! How do we do it, Skids? Where do we go?"

"!¡*calm | determined*¡! We need to go under the caul," he said. "All of us."

I glanced at Hope, then nodded. We had discussed this earlier; we knew what a risky thing it was.

But our way was blocked. To get to the cauls, we had to cross the atrium, and right now that would mean getting past the citizens of Harmony. I looked from my friends and then back out into the gentle parkland of the spire's interior.

Frankhay stood with his dagger-blade protruding, daring anyone to take him on. Marek looked uncertain, but he had gone with them, joined them when he could have fled.

And Saneth...

Saneth sang.

Saneth stood in that clearing with arms spread wide and her-his song swelled and filled the air.

I backed away until I was hard against the wall.

Marek and Frankhay had dropped to their knees, as had some of the citizens.

And then I saw the watchers bulging in the citizens' eye-sockets again, swelling, popping clear, slivers of jelly, near-transparent, glistening in the morning light of the atrium.

They flowed down faces, down bodies, leaving their hosts buckling and collapsing.

A mass of clear jelly gathered on the ground before Saneth, and I thought she-he had won, did not realise then that the ancient chlick was merely buying time.

The mass gathered itself, congealed. A bulge rose from it, the form of a head, neck, shoulders. They rose, pulling a shawl of clear jelly with them, jelly that took form, became arms, torso, hips. The figure rose, towering above Saneth, a giant humanoid form whose face bore no features and whose body was a model of androgynous perfection.

It disintegrated, collapsing in an abrupt flow of individual watchers, an alien shower descending on Saneth, Marek and Frankhay, knocking them from their feet, and they were lost in the gluey mess; lost, I felt sure, forever.

Exogenesis

Chapter Thirty-Eight

"THIS WAY," HISSED Hope, tugging at my arm.

Skids and I followed her, and we worked our way along the wall until we reached a foyer.

We ran at the far wall and it rippled, thinned, spat us out.

The cold hit us, battered the breath from our bodies.

I breathed out, and when I tried to breathe back in again the air was so cold it felt as if it was stripping the lining from my throat and lungs. I put a hand to my mouth, and that allowed me to breathe, but the bare flesh felt as if it were freezing hard already.

Hope gestured, and started to move away.

The world outside the spire was white. Just as Hope had described it, snow piled in high drifts and swirled in the air and our thin clothes offered us no protection against the bitter chill.

I tried to move, but already my boots had frozen to the hard-packed snow.

I heaved and managed to shift one boot, and then the other.

My breath froze in the light fuzz of facial hair I had grown on our journey; my saliva froze on my lips. I kept my eyes slitted for fear that they, too, would freeze.

Ahead, Hope moved determinedly, small and hunched over against the blizzard.

The outer wall of the spire curved gently, and we worked our way through the snow, following the building's base. We had escaped, but we could not survive out here for long. Our best chance was to find another way back in on the far side of the building, closer to where Skids had found the cauls. After a time, we came to a great groove, as wide as a human body, and I realised this was one of the joins between the wide ribbon-walls that wrapped around the tower.

We came to a bank of snow that was taller than any of us, and now Skids and I caught up with Hope.

She paused for breath, then launched herself at the snow, plunging her hands and feet into it and hauling herself up. Skids and I followed. My hands were already numbed by the cold, and now I saw that they were bloodied, torn to shreds by the packed snow and ice, the blood freezing instantly.

At the top of the snow drift we walked for a short distance, then slid down the far side, and here Hope turned to an expanse of blank wall and said, "It's an entrance. It has to be." She was close to collapse.

The wall stood blank before us.

I approached, raised a hand, as if that would make any difference.

At first there was nothing and then, thank the gods, there was a ripple, a thinning.

We tumbled through and lay on the smooth, warm floor as we thawed out. I looked at my damaged hands and saw that Skids had suffered similar injuries. Hope's hands had been scraped raw, too, exposing twists of pale fibre, no blood. She looked at them, and then at me, and then we stood, turned to the foyer, and looked for a way through into the atrium.

* * *

WE TOOK THREE cauls from the tanks, in a room not far from where we had re-entered the tower. Skids selected them and handed one each to me and Hope before taking one for himself.

The thing in my hands was a livid purple, and felt like a slab of meat with a tough, leathery skin. It glistened in the low light, and I expected it to be wet and slimy, but it was dry.

As I held the caul it responded to my touch, swelling around my hands, pressing and scuffing, as if tasting me, sampling me.

Going under the caul was not a thing to do lightly. The chemical rush alone could stun a user into a coma from which they might never emerge; the sensorial shock of embracing the starsinger's window into the All could break minds.

But we had to get through to the Singer of the City.

"!¡*scared* | *decisive*¡! Where do we do this?" I asked Skids.

"!¡*factual reporting*¡! Best is as close as possible to the 'singer," he said. "I just shut myself in one of the rooms off the atrium, but it was weak... The 'singer is really stifled and all its energy is going into maintaining this reality."

"You heard it," said Hope, to me. "You went underground and heard it. That's what you said."

WE SLIPPED AWAY from the caul tank and threaded our way through the fringes of the atrium park, fearful that at any moment we would be confronted by the citizens of Harmony, or by the monstrous reconstituted alien that had smothered Saneth, Frankhay and Marek.

We found the foyer, found the wall with the strange symbols, or artwork, or whatever it was, and descended the spiral ramp.

Darkness again, but the cauls gave off a dim glow. We couldn't see far, but we could see each other, and where our feet fell.

I strained, but caught no hint of the 'singer's presence.

We paused, and I asked, "Where now?" and in the dim light from the cauls I saw Skids shrug.

Then Hope clutched at my arm and I saw that her eyes were wide. "The voices," she said. "I can't hear for them, they're so loud!"

She put hands to her head, dropping her caul with a dull thud. Skids ducked to grab it quickly, and I held Hope as she weakened, and then it was only me holding her up as all strength departed from her legs.

WE HAD NO choice. We had to go through with it. We knew the risks and we had agreed that this was what we would do.

Skids gave me one of the cauls, and then he kneeled by Hope.

She was still conscious, still breathing, eyes sometimes shut, sometimes snapping open and dancing wildly up and down and from side to side.

He smoothed her honey-brown hair back and carefully eased the caul onto the crown of her head.

It spread out immediately, its body thinning, clinging, wrapped like a wet cloth around her skull. In the low light I could see the alien symbiont pulsing rapidly, its purple hue shifting in waves towards a fiery crimson.

"!¡urgent¡! Quick!" said Skids. "She can't be alone."

He took a caul from me and without any preparation pressed it to his head. He rocked back onto his haunches and his eyes widened, glazed. A smile spread across his face, a junkie with a fresh hit, and then he slumped to the ground.

I DID IT.

I raised the thing and I slapped it to the crown of my head, and I felt the All in a sudden, dizzying rush.

THE CAUL STUCK to me, with a grip that might never let go. Needles stabbed my scalp. Sharp pains – I hadn't expected this pain! – lanced through my skull and down my neck. And something happened that felt as if all my perceptions, all that I had ever perceived, had been put together and shaken up and left to settle, seen and felt and heard all over again, but more intensely so, and my head spun and I felt sick and I knew I was crying, crying, crying.

Skids had described the Singer of the City as a mere whimper, a hollow, retiring presence. But something had woken it, something had stirred it up. I could not believe that what struck me next was only a shadow of the real thing.

A sudden blast took me, and I felt like a wisp-seed in a gale. All my bundled perceptions were gone, and I was numbed for a time, deadened. And then the blast came again, and again, and I was a bloodied, broken fighter whose legs would not give in, pounded and battered and beaten. With every wave that swept over me, my head was left ringing, booming, and my body was a single dull mass of pain.

And the blast came again, and again.

I CAME TO on a floating platform of wood, all twisted and gnarled as if partly cut from trees and partly made from driftwood washed up from the river. The wood was white with dark knots in it, the floor smooth, polished.

Overhead hung a great sphere, swirls of white like foam smeared across the deepest blue.

I had seen images like this before. This was our home planet, hanging above us.

My mind rushed, but I didn't care about explanations, was just thankful for the reprieve.

"!¡*calming*¡! Thank... you came through," said Skids, and I looked around, away from the hanging Earth, and saw my old friend sitting cross-legged nearby.

"!¡*fear | concern*¡! Where's Hope?"

Skids looked down. "!¡*concern*¡! I can't find her. This is a bubble reality where the 'singer has confined us. I think it may have cordoned Hope off somewhere else. It's scared of her. She channels so much that it can't know."

"We have to find her," I said.

"!¡*factual reporting*¡! We have to find the starsinger first," said Skids.

He stood, and so did I.

The tangled wooden landscape seemed to go on forever, a dead forest, a ghost forest. "!¡*dismayed*¡! How do we find anything here?"

"!¡*calming*¡! We listen for the song," said Skids, and we started to walk.

"¡*intrigued*¡! What *is* this? A 'bubble reality', you said?"

"¡*factual reporting*¡! We're in our heads," said Skids. "But it's more than that, it's a shared thing. Our heads are channelled through to the All that the starsingers know. But we can't know what they know... They see things differently; they see things so much more deeply, more precisely. Everything is known to them, and these realities are their attempts to sketch out part of the All in terms we can understand."

"¡*contradiction*¡! But not everything is known to them," I said. "We're not. The voices in Hope's head..."

"¡*factual reporting*¡! She scares them. They can handle small levels of uncertainty, but massed together in the condensate it's too much. It's a fundamental shock to them. Saneth says the starsingers are like gods even to gods, but Hope brings them to their knees."

We walked, over roots and branches, for a time that seemed immeasurable.

I listened, but all I heard were our footfalls and breathing.

I longed to know what had become of Hope. She could be lying dead on that basement floor, for all I knew, and I would have lost her and this whole thing would be in vain.

I started to despair and then I heard the song, a child's voice, humming the kind of tune we learnt as small children back in the nest.

It came from beyond a screen of ragged tree stumps, shining a harsh white in the light of the Earth.

We scrambled up over the tangled wood until we could peer over, but the next hollow was empty.

I climbed over the stumps, clambered down to ground level again, and then I kept crawling, kept tumbling, as wood splintered, fragmented, and the ground dissolved beneath me, and the child's song rose to a sing-song screech that filled my head and made my skull feel as if it were about to shatter.

Chapter Thirty-Nine

I WAS IN water. Thick, impenetrable water. I couldn't breathe and my lungs were on fire. I opened my eyes but I couldn't see. I tried to move and it was as if my limbs were cast in clay.

I was dying. I was drowning, and I would die, and in that last glimmer of life I knew that this was brain overload, the caul overpowering my feeble mind... that I would end up in a coma, or dead, and all would be lost.

I burst to the surface, or the surface burst around me, and I was in Laverne again, lying on my back in the middle of a street, the crowded tenements of Cragside looming around me, far more closely than they ever had in reality.

And there, in the windows, were faces, faces masked with tattoos; only, I knew these people, I recognised them.

One of them smiled, and it was Alya, and then on a nearby roof there was the towering figure of Mazar, naked, powerful, and holding a great slab of masonry over his head.

He hurled it and I watched it grow, and then I realised it was heading straight for me.

Still befuddled by my near-drowning, I managed to drag myself away to the side. The masonry hit the ground and exploded, fragments peppering my body.

I peered all around, but I was alone, no sign of Skids.

I saw them at the windows, descending through the buildings. A door opened and a tattooed man emerged, his body all slabs of muscle, limbs gliding easily. A woman followed him, carrying a metal club.

I backed away, but had nowhere to go.

"!¡*earnest*¡! Listen to me!" I cried. "Listen to my story. A story you don't know..."

They wavered, rippled like the wall that was a door, back in the central spiral tower of Harmony.

"A story you're scared of. I can help you know it. *We* can help you know it."

TANGLED WOOD, ALL around me. A cage of twisted branches and roots polished white, twining together to contain me.

I heard a voice, a tiny voice singing songs from my childhood.

Perched on a stump nearby, outside my cage, there was a child. It could have been a boy or a girl, naked, its chubby features androgynous, its genitals obscured by crossed legs. Tucked up behind its back was a pair of feathery wings.

It was not a child, I reminded myself. It was the starsinger. Or rather, it was a manifestation of the 'singer, an embodiment cast in a form I could understand.

"!¡*tentative | respectful*¡! I have a story," I told it, and its face lit up. "Something new."

BACK IN THE atrium, when Saneth had explained that the starsingers could not handle the unknown when it was concentrated into what she-he called the condensate...

Back then, I had recalled Marek's impassioned speech from earlier on our journey, when we had been debating whether to continue the search for Harmony or not. He had argued that humankind had no history, because no one recorded our story. We lived second-hand lives borrowed from alien culture, rather than establishing a life that was truly human. *Harmony is a place for us to learn to be human.* And Saneth had said that Harmony was where we could find our own story.

Back in the atrium, Saneth had told us that the only way to free the captive starsinger was to destroy the human condensate, for that was what the watchers were using to keep the being trapped.

And so now, held captive in a cage of wood, by a starsinger who was itself a captive, I said, "!¡*musing*¡! My kind has a story. A huge and rich story. It's not known to you, and so it's being used to bind you here. What would happen if you were to sing our story for us?"

Hope was a channel to the condensate: that was what her mind had been built to do, and that was why the starsinger feared her. "!¡*explaining*¡! I know someone. Someone who came here with me. Her mind is a channel to the minds of my kind, embedded in the All. What if, rather than imprisoning her, you were to cast another reality altogether and use Hope's mind to channel the condensate there? A new realm. A new Great All."

The feather-winged child sat on its perch, watching me with its head tipped a little to one side.

And still, it sang.

Chapter Forty

HOPE KNEW THAT the risks were high, particularly for her. The caul was risky enough, but she knew she was made differently. It could kill her, or it could do nothing at all.

The thing wrapped itself around her head and sank itself through her skin. Something was happening.

She felt each tendril as a pin prick, felt each fleshy tube penetrate, probe, start to pump its juices under her scalp.

She felt all this very consciously, and that was when she thought it was not going to work, but then it started to, started to seep across her perception of the dimly-lit basement area around her, blurring out the ill-lit faces of me and Skids.

WHEN SHE CAME to, she barely came to at all.

She was conscious, because she could think, although it seemed that even her thoughts were slow, each shape, each word taking years to pull together.

She had no feeling in her body, no sense of hot or cold, no sense of movement, even the shifting of her chest as she breathed. There were no sounds, not even the beating of her heart. No sight, no light, nothing to see.

Nothing at all, except the thoughts, the very slow thoughts, in her head.

* * *

NOT EVEN THE voices, she realised.

No chorus.

Nothing.

THEN, A CHILD.

A small child of maybe seven or eight years, with curly ringlets and furled wings.

Not a child at all.

A starsinger.

A singer of stars, a singer of the Great All.

She lay on her back, naked. Short grass, pressed feather-like against her skin, the ground hard beneath. The air was sweet, the light almost too bright from a deep blue sky.

The child stood over her, peering at her, curious.

Then, with a jerk of the wings, it lifted, hung above her, and started to sing.

SHE DID NOT know how long the child sang for.

It filled her head. That was all.

At some point, as she lay and let the song fill her, she saw a fleck against the blue, and suddenly there were two children, hanging above her, swooping in graceful, playful circles, singing their song.

Soon there were many more, until the air was full of them, and their song was swollen, rich, full of such complexity and tone that it was barely a song at all.

She felt the song in her chest, and then she felt it in her head and it was as if a wall had been broken down and the voices rushed out to meet it, the voices that had been dammed up inside her head.

It felt as if she had been opened up and her insides were spilling out. Like a waterfall. A wild summer storm flood.

The voices roared and rushed and there was no holding them back, no more constraining them.

AND FINALLY, HER head was empty.

The voices had gone.

She was just Hope, and that was a very new thing indeed.

Chapter Forty-One

WE WOKE, THE three of us, and found each other in the dark.

We tore the cauls from our heads, painfully, and hurled them to the ground.

Clutching at each other's arms, we found the spiral ramp and climbed into the light.

It took a moment for our eyes to adjust, but when they did, we saw the carnage that had been wrought.

The trees had fallen, the bushes torn apart as if a whirlwind had ripped through the atrium. Much of the vegetation was dead, withered.

I looked up and saw that only a few storeys above us the spiral tower had shattered, letting the light flood in.

Time had passed. There was no wild blizzard blowing in, although there must have been at some point, killing off the tender vegetation of the atrium.

I looked at my companions, finally, and saw that they were drawn, emaciated. We were all wraiths now.

We sat for a time to regain our strength.

Hope looked serene, more at peace than I had ever seen her before.

"¡*concern*¡! The voices?" I asked.

"Gone," she said. "The starsingers took them from me. The 'singer here tried, but he wasn't strong enough, so they all came, all summoned to him by his song.

They took him away, but first they took the voices. Where did the voices go? What did the 'singers do with them?"

"!¡*factual reporting*¡! They created another Great All," I told her. "A completely new one. They sent them there. Just us, just humankind."

"Just us?" said Hope. "Won't they be lonely there, an All just for themselves?"

I thought of it. A completely new reality, just for humankind. Somewhere, sometime, perhaps there would be a Hope and a Dodge, or two people very like us, sitting and talking, sharing.

I shook my head. They wouldn't feel alone, when they had each other.

LATER, WE FOUND the bones. Humans and one alien.

It was just the three of us, then. But we would not be alone.

Somewhere there was a new Great All, where people like us could discover and explore, where they could find their own story.

And somewhere, back to the west, there was the camp where we had left Ash, Jemerie, Pi and the others, and a story we could start for ourselves.

When they asked, we would tell them that we had not found Harmony, but that somewhere out there a new Harmony was being created.

We could ask for no better story than that.

Coda

"If they existed, they would be here."

They never *were* here.
That was a different All.
Here, it is only us.

The End

About The Author

Keith Brooke is a British novelist with a string of highly acclaimed short fictions and one previous novel from Solaris, a hit with critics, *The Accord*. He lives in the English county of Essex near to the sea. The biggest writers in SF regularly laud his output, and with the release of *alt.human*, the public are set to welcome a major talent into the charts.

ISBN: 978-1-907992-85-8 • US $8.99 / CAN $10.99

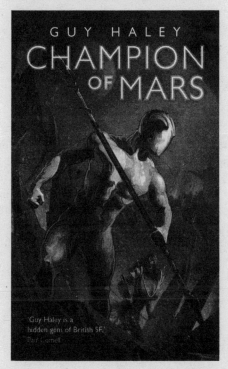

In the far future, Mars is dying a second time. The Final War of men and spirits is beginning. In a last bid for peace, disgraced champion Yoechakenon Val Mora and his spirit lover Kaibeli are set free from the Arena to find the long-missing Librarian of Mars, the only hope to save mankind.

In the near future, Dr Holland, a scientist running from a painful past, joins the Mars colonisation effort, cataloguing the remnants of Mars' biosphere before it is swept away by the terraforming programme.

When an artefact is discovered deep in the caverns of the red planet, the company Holland works for interferes, leading to tragedy. The consequences ripple throughout time, affecting Holland's present, the distant days of Yoechakanon, and the eras that bridge the aeons between.

WWW.SOLARISBOOKS.COM

Follow us on Twitter! www.twitter.com/solarisbooks

ISBN: 978-1-907519-98-7 • US $7.99 / CAN $9.99

When his brother disappears into a bizarre gateway on a London Underground escalator, failed artist Ed Rico and his brother's wife Alice have to put aside their feelings for each other to go and find him. Their quest through the 'arches' will send them hurtling through time, to new and terrifying alien worlds.

Four hundred years in the future, Katherine Abdulov must travel to a remote planet in order to regain the trust of her influential family. The only person standing in her way is her former lover, Victor Luciano, the ruthless employee of a rival trading firm.

Hard choices lie ahead as lives and centuries clash and, in the unforgiving depths of space, an ancient evil stirs...

Gareth L. Powell's epic new science-fiction novel delivers a story of galaxy-spanning scope by a writer of astounding vision.

WWW.SOLARISBOOKS.COM

Follow us on Twitter! www.twitter.com/solarisbooks